REALMS

SEA

Grey Lady

THE VALE

Fellsmarch

Wizard Head

Marisa Pines Camp

Firehole R.

Chalk Cliffs

Fortress Rock

Marisa Pines Pass

Way Camp

Hunter's Camp

Alyssa Plateau

The Harlot

Spiritgate

Delphi

North Rd.

KINGDOM of ARDEN

Heartfang Mtns.

Middlesea

Temple Church

Ardenswater

Bittersweet Keep

Ardenscourt

East Rd.

Baston Bay

THE INDIO OCEAN

Ardenswater

Heartfang R.

Bright Stone Keep

Bitter Springs R.

Watergate

Gryphon Pt.

The Wastes

WE'ENHAVEN

Hidden Bay

The Claw

Northern Islands

Demon's Wounds

JARTHIS

Deepwater Cou

Salt Sea

Dragonback Mountains

Tarvos River

Guardians Tarvos

Scorched Lands

The Indio Ocean

Endru

SHADOWCASTER

Also by Cinda Williams Chima

THE SHATTERED REALMS SERIES
Flamecaster

THE HEIR CHRONICLES
The Warrior Heir
The Wizard Heir
The Dragon Heir
The Enchanter Heir
The Sorcerer Heir

THE SEVEN REALMS SERIES
The Demon King
The Exiled Queen
The Gray Wolf Throne
The Crimson Crown

CINDA WILLIAMS CHIMA

SHADOWCASTER

A
SHATTERED REALMS
NOVEL

An imprint of HarperCollinsPublishers

Shadowcaster
Copyright © 2017 by Cinda Williams Chima
All rights reserved. Printed in the United States of America.
No part of this book may be used or reproduced in any manner whatsoever
without written permission except in the case of brief quotations embodied
in critical articles and reviews. For information address HarperCollins
Children's Books, a division of HarperCollins Publishers, 195 Broadway,
New York, NY 10007.
www.epicreads.com

ISBN 978-0-06-266291-0 (international edition)
ISBN 978-0-06-238097-5 (hardcover)

Typography by Erin Fitzsimmons
17 18 19 20 21   PC/LSCH   10 9 8 7 6 5 4 3 2 1

First Edition

To the booklovers—teachers, librarians, booksellers, family,
and friends who taught me that books are the gateway to dreams.
Some of them even come true.

LODGE OF THE EXILES

Lyss's feathered fly sparkled in the sunlight before it dropped lightly onto the thrashing surface of Weeping Creek. Planting her feet, Lyss pulled back on the rod.

"Don't yank on it," her brother Adrian whispered. "Let it come to you on the current. Mayflies don't swim."

"Maybe mine do," Lyss retorted.

"If you want to pull it along, you should use a streamer fly," Adrian said. He reached for his carry bag. "I have one that you might—"

"Would you *stop* bossing me around?" Adrian was thirteen—only two years older than Lyss—so he didn't have to act like an expert on everything. Even if he was.

"*You* stop yelling, or you'll scare the fish," Adrian said, reaching for her rod.

Trying to avoid his questing hand, she stepped back from the water's edge. Her foot slipped on a loose rock and she landed, hard, on her backside. "Blood and bones!" she swore, rubbing her tailbone.

Adrian collapsed beside her on the riverbank, helpless with laughter. Lyss would have punched him, but then she realized that it was the first time she'd heard him laugh since their sister Hana died.

Still. *She* needed something to laugh about, too. So she pushed him into the creek.

He surfaced, sputtering, but still laughing, his head sleek as an otter's. He reached the shore with a few quick strokes (he was an expert on swimming, too) and hauled himself up on the bank.

"Well," he gasped, "we may as well quit fishing. By now there's no trout within miles of here."

"Does that mean we have to eat dried venison *again*?"

"I'm not the one who scared the fish."

Lyss struggled to control her temper. That came hard. Her mother the queen always told her to think before she spoke, but thinking always seemed to happen after.

Her older brother was different. It was nearly impossible to start an argument with him. Their father always said that Adrian had a long fuse. Once lit, though, it smoldered on forever. There was no putting it out. Never ever.

They lay on their backs, side by side, squinting against the late summer sun that filtered through the shivering aspen leaves overhead. Adrian was shivering, too, and Lyss felt a flicker of guilt. It wasn't his fault their sister Hana was dead and her life was in shambles.

"I don't want to go back," Lyss said.

Adrian grunted in reply.

"I'm serious. We could stay up here and live off the land."

"Guess it'd *have* to be the land. We'd better not rely on fishing."

"I'm good with a bow," Lyss said. "Da says so. And you know all the plants and where to find them. We could build our own lodge before the snows fall. Or move into the ruins down there." She waved toward Queen Court Vale below. "We could call it Lodge of the Exiles."

Adrian closed his eyes and breathed out a long, shuddery breath. She could see the lines of pain in his face. They both needed to get away—she just had to convince him of it.

Sitting up, Lyss pulled her journal from her own carry bag and wrote the name down. *Lodge of the Exiles.* Then sketched it—a crude rendering of the broken summer palace, smoke curling from the twin chimneys, with the two of them looking out of the windows.

Nudging her brother, she thrust the journal toward him. He usually admired her stories and drawings, but this time he shook his head. "How long do you think it would take for the clans to find us?"

"Until they do, somebody else will have to be queen."

"Somebody else *is* queen. Our mother isn't going anywhere. You won't even be named princess heir until your sixteenth name day. That's five years away."

"But once I start walking that path, there'll be no turning back, or to either side." She paused, eyeing him. "Why can't we have a king once in a while?"

"If you're thinking of me, the answer is no," Adrian said, giving up on ignoring her. He scooted into a sitting position and rested his back against an aspen tree.

"What about Finn?"

"Finn?" Adrian rolled his eyes. "I know you're sweet on him, but—"

"I am not sweet on him!" Lyss said hotly.

"Look, nobody wants a king, let alone a wizard king. The clans would go to war over it, and Arden would walk in and take over." He slid a look at Lyss. "Speaking of Arden, King Gerard—*he'd* love to step in."

"I didn't mean him," Lyss said, her voice trembling with rage. "He will never, ever get his hands on the Gray Wolf throne. Somehow, someday, I'll make him pay for murdering Hana." Their sister Hana had died in a skirmish with southern soldiers in the borderlands. Though the king of Arden hadn't swung the blade himself, it was his soldiers, his orders, his fault.

"Don't you think that might be easier to do if you were queen?" Adrian said. He had a habit of telling her things she knew, deep down, but didn't want to dredge up.

Lyss closed her eyes, but it was too late. A tear escaped from under her eyelids and trickled down her cheek. "It isn't fair," she whispered, a sob shuddering through her. "I was never supposed to be queen."

Adrian reached out and took her hand.

Feeling magic trickling through his fingers, she yanked her hand back. "Stop that!" she snapped. "Stop soothing me."

Adrian frowned. "Aren't you wearing your talisman? Didn't Fire Dancer tell you that you should never take it off?"

"I didn't think I'd have to protect myself against my own brother."

"It doesn't matter who you're with, you wear your talisman," he said, going straight back to bossy. When she didn't respond, he continued, in a softer voice. "What's wrong, Lyss? What are you really afraid of?"

"Everybody loved Hana," Lyss said miserably. "She would've been a great queen. I'm just not cut out for it."

"That's not true. Just because you're not Hana doesn't mean you won't be a great queen," Adrian said. "You're strong in your own way."

"Such as?"

It took him a minute to come up with anything. "You tell the truth."

"Maybe I do," Lyss said, "but it only seems to get me in trouble."

"You don't put up with scummer."

"That's what queens have to do all day long. Plus shovel some of their own."

He laughed. "See? You know a lot about being queen already."

Lyss just grunted. She saw no humor in her situation—none at all.

After a moment, Adrian started in again. "You're a rum observer—you notice everything. You're great at tracking game, good on horseback, and a deadeye with a bow. And you're really good at writing and drawing and playing the basilka. The songs you write go straight to the heart."

It was true. When she put things in writing, it gave her time to think and edit. Unlike when she opened her mouth.

"Maybe I'll write King Gerard a nasty note," Lyss said, rolling her eyes. "That should send him packing. They can put that on my tomb: 'Better on the Page.'"

"Is that what you're afraid of? What people will say about you?"

"That's part of it," Lyss said. "The queendom has been here for more than a thousand years. I don't want people to remember me as the queen that ruined it."

"If the queendom is ruined, it won't be you that does it," Adrian said, his jaw tightening.

"I'll get the blame. I need to be queen during a boring time—not when we're in the middle of a war."

"There's no boring times around here. Things were a

mess twenty-five years ago, when our mother took over. They're a mess now." He waited, and when she didn't say anything back, went on. "The war can't last forever. Anyway, you have to do it, there's nobody else."

"What about Julianna? At least she *looks* like a queen."

Julianna was her cousin, her aunt Mellony's daughter. She was slender and graceful, and she always seemed to say the right thing. People loved Julianna.

Adrian snorted. "You really think she would be better than you? She doesn't have the backbone that you do. Or the heart."

Anybody would be better than me, Lyss wanted to say, but she knew it wasn't true. Maybe she didn't want the job, but she didn't know who else should fill it.

"Don't be so hard on yourself," Adrian said. "You've just had your eleventh name day, and Hana was twenty when she died. You've got to stop comparing yourself to her."

"Everybody else does," Lyss muttered.

"You'll probably be an old woman when you take over," Adrian said. "You'll have a lot of time to figure it out."

"It's easy for you to say," Lyss said, though she knew that wasn't true. "You can do what you want. You'll go off to Oden's Ford and never give us a thought."

Adrian scooped up a flat skipping stone and sent it skittering all the way across the river. "I don't know if that's even going to happen now."

Lyss stared at him. "What do you mean? I know it's a few more years until you're old enough to go to Mystwerk, but—"

"I'd like to go now, and train with the healers," Adrian said.

"A wizard schooling with healers? I never heard of that."

"That's what everyone says when I bring it up. And now, since Hana was killed, Mama won't even talk about Oden's Ford."

Lyss found her own stone and side-handed it, but it only skipped twice before it disappeared into the water. "She'll change her mind."

"Why is it always easier to be optimistic about somebody else's worries?" Adrian said with a bitter laugh. "Anyway, we didn't come up here to talk about me and my problems."

Lyss bit her lip, feeling selfish then. "We can, if you want."

He shook his head, his blue-green eyes fixed on her face. "I didn't bring you here so you'd have a better hideout. I brought you to the old capital because you descend from a line that ruled the entire continent from here. Sometimes you have to get away to remember who you are. Believe in yourself, Lyss. You're strong and smart enough to do this job. Never let anyone tell you different. You love these mountains, and our people. You're honest, you know what's right, and you don't back down. You're tough, and you're not full of yourself. That's the kind of queen we need. I'd rather have one of you than fifteen Juliannas. Or five hundred Finns."

Lyss felt a spark of hope that quickly sputtered out. "I just keep having these dreams, where everyone's dead and I'm all alone on Hanalea Peak, just me and the wolves."

"You won't be on your own. Mama will teach you, and Da will help, and you'll have a bound captain like Captain Byrne. And I'll help you, too, any way I can, whatever you want. Even if I do get to go to Oden's Ford, I'll come back and help when I've finished."

I'd rather *help* the queen than *be* the queen, Lyss thought. Still, it would mean a lot to know that her brother would be at her side. She came up onto her knees, facing him.

"You promise?" she said, taking both his hands. "You promise you won't leave me on my own?"

"I promise," he said, looking straight back at her. "You will write your own story as queen, and I'll play whatever role you give me."

It was like a benediction. They remained, knee-to-knee, for a few more seconds until he said, "Now we'd better find a good camping spot before the sun goes down."

WEEPING CREEK

Lyss dipped a cup of water from Weeping Creek and used it to wash down a dry mouthful of cheese and waybread. She wished she could wash down her memories as easily.

The rest of her squadron was sprawled around her on the creekbank, grabbing a quick rest and a bite, once they'd made sure that their ponies were well watered.

Lyss followed the waybread with a few strips of leathery venison and a handful of dried fruit and nuts. She was so bloody tired of campaign rations. An army on the move had no time for hunting or roasting fresh meat.

Just four years ago, Lyss and her brother Adrian had camped on the banks of this creek after Hana died. Four years ago, her brother had made her a solemn vow.

You won't be on your own.

And then, just a few months later, at Solstice, her father and her brother were ambushed in the streets of Fellsmarch. Her father was murdered, and her brother Adrian carried off, leaving his blood-smeared remedy bag on the cobblestones.

They'd buried her father next to Hana in the Cathedral Temple, then waited on tenterhooks for news of Adrian. What they expected was a demand for an impossible ransom from the king of Arden, or some grisly token proving his death. What they got was . . . nothing. After four years with no word, Adrian was presumed dead—by nearly everyone but Lyss. Despite evidence to the contrary, she still believed in miracles. She couldn't help hoping that he might be alive, held captive, perhaps, in a southern dungeon, even though common sense told her that he'd be better off dead than Arden's prisoner.

If he was dead, I would know it.

At first, she'd seethed with plans to go looking for him. Her mother had strictly forbidden any adventures of that sort, and had assigned a full-time guard to her sole surviving child to make sure she didn't sneak away.

Eventually, over Lyss's strenuous objections, they'd held a funeral for Adrian. Eventually, Lyss grew up enough to know that, even if Adrian lived, she'd have no idea where to start looking.

She still had dreams that he showed up at their door,

demanding to know why no one had come looking for him.

This is the land of broken promises, she thought. Get used to it. I've been kind of busy since you left.

Lyss skipped a stone across the water, but it sank before it reached the other side. Next to her, Sasha dug in her kit, no doubt hoping to surface some scrap of food she'd missed. Nobody in this mixed bag of soldiers had an ounce of fat on them, but Sasha was big, and she had an appetite to match.

"Here," Cam said, tossing her a sack of dried berries. "I've had my fill."

Sasha tossed it back. "Eat up, Private. I've got a lot more meat on my bones than you do."

It was true. Cam always looked like he could use some feeding up—he was thin as a reed, with hands and feet that hopefully he'd grow into one day.

Sasha Talbot and Cam Staunton were the two members of the queen's Gray Wolf guard assigned to Lyss during the marching season. Though they wore the spattercloth of the regular army, they had one purpose and one purpose only—to keep the heir to the Gray Wolf throne alive. That job was getting harder and harder as the war dragged on and Lyss's patience eroded.

Staunton was relatively new to the guard. His mother had been a corporal in Lyss's squadron. She'd been killed in the Fens the previous year, leaving Cam to support two younger brothers.

The funeral fires were barely out when twelve-year-old Cam came to Lyss, asking to enlist in the Highlanders. "I'd like to fight for you, ma'am," he said, chin up, shoulders back, already at attention. "Everyone says I'm sure to see some action if I'm with you."

"Stay at home a little longer, Cam," she'd said. Though Lyss was only two years older, it felt like decades.

"You was fighting in the war at twelve," Cam said. "Mama told me that. When you was thirteen, you grabbed the Gray Wolf banner from the cold, dead hands of your commander and led the charge that drove the southerners into the sea at Hallowmere. And, just last year, you—"

Lyss held up both hands. "Don't believe everything you hear," she said. "Stories have a way of growing. And there's a lot they leave out."

Cam clenched his jaw. "There's lots of my age-mates in the Highlanders. The only reason I never signed up is Mama wouldn't let me. She always said I had to look after my brothers."

Lyss knew that any other commander would have signed him right up. He was likelier than many they had in the field. There was nothing to stop him from going elsewhere if she refused.

"Who'll look after your brothers if you go to war?" she'd said.

"I have older cousins near West Wall," Cam said. "They can stay there during the marching season."

"What about school?"

"I'm pretty much finished at the Temple School. But I'll study hard, when I'm home."

Lyss sighed. She knew what happened to that kind of promise. "Why do you want to go to war? Find an apprenticeship. Something you can carry on with, after the war."

"After the war, ma'am?" Cam looked baffled. "Do you really see an end to it anytime soon?"

And Lyss could not lie to this boy who'd lost so much already. "I don't know," she said.

"Then I want to help," he said. "I want to go after the ones that killed my mother."

In the end, Lyss had put in a word with Captain Byrne, and Cam had been allowed to sign up with the Gray Wolves. That would keep him off the battlefield, and he could be posted close to home. This summer, though, he'd managed to get assigned to Lyss, so he'd found his way to the battlefield, anyway.

Who's to say the Vale is any safer? Lyss thought.

The queens of the Fells were bound by blood and history to the Spirit Mountains. Their Gray Wolf ancestors were the guardians who dwelt in the forests and high mountain passes. The peaks had always stood as an impenetrable barrier to the south, holding evil at bay. Twenty-five years ago, when her mother, Raisa, was a young queen, the monstrous Gerard Montaigne, king of Arden, had breached that barrier. His armies had marched all the way to the gates of Fellsmarch, demanding surrender.

They'd driven him off then, and reinforced the borders, and through twenty-five years of war they had kept him at bay. Then, four years ago, the killings began. They started with her father and brother, but were not limited to the royal family. It was most often wizards, but included military officers, clan warriors, government officials, and members of the nobility. What they had in common was their importance to the war effort, or their close connection to the queen.

How were they supposed to protect themselves against an enemy who could be anywhere, and might strike at any time?

Lyss dipped her waterskin into the bone-chilling creek, refilling it for the ride ahead. The streams that ran down from Alyssa Peak were always cold—fed by snowmelt that ran from spring until the new snows cloaked her rocky summit in late summer. The southerners had a different name for her—the Harlot, because she was a mountain that broke men's hearts.

Ardenine hearts, maybe, Lyss thought.

Over the past several days, they'd ridden hard from Way Camp to join the rest of their salvo in Queen Court Vale. The queendom's eyes and ears had sent word that the Ardenine general Marin Karn had landed a large force at Spiritgate. Their intended target could be Fortress Rocks to the north or Queen Court Vale, which spread out in front of them, a checkerboard of small farms in the middle of the harvest season.

"Somebody's coming," Sasha said, pointing over Lyss's shoulder. Her eyes narrowed in disbelief. "It looks like Shadow Dancer."

"Really?" Lyss said. "I thought he was still at Demonai Camp." She turned to look, squinting against the morning sun at the horseman riding hard from the direction of the command tent across the Vale. "You're right. It *is* him. I wonder what he's doing here."

Shadow reined in next to Lyss, saluted, dismounted, and produced a dispatch tube with a flourish. "From General Dunedain, ma'am," he said.

Lyss threw her arms around him, ignoring the dispatch for the moment. The scent of flux and charcoal and metal said that he hadn't been too long away from the forge. "What are you doing here?"

"I dropped off a load of new gear to your quartermaster," Shadow said.

That made sense. At sixteen, Shadow was already one of the most talented flashcrafters in the queendom—clan artisans who made weaponry and magical tools in support of the northern war effort.

That still didn't explain why he was delivering dispatches. "Since when are you playing messenger?"

"I heard that there might be a chance to kill southerners today, so I decided to extend my visit." The many braids in Shadow's hair were evidence that he rarely said no to a fight, and that he usually came away with a kill. Though the work he did in his shop was critical to the war effort, it was all but impossible to keep him off the battlefield. He was the fiercest metalsmith in the queendom.

Shadow had a private's colors knotted around his neck, as much of a uniform as he'd ever put on. He might have inherited his gift for flashcraft from his clan-born, gifted father, but his looks and reckless, independent spirit came from his Southern Islands mother.

Cat Tyburn had been spymaster for the queendom, until two years ago, when somebody cut her throat and dumped her body in the Dyrnnewater. Cat was the savviest street-fighter in the realm. Lyss couldn't understand how she'd been caught unawares.

Cat might be gone, but she lived on in her headstrong, mercurial son. Lyss and Shadow had been inseparable as lýtlings, but these days their paths rarely crossed in the marching season. And now . . .

"I would have thought that you'd have better things to do," Lyss said. "Didn't I hear that you're planning a wedding?"

Shadow nodded, a bit of color staining his dark cheeks. "News travels faster than I do, it seems."

"Have you set a date?"

He shook his head. "My father wants us to wait another year or two. Aspen and I are buried in work, anyway, so it likely won't be until sometime next year. Don't worry—you'll get your invitation as soon as I know when and where it will be."

Lyss had met Shadow's betrothed, Aspen Silverleaf, several times at clan markets. Aspen was known throughout the Seven Realms for her fine leatherwork. Her workshop was in Fortress Rocks, a midsized town to the north and east, where she looked after four younger brothers and sisters.

We are a land of orphans, Lyss thought, doing the work of dead parents.

Aspen was steady, practical, and wiser than her years. She'd been good for Shadow. In the time they'd been together, he'd begun taking better care of himself.

Still, Lyss was having a hard time with the notion of Shadow marrying and settling down, even if it might keep him alive a little longer. For years, even when they were apart, they'd been comrades, focused on a common goal: keeping the king of Arden's army from overrunning their homeland. Wasn't it tempting fate to be settling down to a life with this war still going on?

"Where do you think you'll live? After you're married, I mean." If he moves to Fortress Rocks, I'll never see him, she thought. Which she knew was selfish.

"One thing at a time," Shadow said, laughing. "I'm still getting used to the idea of getting married." He waved the dispatch tube under her nose. "Don't you want to read this after I've carried it all this way?"

Lyss unfurled the paper inside, scanned it, and crumpled it in her hand.

"What?" Sasha said, instantly alert.

"The gutter-swiving mudbacks have committed themselves," Lyss said. "They are heading for the pass. Mason and Littlefield are meeting us there."

Sasha pulled out her spyglass and scanned the shoulder of the mountain. "How many?"

"She doesn't say, but they must have slave mages with them. They're sending Finn along with us."

"Sul'Mander's here, too?" Shadow looked from Sasha to Lyss, his expression flat and unreadable. "Last I heard, he was in the borderlands with the queen."

"He was," Lyss said. "He was wounded back in the spring, and he's been in hospital since. He just arrived from the capital. They must think we can use a little more talent."

Even though Shadow and Finn were distantly related (Shadow's grandfather was a Bayar), Lyss always got the impression that he somehow disapproved of Finn. Lyss didn't think it was the old mistrust between uplanders and wizards—Shadow's father was a wizard, after all.

Maybe it was because they were both intense, in different ways.

"Let *me* ride with you," Shadow said, fondling the bow in his saddle boot. "*I* have talent."

"I know you do," Lyss said, rolling her eyes. "But can you follow orders?"

"I can follow orders as well as any Demonai," Shadow said, which was setting a pretty low bar. "Anyway, General Dunedain already said yes."

"Fine," Lyss said, irritated that he'd gone around her. "Just remember—I don't want to hear whining when the going gets tough." She didn't say aloud what else she was thinking—that this Ardenine offensive must be a bigger threat than they'd thought if Dunedain was recruiting their flashcrafter.

"Let's go!" she said, rousing the rest of her squadron. "Get ready to ride!"

By the time Lyss had loaded her gear, she saw another lone horseman galloping toward them, his pale hair glittering in the slanting morning sun.

Finn. Lyss's stomach did its usual somersault. She'd had a crush on Finn sul'Mander since she was eleven years old. She'd often see him with Adrian and his friends, at a time when her worship of her brother extended to everyone around him.

Back then, she'd tried to pump Adrian for information in her clumsy way. "Is he really your friend, Adrian?" she'd ask.

He raised his eyebrow. "Of course he is. I wouldn't spend so much time with him if we weren't friends."

"But he's a Bayar," Lyss said. "Da says we shouldn't trust Bayars, right?"

"He's a Mander," Adrian said. "Anyway, he's different. He's not like the rest of them at all."

Lyss didn't know what he meant by that, but it was enough to ease her mind. She'd always thought of Finn as solemn, intense, mysterious, and deep. That hadn't changed. In wartime, many of their age-mates fought young, loved young, and died young. Some tried to live a lifetime before they turned twenty. Despite plenty of opportunities, Finn didn't seem to play the romantic games that others did. If he'd had sweethearts in the past, it was a closely guarded secret.

Maybe that was why Lyss liked him. Wooing and romantic banter were not in her arsenal, either. When you fall in love with somebody, they just go and get themselves killed. When I marry, she thought, I'm going to find somebody with an army and some warships and a big bag of money. Then I'll do my dancing on the battlefield.

Finn hadn't been around much these past four years— he was always either away at the academy at Oden's Ford, or fighting in the borderlands. The stories Lyss had heard about his steady courage under fire did nothing to diminish his appeal.

She'd had lots of crushes back when she was eleven. This was the only one that had lasted.

"Lieutenant Gray," Finn said, reining in and saluting her. "I am, as always, at your service."

For a moment, Lyss was speechless. Finn was still handsome by any measure, but his time in the healing halls had changed him. He looked thin and haggard, his black eyes undershadowed with weariness and pain, his skin nearly as pale as his hair.

Lyss leaned in to take a closer look, worry squirming inside her. "Are you all right? I mean, I heard you were wounded."

Finn tightened his reins so that his horse danced a few steps back. "I'm well," he said, his tone of voice and expression telling her to back off.

"Good," Lyss said, lifting her chin. "Glad to hear it."

Finn grimaced, and said more gently, "Isn't that what soldiers are supposed to say, whether we are or not?" He sighed. "It's just . . . so many have died, and for what? We can win every battle and still lose the war. It's such a waste."

"Is there something you think we should do differently?" Lyss said.

"Everything," Finn said. "I'm willing to give my life for the realm, but I don't see that making a difference." He looked away. "Never mind," he said. "I shouldn't have said that."

"I'm glad you did," Lyss said. "My father had a saying: 'If you keep doing what you've been doing, you'll get what you've been getting.' In our case—an endless war."

Finn turned back to her, studying her. "You *do* understand," he said.

"I don't just understand," Lyss said. "I agree."

Finn smiled, and Lyss melted. She knew a dozen girls

who would kill to win a smile from Finn sul'Mander, but he bestowed them sparingly.

"We'd better go," she said. "Mason and Littlefield are meeting us at the near end of the pass."

Lyss wheeled her horse, and Finn wheeled with her, so he was riding beside her. Sasha and Cam took their usual positions, one just ahead of Lyss, the other just behind.

As they rode east, the early sun disappeared behind the shoulder of the great mountain, and the air grew noticeably cooler, sending a finger of chill down Lyss's back.

"There's something else I should tell you," Finn said, leaning closer. "I'm not going back to the academy this year."

"You're not?" Was this the reason for his unusually gloomy attitude? "Why not?"

"I'm going to stay home. I've decided to train with Lord Vega in the healing halls," Finn said.

"But . . . you always talk about how you *love* Oden's Ford."

"I *do* love Oden's Ford," Finn said. "But it's time to stop being selfish and do what I can for the realm."

"Finn . . . you've been a major asset on the battlefield," Lyss said. "You were seriously wounded fighting for the queendom. That hardly seems selfish to me."

Finn shrugged that off. "I just think I need to contribute to the war in a different way. After spending months in the healing halls, after seeing the important work they do there, I realized that's where I belong. Lord Vega has truly been a mentor to me."

This was almost as surprising as Finn's decision not to go back to the academy. Lyss recalled Adrian complaining about Lord Vega, and she'd heard much the same from his friend Ty Gryphon. According to them, the wizard was definitely not the mentor type.

Well, she thought, good for the both of them. Vega's been griping for years about the lack of recruits to the healing service. Either he's realized that his own behavior is the root of the problem, or at least he's found somebody who'll put up with him.

Lyss tried to keep an open mind about Harriman Vega, but, to be honest, she despised him. She hoped it wasn't because she couldn't forgive him for failing to save her father's life. He'd been the one to pronounce him dead in the street.

"Does General Dunedain know? That you're leaving the Highlanders?"

Finn shook his head. "I plan to tell her when we return to the capital in the fall."

"It goes without saying that we'll miss you," Lyss said.

Finn smiled. "Go ahead," he said. "You can say it anyway."

Lieutenants Mason and Littlefield met them at the near end of the pass, along with Captain Starborn, the commander of the salvo. Starborn was one of the rare Demonai warriors who'd enlisted in the regular army.

"Good news!" Starborn said, with a broad grin. "We have many, many flatlanders to kill today."

"Typical Demonai," Sasha muttered, shooting a worried look at Lyss.

"How many?" Lyss said.

Starborn rocked his hand. "Our scouts think that it might be a full brigade."

"A *brigade!*" Littlefield turned an odd shade of gray.

Starborn nodded. "So." He rubbed his hands together. "There'll be plenty to go around."

"Shouldn't we wait for reinforcements?" Littlefield persisted.

"We can't afford to wait," Starborn said. "We have to keep them in the pass—that way we'll face only a few at a time. If they spill out into the Vale, they can use their numbers against us."

Lyss leaned forward, and Mincemeat shifted under her, sensing her impatience. "Shall we ride, then, sir? My squadron can take the forward position, where Finn will be at his most effective."

Starborn eyed her appraisingly, then nodded. "Carry on, Lieutenant Gray. We'll be right behind you."

Lyss waved her troops forward, settling into the lead with Sasha and Cam on either side of her, Finn and Shadow just behind.

"Do you always have to take the forward position, Lieutenant?" Sasha hissed. "Could you try and remember who you are, sometimes?"

"I never forget who I am," Lyss said. "That's why I take the lead."

MATELON

Halston Matelon would never admit that he was looking forward to a fight—but he was. After an endlessly frustrating season watching his back in Delphi, the prospect of leading an army into battle seemed positively appealing. Even if it wasn't a fight he would have chosen.

A soldier doesn't choose his battles, Hal's father always said. *His job is to win the one before him.* By that measure, Hal was a good soldier. He'd moved up quickly in the empire's army. At seventeen, he was already a captain. His men were good soldiers, and loyal, and he won more battles than he lost. Only that, all of a sudden, was a problem.

Nine months ago, at Solstice, he'd received new orders—King Gerard was relieving him of his command

and sending him to the conquered city of Delphi as the administrator of martial law.

"Why would he do that?" Hal had asked his father over his second tankard of ale. "I've been a good soldier. Why would he send me to do a job I have no preparation for?"

"Right now it doesn't suit King Gerard for you to be a successful soldier," Lord Matelon said. He rubbed his chin with the heel of his hand. "That's likely my fault. I've been too outspoken in my criticism of the war."

"But . . . if he wants to win the war, why would it make sense to make a boneheaded move like that?" Hal took a quick look around to make sure no one was in a position to overhear. This even though they were sitting on the terrace at White Oaks, the well-fortified Matelon holding in the countryside.

"King Gerard doesn't want you marching around at the head of an army if he makes a move against me," his father said, with a sour smile.

"Do you think that's a possibility?" Hal said, lowering his voice anyway.

"It's what the king thinks that's important," Lord Matelon said. "King Gerard is always short of money, especially now that the council has tightened the purse strings. One way to resolve that—temporarily, at least—is to name one of us a traitor to the crown and seize his holdings. Right now I'm likely at the top of his list."

Hal glared out over the green hills and forests of the

estate he called home. Just below, he could see his mother and sister—moving spots of color—gathering winter blooms in the garden. He needed to protect them, this place, this sanctuary. "If he comes after you, I'll give him reason to regret it," he said grimly.

"I dearly hope so," Lord Matelon said, with a hoarse laugh, "but that's precisely what King Gerard's afraid of." He paused, leaned in. "We also have to consider the possibility that he means to make sure that you never get out of Delphi alive."

Hal slammed his hands down on the table. "And you *still* think I should go?" To Hal, politics was that thing you did when you were too old to be of any use on the battlefield. Though he had to admit, his father had always been good at both.

"You must go," Lord Matelon said. "You cannot give King Gerard an excuse to take you into custody and hold you hostage against my good behavior. Delphi is a nasty place, but the king's gaol is nastier. So, yes, I think you should go, with your eyes open to the danger you're walking into. This is not the battlefield you're used to fighting on. Don't trust the King's Guard—they serve the king. Take a half dozen of your best soldiers with you, and trust no one else. People die in Delphi every day, and you don't want to be among them."

Hal rose and began pacing back and forth, seething. "Do you think there's a chance the king will realize that posting me to Delphi was a mistake?"

"Aye, there's a chance," Lord Matelon said. "There's a chance that an earthshake might swallow him up. Just don't try to hurry it along by failing on purpose. Even if the job you're assigned is not to your liking, a Matelon will see it done."

Of course. Hal had been hearing that all of his life. By now it was engraved on his bones.

"Other than watching my back, do you have any other advice about how to succeed in Delphi?"

"As military commander over a district, you need to make yourself visible and accessible. Listen to what people have to say. Let them know what the rules are, and then enforce those rules consistently. Be ruthless when you need to, but be fair about it. They still won't like you, but they'll respect you, and that's the best way to stop trouble before it starts."

Now, nine months into his posting, Hal was finding that following his father's advice was easier said than done. It seemed that whenever he made a little headway toward a working relationship with the Delphians, the King's Guard undid it through cruel, vindictive, and arbitrary tactics. As the police force in the city, they were the face of Arden to most citizens, and it was an ugly one.

During his first four months in the city, Hal had also survived three assassination attempts. Once, it was poison; once, an ambush in the streets; and once, someone had carefully frayed the cinch strap on his saddle. He didn't know whether the perpetrators were Delphian Patriots or agents of the king, since the blackbirds never caught them.

After that, Hal moved his headquarters into a compound north of the city. His excuse was that he wanted to keep a closer eye on the mines and the northern border. That was true enough, but that was only part of it. This way, he could keep his soldiers away from the city and avoid being pulled into criminal and civil disputes. Some would say it was a coward's way out, but he had no stomach for beating people into the ground. What's more, he had no plans to die in Delphi, and he was more likely to survive when he didn't have to walk through the city's crowded streets.

Why is it that when a man is successful on the battle-field, they ruin his life by making him an administrator?

But now, in a twist of luck, the war had come to him. General Karn had landed an entire brigade at Spiritgate in an attempt to wring a small victory from a bitter stalemate of a summer. Karn was desperate to win a little territory in order to placate the Thane Council. Hal's father wasn't the only one losing interest in funding King Gerard's grudge match against the witch queen of the Fells.

The plan was to march across the Alyssa Plateau, around the flank of the Harlot, and straight into Queen Court Vale. Karn was in need of an experienced commander who knew the territory. At least that was the reason given when Hal was detailed to join this late-summer offensive.

Hal was cautiously optimistic. Maybe it meant that the king had realized that he couldn't afford to send good soldiers to the backwaters of Delphi to die. He hoped it represented a chance to demonstrate his value to the empire.

He met up with the army at Spiritgate. Karn put him in charge of an entire battalion—a third of the brigade. Hal had brought his half dozen seasoned men with him, but he soon discovered that the rest of the soldiers in his command were raw recruits from the down realms, men who scarcely knew how to cock a crossbow. They were as green as grass, with less than a week until they marched.

Hal called his handful of veterans in and said, "Good news. You're all being promoted to lieutenant."

They looked at each other, shuffling their feet, murmuring thank-yous, waiting for the rest of it.

"I'm going to split this battalion into five columns of twenty-four. Each of you will take charge of a column. You'll march with them, eat with them, sleep with them, get to know who's who, and surface any talent you can. Until we engage, I want you to drill them hard. Focus on crossbow drills, the five standard orders, fighting formations, and the care of weapons. Once we engage, I want you to do everything you can to keep all of your scrips alive."

"But Captain," now-Lieutenant Cousineau protested, "what about you? Who'll watch your back if—?"

"Do it," Hal said, and turned away.

Once Hal's hurry-up boot camp began, his men were up at dawn, drilling, every single day, while the other battalions slept in.

Part of the mission was to undo the damage done to the recruits already. The newlings had been stuffed full of stories by the veterans—tales of the sorcerous land up north, of the witch queen and her terrifying twin daughters who drank the blood of the faithful and rode saber-toothed horses naked through the skies. Of the northern warrior they called the Gray Wolf. Impossible to kill, he turned into a huge gray wolf when the battle fever took him, savaging any poor soldier unlucky enough to cross his path.

Hal wasn't going to rule anything out, but he'd fought several campaigns in the north and had seen nothing of the sort. There *were* wolves in the mountains—Hal had seen and heard them. He reasoned that any wolf looks like a giant when he's bearing down on you, and grows considerably after, in the telling.

"The northern soldiers are just men," Hal told the men in his command. "And women," he amended. "When you cut them, they bleed, just like us."

It was true that northern women fought as fiercely as the men—so fiercely that, on the battlefield, it was difficult to tell them apart. Several times in the past, Hal had discovered that the man he'd just killed was actually a woman. He just couldn't get used to that. Maybe that was the root of the rumors—it was easier to think you'd killed a witch or a ghost warrior than a woman.

They left Spiritgate a week after Hal's arrival. The countryside they marched through had been stripped of anything edible or useful. Many of the farms and villages had been destroyed and abandoned over the course of the war. And yet the northerners kept on fighting, year after year. The church said it was because they'd been enslaved by their sorcerous queen, and the true sons of Malthus would be welcomed as liberators.

Hal was still waiting for that.

They met little resistance, save the usual copperhead hit-and-run attacks. Karn made no attempt to pursue, apparently considering the loss of a few soldiers here and there the price of making good time.

Hal's battalion was still more likely to kill one of their fellow soldiers than to give the northerners anything to worry about. It gave Hal plenty to worry about, though.

They were young, too—many had not yet got their growth. Some didn't even speak Common. Hal set about to try to learn their names. Ty. Bakshi. Raynaud. Skye.

The only veterans attached to his battalion, aside from the ones he'd brought himself, were four captive mages. One of them was a blade-faced man named Pitts. Every time his droop-lidded gaze brushed over Hal, it gave him the chills. The mages had little to say to Hal, despite his attempts to engage them. That wasn't unusual. Collared mages were often sullen—resentful of being ganged into the southern army. Hal usually got on well with them once he won them over—but that took time he didn't have.

Hal couldn't help wondering why these men had been sent into the fighting so soon after recruitment, why they had been assigned to him, and why he and his were marching ahead of the veterans to the rear.

He didn't know for sure, but he had some theories.

They'd reached the eastern end of the pass before Hal managed to corner General Karn.

"Sir. I've been evaluating the men assigned to my battalion and I'm worried that their inexperience might endanger the brigade and interfere with the mission," Hal said, the words tumbling out quickly before he could be dismissed.

"So you're *worried*, Captain Matelon," Karn said, planting his hands on his hips. "I hope it's not keeping you up nights. As you should know, we're dredging the bottom of the barrel when it comes to new recruits. You'll have to work with what you have, just like the rest of us."

"Sir," Hal persisted, "I'm not complaining about the quality of the men under my command. I believe they can become good soldiers with time. I'm concerned about their youth and—"

"You're scarcely dry behind the ears yourself, and you've done all right," Karn said.

"I've been fighting for the empire since I was eleven," Hal said. "What most concerns me is their lack of training and experience, coupled with their concentration in one unit. It seems to me that if they could be mingled with more experienced troops in all three battalions, they could learn from their comrades and the veterans could help them survive until they develop some skills."

"Are you questioning my orders, Captain?"

Yes, Hal thought, I definitely am.

"No, sir, I'm merely suggesting that—"

"I need my veterans to fight, Captain, not to babysit new recruits," Karn said. "I've organized my battle plan to make the best use of all my assets. Everyone keeps telling me you're a brilliant field officer. That's why I put these scrips with you. You and your battalion will have an important job to do."

"Which is?"

"Your battalion will take the lead in the invasion of Queen Court Vale," Karn said.

If it had been anyone else, Hal would have assumed he'd somehow misunderstood. But when he looked into Karn's face, when he saw the sneering triumph there, he knew that he'd heard right.

"Could you . . . elaborate, sir?" Hal said. Somehow, he managed to keep his voice calm, steady, matter-of-fact.

"You will fight your way through the pass," Karn said, as if Hal were too stupid to divine his true meaning. "Once through, you will clear the valley of civilians, loot the town of all valuables, and burn everything to the dirt."

Karn paused, as if he expected a hearty thank-you for this suicide assignment.

Hal straightened, broadened his stance, and looked the general in the eye. "And after that?" he said evenly.

For a long moment, Karn was at a loss. Hal knew he hadn't made a plan for after, because Hal and his battalion weren't supposed to survive.

"After that, you'll . . . await further orders," Karn said.

"If I may ask, sir, what will the other two battalions be doing in the meantime?"

"We will be right behind you," Karn said, with a predator's smile, "sending replacements up as needed." The general paused long enough to let that sink in. "Now, Captain, you'd best get some rest." With that, Karn turned and walked away, not waiting for a salute. Which was good, because Hal was not about to give him one.

His father's words came back to him. *Right now it doesn't suit King Gerard for you to be a successful soldier.*

Hal added his own coda to that.

But it does suit him for you to be a dead one.

He was boxed in. If he refused Karn's orders, he'd be court-martialed and executed. If he deserted, he'd be hunted down and executed. He could turn traitor, and throw himself on the dubious mercy of the witch queen. Any of those options would disgrace his father and help build the king's case against him.

If Hal walked off a cliff, would that be a virtuous death?

What would happen to his battalion? Would Karn fold them into his other forces or would they be sent out to slaughter on their own? Truth be told, Hal wanted to live, and he wanted to save as many in his battalion as he could. He was just beginning to learn their names.

Even if the job you're assigned is not to your liking, a Matelon will see it done.

Hal considered his options. He had just a handful of mounted soldiers—the vast majority were infantry. But in the narrow pass, the terrain was a double-edged sword. It would protect his flanks, but it would also prevent him from using his numbers, which was the only card he had to play. His best hope was the element of surprise. He needed to get his battalion through the pass and into the open field before the northerners could block their path. Then he could do with numbers what he couldn't do with talent and skill.

"Sir!" he called after Karn.

The general stiffened and turned. "Yes, Captain?"

"Permission to march now, sir."

Karn blinked in surprise. Eyed him suspiciously. Then bared his teeth. "Captain," he said, "you can march whenever the hell you want."

QUEEN COURT VALE

Lyss's squadron met the army of Arden midway through the pass, where the steep shoulders of the mountains nearly touched, and the enemy had to file through, two or three abreast. Lyss and her soldiers stood directly in their path, a briar of swords, axes, spears, and magic. She sent her best archers—Shadow among them—scrambling up the hillside so they could shoot down from above.

It was hard to tell how many of the enemy there were, since they were strung out in a line. It doesn't matter, Lyss told herself, if we only have to face a few at a time. The mudbacks were known for their precision columns and formations, but this batch seemed just a bit ragged.

Lyss counted four slave mages to her squadron's one

wizard. She could see them, their collars glittering in the noonday sun, just behind the enemy's front lines. Finn was kept busy on defense—raising shields against attack magic and pinning down enemy wizards who attempted to improve their firing position by climbing higher. That left him little opportunity to assist the Highlander offense. So it was up to the line soldiers of the salvo to make the southerners pay a dear price for every bit of ground.

And pay they did. The southerners lost three soldiers for one of theirs, but the mudbacks kept coming, filling in the gaps created when one of them went down, bringing up more weapons, and carrying away bodies. Lyss imagined a long line of mudbacks reaching all the way to the coast. The only constants were the four mages and a young officer with raven hair who seemed to be everywhere, riding his dun-colored horse up and down, correcting their formation, ordering replacements forward, and shouting encouragement. At one point, Lyss saw him lean down from his horse and scoop up a soldier who was staggering around aimlessly, blood pouring from a head wound. He carried him to the rear, then immediately returned to the front, his tunic now soaked with blood.

As the afternoon wore on, the cacophony around Lyss seemed to recede to a dull roar, as she focused on the enemy in front of her. Her sword grew heavy in her hands and her shoulders ached. They seemed to be at an impasse as the killing continued, with neither side making forward progress. Healers came and went, carrying the wounded and dead away. Lyss shouted encouragement to her weary soldiers, sending some to the rear and bringing up fresher fighters from the other squadrons. Only Lyss, Finn, Shadow, Sasha, and Cam stayed on the front line.

She tried to shut down the voice in her head that said that her side would run out of soldiers and weapons eventually, and then they would be overrun.

"Look out, Lieutenant!" Cam slammed his horse into hers so that she all but lost her seat. The incoming arrow passed harmlessly over her shoulder, but she heard someone scream when it found a mark to the rear.

"Mander's down!" Shadow shouted from his vantage point atop the hill. Lyss turned and looked, but couldn't see Finn.

If Finn is down, his shields are down, Lyss thought. Once their mages figure that out, we're all sitting ducks.

Sasha had reached the same conclusion, because she angled her horse between Lyss and the Ardenine mages, shouting, "Go! Lyss! Get out of here now!"

Lyss wheeled her horse so she faced the enemy and saw all four of them, right arms extended, left hands on their amulets, preparing to fire. At this distance, there was no way they would miss.

Lyss wore her father's clan talisman, which provided protection against a direct hit of attack magic. As far as she knew, she was the only one on the field with one. But

Mincemeat was unprotected, and they'd both go down if the mages were smart enough to target him.

The mages hadn't seemed to notice her yet. In fact, they seemed distracted, aiming off to one side.

Well, then, Lyss thought. "For the queen in the north!" she cried, spurring her horse forward. Behind her, she heard Sasha and Cam shouting at her, then the rattle of hooves as they followed.

The mages never saw her coming. Mincemeat crashed into the nearest mage, sending him flying. He landed flat on his back nearly under her pony's hooves. Leaning low out of the saddle, Lyss finished him with a sweep of her ax, then ducked as a mudback aimed a blow at her skull. She could feel the buzz as bolt after bolt of attack magic sizzled into her talisman. And then, blessedly, the bolts stopped coming.

Lyss looked around and saw that Sasha and Cam had done for two more of the mages, but the last one had retreated behind a wall of mudbacks and was lobbing flame and attack charms over their heads. As she watched, one of his bolts all but hit the young Ardenine officer.

That was when she realized: this mage wasn't aiming at her at all—he was aiming at his own commander.

Sasha scooped up a mudback by his scruff and breeches and used him as a shield as she spurred her pony into the line of southerners. The line broke, opening a path to the fourth mage. Lyss's first arrow bounced off his silver collar, but her second found a home, and he toppled backward.

Four mages down, Lyss thought, but her cheer faded when she looked around and saw nothing but a sea of mudbacks around her, and the young officer facing her, his crossbow aimed at her heart.

THE GRAY WOLF

Despite Hal's forced march through the pass, the northerners met them before they'd reached the Vale. They made their stand at the narrowest part of the pass. Their archers had positioned themselves on the heights, where they could direct withering fire onto his men as soon as they appeared.

As planned, his veterans split up, each taking charge of a column. Six officers who know what they're doing can accomplish a lot more than one. It also allowed Hal to keep one eye on the shape of the battle and the other on his mages.

Clearly, the northerners had at least one mage on hand, because he was busily putting up barriers to deflect their attempts to clear off the bowmen. Hal searched the enemy lines until he spotted him—a young man whose pale hair made him a good target. Hal's own mages were veterans— so they should have known what to do on their own. Yet they wove magical barriers around themselves but initiated no offense.

"Pitts!" Hal shouted, pointing. "It's four against one. Can you do anything about their mage?"

Pitts complied like a man half-asleep.

"A gold crown to whoever can take out their mage," Hal called out to his own bowmen. They did their best, though they could have benefitted from a few more years of drilling. Once they'd launched their bolts, it seemed to take them forever to reload. The northerners, on the other hand, used longbows, and they were excellent shots. Their frontline soldiers fought as fiercely as any he'd seen. Though their numbers were fewer, each well-trained northern soldier was worth four of Hal's men.

They are fighting on their home ground, Hal thought, and it shows.

As the battle dragged on, Hal was losing two or three soldiers to every one of theirs. Soon, the empire's advantage in numbers would evaporate. When he looked to the rear, the other two battalions were nowhere in sight.

I've been set up for failure, he thought, as his losses mounted. But I won't fail. I need to find a way to win.

Hal looked for the Fellsian field commander and

eventually spotted him, wearing a yellow lieutenant's scarf, mounted on a smoky-gray pony. As the lieutenant rode up and down the line, two other soldiers moved in tandem with him, as if they were linked by an invisible tether. He has a personal guard, too, Hal thought, surprised.

The guards (if that's what they were) had their work cut out for them. The lieutenant wasn't afraid to wade in himself. It was like he had eyes in the back of his head. If I could eliminate their commander, Hal thought, it might give us a fighting chance.

"Pitts!" Hal shouted. "Target their field officer." He pointed.

Pitts looked, then shook his head, making the sign of Malthus. "Won't do any good," he said. "That's the Gray Wolf."

Hal heard a murmur go through the troops like a collective shudder. *The Gray Wolf! It's the Gray Wolf!*

Hal looked again. Granted, the lieutenant was a distance away, but Hal didn't see anything wolfish about him. "What makes you think it's him?"

"I've seen him before, in the borderlands, and in the Fens. He always fights with two guards at his side. He's a demon. If you try to kill him, he turns into a wolf."

Hal struggled to be patient. "You've seen this with your own eyes?"

Pitts shook his head. "Nobody's seen it and lived to tell about it."

Hal could sense panic rising all around him like a flood tide. He needed to put a stop to it.

"I don't know about you," Hal said, "but I'd rather face a wolf than a demon." He urged his horse forward, closing the distance between them as much as he dared. Unslinging his bow from his shoulder, he reached into his saddle boot, drew out an arrow, nocked it, and let fly.

Hal was not the best bowman in the king's army, but at that distance, he might have hit his mark had the Gray Wolf's guardian not shoved the lieutenant aside so that the arrow flew harmlessly over one shoulder. Hoping for a second shot, Hal wheeled his horse. Then, out of the corner of his eye, he saw Pitts, his hand on his amulet, loose a torrent of flame straight at him.

It struck his gelding dead on. The horse screamed and went down, but Hal had already leapt free. He landed, rolling to his feet in time to see another one of his mages taking his own shot at him. That missed, too, but Hal knew that his luck couldn't hold forever.

Hal ran a zigzag toward them, sending up a prayer, all the while knowing there was no way he could get to all of them before one of them got lucky. He imagined the message his father and lady mother would receive—that he'd been killed in a losing battle. Would his father suspect the truth?

His prayers were answered in an odd sort of way when three spatterbacks plowed into the mages, sending them flying.

It was the Gray Wolf and his two guardians.

Hal stood frozen, watching them make quick work of three of the mages. But Pitts retreated a short distance away, set his feet, and slammed bolt after bolt of flame into the officer he called the Gray Wolf. The lieutenant did not turn into a wolf. In fact, he scarcely seemed to notice. Did that mean that Pitts was right, that the Fellsian officer was some kind of witch or demon?

With that, Pitts must have spotted Hal, because he shot a torrent of flame straight at him, nearly incinerating him.

That broke into Hal's trance, stirring him to action. He ripped a bow and packet of arrows from the grip of a dead soldier, mounted a riderless horse, and charged toward Pitts just in time to see the mage go down, an arrow transfixing his chest.

Hal wheeled, nocking an arrow, and found himself face-to-face with the lieutenant, who'd just taken the shot. Hal understood several things in rapid succession.

First, demon or not, this enemy officer had withstood a torrent of magical attacks with no apparent damage.

Second, the lieutenant was a woman. Though she was tall as many men were, her features were unmistakably feminine, and her long hair was woven into a thick braid the color of autumn wheat. Her skin was darker than that of many northerners, her brown eyes as fierce and proud as any raptor's.

Third, she and her companions had just saved his life by

killing four mages who were supposed to be on his side.

Fourth, all he had to do was let fly, and the so-called Gray Wolf would be done for—assuming arrows worked better on her than magery.

But he couldn't. For what seemed like an eternity, they sat on their horses, staring at each other. Two soldiers on opposite sides, each trying to survive. Hal realized that he had a lot more in common with this fierce lieutenant than with the thrice-damned king of Arden. And he owed more to the men under his command, who had fought so fiercely in the service of a man who had betrayed them.

Hal lowered his bow. The battle is lost, anyway, he told himself. Those dead mages were the only edge we had.

The lieutenant grinned, her eyes crinkling in amusement. "Better watch your back, flatlander," she said. She turned her pony and galloped back to the safety of her forward line.

With that, Hal called the retreat, hoping that his decimated troops still remembered that command.

AFTER THE DANCE

Lyss walked the now-quiet battlefield with General Dunedain, Shadow Dancer, Mason, and Littlefield. Darkness was falling. As the sun descended in the west, the Spirit Mountains sent long shadow fingers across Queen Court Vale, reaching for Alyssa Peak. The dead from both armies were still being carried from the field. In the surrounding hills, funeral pyres were burning, smudging the face of the rising moon. One of them burned for Captain Starborn, who'd died doing what he loved best—killing southerners. Even the usually impassive Dunedain wept when she heard the news. This was a loss they could ill afford.

Even when we win, we lose, Lyss thought.

Most of the queendom's dead and wounded were from

Lyss's own squadron. She'd fought with some of them since the summer she'd turned twelve, just a year after Arden stole her father and brother from her.

A battle is like a deadly sort of dance, Lyss thought. We learn the steps by sparring in the practice yards, by marching up and down the field in the hope that we'll remember the moves when we're distracted by the smell of blood and the shrieks of the wounded and death howling toward us from all sides. We go into battle to the cadence of drums and guns, but our dance cards are blank. We have no idea who we'll dance with that day, when death might cut in, and who'll leave the floor alive.

Officers attempt to call the steps, but after a certain point, nobody is listening. It all comes down to what happens in each of dozens of intimate meetings: advances and retreats, moves and countermoves. As an officer, Lyss had to try to manage the field, but, like any other soldier, if her time came, she would die alone.

The wounded had long since been delivered to the healers in the town. Among the wounded was Finn, who'd suffered a blow to the head. Lyss had already been to the healing halls, where she'd spoken to all who were well enough for visitors. Finn refused to see anyone, which was one more worry. He shouldn't have gone back into battle so soon, Lyss thought. No wonder he wants to serve the queendom a different way. Still, the healers said that Finn would recover, and that was something to be grateful for.

The story of the charge against the southern mages had spread like wildfire, adding more glitterbits as it traveled. Soon it would be an entire battalion of mages, led by the king of Arden himself. The only thing Lyss liked about that version of the story was the thought of having Gerard within bowshot.

Lost in a muddle of thought, Lyss trailed after the others. On the one hand, they had won an important victory against what had appeared to be impossible odds. On the other hand, she now knew that a good part of the battalion they'd faced was as young and green as the grass along the Dyrnnewater in June. Untrained, untried, untested on the battlefield—lucky to know which end of a sword to poke with. Yet they'd been sent into the van with their young captain like sheep to a slaughter while Karn's more seasoned troops melted away. And a slaughter it was. The enemy losses were extraordinarily high, compared to their own.

The difference between us and them is that the king of Arden doesn't care.

If they were sheep, the mudback captain was the sheepdog, by turns leading them into the fray, turning them away from danger, snapping at their heels, calling them to order when they fell apart. She could see the bones of his tactics. He'd done what she would have done in his place—fashioned a simple attack strategy in the hope that they could carry it out. He'd done the best he could with a bad situation. And, then, in the end, he was betrayed.

Sasha and Cam said she must be mistaken, but Lyss knew what she'd seen, and what she'd seen was four mages turning on their commander—gunning for him instead of the enemy on the field. And that same commander standing down when he had the chance to put an arrow in her throat.

Why would Karn lead with these younglings? And why wouldn't he relieve them when they needed it? Didn't he care whether he won this battle or not? More importantly, where was Karn now?

Was it all some sort of distraction or decoy? A red herring? Was Karn teaching someone a lesson? Were the mages rising up against their southern handlers? There was a story there—Lyss knew there was a story, but she would probably never hear it. All in all, it was a hollow sort of victory.

"Lieutenant Gray!"

Startled, Lyss looked up to find herself the center of attention.

"Wherever you were, I hope it was a pleasant journey," General Dunedain said.

"Oh, uh, no, not exactly," Lyss said. "It's just that, after a battle, there's a lot to think about."

"I agree," Dunedain said. "I've been thinking, too." She held out her hand. "Give me your scarf."

Lyss, confused, blinked at the general. "I'm sorry, ma'am, I don't understand."

"Your scarf, Lieutenant," Dunedain repeated impatiently. Patience was not the general's strong suit.

Lyss reached up and fingered the yellow scarf around her neck. Her battle-weary mind stumbled around, unable to hit on an explanation. "I know it needs washing, but—"

"It doesn't need washing," Dunedain said. "It needs replacing. Now give it here."

Was she being demoted? Booted out? Lyss managed to undo the knot, slipped the scarf off, and handed it to Dunedain. The general tucked it into her carry bag and pulled a wad of fabric from her pocket. She thrust it at Lyss. "Here's a new one."

It was blue. Captain's blue.

"I know you don't stand on ceremony, Captain Gray," Dunedain said, grinning, "so you won't be disappointed by a field promotion. This salvo needs a new commander, and I've chosen you."

Lyss stood clutching it. "But . . . Littlefield and—and Mason . . . they've got a lot more experience than I have, and—"

"I don't want the job," Littlefield said. "Blue clashes with my eyes."

"And I can't count high enough to be a captain," Mason said.

Shadow took the scarf from Lyss and knotted it around her neck. "It's you, Captain Gray. Deal with it. And when we get to town, you're buying."

"You're the one getting married," Lyss said. "You're buying."

"I'm buying on my wedding day," Shadow said. "You'll have to wait until then."

And then they were all laughing, and embracing, and making the kinds of threats and promises that comrades make when one battle is over and the next not yet begun.

They'd just reached their horses when they heard a pounding of hooves and saw the silhouette of a rider against the night sky. He reined in next to them, saluted General Dunedain, and handed her a dispatch tube. "We had a bird from Fortress Rocks, ma'am," he said. His expression said it was bad news.

Fortress Rocks! Lyss glanced at Shadow. His betrothed, Aspen, lived at Fortress Rocks.

Dunedain weighed the tube, unopened, in her hand. "And?"

"While we were occupied in the pass, Karn took the rest of his brigade north." The soldier swallowed hard. "It's bad, ma'am. The town's destroyed. They burned everything that was burnable, stole everything that was stealable, and blew up the keep. They slaughtered everyone."

Lyss's heart sank. Fortress Rocks was a beloved symbol of northern resistance. It had never fallen to a foreign invader—not even during the Wizard Wars. Until now.

Shadow had gone dark and still, in the way only an uplander can. "Civilians? They killed civilians?"

The soldier nodded. "It was nearly all civilians," he said. "Since it's far from the border, there's only a handful of soldiers stationed there, as a rule. I guess they figured it was an easy mark."

"What about survivors?" Shadow persisted.

The soldier shook his head. "I don't know."

Dunedain pulled the paper from the tube, scanned the message, and swore.

"May I see it?" Shadow stuck out his hand.

Dunedain didn't want to hand it over, Lyss could tell, but she did. Shadow read it, twice, then handed it back. He looked like he'd been gutted, yet was somehow still on his feet. Lyss took a step toward him and put her hand on his arm, but he shook her off.

"This brigade of Karn's," he said to the messenger, his voice icy and flat. "Do we know where they are now?"

"We thought they might go straight on to Chalk Cliffs, but it appears they've turned back south, hotfooting it back to Spiritgate. By now they've likely met up with what's left of them that we fought. There's no way we'll catch them now."

"If they are in the Seven Realms, I'll find them," Shadow said.

Lyss knew, in her bones, that Aspen was dead. That was bad enough. But somehow she had to prevent her friend from throwing his life away, too.

She gripped his shoulder. "Shadow, please. Let's ride to

Fortress Rocks," she said. "There . . . there may be people there who need our help. That's what's important now."

He just stood there and looked at her, his face as expressionless as any granite face of Hanalea Peak, his eyes black and opaque as twin caves.

"Please, Shadow. The bastards will still be there when we go hunting them."

That had the force of truth. Evil always seems to flourish, while the good die young.

After a long pause, Shadow nodded. "All right," he said. "Let's go."

7

BACK IN THE CAULDRON

Lyss and her party began the long descent from the eastern mountains, following the valley of the Dyrnnewater down into the Vale. It had been nearly three months since Queen Court and Fortress Rocks—events Lyss needed to remember, and learn from.

Now, November snow was already piling up in the high passes. It was late to be going home. It had been a long and bloody marching season.

The scene at Fortress Rocks had been even worse than Lyss had imagined. The slain totaled close to six hundred, including Aspen Silverleaf, who'd gone down in the street with her knife in her hand and two dead mudbacks to show for it. The Ardenines had put everyone to the sword—adults, lýtlings, even the livestock.

Lyss's salvo spent days clearing away rubble and constructing the funeral pyres that burned on for days. They were writing the epitaph to hundreds of sad stories. In most cases, Lyss and her soldiers were the only mourners—there was no one else left alive. Finn had insisted on riding along to see if he could help with the wounded, but there were very, very few. He seemed to be recovering from his injury, though he still had little to say.

There was one bit of good news. Aspen's younger siblings were not among the dead. They'd been staying with family at Marisa Pines Camp so that Aspen could catch up on her orders. They returned to find their eldest sister dead and their home in ruins.

The only other survivors were a few townspeople who had managed to flee into the surrounding hills or hide from the soldiers until they marched away. Lyss, Shadow, and Dunedain questioned them, collecting details, assembling timelines, as if this would somehow prevent it from happening again.

The only way to prevent this from happening again is to win this war, Lyss thought. And we are not winning.

Lyss kept thinking about the young captain, leading his soldiers to slaughter in the pass while, farther north, his comrades were slaughtering civilians. How much did he know about the plan of attack? Was he a willing or unwilling participant? A dupe or a co-conspirator? Was that why his own mages had turned on him—was it because they knew they were being sacrificed?

It doesn't matter, she told herself. Then why did she keep dwelling on it?

They laid Aspen to rest in an embroidered deerskin robe made by her own hands. Shadow put her awl and needle in one hand, her dagger in the other, a pile of furs and deerskins at her feet. He held on to her hand until the rising flames forced him to let go. Lyss released a breath of relief when he did. She'd been afraid he might choose to burn with her.

They spent their remaining time at Fortress Rocks rebuilding the temple and enough dwellings to house those few who remained. When Lyss's salvo received marching orders, Shadow stayed behind to help rebuild Aspen's shop. Her younger sister, Sparrow, was determined to take it over and make a living for what was left of the family. Their grandmother came from Marisa Pines to help.

Lyss and her salvo had spent the rest of the autumn skirmishing with the enemy at Spiritgate and along the southeastern border. Accomplishing nothing.

Now they were going home. Most of her salvo had gone ahead of them. Lyss, Sasha, Cam, Finn, and Littlefield had detoured and collected Shadow at Fortress Rocks.

They rounded the flank of the mountain, and Lyss found herself looking down into the home vale. In wintertime, it was like looking down into a sea of cloud formed when the steam from the hot springs and geysers met the cold mountain air.

Her father used to call it the Cauldron. Lyss couldn't help thinking that wasn't too far from the truth.

As they descended, the air grew noticeably warmer, thanks to the heat that seethed beneath the ground and leaked out in places. The moist air formed layers of ice on cliffs and trees, producing a glittering fairyland when the sunlight hit it. It still snowed in the Vale when the witch wind blew down over Hanalea and dumped its blizzards into the valley. But there were glens and niches that remained green all year long.

Dusk was falling when they finally penetrated the last layer of cloud and Lyss saw the city spread before them, prickling with temple spires. The lamplighters were already moving along the streets—young wizards who spun spheres of light between their hands and lifted them to the tops of the lampposts. Crowds of children trailed behind, hoping the lamplighters would play catch with them before they moved on, the wizard light streaking through the darkness. Sometimes the lighters would lift the lýtlings on their shoulders and allow them to grasp the brilliance between their hands and set the lights themselves. Even now, in wartime, with so many losses, some traditions continued.

Light spilled from doorways into the dusk. Lyss heard the faint sound of music as the last of the shops closed up and the inns and music halls opened their doors. People filled the streets, moving from work to play, going home to their families, or meeting lovers and friends. Once, Lyss would have been among them. As a child, she'd loved walking the familiar streets of Southbridge and Ragmarket with her father, cloaked in anonymity, visiting the markets and attending music programs in the temples. Letting the music lift her and take her away.

Not anymore. Maybe it was the gathering dark that meant it was the beginning of the month-long solstice season. This time of year always brought with it memories of past grief and apprehension about the future. Solstice would be forever tainted by the deaths of those she loved. As the monstrous king of Arden no doubt intended.

Once their horses realized where they were going, their steps quickened, and it was more a matter of reining them in than of urging them forward. Mincemeat tried to take the bit in his teeth and forge ahead.

Everyone's glad to be going home but me, Lyss thought. She looked up at Shadow, riding just ahead of her, shoulders still rounded from grief. Almost everyone.

Lyss's sixteenth name day hurtled toward her, bringing with it her coronation as the princess heir and her launch into the marriage market.

Lyss had a few memories of her sister Hana's naming party, in the optimistic past. Lyss's father had danced with her, his serpent amulet glittering at his neck, a proud grin on his face.

"Did you know that I hired your mother to teach me how to dance?" he'd said, leaning close to speak into her ear.

"What?" Lyss had frowned at him, convinced he was teasing her.

"It's true, I swear on the dead queens," her father had said. "It was the only way I could think of to get her to dance with me."

"Well," Lyss observed, "she did a *fair* job, I suppose."

Her father had come out of the slums of Fellsmarch, a charismatic streetlord whose silver cuffs signified a magical legacy. He had become the queen's bodyguard, then a member of the Wizard Council, and finally High Wizard and consort to the queen. Never a king. He'd never wanted to be king. What he wanted was the queen, and he'd paid a heavy price.

We're a lot alike, Lyss thought. He didn't want to be king, and I'm not so keen on being queen.

If Hana still lived, Lyss's naming would have signified nothing more than a milestone, a festive party that signaled her entry into a career. Once she'd thought to be a musician or a poet; now she'd probably choose a military career. As it was, more and more, she'd be pulled from the battlefield, where at least she knew what she was doing.

Lyss inhaled the mingled scents of Fellsmarch. Flowers of all kinds, and the little charcoal burners the street vendors used to grill the sausages and flying fishes that they wrapped into flatbreads. The lights from the carousel sparkled out on the green like raindrops on a window-pane, blurred by the tears in her eyes. Her father had brought it in pieces through the mountains and ordered it reassembled so all the lýtlings in the city could ride flying horses, too.

Four years, she thought. Four years since the last attack on the royal family. Did it mean that King Gerard had turned to other targets? Or did it mean they were due?

"Captain?" Sasha urged her pony up beside Mincemeat. "Are you all right?"

"I'm fine," Lyss lied. "The smoke burns my eyes is all."

"It does that every time you come home," Sasha said, with a sympathetic smile. "Nothing that a meat pie and a pint won't cure."

"Have I ever told you that I love you, Talbot?" Lyss said.

Sasha snorted. "Me, I'm happy to be home. I can't wait to see my nieces and dig into some Solstice cakes."

"I can't wait to dig into some hot wassail," Littlefield said.

Lyss glanced over at Finn, who seemed lost in his own thoughts. "Finn? What are you looking forward to? Will you be working in the healing halls right away?"

The question seemed to take him by surprise. "Oh! I'll . . . look forward to seeing people . . . I haven't seen for a while," he said. "And I'll begin working with Lord Vega as soon as . . . I'm needed."

"I hope you'll take a little time off, Finn," Lyss said. "After everything that—"

"I'm *fine*," Finn snapped. "Why won't anyone believe me?"

"Easy, sul'Mander," Shadow said.

"What about you, Shadow?" Sasha said, then clamped her mouth shut as if sorry she'd asked the question.

"I won't be home long," he said. "I'll stay a few days and see my father, but then I'm going back east."

"What?" Lyss said, startled. She'd been counting on spending time with her friend while they were both in the capital. She wasn't good with matters of the heart, but she still hoped she could find a way to help him the way Adrian had helped her after Hana died. "You won't be home for Solstice?"

He shook his head.

"Are you going back to Fortress Rocks?"

"I plan to make a stop there, and drop off some more supplies to Sparrow, but I have business on the coast in a week. I'll be working at Demonai Camp through the spring, so there's not much point in traveling all the way back for the holiday."

"Yes, there is," Lyss said, thinking fast. She didn't believe that story about business on the coast. If he was traveling east, it might mean he planned to follow through on his promise to go after Marin Karn. Shadow had always danced on the edge, but now there was a recklessness about him that she'd not seen before. Worry squirmed in her middle—the worry that he would never come back.

She groped for a way to keep him in the Vale, or bring him back for the Festival of Light, at least. "But . . . I was counting on going hunting together to put some meat on the table for the holiday. If I have to eat barley all winter, I'll cut my throat."

"You're a better hunter than I will ever be," Shadow said. "You'll do better on your own."

"No, I won't," Lyss said. "Anyway, you can't fight this war every minute of every day."

"Hang on," Sasha said, staring at Lyss. "What did you just say? I think something's gone wrong with my ears."

"Shut it, Talbot," Lyss growled, her mind still churning, trying to surface an excuse to convince Shadow to stay. "The thing is, there's something else I need your help with."

Shadow's eyes narrowed. "Something else?"

"Right," she said. "Something else."

"Like?"

Before Shadow's name day, when he took up flashcraft, music had been a connection between them, and central to his existence. She could use that.

"Remember how we used to take music lessons together at Southbridge Temple? And how you were always better than me?"

"Barely," Shadow said, as if he thought he might be

walking into a trap. "That was a long time ago."

"So, you know how Speaker Jemson holds that benefit for the Briar Rose Foundation every winter solstice?"

"Ye . . . es," Shadow said, scrubbing his hand through his curls. "So?"

"I promised Jemson that the two of us would do a set for the twenty-fifth anniversary of the Briar Rose Ministry."

"No."

"But I promised."

"You promised, I didn't," Shadow said. "It's been forever since I've picked up a basilka."

"That's something you never forget," Lyss said, with false confidence. When Shadow kept shaking his head, she rushed on. "If you'd seen Jemson's face, there'd be no way you could say no. He was so excited. You know how sentimental he is about his former students. And you know the ministry is more important than ever these days. So many people are going hungry during the holiday."

"All the more reason to focus on the war," Shadow said. "You don't need me. You're the one that will draw the crowds. You're a war hero, and the heir to the throne. Who could resist?"

It was down to begging. Lyss leaned out of her saddle, gripped both his hands, and looked him in the eyes. "Please, Shadow," she said. "Don't make me get up there alone. I would rather face a hundred howling southern mercenaries than a temple crowd."

Shadow laughed, a rare and precious sound these days. "I do believe you would," he said. "All right. I'll do it. But I won't be back until just before the holiday. Let me know what pieces you want to play and I'll try to get in some practice while I'm gone."

"Thank you," Lyss said. "I owe you. I can't wait to tell Jemson."

She watched Shadow wheel his horse and ride away, thinking Jemson would likely be the most surprised of all.

Littlefield, Mason, and the remaining Highlanders peeled off as they entered the city, heading for the garrison house. Lyss, Sasha, Cam, and Finn continued on, making for the castle close and the tower of Fellsmarch Castle, poking above everything else.

"Will you be staying in town?" Lyss asked Finn, hoping that was a safe question. She'd expected that Finn would break away and go directly to his family's compound on Gray Lady Peak.

"I'll be staying in the palace," he said. "The princess Mellony has arranged housing for my family over the holiday."

"Really?" Lyss said, surprised. "Aunt Mellony did? Does that mean I'll be seeing more of you than usual?"

"Yes," he said. "You will."

"As long as you're in town, you can come dine with us on the holiday," she said impulsively.

"That's the plan," he said. Looking over her shoulder, he added, "Here comes the queen."

Lyss turned to find her mother crossing the stable yard, Captain Byrne at her heels, Lyss's aunt Mellony and cousin Julianna following close behind.

"Look!" Lyss said, pointing at Lord and Lady Mander bringing up the rear. "Your parents are here, too."

Finn nodded, shifting his shoulders. He didn't seem surprised.

Lyss opened her arms and pulled her mother close. As usual, Lyss felt like an awkward blond giant.

"Thank the Maker you're home safe," Queen Raisa said, tears shimmering in her eyes. She tolerated Lyss's battlefield adventures because they were part of the role of a Gray Wolf queen. The only part Lyss had enthusiastically embraced. A little *too* enthusiastically, as far as the queen was concerned.

"How long have you been home from the borderlands?" Lyss asked, holding her mother out at arm's length.

"Just a week," her mother said. "I'll want to hear all about the campaign in the east."

It's always the same story, Mama, Lyss thought. They march north, we kill some of them, they kill some of us, and then they march south again.

Out of the corner of her eye, Lyss saw Lady Mander sweep Finn into her arms, embracing him with more enthusiasm than Lyss had ever seen her display about anything. His father kept slapping his back and murmuring into his ear. When that trio finally broke up, Aunt Mellony greeted Finn, beaming, as if he were her long-lost son. Then it was Julianna's turn. If anything, her greeting was warmer than her mother's.

Everyone's sure glad to have Finn home, Lyss thought. Not that they shouldn't be, but . . . it was all just a little overdone, like a play in its first run-through.

Eventually, the lovefest was over. The Manders walked off together, Lord Mander with his arm around Finn's shoulders.

That was when Aunt Mellony noticed Lyss. "Welcome home, Alyssa," she said, warmly embracing her. "Julianna and I have been looking for you every day."

As soon as Aunt Mellony released her, Julianna gripped both her hands. "Lyss. I never feel the marching season is really over until you're home safe."

"You're looking well," Lyss said, because it was true. Her cousin's eyes were shining, and her cheeks were pinked up from the cold, or excitement, or maybe that's just the way they were.

"We have so much to talk about. Aunt Raisa and I have been discussing ways to prevent another Fortress Rocks, and we wanted to get your insights."

"Good idea," Lyss said. She couldn't help noticing that her cousin's hands were soft, the nails clean and manicured. It made Lyss hyperconscious of her own hands—callused and cracked and dirt-stained.

Taking a step back, her cousin looked up at her. "You always have so much more color in autumn than you do when you leave in the spring," she said.

"Actually, it's dirt," Lyss said. "We've discovered that a thick layer of dirt is great camouflage. In fact, out in the field, a good scrubbing could cost you your life."

Julianna, brow furrowed, gazed at Lyss. "Really?" she said finally, as if she didn't believe it but was afraid to call her on it.

"That's not all," Lyss said, some devil inside her driving her on. "Mud, it turns out, is an excellent treatment for the complexion. I've brought a supply home so that I can apply it on a regular basis here at court." At that point, her mother caught her eye, scowled, and shook her head slightly.

Julianna pretended not to notice.

Lyss couldn't say why she was so thin-skinned when it came to her cousin. Was she jealous that Julianna was built like a princess and not a lodgepole pine? Or was it that Julianna had all the traits Lyss lacked—social skills, diplomacy, political smarts, and breasts?

Was it because her cousin was one of her mother's trusted advisers, though she was only two years older than Lyss? Julianna had become an expert in foreign relations and had recently assumed responsibility for the queendom's intelligence service. It had been floundering since Lady Tyburn was murdered.

Strange. Lyss couldn't remember Aunt Mellony ever showing the least bit of interest in politics. Julianna took to statecraft like a—well, like a pig to mud, demonstrating the kind of clever, quick wit required to navigate agendas at court. It seemed like Lyss had spent a lifetime hearing Julianna gently correct her in meetings.

"Well, the fact of the matter is . . . ," she would say, tapping her long fingers on the reports in front of her. Or, "I can see why you might think that, Your Highness, but . . ." Or, "Our latest intelligence actually suggests that . . ."

Lyss could only conclude that her cousin had inherited that interest and talent from her dead father. However she'd come by it, it seemed like Julianna and the queen could finish each other's sentences without a hitch.

Good for her, Lyss thought. I wouldn't want to waste the marching season in one meeting after another.

"Congratulations on the victory at Queen Court, Your Highness," Captain Byrne said.

Immediately followed by the massacre at Fortress Rocks, Lyss thought.

"Finn says that you're the most ferocious woman he knows," Julianna added.

Ferocious? That was a compliment of sorts, but it wasn't exactly what Lyss was going for.

"Julianna and I have been following your accomplishments," Aunt Mellony said. "They are the talk of the court. Imagine, downing four slave mages with one swipe of your sword."

"That's not exactly how it happened," Lyss said.

"The ambassador from the Fens tells me that Lord Dimitri is ready to adopt you," Julianna said, "or at least marry you off to two or three of his sons."

"I'm not marrying anyone," Lyss snapped. And then, taking a deep breath, she added, more graciously, "Anyway, Lord Dimitri is too generous. All the credit for our success in the west should go to the Waterwalkers. I'm just glad they're on our side."

"Perhaps we should send some of them to our southern borders," her mother said, with a wry smile.

"Perhaps we should send them *beyond* our southern borders," Lyss said. She looked at her mother, and her mother looked back, each knowing what the other was thinking, their ongoing disagreement about tactics hanging heavy between them.

Let's not get into an argument before the sun has set on my first day home, Lyss thought. Especially not in front of Mellony and Julianna.

"I'd better see to Mincemeat," she said, stroking the pony's nose.

"Dinner's at seven," her mother said. "Julianna and your aunt Mellony will be there, too. I can't wait to catch up."

8

SPARRING LESSONS

"Heads up, Lyss!"

Lyss gritted her teeth and raised the tip of her sword to counter Sasha's swing. When their blades met, the force of the blow all but rattled the teeth from her head. Her ears were ringing from the clamor of steel on steel and her arms were so tired she could barely lift her sword. The cold wind somehow found its way into the practice yard and dried the sweat from her face as soon as it appeared, but her clothing was soaked through. When the bells from the cathedral tower signaled time, she fell forward onto her face in the snow.

They were usually fairly evenly matched, heightwise, at least, though Sasha had about fifty pounds on her. But Lyss couldn't remember ever being worked this hard.

"Blood and bones," Lyss muttered, scrubbing snow over her face. "Tell me, Talbot, is it something I said? If so, I'm very, very sorry."

"Special request from your salvo," Sasha said, extending her hand to help her up. "They asked me to wear you out so they wouldn't have to drill this afternoon. Some people have lives, you know."

"Ha," Lyss said. "Well, you've worn me out for nothing. Drill is cancelled this afternoon, anyway. The war council is meeting, and then we're having an early dinner because of the concert."

"Oh," Sasha said, grimacing. "In that case, I'm very, very sorry I worked you so hard."

"I should probably just leave my armor on for this meeting," Lyss said, as they walked into the deserted duty room.

"You're expecting heavy fire?"

Lyss nodded. "Nobody wants to hear what I have to say."

"Is it what you say or how you say it?"

Lyss sighed. "Probably both. I always think that if I tell the truth, people can't help but agree. When they don't, I lose my temper and everything goes south from there."

Sasha snorted. "That's your mistake—thinking politics has anything to do with the truth."

"So it doesn't matter what you say, as long as you make it pretty," Lyss said. "I should write that down." She peeled off her padded sparring coat, leather armor, and the weights she used to strengthen her arms. Sasha stripped down, too. Lyss could tell she was chewing on something, trying to decide whether to spit it out.

"What?" Lyss said finally.

"I keep thinking about something my da told me about making a sale."

Sasha's da had died when she was just a lýtling, but he seemed to have been a gusher of wisdom, because she was always quoting him.

"What did he say?"

"Well, you know he had a stall in Ragmarket," Sasha said.

Where he fenced stolen and smuggled goods. Lyss nodded.

"He said when you're trying to sell a lady a shawl, you don't plunge in talking about upland sheepswool or indigo dye or hand-knotted fringe."

"You don't?"

"Maybe she don't care about any of that. No. You find out what she wants, what's missing in her life, and then you show her how that shawl fills the bill."

"So, if she's starving, you tell her she can eat the shawl?"

"Never mind," Sasha growled, cheeks flaming. "I was just trying to help."

"Hang on," Lyss said, putting her hand on Sasha's arm. "I'm sorry. Can you give me an example?"

"So she says she don't need a shawl, it's too expensive, and she's got a warm coat already. But you're talking, and you find out she loves her grandchildren, and wishes they'd visit more often. So you paint a picture of her sitting at the fireside with all those grandchildren, snuggled up in that shawl. *That's* what she's buying, not just a shawl."

Lyss laughed. "Thank you. I'll try to remember that."

Sasha gathered up the equipment and practice swords, cradling them in her arms like a load of kindling. "Everybody's excited about the concert tonight," she said. "There's banners up all over town. I think your whole salvo's planning to be there. Littlefield and Mason, anyway."

Great, Lyss thought. What if they show up and Shadow doesn't? I'll never hear the end of this.

"What are you planning to wear? Wait—let me guess— your mourning coat."

That was Lyss's standard dress-up garb—it seemed to suit every occasion. But not this time. "Aunt Mellony's lending me a dress," she said.

"Hmm," Sasha said, her lips twitching as she fought back a smile. "That'll be a sight to see."

"It's not like you haven't seen me in a dress before."

"Not one of Princess Mellony's dresses. What about Shadow? What's he wearing? I don't think I've ever seen him dressed up."

Lyss shrugged. "I don't know. He's not back yet."

"He's not?" Sasha struggled to wipe away the surprise

on her face. "Oh. I thought you'd be practicing."

"I've been practicing some, on my own," Lyss said. "Probably he has, too. We're both writing new songs that we'll do solo."

Sasha bit her lip. "Have you heard from him?"

Lyss shook her head. "I'm not worried," she lied. "He said that he wouldn't be back until right before the concert."

"You mean like now? It *is* right before the concert."

"He'll come," Lyss said. "Music was always really important to him. Besides, he won't let me down." Unless something's happened to him.

Just then, the bells of the cathedral tower bonged the half hour. "Bones," Lyss said. "I'd better hurry and clean up, or Julianna will think I've gone back to wallowing in the mud."

"Good luck, Lyss," Sasha called after her.

When Lyss walked into the library, a cheerful fire was blazing on the hearth. The council members were scattered around the room, chatting informally. Her mother was poring over maps she'd spread across the large central table—maps of the Fells and neighboring Tamron and Arden.

Why do you need maps of places you never intend to set foot in? Lyss thought.

Lyss had maps on her walls, too—drawings of military targets south of the border; schemes for how to get a northern army in and out.

You should talk, she scolded herself. *You aren't going anywhere, either.*

When Lyss entered, the queen looked up and nodded briskly. "There you are. Help yourself to some tea, if you'd like. We'll get started in a few minutes."

To Lyss's surprise, Finn sul'Mander was at the sideboard, stirring honey into two cups of tea. He'd never attended the council before.

"What are you doing here?" Lyss whispered, coming up beside him and looking over the meager spread on offer.

"My father asked Uncle Micah to bring me to this meeting," Finn said, sipping at his tea and adding a little more sweetening. "He wants me to know more about decision-making here in the capital and how to plan battle strategy. Especially since I'll be here in the city full-time. Lord Vega says that maybe I can take his place at some of the meetings related to the health service."

Spend a little time at these meetings, and you might find you prefer the battlefield, Lyss thought. Though she'd swap Vega for Finn any day.

"Here's a tip," she said. "Try to stay awake. Everyone notices if you fall asleep."

Finn pretended to scowl. "Oh, too bad. I thought I could get a nap in so I'll be fresh for the concert tonight."

Lyss all but choked on her tea. "You're coming to that?" It was beginning to register that the audience would be made up of actual people that she knew, that she'd see again.

He nodded. "I wouldn't miss it. Besides, your aunt Mellony seems to be eager to show you off, and Julianna's really excited about it."

She is? Lyss thought, watching him carry two cups of tea back to the table, setting one down in front of Julianna and taking a seat between her and his uncle-cousin, Micah Bayar. With the two wizards side by side, their heads together, talking, the resemblance was striking, save that one was dark, the other light. Bayar was draped in the High Wizard stoles that had once belonged to Lyss's father. As long as she lived, she would never get used to that.

Lyss took her usual seat to the right of the queen. She looked around the table, thinking about what Sasha had said. She'd known most of the council members all of her life. But what did they really want?

Her mother was easy. She wanted to preserve the queendom and the Line. She wanted to protect what was left of her family, that being Lyss. That tended to make her more cautious—less eager to take chances. The key would be convincing her that doing nothing brings its own risks.

Captain Byrne sat to the left of her mother. As the queen's bound captain, he wanted to protect the queendom and the Gray Wolf line. He might back a change in strategy if he believed that the Line was in danger otherwise.

Beside him was Shilo Trailblazer, clad in her deerskin leggings and coat, her hair entirely beaded and braided, signifying her many kills. Shilo was matriarch of Demonai

Lodge and commander of its famous clan warriors. The Demonai were born to fight, but they preferred to do it in their beloved mountains, where they had the upper hand. Lyss would have to make a good case to move them to a different field of battle.

Randolph Howard drummed his fingers on the table, then riffled through the notes spread out before him as if he had places to go and better things to do. A merchant and member of the Vale nobility, he served as a quartermaster of sorts—arranging for supplies for the Fellsian fighting forces. Howard could always find a way to make money, in peacetime or wartime.

Char Dunedain commanded the regular army—the Highlander forces. She was smart, tough, and experienced, with an extra share of courage. She wanted a strategically important mission with clear goals that would not spend her soldiers' lives thoughtlessly.

Bayar represented the Wizard Council. When it came to offense, they were likely to balk at crossing into Arden, where they might be captured and collared. Still, wizards might be her most reliable allies if she could make her case. They'd seen what happened to the gifted in the empire and they had no desire to see that replicated in the north.

Lord Vega sat to Julianna's left, but he kept leaning across her to speak with Finn. Vega was the health minister and overseer of the healing halls. Lyss couldn't imagine why he'd chosen that profession—he was arrogant, mean-spirited, and totally lacking in empathy.

What Lord Vega wanted was to go back to some golden age in his imagination when people knew their place and wizards were kings.

At the far end of the table, Hadley DeVilliers met her gaze and brought her fist to her chest in a mock-solemn salute. Hadley was the commander of the fledgling Fellsian navy. She wasn't much older than Lyss, but she'd built the navy from nothing in a few short years. Hadley tended to avoid politics, but she was a friend who could usually be counted on.

Across from Hadley sat Lyss's cousin Julianna, next to her mother, the princess Mellony. Mellony had never had much to say, but Julianna was cut from different cloth. She tended to be outspoken. She asked a lot of questions and offered her opinions freely.

Though she'd known Julianna nearly all her life, Lyss realized that she had no idea what Julianna wanted. How could that be?

"I hope you've enjoyed lounging about here in the luxury of the capital," the queen said, by way of a beginning. "What's it been—three weeks, now?"

Laughter rippled through them. Though a step up from their summer encampments in the borderlands, wartime Fellsmarch was not exactly luxurious.

"The beds are too soft," Trailblazer grumbled. "All wrong for my Demonai bones."

"All this rich food," General Dunedain said, pinching the nonexistent fat at her waist. "I can scarcely fit into my uniforms."

Even Bayar joined in. "The nonstop parties grow tiresome after a while," he said wryly.

"I'm so glad you feel that way," her mother said, "because we have work to do. As you know, the fallow season is when we discuss our military strategy and consider whether we need to make any changes. That's what I would like to focus on today. As usual, I would encourage you all to speak freely, knowing that what we say here will stay in this room."

Lord Bayar stood. "Your Majesty, before we begin, I would like to introduce my cousin's son, Finn sul'Mander, and to thank you for allowing him to sit in and observe our proceedings."

"Welcome, Finn," the queen said. "Feel free to ask questions as we move through the agenda. Now, General Dunedain, let's start with you."

And so it began, the annual ritual that Lyss had grown to detest. No matter what had happened on the battlefield during the year, the outcome was always the same—let's keep doing what we've been doing.

Dunedain reviewed the "victory" at Queen Court and the massacre at Fortress Rocks. This was old news to most of the council.

"One point of clarification," Lyss said. "Since it seems

clear now that Queen Court was just a diversion from the attack on Fortress Rocks, I don't think we can call it a win."

"Yet the southern forces at Queen Court suffered heavy losses," Dunedain said.

"True," Lyss said, "but the troops they lost appeared to be poorly trained conscripts from the down-realms. It's not like Arden had a lot invested in them."

"There you go again," Hadley said, wincing. "Snatching defeat from the jaws of victory. Can't you just bask in glory for once?"

"I just don't want to mislead anyone," Lyss said.

"Still," Raisa said, "isn't it true that the Ardenine battalion was decimated, and they lost four mages?"

"That's true," Lyss said. "The difference between us and them is that the king of Arden doesn't care."

"Stipulated," the queen said, and amusement rippled through the council. She turned back to Dunedain. "Continue."

"Lord Dimitri and our allies in the Fens have been keeping the enemy busy in the west," Dunedain said. "They've also captured quite a bit of ordnance, along with supplies and foodstuffs, which should help us through winter and again in the spring."

Lyss knew what the summation would be. At the end of the marching season, neither side had gained ground. The southerners had sustained more casualties—in absolute numbers, anyway. But the queendom had lost hundreds of civilians and millions of crowns' worth of property.

"Each one of our soldiers is worth three of theirs," Howard said, with the kind of fierce pride displayed by those who've never raised a sword themselves.

"Our soldiers have to be," Dunedain said. "The south can field three times as many troops as we can."

"Southern weapons can't compete with clan-made blades and longbows," Shilo said.

"Aye, our weapons are better," Dunedain said. "It's just difficult to lay our hands on enough of them."

"The problem is the Ardenine blockades of our ports," Howard said, looking pointedly at Hadley.

"Which brings us to Lady Barrett," the queen said, ignoring Howard's glare. "How goes our negotiation with the port masters in the Southern Islands?"

Julianna grimaced. "Negotiating with them is like trying to catch a fish with your bare hands. Just when you think you've got a grip on them, they slip away. They'll build ships for us—our money spends as good as any—but they're wary of opening their ports to us for shipping or for military use. They're just too vulnerable to Arden."

"Is there any news from Arden?" Captain Byrne asked. "From within the realm, I mean?"

Lyss came instantly alert.

"From what we're hearing, Montaigne is at odds with the Thane Council over the war," Julianna said. "He sold them a quick win, with spoils for everyone who agreed to supply men and money. Some are questioning whether our rocky bit of ground is worth what they've spent in men and treasure."

"Do you think it will amount to anything?" Bayar asked.

Julianna shrugged. "Hard to say. King Gerard has a history of ruthlessly quenching any spark of rebellion. Ask his six dead brothers."

The queen smiled sourly. "Anything else?"

"They seem to have tightened their grip on Delphi," Julianna said. "Recently the blackbirds have restricted travel into and out of the city. It's made it more difficult to stay in touch with our eyes and ears there. Arden must be expecting some kind of trouble."

"Let's hope they are right, Lady Barrett. Lord Bayar? Your assessment of our magical resources? Is there a shortage of flashcraft as well?"

Bayar shook his head. "Not really, Your Majesty. So many of the gifted have been killed that we have more than enough amulets to go around."

He looks tired, Lyss thought, feeling an unexpected flicker of sympathy. And discouraged.

"They seem to be growing more and more sophisticated in their use of magic," Bayar went on, "which means that we are losing some of our advantage in that arena."

"Thank you, everyone, for your insights," the queen

said, scribbling a few notes and putting down her pen.

Here it comes, Lyss thought.

"In summary, the war goes on, but we've done well against superior numbers and vastly greater resources. I think we can be proud of our Highlanders, our clan warriors, our young navy, and all of the citizens who have sacrificed so much to keep us all free."

She raised her glass, and the others followed suit, murmuring, "Hear, hear!"

That was always the postmortem—we've done well, considering. Against all odds, we've survived one more year. Raise a glass to that.

"Does this feel like freedom?" Lyss said, pushing to her feet. "Or a life sentence?"

There followed an awkward silence.

"In regard to . . . ?" Captain Byrne said.

"In regard to all the things that make life worthwhile," Lyss said. "Can upland traders travel throughout the realms the way they used to do?" she said, looking at Trailblazer. "Can metalsmiths create the amulets and jewelry that made them famous throughout the Seven Realms, or do they spend all their time producing weapons? Can children roam the forests freely, the way our parents did? Can we sail from our ports without risking being taken by the enemy? Do our wizards sleep well at night, knowing that they might be collared and enslaved? Can the blooded queen of the realm walk through the streets of the capital without looking over her shoulder?"

"I don't know why not," Lord Howard said, a little huffily. "There hasn't been an attack on the royal family for nearly four years."

"But people keep on dying, don't they?" Lyss said. "People we can't afford to lose. Do *you* think we're safe, Captain Byrne?"

Lyss felt bad, putting him on the spot, but Byrne didn't flinch. "I don't know, Your Highness," he said, "but I'll do everything in my power to make it so."

"I know you will," Lyss said. "But, as we've seen, sometimes that isn't enough. We all agree that we're doing better than anyone expected. But how many of you think that we are winning?" She looked down the table. No one raised a hand.

"Maybe we're not winning," Trailblazer said finally, "but we're not losing, either."

"I disagree. We're losing plenty," Lyss said. "What we've lost is irreplaceable. I'm not just talking about Hana, and Adrian and my father. We're losing our future. We're losing opportunity. Think of what we could do with the money we're spending on the war. We've got lýtlings in the mines and fighting in the mountains instead of going to school, or the academy, or apprenticing in the trades. Where will the Demonai get their weapons when no one is left who knows how to make them?"

"Shadow Dancer has been learning from his father,"

Trailblazer said. "The work he is doing is as good as any I've seen."

"That's true," Lyss said, "but both Shadow and his father are walking dangerous trails these days. Death will find them, if the war goes on long enough. Our officers are strategic geniuses compared to the southerners, but, General Dunedain, how long can you continue to work miracles with the soldiers and ordnance that you have? How many battles might we have won outright if we'd had more in the way of resources?"

"That's hard to say," Dunedain replied. "I'm not a seer."

"If I threw down the scrying bones and told you that the empire would never claim the queendom, but the war would go on forever—how many of you would want to sign on?"

They all shifted in their seats and looked away.

Hadley held up her hand, her forefinger and thumb an inch apart. "Damn, Lyss, I was just this close to being happy."

"Your Highness," Lord Vega said, verbally patting her on the head. "We all wish the war would go away. Until it does, we haven't a choice."

"The war doesn't go away until we make it go away," Lyss said. "The only way to make it go away is to take a risk."

"Do you have something specific in mind, Alyssa?" Queen Raisa said, with a trace of impatience.

"We need to draw blood on their side of the border. We should let them know that we have teeth. Wolves honor no borders when they are on the hunt."

Trailblazer frowned. "Are you suggesting that we deploy our own assassins into Arden?"

"Isn't that exactly what Montaigne will expect?" Hadley said. "He sends out assassins, and we answer back in the same way. I'll bet he's harder to get at than our royal family."

"He is," Julianna said, folding her hands in front of her. "There have been several attempts on the king of Arden's life already—all unsuccessful." The others looked at her, waiting for her to elaborate, but she didn't.

"Meadowlark," Trailblazer said, using Lyss's clan name, "I don't blame you for wanting to get revenge on the southerners, after everything that has happened, but—"

"I'm not talking about revenge," Lyss said. "I'm talking about a strategy that might help us win the war. And I'm not talking about assassins, specifically. We need to launch an offense that will get their attention."

"If you're thinking of an invasion, we're spread thin as it is," Dunedain said. "It's not just recruiting and training the soldiers, it's maintaining a supply chain, once they get down on the flatlands. I've fought there before, and it's a different kind of war, and not one that plays to our strengths." She paused. "Our soldiers are tired, Your Highness. Many are recovering from wounds. We've always used the dark season to recover. Would you ask them to march out again?"

Lyss groped for an answer, conscious that she was losing ground. "We don't have to march to Ardenscourt," she said. "We just need to put a dent in their wall of invincibility."

"I agree with Alyssa," Julianna said, which startled everyone into silence, including Lyss.

What's that about? Lyss thought, staring at her cousin.

"I do, too," Hadley said, planting her hands on the table and thrusting out her chin.

"And I," Finn said.

"We can't afford to risk soldiers just to put a scare into the southerners," Dunedain said.

"What the princess heir is talking about is not an empty gesture," Julianna said. "If their council is weary of the war now, imagine their reaction if they actually begin to lose territory to us. The cost of this war is going to seem awfully high. A nasty turn in the war might be just what is needed to shift the balance of power and make Montaigne's overthrow seem possible."

"We've been at war for my entire life," Hadley said. "Too many of my friends have died young. I hear the elders talk about the good old days, knowing that they're never coming back. That's a pretty low standard for success."

"I don't understand why we need to change our tactics, Your Majesty," Trailblazer said. "We have always waited for Arden to come to us. They impale themselves on our slopes, and our archers finish them. These younglings have not yet learned the value of patience."

That was when Lyss realized that every one of her age-mates was on her side. "I don't want to send my children to war," Julianna said fiercely, which Lyss found surprising because her cousin had none. She wasn't even married.

The queen smiled faintly, her lashes wet with tears. "I never wanted to send my children to war, either," she said, lacing and unlacing her fingers.

That was like a knife to the gut.

Bayar glared at the three of them. "It is easy for the young to look back critically at what their elders have done. Do you have any idea what this queen has accomplished over these past twenty-five years? She has done the impossible in keeping the red hawk of Arden outside our borders. That may not be everything we want, but it will have to be enough."

Lyss hadn't intended to sound critical of her mother's war strategy, but that was the way it was coming off.

"We don't have to decide this issue now," her mother said. "I suggest we defer this topic until we meet after the Solstice holiday. It may be that we can come up with some changes in strategy that will satisfy all parties in time for the next marching season."

If it's not too late, Lyss thought. "Sometimes there is more risk in doing nothing than in doing something," she said. She paused, memory washing over her like dark waters closing over her head. "When I was nine years old, my brother and I were out in a small boat and it capsized. I managed to grab hold of a rock just offshore. The tide was coming in, and I knew that I had to swim to my brother. But that meant I had to let go of the rock. I did it, but it was one of the hardest things I've ever done."

Trailblazer nodded thoughtfully. Uplanders often used stories to make a point.

"What does your boating accident have to do with the war?" Lord Howard said.

"My point is, we need to let go of what we have been doing and take a chance. If we do what we've always done, we'll get what we've always gotten—this never-ending war. We can't tread water forever. Eventually, we will drown."

9

BREON

It might have been the craving that woke him—that was the usual. Or the sound of stealthy movement, which was not. Breon's hand found his shiv before he cracked open his eyes. Someone crouched on the filthy floor next to him, rooting through his things.

"Goose," he said through parched lips, "don't waste your time."

Goose lurched backward, landing on his ass. "I wasn't . . . I was just . . ."

"Just . . . shut it." As always, Breon regretted waking up. Every part of him hurt, and, as was happening more and more often, he had no idea where he was. It was too cold for the clothes he wore, the air seemed thin, and he could no longer smell the sea. It only made his own stench more apparent. He smelled of sweat and stingo, leaf and fish.

Fish?

It must be daytime; he could see light leaking in around the window shutters. He must have slept like the dead. He propped up on his elbows, in a sudden panic. But his jafasa still lay next to him in its padded bag. He ran his hand over it, making sure it was real. It would have gone missing long ago, but the others knew better than to touch it. Whacks found it useful for Breon to keep it. It was a tool of the trade in their traveling show.

They were in a city; he heard temple bells close by. That muddle of blankets in the corner would be Aubrey. Out of their original dozen, they were the only four left. Breon supplied the talent, Aubrey the looks, and Goose— he was a fine acrobat when he was feeling well, which was almost never, these days. Whacks was supposed to handle the business end—book their shows and arrange for travel. But he mainly made his money dealing leaf.

Whacks was a sorry codshead of a manager, to tell the truth. Breon had plans. He was leaving, too, any day now.

"I thought Whacks would be back by now," Goose whined. "I could use a wake-up, if you know what I mean."

I *do* know what you mean, Breon thought. His head throbbed like a drum that'd been pounded all night. "Where are we again?"

"The capital," Goose said. "Fellsmarch. In the mountains."

"For real?" Breon said with a spark of interest. "I always wanted to see the mountains." He stood, all but losing his breeches in the process. He was losing weight again. There was never any food around these days, and when he was using leaf, he burned it up like a furnace.

Goose, as usual, stayed on point. "Do you think they even *have* leaf here? I mean, it's all snow and ice, in't it?"

"You can get whatever you want here," Breon said. "It's the capital." Like he knew any more than Goose. He paused. "How'd we get here again?"

"Whacks got us a spot in a fishwagon from the coast," Goose said. "Remember?"

Right. That explained the smell clinging to his clothes.

Breon walked out to the privy, which looked and smelled like privies everywhere. They were in a narrow lane in a tangle of streets lined with tenements and warehouses. It might be the capital, but it wasn't much of a step up from the coastal towns he was used to. It *was* colder than the coast, but warmer than he expected it would be, in the mountains. The streets were cobblestoned, not mud like some. And, on every side, snow-covered peaks loomed up behind the buildings like the walls of a stone prison.

Or a palace, depending on how you looked at it. *It's all about attitude*, Whacks liked to say, when he got them yet another gig in a rundown tavern or clicket-house.

A few blocks up, he could see towers poking up above the buildings. Must be the temple. Slitting his eyes against the painful sunlight, he followed the wall out to the high street to see what he could see. Sometimes the temples had food on offer. He needed to fill his belly before Whacks came back. Another hit of leaf, and he'd forget he was hungry at all.

In that, he lucked out. On the plaza in front of the temple, dedicates were handing out bread and oranges.

Oranges! That struck a chord deep inside him. Where would he have tasted oranges before? Breon had no idea. It was like somebody had wiped huge chunks of his life from his memory. His mouth remembered, though, because it watered as he lined up with the others. Looking forward, he saw that Aubrey had somehow got in line ahead of him. She turned and smirked at him. That was Aubrey—two years older and always two steps ahead.

The dedicate offered a blessing along with the bread and fruit.

"Could I have another?" Breon asked. Meaning the food, not the blessing. "For my friend?"

The dedicate gave Breon a good look-over as he handed off seconds. "If you need help," he said, "you'll find it inside." He tipped his head toward the temple.

Breon shook his head. "I'm not much for religion," he said, around a mouthful of bread.

The dedicate smiled, showing perfect blueblood teeth.

"It's not only religion," he said. "We offer help of a more practical kind—classes, housing, a chance to get clean."

Breon raised the hand clutching the bread. "This is all I need right now," he said. "Thank you—" He cast around for the proper title, then finished with "Your Honor."

"Call me Samuel," the dedicate said.

"Samuel." Breon got off a little bow and started to turn away.

"There's a free concert tonight," Samuel persisted, pointing to a banner draped across the front of the temple.

The Briar Rose Ministry Presents HRH Alyssa ana'Raisa in Concert Tonight, with Rogan Shadow Dancer and the Temple Dancers. One night only. Southbridge Temple. Freewill offering.

"It says that—"

"I can read," Breon growled. When and where he'd learned, he had no clue. People said that leaf fried the brain, and maybe that was true. He could quit anytime, and maybe he should.

"Since you can read, you might enjoy our library," Samuel said, gesturing toward the temple. He seemed to be one of those dedicates who are so hot to do good, they don't know when to give up.

"Thank you, Your Honor. I need to go see my friend over there." He nodded at Aubrey, who was watching, doubled over with laughter.

"Sometimes you need to feed the spirit along with the body," Samuel called after him. He turned to his next customer, who'd been shifting his feet, probably worried he'd starve to death during the sermon.

The temple was a stone's throw from the river, and Aubrey was sitting on a bench overlooking the water. She scooted over to make room for Breon. That's when he noticed she'd snagged *three* helpings, and was finishing off the first.

"How'd you get three?" Breon scowled at her.

Aubrey patted her midsection, where her belly should have been, and put on this vacant, cow-eyed look. "I lied. I told him I had a bun in the oven." From the look on her face, you'd think she had no idea how it got there.

Breon laughed. Aubrey was a natural felon. She'd been the one to teach him how to survive on the streets of a harbor town. She'd taught him other lessons, too, after the lights were out.

She wasn't much of a musician, but she brought in the men in droves to see their sorry little show. Sometimes, when Goose was feeling good, he and Aubrey would do funny bits together.

Sometimes Breon thought he might be in love with her—how was he to know, since he'd never been in love before? Leastwise he always enjoyed what she had to teach him. She was the only person in his tattered memory who had ever been kind to him. But lately she'd seemed more snappish and standoffish.

Breon peered over the stone wall at the river. It was the

cleanest he'd ever seen in any city. Though it was nearly midwinter, tiny flowers cascaded over the wall. He picked a few and held them out to Aubrey. She sniffed at them, then set them on the bench beside her.

Encouraged, Breon scooted closer. "It's kind of romantic, having a picnic by the river." Putting his hand on her knee, he leaned in for a kiss, but Aubrey turned her head away.

"Tell me that again when you an't stinking of fish." She licked her fingers and wiped them on the bench.

She's sure moody, he thought.

When Breon and Aubrey ducked back through the door of the crib, Whacks was back, and having a litter of kittens.

"Where've you been?" Whacks gripped the front of Breon's jacket and gave him a shake. "Why is it you always wander off just when I need you?"

"Take it easy," Breon said, wrenching loose. "If I'd of known you needed me, I wouldn't of wandered off." He eyed Whacks warily. It had been a long time since Breon's self-styled manager had shown that much interest in him. Whacks could be much too creative when it came to ways Breon could earn his keep. Ways that crossed the boundaries Breon had set for himself.

He'd been with Whacks since he was a pretty blond ten-year who needed protection in the southern harbor town of Baston Bay. He was grown, now—sixteen years old and able to make his way on his own. More and more, he was beginning to question whether staying with this lot did him any good.

Aubrey would be fine. She knew how to land on her feet. Lately she'd been gone a lot, and Breon suspected she had her own game going. He was surprised she'd stayed this long.

But what about Goose? What would happen to him if Breon left? Breon was bringing in most of the money these days. And Whacks could be ruthless when crossed.

He could be ruthless anytime he thought it would do him some good.

"So what's up?" Breon said. "Did you bring anything back for us?" Breon could take or leave the leaf, but Goose was in a bad way.

Whacks's gaze flickered away. "I got nothing for you now," he said, "but we'll be in gravy tonight. You'll just have to tough it out until then."

Breon clamped his teeth to keep his thoughts from spilling out. Then opened them enough to say, "What happens tonight?"

"That gig I was talking about? It's on." Whacks rubbed his thumb and fingers together. "It's real money this time. I told you the capital was the place to be." His eye lit on the food Breon was clutching. "Is that an orange? Where'd you get that?" He grabbed it out of Breon's hand and began peeling it.

Breon tossed the remaining bread to Goose before it

went the way of the orange. It wasn't what Goose wanted, but it was all Breon had.

"I'll need a hit if we've got a show tonight," Goose whined, taking a big chomp out of the bread.

"It's just Bree," Whacks said, jerking a thumb at Breon. "Not you."

"Hang on. What kind of a gig are we talking about?" Breon asked, instantly on guard.

"It's, you know, a—a private concert," Whacks said. "Somebody heard you play back at Baston Bay and nothing would do but you'd come and play for him here."

"A *private* concert?" Breon raised an eyebrow. He'd heard that before.

"I got you some new clothes," Whacks said. "And I've arranged for a bath at an inn across the river."

An inn. Right.

"Forget it," Breon said, his cheeks burning. He sat down on the floor next to his jafasa, wrapping his arms around his knees. "I've said it before, and I'll say it again—I'm a musician. Not a fancy."

"No, no, no," Whacks protested, shaking his head. "You've got it all wrong. It an't like that."

"Oh?" Breon undid the buckles on the case and lifted the instrument out. "What's it like, then?"

"It's a concert," Whacks insisted. "In front of quality. You can't go into it stinking of fish."

"Who's the audience?" Breon demanded. "Who's

paying, and what's the money? And where's the concert?"

"The concert an't at the inn," Whacks said. As usual, he picked the question he wanted to answer.

"Where is it, then?"

"Ah, Bree," Whacks said sadly. "I remember when you were such a charming, trusting boy, who relied on me to—"

"I've learned that charm an't enough," Breon said. "And trust has to be earned." And that I can't rely on you to tell the truth.

Whacks heaved a put-upon sigh. "You'll be singing for a girlie," he said. "She'll be attending a concert at the temple around the corner."

Breon recalled the banner draped over the entrance to the temple. That must be the one.

"You'll begin singing and playing when she passes by. You know it's on the up-and-up because it'll be out in public."

How does *that* make it on the up-and-up? Breon thought. Bad things happen in public all the time.

"She walks by, I sing to her, and that's it?"

Whacks nodded. "See? Easy money."

"Why?"

"Why what?"

"Why does this client want me to sing to this girlie?"

"He wants you to woo her for him."

Well, that explained the bath and the change of clothes.

But it didn't explain Whacks's shifty-eyed look.

"That kind of thing can go wrong, you know," Breon said. "A girlie is not like a pork bun. It's not like I can woo and win her and then hand her off to someone else."

"I guess he just wants you to put her in the mood," Whacks said, licking his lips in a suggestive way, which wasn't at all appealing on him. "Sing some romantic ballads to soften her up a little. She's a blueblood, and he's not. He's hoping you can help him make his case."

"I don't like it," Breon said, running his fingers over the strings, hearing the notes float up like magic. "Every other spark in town uses blue ruin to talk a girlie into making a bad decision. I'd just as soon not get mixed up in that."

"He's offering forty crowns," Whacks said, playing his trump card.

"Blood and bones," Goose muttered. "Forty girlies? For a love song?"

"Girlie" was also the popular name for the coin of the realm, which bore an image of a crown on one side and a silhouette of a royal on the other. It was rare that *one* girlie crossed Breon's palm, let alone forty. That was a small fortune. And if Whacks quoted forty, it likely meant the lovelorn suitor had offered sixty.

"I thought you said this cove wasn't a blueblood," Breon said. "Where would he get that kind of money?"

"It's not just bluebloods that are rich, you know—"

"Right, there's rushers and thieves and streetlords,"

Breon said, "and I don't want to mix with none of them."

"Forty girlies, Bree," Goose said, picking at his blankets with his busy hands.

"Don't you want to bring these young lovers together?" Whacks pressed him. "He just wants to talk to her."

"*Talk* to her? Are you sure that's all he means to do?"

"Look, when the concert lets out, there will be all kinds of people in the streets and bluejackets everywhere. What could happen?" Whacks stroked his wispy beard.

Breon sighed, running his hand through his filthy hair. It wasn't just Goose that was hurting. It had been a very lean year. "All right," he said, already working out a set list, "I'll do it."

"Good boy!" Whacks said, all smiles. "Now we'll just—"

"If," Breon added.

Whacks blinked at him. "If what?"

"I know this cove gave you money down," Breon said. He stuck out his hand, wiggling his fingers.

"He did, but I spent it on your new clothes, and the bath and all," Whacks whined.

"Not all of it," Breon said. "We all need a good meal, and me and Goose an't going to wait until tonight. When the payment's made, I get twenty-five girlies, Goose and Aubrey each get five."

"Why do they get five? They didn't do nothing to earn it."

"'Cause we're all in this together," Breon said. "Isn't that what you always say? Share and share alike?"

"What about my finder's fee? Only five crowns?"

"I'm guessing you've already claimed your fee," Breon said. "Take or leave."

"All right," Whacks grumbled, and the fact that he gave in told Breon all he needed to know. Whacks dug in his carry bag, pulled out a purse, and handed it over. It wasn't all that heavy, and no doubt it was stuffed with steelies and not the girlies Bree was looking for.

"How will I know who to sing to?" Breon asked. "Do you have something that belongs to her?" Breon could charm almost anyone as long as he had an instrument to channel through. It helped if he could look the person in the eyes. It helped even more to have a connected object— a beloved object was even better.

"You'll be meeting your client on the corner of South Bridge and River Street. Just the other side of the river from the temple. He'll have something of hers to give you."

"Do you even know what her name is?"

"Nah." Whacks slapped him on the back, nearly knocking him over. "No worries. I have faith in you. Just sing. What with that and your pretty face, she'll come."

10

OUTPLAYED

Dinner was early, and even more informal than usual in these lean times. The queen had issued an all-hands invitation in honor of the concert later that evening, proclaiming it the launch of the holiday season.

The dining room was already crowded when Lyss walked in. Automatically, she scanned the room for potential ambushes. She hated this kind of gathering, with everyone jostling for position.

Seeing the diverse mingle of people, Lyss relaxed a little. She spotted Cam Staunton in his dress blues, scouting the dessert table. As she watched, he scooped up two biscuits and stuffed them into his mouth. When he turned and saw Lyss watching, his face went scarlet, which contrasted nicely with the powdered sugar around his mouth.

"You look for witnesses *before* you snitch the biscuit, Private," Lyss said.

"Yes, ma'am," Staunton blurted, spewing a few crumbs. "Sweet Lady of Mercy," he muttered, then saluted and hurried away.

"Your Highness."

Lyss turned and saw that it was Finn sul'Mander, in a midnight blue velvet coat that set off his silver-blond hair and his black eyes, his fellscat stoles over top.

Finn bowed and kissed her hand, his lips leaving the buzz of wizardry on her skin. "Your Highness. I want you to know that I agreed with what you said in the council meeting today—that we're losing the war, but no one will admit it."

"I didn't exactly say we were losing," Lyss said. "I only questioned whether we were winning. There's a difference." She was sure there must be, though she'd be at a loss to explain it.

"Still. There are many who believe that we are on a path to disaster." He gripped her hands hard, and his voice shook a little.

"Hey, now," Lyss said. "It's been a long season. As for the council, sometimes it just takes time to win people over to a new way of thinking. It's not supposed to be easy." Even as she said this, she couldn't believe those words were coming out of her mouth.

"What they don't understand is that time is running *out*," Finn said. With that, he seemed to gather himself and remember that he was in a room full of people. "I apologize," he said. "After all, we have lots to celebrate tonight."

We do? Lyss thought, as he bowed and turned away. Biting her lower lip, she watched him cross the room. The war doesn't end when the fighting stops, she thought. There were so many walking wounded among her friends. If the war ended today, how long would it take the realm to heal?

Sighing, she headed for the food and drink herself.

The recent winter court arrivals were swarming the meager spread after months of trail food. Greeting several hungry members of her salvo, Lyss helped herself to a biscuit and a glass of wine. Turning away from the sideboard, she found herself face-to-face with Quill Bosley, resplendent in his dress Highlander uniform.

"Sweet Alyssa," he said, with a bow. "I hoped you would be here."

And I hoped you wouldn't be, Lyss thought, looking around for an excuse to escape, and seeing none.

"Lieutenant," she said, inclining her head in greeting.

"I just heard the good news," he said. "I understand that congratulations are in order, Captain. Or should I call you the Gray Wolf?"

"Captain will do," she said. "It was an honor to be selected, when there are so many more experienced officers to choose from."

"Well, it's not surprising that General Dunedain would want to get into your good graces. I'm not saying you didn't deserve it, of course." Bosley winked at her, as if her promotion were some kind of cozy insider joke.

Bosley was one of several suitors who had displayed interest in Lyss last social season. These overtures were mostly quick forays and quicker retreats. Bosley had been more persistent than most, showing up on her dance card repeatedly despite her penchant for awkward conversation and stepping on feet. The youngest son of a member of the Vale nobility, he seemed to be pursuing an alternate route to advancement.

Lyss had been polite at first, reasoning that at least, as soldiers, they'd have something in common to talk about. But the more time she spent with him, the less she liked him. It seemed that he was more interested in getting under her smallclothes than in anything she had to say about strategy. Now he seemed to think that he had staked some kind of claim.

Though he'd called on her several times since she'd been home, she'd managed to avoid a face-to-face. With the advent of the Solstice social season, that respite was over.

"I must say, I am disappointed that I've not seen more of you since we've been home," Bosley said.

"I've been pretty busy," Lyss said vaguely. "Our time at home goes by so quickly."

"Which is why we need to make the most of it."

Reaching out, he took both her hands. Why did people keep taking her hands? "I wondered if you had plans after dinner," he said, leaning in close so she could smell the stingo on his breath. "We could go somewhere and exchange war stories."

If he'd really meant that, she might have been tempted. Especially if the conversation took place in public.

"Too bad," Lyss said, pulling her hands free. "I have a recital tonight. In fact, this entire season is incredibly busy. Since I'm out of town so much, there's a lot to pack in. Drilling, marching, meetings, more drilling . . ."

Bosley shifted his weight and fisted his hands. "I understand that your social calendar must be complicated, what with the holiday and all, but surely you—"

"Speaking of social calendars," Lyss said, looking over Bosley's shoulder, "here comes Lord Thornleigh." She couldn't ever remember a time when she was glad to see Thornleigh. Until now.

Caddis Thornleigh, assistant minister of state, was bearing down on them. Or maybe *gliding down on them* was a better description.

"Your Highness," he said, executing a perfect bow and ignoring Bosley. "Welcome back from the hinterlands. You must be in an absolute *frenzy* of excitement. Can you believe that we are on the cusp of the most important night of your life?"

For a moment, Lyss was lost. "Oh," she said finally. "If

you're talking about the concert, I—"

"Concert?" Thornleigh furrowed his brow. "I'm talking about your name day, Your Highness. Your debut."

"Oh," Lyss said, her confusion clearing. "That's still months away."

"Exactly my point," Thornleigh said, taking her arm and drawing her away from Bosley. In Thornleigh's case, that would be an intentional snub. "I know you've been busy, but now you are here, and time is of the essence. I told the queen that I would assume responsibility for planning an exquisite ceremony and celebration. We'll need to put our heads together soon to discuss an invitation list."

Lyss's stomach clenched into a knot. "I couldn't ask you to take that on, what with all your other responsibilities, like, you know, diplomacy . . ."

"Your Highness, I can't think of any diplomatic endeavor more important in the new year than seeing you well married."

Hang on.

"My *name day* is coming, Lord Thornleigh," Lyss said. "Not my wedding. Not for a long time." She swung around to find Bosley still hovering. "Good–*bye*, Bosley," she snapped.

Bosley bowed stiffly. "Perhaps, Your Highness, I will see you at your name day party," he said, his jaw tight. He turned and walked away.

Thornleigh watched him until he was a distance away,

then said, "That whelpling is arrogant, isn't he? What makes him think he would be invited?"

"Look, I'm not really interested in a lavish bash," Lyss said. "We don't have the money, and I don't have the time. Summer is the marching season and no doubt I'll be out of the city. I think we should handle name days the way they do in the uplands—with two big ceremonies a year, honoring everyone who's turned sixteen. Each family could contribute a haunch of venison and a keg of ale."

Thornleigh's face just kept twisting until it resembled a sailor's knot of disapproval. "Your Highness, with all due respect, I—"

"We would have to have a very large cake, in order to fit all the names," Lyss said. "Or maybe it could just say, 'To whom it may concern: Congratulations!'"

The diplomat's face gradually smoothed into a mask of solicitous concern. "You may think of your debut celebration as frivolous, but it's an important investment in the future of the queendom. We are in dire need of allies, resources, and money. The right marriage can deliver all that. In order to attract a useful match, we will need a display of power and wealth." He leaned in closer. "Be realistic, Your Highness. You're not the beauty that your mother is, or your sister, Hana, may she rest in peace, or your cousin Julianna—such a lovely girl—but there's a lot can be done with the proper staging and—"

"Lord Thornleigh, I am well aware of the importance

of choosing wisely when it comes to an alliance. Rest assured, when I marry, I won't be looking for a pretty face, either. I'll find somebody who brings assets that will help us win this war." Lyss's voice was rising, and now people were turning to look. Bloody bones, she thought. "Now, if you'll excuse me . . ."

Without waiting for a response, Lyss made her escape before more thoughts slipped past her lips. In her case, that was the key to diplomacy—escaping before you said what you really thought.

Anyway, she'd seen somebody that she actually *wanted* to talk to—Hadley DeVilliers.

"Hadley!" she exclaimed, embracing her. "I didn't know you were back until I saw you at that meeting this morning."

Hadley always evoked thoughts of faraway places. After months away, she looked more exotic than ever, with her sun-bronzed skin, piercings, and tattoos, her hair a deep black streaked with blue.

Lyss held her out at arm's length, studying her. "Last time I saw you, wasn't your hair—?"

"Pink made too good a target," Hadley said, grimacing. "After a few near misses, I decided to go with something less visible."

"Good idea," Lyss said. "I can't wait to hear stories about exotic ports and naval battles on the high seas." Stories were all right. Just don't try to get me directly involved.

"I wouldn't exactly call it the high seas," Hadley said, laughing. "Between the Ardenine warships and Carthian pirates, we spent most of our time creeping in and out of inlets and trying to avoid running aground. We never got all that far from shore, but we did keep them busy."

"Did you really see pirates?"

Hadley nodded. "Never very close up, though, and usually sailing the other way. Pirates don't like to tangle with ships that shoot back, especially since we don't carry the kind of swag they're after."

"How long will you be home?" Ardenine ships prowled the seas year-round, so there was no defined fighting season for Hadley.

Hadley shrugged. "I haven't received orders yet, so who knows."

"When can we catch up over a few beers?" Lyss said.

"How about tonight?"

"I don't know whether you've heard, but I'm doing this concert tonight—"

"Oh, I'm coming to the concert," Hadley said, grinning. "I wouldn't miss it. Maybe after the concert, we can get a group together."

"Let's do it," Lyss said, absurdly happy. "It's been too long."

Hadley hesitated, as if debating whether to speak up. "Just so you know, I'm on board with the idea of an attack on Arden. I assume you have a target in mind."

"Several," Lyss said, with a grim smile.

Dinner was served, and still no Shadow. Lyss's concern turned to worry. He'd said he would come, but—what if something had happened to him? As she'd said in council, he walked a dangerous road—especially since Aspen died.

Dinner was being held early, because of the concert, and pretty much everyone at court was invited. Aunt Mellony was hosting. Raisa and Julianna sat up front with her, along with Finn and his parents. Aunt Mellony was dressed up, of course, and Julianna resembled a rare flower, with her porcelain skin and smoky eyes, her hair pulled up to show off her graceful neck.

For once, Lyss hadn't been included in the seating plan. Since she had a choice, she ate with Hadley, Sasha, Mason, and Littlefield toward the foot of the table.

Lyss poked at her roast chicken, usually one of her favorites, not being barley, but her stomach was in a turmoil of worry. She'd been sure Shadow would show up for dinner.

During dessert, talk inevitably turned to Arden and the war. Can't we ignore the war for just one night? Lyss thought. If you're not going to *do* anything different, then why not talk about something else?

Be careful what you wish for.

Her mother stood, and the room quieted. She was that kind of a person. "I would like to welcome you all to the opening of the season of Solstice, when we celebrate the return of the light. We're also celebrating the return of many of you from the battlefield, and honoring those who will never return to us." She raised her glass, and everyone followed suit. "I hope all of you will find joy and peace this holiday season, and the time and space in which to mend your spirit."

They all drank.

"It is during this festive season that the spark of romance often kindles," the queen went on. "Marriage represents a hope for and belief in the future—something direly needed in a time of war. In that spirit, your host and my sister, the princess Mellony ana'Marianna, has an announcement." She gestured, and Aunt Mellony rose to her feet amid a buzz of speculation.

Aunt Mellony is getting married again, Lyss thought. Good for her. Lyss scanned the table for possible candidates. Not Lord Mander. He was sitting next to her, but he was already married.

Could it be Micah Bayar? Could they have finally come together after all these years? Lyss looked down the table to where the wizard sat. He was looking on, smiling, but he displayed no flush of romance.

"Your Majesty, ladies and gentlemen, it is my very great pleasure to announce the betrothal of my daughter Julianna ana'Mellony to Finn sul'Mander."

Wait . . . what?

Lyss looked down the table to where Finn and Julianna sat next to each other, blushing and smiling. Well, Julianna was blushing and Finn was smiling. Julianna held up their joined hands to display her engagement ring. A confection of emeralds and diamonds, it glittered in the candlelight.

Instantly, Lord Mander was on his feet, raising his glass. "A toast to the happy couple!"

Micah Bayar joined him, smiling, raising his own glass. "Hear, hear!"

Then Lord Vega. "I couldn't be happier," he said, with a broad smile. "You are the kind of fine young couple this queendom needs more of."

There followed a flurry of toasts and best wishes and questions about wedding plans. Lyss dutifully toasted her cousin, then sat, silent as a stump, a smile pasted on her face.

It wasn't that she was in love with Finn sul'Mander. True, she'd had a crush on him when she was younger, but she'd grown out of that. Pretty much, anyway. It wasn't that she was jealous, exactly. It was just that Thornleigh's words kept echoing in her head: *You're not the beauty that your mother is, or your sister, Hana, may she rest in peace, or your cousin Julianna—such a lovely girl.* . . .

It was just that Finn and Julianna were so perfect together, like a matched pair of thoroughbreds.

It was just that Lyss had had no clue this was coming until it actually happened. Finn hadn't said a word about it on the long trail home.

It was just so damned humiliating.

THE CLIENT

The "inn" was called Mabry's, and it *was* a clicket-house, as Breon had suspected. But the place was clean and well kept, and there was no reason he couldn't take a bath there as long as he locked the door and kept his shiv by his side.

Long, hot baths were rare in Breon's world. It was unusual, too, to get to be first to the tub. Truth be told, it had been a while since he'd had his clothes off, and he was shocked at how thin he'd become. He'd grown taller, and it was like he'd been stretched out, his ribs prominent under his skin.

You need to leave the leaf alone, he thought, and he would. Soon.

He was surprised at how good it felt to stew until his

skin got wrinkly, the water turning murky gray around him. When he finally rose, dripping, from the tub, his hair was two shades lighter and the stench of fish was gone.

As soon as he unfolded the bundle of clothing, he knew Whacks hadn't picked them out. He found soft wool breeches, a snowy linen shirt with bloomy sleeves, and a velvet doublet in a rich emerald green. There were warm hose to wear underneath, and a fine hooded cloak with velvet trim to wear over. Everything fit well enough, though he had to cinch in the breeches to keep them from sliding down over his bony ass.

He was admiring himself in the mirror, striking poses, when somebody knocked at the chamber door. Breon grabbed up his shiv and said, "Occupied."

"Open up quick. It's Aubrey."

He stowed the shiv and padded to the door.

Aubrey stood outside, holding a pair of boots. Her eyes widened when she saw Breon. "Bones, Bree, will you look at you? You could walk right into any palace and be at home."

"Until I opened up my mouth," he said, stepping aside so she could enter.

She walked in, stuffing the boots into his arms as she passed. "Try these on," she said. "See if they fit." She glanced into the tub. "Whoa," she said. "Plow that up and you could grow barley."

Breon, touched and surprised, cradled the boots. "These are for me?"

"Naw, they're for my other sweetheart with feet the exact same size as you."

Sweetheart? That was encouraging, in a peculiar way. Breon sat on the edge of the bed and pulled on the boots. They were loose, but another pair of hose or another year's growth would fix that.

"Thank you," he said, sticking out his feet so he could admire them. "Where'd you get these?"

"They were sitting outside one of the other rooms, and they looked like the right size. We'd better be gone before the owner misses 'em. But, first—" Aubrey sat down beside him. Sliding her arms around him, she kissed him, long and deep, pressing him back onto the pillows until his heart was thumping under the fancy doublet.

"What was that for?" he said, when she broke it off. Not that he was complaining, but it had been a long time since she'd kissed him like that.

"I wanted to see what it was like to kiss a gentleman," she said.

"Well, then," Breon said, "as long as we're here, would you like to see what it's like to—?"

She shook her head and put her fingers to his lips. "Like I said, we need to go before the cove down the hall comes looking for his boots," she said. "But I wanted to talk to you in private." She slid her hands down until they circled his neck, and her fingers caressed the magemark on the back of it. Then she pushed his head down so she could take a closer look. Gooseflesh rose on his back and shoulders.

"Don't," he said, pulling free.

"Why not?"

"Because I said so."

Aubrey blinked at him, then dropped her hands into her lap. Breon guessed she wasn't used to hearing no. Not from him, anyway.

"It's time we went out on our own," she said.

Breon sat back a little, resting his hands on his thighs. He waited.

"Whacks does nothing for us, only gets in our way," she said. "A streetlord that can't support his crew doesn't deserve to have one."

"He's not a streetlord," Breon said. "He's a manager. We're not a crew, we're a musical troupe." He couldn't say why it was so important to him to maintain that distinction.

Aubrey flipped her hand, as if to say, *Whatever.* "You're the one bringing in all the money. Now we have some coin, there'll be more coming in, and you have some fine clothes. I say we leave after the gig tonight."

"And go where?"

"We'll go back to the coast. I've been doing some business on the side down at the harbor. Plus, we can sail anywhere from there. *I'll* be your manager from now on."

"What about Goose?"

She scowled. "What about him?"

"What happens to him?"

"He . . . stays with Whacks, I guess," she said, shrugging.

"What's he going to live on, with us gone?"

She shrugged again.

"Whacks can fend for himself," Breon said. "But if we leave, then Goose comes with. He needs a chance to get clean." If they left Whacks, if his source was gone, it might be easier.

"All right," Aubrey said, rolling her eyes and loosing a put-upon sigh. "Goose comes with." She stood. "We'd better go back," she said, all brisk and businesslike.

"You go on," Breon said, saying no for the second time that day. "I'm going to walk over to Southbridge early and see what's what."

Aubrey studied him for a long moment. "All right," she said. "Be careful. I'll get things together so we can leave soon as you get back." She kissed him again in a promising kind of way and swayed out the door.

Breon shook his head, laughing at himself. That girl could turn the charm on and off like a spigot. He knew he shouldn't trust her, and yet—this thing they had was maybe as close as he'd ever come to being in love.

You sing love songs all day long, he thought, but you wouldn't know love if it came up and bit you on the ear.

Time was wasting. Breon picked up his jafasa, loped down the stairs, and walked briskly through the common room, careful not to make eye contact with any of the patrons or respond to any of the suggestive comments that came his way. Once outside, he crossed back to the temple side of the river and entered the big front doors.

A dedicate sat at a small reception table just inside the doors, paging through a large illuminated manuscript.

"I was told there was a library?" Breon said, when she looked up.

He half-expected her to demand why he wanted to know, but she just pointed. "Down this hall to the right. Go all the way to the end and you can't miss it." She returned to her reading.

Must be the new clothes, he thought, brushing his fingers over the velvet.

The library was the biggest he'd ever seen, three stories tall and all paneled in dark woods. They had rolling ladders you could use to reach the highest shelves. Another wall was all little niches with rolled manuscripts poking out of them.

Dedicates were seated at tables here and there, heads bowed over their work. In one corner, a scholar was reading a book to a group of children. At the front desk, a man looked up at Breon's approach, keeping his place in his book with his forefinger.

"I was wondering," Breon said, "if you have any books about ships."

As it turned out, they did.

Breon could spend hours reading about ships and the sea. Maybe it was because he'd grown up in a harbor town, watching ships come and go, wishing he were aboard. This one time, a shipmaster had seen him staring longingly at the ships in the harbor and offered to row him out to take a closer look. Breon had been seized with an unreasoning panic, and fled.

Books were the safer way to go. It was easy to get lost between the covers of a book. He imagined what it would be like, living right here in the temple library, where he could read and read and read, venturing out to the square now and then for bread and oranges. On temple days, he'd go to the clicket-house for a bath.

Before he knew it, the bells overhead were bonging and it was seven o'clock and time to meet his contact about the gig.

Slinging his jafasa over his shoulder, he walked back down the steps, stopping at the table by the door in case they wanted to search him for whatever he'd pocketed. The dedicate just waved him on, out the front door of the temple, under the banner proclaiming the concert.

A light snow was falling as Breon crossed back over the bridge to the neighborhood known as Ragmarket and turned down the first alley on the left. The alley ran along the rear of a series of riverfront taverns, clicket-houses, and tenements.

At the end of the first block, he saw a cloaked figure

leaning against a lamppost on the corner. When the lamp-leaner spotted Breon, he straightened, eyes glittering within the shadow of his hood. The rest was all darkness, like he was one of those demons, from scary storybooks, that are looking for a new body to live in.

Was *this* the lovelorn suitor? No wonder he was having trouble romancing his girlie.

And yet—there was a familiar shine to him, a blue-white glow that Breon had always associated with mages. That can't be right, Breon thought. Mages never have trouble finding a lover. That's what he'd heard, anyway.

Maybe he was mistaken. With the client wrapped up as he was, he couldn't get a good look.

"I'm here about a street concert," Breon said, wanting to establish the rules of the game up front. "Are you?"

"You're the spellsinger?" The client's voice was as cold as a dead fish across the face, and flat, as if he were trying to disguise it.

"Yes," Breon said, not being in the business of splitting hairs and not knowing what Whacks might have told him.

"Are you able to charm a person, even if she is wearing a clan-made talisman?"

"Yes," Breon said. He really had no idea, but he was beginning to think that the answer had better be yes. Was that why he'd been called in? Because this mage had tried and failed? Breon puffed out his chest a little.

The stranger looked up and down the street, then

motioned for Breon to follow him. Breon did so with a prickle of unease. Whacks wasn't all that choosy about who he did business with. Not that Breon had much money in his pockets. He'd spent most of Whacks's light purse on some leaf to tide Goose over. And a little for himself.

"You'll be on this corner," the client said, pointing out of the snarl of alleys to where the main road crossed the bridge. "When she comes, you'll move this way down the riverbank and bring her along to the riverside park. Stop there."

"How will I know who to sing to? What does she look like?"

"She's tall," the client said, "and big-boned. Awkward. She'll be wearing a green dress. And a shawl."

That didn't sound like somebody's description of his sweetheart. Breon waited for more and got none. "Is that it?"

"That isn't enough?"

"I don't want to charm up the wrong girl," Breon said. If it'd been anyone else, he would have made a joke of it. "Ah . . . what about her hair? What's it like?"

"It's long, and it's a kind of an ochroid color."

"Ochroid?" Who says "ochroid"? It sounded like some kind of a disease.

"Like old gold or amber," the client said impatiently. "She may be carrying an instrument case."

"An instrument case?" Breon said, with a spark of interest. "She's a musician?"

The client ignored the question. Instead, he fished

inside his cloak, and Breon heard a soft clink of metal on metal. When the client extended his hand toward him, Breon couldn't help taking a step back.

The client released an exasperated breath. "I was *told* that you need something of hers in order to spell her," the client said. "Do you want it or not?" He opened his fist and dropped a locket into Breon's hand.

Breon weighed it in his palm. It appeared to be gold, and it was inscribed on the outside with a rose. When he pried it open with a thumbnail, he saw that it contained tiny painted portraits of bluebloods that seemed to shift before his eyes.

He looked up at the client. "Was this . . . something with sentimental value that—?"

"Yes." When Breon kept studying it, the client hissed, "Put that thing away before you lose it. And don't let anyone see it."

Breon tucked it away in his breeches pocket, lowering his head to hide the scowl on his face. He did not like this client much at all.

Looking up and down the street, the client drew his hood forward, his cloak closer around him. Maybe it was the cold wind, but Breon got the impression that he didn't want to be seen with the likes of him, even in his new clothes. "I want you to go on playing and singing and keep her there until I come. Then you can go."

Breon shifted the jafasa on his back, uneasy about greasing this meeting. "Does the girlie know you? Is this something she'll—? You an't planning to—?"

"Do you want this job or not?" The client gripped the front of Breon's fine coat and gave him a shake. Again, there came a soft clinking of metal.

Does this cove have a whole pocketful of lockets from all the girlies he wants to woo?

"You're being paid—well paid—to sing, not to ask questions."

Breon hesitated. This gig stunk to high heaven, but he really needed it, especially if he and the others were leaving Whacks. They'd want traveling money.

If he could get money up front, he'd go back and collect Goose and Aubrey and hit the road without any ethical dithers. It was worth a try. He stuck out his hand. "I need a down payment. Twenty-five crowns."

"I gave the down payment to your . . . handler," the client said. "I'll pay him the rest when you deliver the girl. The concert should be over about nine-thirty. I want you here at quarter after. You can keep time by the temple bells. Understand?"

Breon didn't like it, but Whacks had already made the deal, so it was hard to argue the point. He nodded. "Got it."

"One more thing." Reaching inside his cloak again like some kind of street magician, the client produced a bunch of flowers wrapped loosely in a cloth and thrust them at Breon. "Give her these."

That was odd. It seemed like his client would want to

hand off the flowers himself and make sure he got credit. "You want *me* to give them to her?"

"Isn't that what I just said?"

Breon took the bouquet. "What if she asks who sent these? What should I say?"

"Tell her it was Darian," the client said.

Darian?

"Now, remember—keep her there until you see us meet face-to-face."

"Right," Breon said, just wishing this awful client would leave.

But Darian had one more thing to say. "Just remember—if you disappoint me, you'll wish you'd never been born." He turned, the snow eddying around him, and walked away, boots crunching on the icy cobblestones. Breon watched him until he turned a corner and disappeared.

Breon stood there, as if frozen to the spot. His hands were full, what with his instrument case and the flowers. Finally, he set his case down in the snow, unbuckled it, and slid the flowers inside, thinking they would make a pretty poor show by the time he handed them off.

He really didn't care. He never should have agreed to this gig. He knew that now, but he couldn't see any way out of it.

I'll see how things look, he told himself. If it smells too fishy, I'll find a bluejacket. That's what he told himself, but he knew in his heart he wouldn't.

THE PLAYERS TAKE THE STAGE

As soon as Aunt Mellony heard about the concert, she'd insisted that Lyss borrow a gown from her for the performance. Lyss's aunt had a kind of gown museum in her closet, each garment lovingly preserved in a linen wrapper. They were the kind of dresses that nobody could afford these days, even if they could find them. Lyss had to try on a dozen before she found one green dress that she could squeeze into. And even that one was so narrow that she could scarcely walk, and it was really too short on her.

"You're just big-boned, dear," Aunt Mellony had said, chewing her lower lip and looking Lyss up and down. "There's nothing wrong with that."

It wasn't just bone. Anyone who spent so much time

sticking and sparring and practicing with a bow, who spent days on horseback, and digging latrines, and the like, tended to add layers of muscle. That was a good thing, most of the time. Except when a body was trying to get into one of Aunt Mellony's slinky dresses.

"I appreciate the offer, Aunt Mellony, but maybe this isn't going to work out," Lyss had said. "I'm sure I have something that I—"

"Nonsense," Mellony said. "Make your choice, and I'll have it altered."

"I don't want you altering your dresses to fit me," Lyss said. "Then they won't fit you. I'll just wear my clan coat. That will—"

"Your funeral coat is certainly memorable," Aunt Mellony said, scrunching up her face, "but I think for this occasion you'll want a more festive look."

In the end, Lyss went with the too-short green dress, figuring that she could get through the performance, anyway. Still, it was a good thing Sasha dropped by and helped her on with it, or she would have been late.

"You sure you don't want me to slice it up the sides so you can walk?" Sasha said dubiously, resting her hand on her belt knife.

"It's a borrowed dress, Sasha," Lyss said. "I'll just have to live with it for a little while. I'll wear my shawl over it, and bring something more comfortable to change into right after."

"Suit yourself," Sasha said, fumbling with a row of tiny buttons. The whole thing was faintly ridiculous—Sasha playing chambermaid, helping her into petticoats and lace instead of weapons and armor.

"So, how about that—Julianna and Finn," Sasha said, around the buttonhook gripped between her teeth. "Did you see that coming?"

"No, I didn't."

"I didn't have a clue, either," Sasha said, "but I thought maybe Julianna would have told you ahead of time."

"We're really not close," Lyss said. Despite all her efforts, her voice trembled. With that, Sasha left off buttoning and walked around until she could look Lyss in the face.

"He's not a good match for you, Lyss," she said gently. "You're stronger than him in a dozen ways. You can do better, and you will."

Lyss was mortified. Am I that easy to read? Does everyone know I've been mooning after Finn sul'Mander? Am I the laughingstock of the entire court? Or, worse yet, the object of pity?

"No," Sasha said, answering her unspoken question. "Likely, I'm the only one that knows, and I'm not telling anyone."

When Lyss and Sasha emerged into the stable yard, there were three coaches lined up in front of the door and a small crowd of people waiting to board.

Lyss spotted Julianna right away. As usual, she was surrounded by a crowd of friends, and they were buzzing about the engagement. Lyss made a wide circle around that, as she would a hornet's nest. She knew she should congratulate her cousin on her engagement, but she just wasn't in the mood. At least Finn wasn't with Julianna—a small blessing.

But Julianna saw her, and turned away from her friends. "Alyssa! Wait! Let me see!"

So Lyss had to stop, and turn, and show off her dress with the tiny, mincing steps that were all she could manage. Her cousin wore a long, sinuous dress in a smoky purple, a flatland lily in her midnight hair. It was no wonder Finn was smitten with her.

"You look lovely, Alyssa," Julianna said, gracious as always. "I'm so glad to see that dress put to good use. Mother insists on keeping them, but she never wears them. You've really made it your own."

Not for very long, Lyss thought.

"Let me see!" It was Bethy Musgrave, the daughter of a landowner near West Gate. Someone Lyss scarcely knew and didn't want to know better.

Bethy tapped her rouged lips with her forefinger, frowning. "You do look statuesque," she said, as if savoring the word. "Though I wonder if you should have added a flounce at the hem to take care of the ankle situation."

Lyss looked down to where the hem of her gown just

grazed her shins. Then looked up at Bethy. "At least that's fixable," she said. "Being an asshole isn't."

For a long moment, Bethy stood frozen, a stunned expression on her face. Then she picked up her skirts, tossed her head, and said to Julianna, "Don't forget, we're playing cards next week with Cecily and Geoff." She flounced away.

To Lyss's surprise, Julianna began to laugh. Once started, she laughed until she blotted tears from her eyes with her sleeve. "Did you see her face? She deserved that. I just wish I could speak my mind like you do."

"Not everyone wants to hear what's on my mind," Lyss said.

"But they need to hear it," Julianna said. "I thought what you said in council today was brilliant. We need some new ideas. I get so frustrated sometimes. . . ." She trailed off.

You too? "Oh. Well. Thank you," Lyss said. "I . . . ah . . . appreciate your support. I . . . didn't get to congratulate you personally on your engagement. You and Finn are so beautiful . . . so beautifully well matched."

"Do you really think so?" From the expression on Julianna's face, it seemed she really cared what Lyss thought. "The queen has given her blessing, and Mama couldn't be more pleased. I didn't expect . . . well . . ." She hesitated, then rushed ahead. "Listen, I know this is probably the wrong time to ask it, but I've scarcely seen you since you returned to court. I know how busy you are, but . . . it would mean so much to me if you would stand up with Finn and me at our wedding."

Lyss opened her mouth, and for once nothing came out. She'd been blindsided once again. How could she be so good at dodging arrows on the battlefield, and such an easy target at court?

When Lyss said nothing, Julianna rushed on. "Finn and I talked about it, and he thinks it's a perfect idea. We both admire you so much and we can't think of anyone else we'd rather share our day with."

"Well, ah, this is such a surprising . . . surprise. I . . . ah . . . don't know if I—"

"You don't have to give me an answer now," Julianna said. "I know you have other things on your mind tonight. We don't even have a date yet, but we're thinking sooner rather than later. If you say yes, we will try to work around your schedule." Her cousin squeezed her arm. "You're the closest I have to a sister, so I hope you'll at least consider it."

"Great," Lyss said. "That's . . . I'll sure look forward to that." Like having a tooth pulled.

Why didn't I see this coming? she thought. I'm Julianna's only female relative who's under forty years old. Of course she'd ask me to be in the wedding. Not to mention that it was a smart political move. The kind Julianna was so good at.

When she looked up, Julianna was watching her with this expectant look, so she said, "Where is Finn, by the way? I thought he was coming, too."

"He's going to meet us there," Julianna said. "He couldn't get away any earlier. Now I'd better go see which carriage we're supposed to take."

Lyss, her mind in a tumble, watched her cousin as she walked away toward the waiting carriages.

"Your Highness."

Lyss turned to find Cam right behind her. He was now dressed in his blues, with not a speck of powdered sugar anywhere. "Your Highness, I'm to escort you to the middle carriage," he said. "We'd better get under way if you're to make your time. I've loaded up your instrument case, and Princess Julianna is already on board." Looking forward, Lyss saw that the middle carriage was surrounded by more Gray Wolves on horseback.

"You haven't seen Shadow, have you?"

He shook his head. "No, ma'am. Captain Byrne said he was supposed to ride with us, but I an't seen him yet. Maybe he's decided to meet us there."

Her mind in a stew of worry, Lyss allowed herself to be led to the designated carriage. Cam gave her a hand up, then climbed in after her. "Captain Byrne said I should ride inside," he said, as if feeling the need to justify his presence. "Talbot will be riding alongside."

"Great," Lyss said automatically. "That's great."

Cam settled in next to Julianna on the opposite seat, but Lyss scarcely noticed. *I shouldn't have pressured Shadow to perform at this concert*, Lyss thought. *The last thing he'd want would be to get up in front of people so soon after Aspen's death. He's the kind who'd want to deal with grief in private. I don't care if I have to perform alone. Just let him be all right.*

"Alyssa? What's wrong?"

Lyss looked up to meet her cousin's worried eyes and furrowed brow. "Nothing. Just trying to remember my—"

Just then, the carriage rocked a little as someone climbed in.

It was Shadow.

"Hello, Meadowlark," Shadow said, claiming the empty space next to Lyss and setting his basilka between his knees. He nodded to Cam and Julianna. "Sorry I'm late. I hope I haven't held you up."

"Shadow!" Lyss threw her arms around him. "Thank the Maker. I was beginning to think you weren't—that you were coming straight from Demonai Camp."

"I arrived a few hours ago. I thought I should wash the sweat off before I went to temple." He cocked his head. "Are you all right?"

"Perfectly," Lyss said. "I was . . . I just didn't want to be late. Will your father be here?"

He nodded. "We came back together. We've been working on a project."

Shadow was clad in leggings and boots, a talisman around his neck. Over top, he wore a fine deerskin mourning coat decorated with aspen trees. He looked Lyss up and down, taking in her dress and hair. "Let's hope our music is more in harmony than our clothes," he said.

"It will be," Lyss said. She dug in her carry bag and pulled out her set list. "Now, let's make sure we're singing off the same sheet. What do you have?"

Their duets were songs they'd been singing their whole lives. Shadow had brought two new compositions for his solo pieces. So he *had* been writing music while he was away. It was just like old times, heads together, arguing over music.

In no time, they clattered over South Bridge and pulled up in front of the temple. Concertgoers, a mingle of the diverse peoples of the Fells, filled the entire street. Wizards and members of the Vale nobility descended from carriages, lighting up the square with their finery. These would be patrons of the Briar Rose Ministry. Some of them were longtime supporters of the cause. Others, no doubt, were currying favor with the queen.

Apprentices wore the rainbow badges of their guilds, soldiers their dress uniforms. Clanfolk were well represented, too, clad in traditional finery. Now, at the end of the marching season, some had descended into the Vale for their semiannual visits. Music, dance, weddings, funerals, and politics were the only things that could bring them into a place they considered the flatlands.

Southbridge and Ragmarket parents herded children forward, dressed in their best and sometimes only clothes.

Their blue-jacketed guards directed the carriage driver around to the less-crowded alley behind the temple, where Lyss and her companions could enter via the back door.

Just inside, Finn and Hadley were waiting for them. He and Julianna embraced as if it had been months and not hours since they'd seen each other.

"I'm sorry I couldn't ride along," Finn said. "I seem to have too many people running my life these days. My father has absolutely no sense of urgency when it comes to anything other than war and politics. Lord Vega is the same with regard to the healing service." He kissed Julianna again. And then again.

"Hey, Lyss," Hadley said, as if to draw her attention away from the kissing. "Is that a new dress? I don't think I've seen you wear that before."

Lyss examined Hadley's face for any sign of a smirk, but saw none. "It's Aunt Mellony's," she said, resisting the urge to yank at the fabric. Hadley looked a lot more comfortable in her leather breeches and silk shirt, a mariner's sash at her waist.

Hadley studied her. "You should wear dresses more often," she said, stroking her chin, nodding thoughtfully.

"Quit shoveling it, Hadley, you know I—"

"I didn't say *that* dress," Hadley said, grinning. "Just dresses in general."

It seemed that Finn and Julianna were done kissing,

because Finn broke into the conversation. "We need to go sit down," Finn said, "but we're going out after. Do you want to come with us?"

"We" meaning Julianna and Finn? Three would definitely be a crowd. "Well, ah . . . I'd love to, but I actually promised Hadley I'd—"

"Hadley, you come, too," Julianna said, her happiness sloshing over the two of them like a rogue wave. She turned to Shadow. "What about you, Shadow? Do you have plans after the concert?"

Shadow hesitated. "No," he said, "but I don't want to—"

"Please come!" Julianna said. "I need to find out what you've been seeing and hearing out east."

"No working," Finn said, rolling his eyes. "Only playing. The more the merrier."

"The more the merrier," Lyss said, thinking that at least the happiness would be diluted a little. What do you get when you mix giddy and grieving?

"Right. It's settled, then." Finn took Julianna's elbow. "We'd better go, before we lose our seats." And the two of them walked away, arm in arm.

Backstage, the assembled players bubbled like a pot coming to a boil, with dancers in costume darting this way and that.

Speaker Jemson hurried past, looking harried, pursued by three dedicates, who were bombarding him with questions. When he saw Alyssa and Shadow, he said, "Thank the Maker," and crossed something off on a list. "Trying to organize this thing is like herding fellscats."

Lyss peeked through the curtains and saw that the sanctuary was crowded already, with chairs set up on every level surface. Security was tight; blue-jacketed guards were stationed in the balconies and at the entries, and were peppered through the front few rows.

"All right," Speaker Jemson said. "We'll open with a prayer, then the handbells, then the choir, and the Temple School dancers. After the intermission, we'll bring you on. For 'Hanalea,' we'll have the full choir and the handbells back. Sound good?" Not waiting for an answer, he sprinted stage right to where a young acolyte was struggling with one of the larger sets.

Lyss pulled out her notes and went over the new lyrics. She'd be on her own for those.

The crowd was growing more restive, and Alyssa knew it must be close to eight o'clock. Overhead, the bells in the tower began to sound, signaling that it was showtime.

Somehow, miraculously, through divine intervention, perhaps, all of the musicians and singers were in place, in costume, ready to go when Speaker Jemson walked out to the front of the platform. "One thing about working in a temple," he said, looking up into the bell tower, which was still resonating. "You always know what time it is."

STAGE DEBUT

The first half of the concert passed in a sensory blur: young voices echoing in the nave, the scent of candle wax, hundreds of upturned faces in the audience. Lyss stayed backstage, her apprehension warring with the pure, sweet magic of the music.

At intermission, Aunt Mellony came backstage to help Lyss with her hair.

Mellony unraveled Lyss's usual thick braid and arranged her hair in a soft twist on the back of her head so it showed off her long neck and her grandmother Marianna's diamond earrings, another loan from Aunt Mellony.

"You should wear your hair like this more often," Aunt Mellony said. "It's very becoming."

"Maybe," Lyss said, studying herself in the mirror. A stranger looked back at her, one with color on her eyes and lips and a dress that exposed her shoulders. On a chain around her neck Lyss wore the rowan talisman she'd inherited from her father, which was meant to protect her from magical attacks. The one that had saved her life at Queen Court.

She'd planned to wear it alongside the locket her father had given her on her eighth name day. "You can put images of your sweethearts in there," he'd said. "Stacked one on top of the other."

I'm not my mother, Lyss thought. One will do.

In the dark days after Hana's death, Adrian had gone to clan artists and commissioned tiny portraits of each person in their family—himself, Hana, Alyssa, their father, and their mother. With help from Shadow's father, Fire Dancer, Adrian had mounted them into the locket. The images were cunning flashcraft. When she touched it, the portraits would shift, displaying first one person and then another.

He'd demonstrated the trick of it, fastened it around her neck, and said, "See? We'll be with you, every day. You'll never be alone."

Not anymore. The locket had gone missing two weeks ago.

This latest loss had hit Lyss hard. They're still in your heart, she told herself, but she missed having something physical that she could hold on to. The last gift her brother had given her.

She'd not told her mother—she'd not told anyone. Surely she'd find it before long, trapped between the bed frame and her mattress or along one of the paths in the glass garden on the roof of the palace or at the bottom of a trunk of clothing. Never mind that she'd already looked in all of those places. She couldn't admit to losing one more precious bit of memory.

"You seem preoccupied, Alyssa," Aunt Mellony said as she applied the finishing touches. "Is everything all right?"

Lyss realized she'd barely spoken a word while her aunt fussed over her.

"Oh! I'm sorry," Lyss said. "This time of year always stirs up a lot of memories."

"For all of us, sweetheart," Aunt Mellony said, resting her hands on Lyss's shoulders. "In times like these, it's difficult not to think of what might have been." She smiled at her. "You look lovely. So grown up. Your mother is so proud of you."

"Is she?" Lyss blurted.

Mellony cocked her head, frowning. "Of course she is. Raisa will be right in the front row tonight. Why would you doubt it?"

"It's just . . . it always seems like my mother and me—we're pulling in different directions. She's never here, or if she's here, I'm gone. And when we *are* together, I feel like she's watching me, waiting for me to do the wrong thing."

"Oh, I don't think that's true," Mellony said, licking her finger and smoothing down a wayward strand of Lyss's hair. "It's just that she's worried about you. She's had so many losses already."

"She's always correcting me, pointing out how I could have done better. It's like she's constantly comparing me to Hana."

Mellony hesitated, as if choosing her words carefully. "Well, if she is, she shouldn't be. Hana was . . . remarkably gifted, and Raisa spent years grooming her to be queen. She shouldn't expect so much of you. I think she's just conscious of a . . . a shortened timeline."

"It's not like I want her to go easy on me," Lyss said. "I want to be a good queen."

"Of course you do."

"You and Julianna are so close, it's like you share everything," Lyss said.

"Not everything," Aunt Mellony said. "She's really her father's daughter. Sometimes I—" She stopped and bit her lip.

Lyss groaned inwardly. Lord Barrett had died young, too, of a fever, just a year after her own father. Their loss was even fresher.

"I'm sorry, Aunt Mellony," Lyss said. "I didn't mean to unload on you."

"There's nothing to be sorry about, dear," Mellony said

lightly. "I'm not as fragile as you think. Just be fair to your mother, Alyssa. I have a lot more time to spend with Julianna, and there's less pressure on the two of us, so it stands to reason that we would get along." She kissed Lyss on the forehead. "Now. I'd better go back out front before they start up again. And don't worry. Tonight is your night to shine. I can't wait to see you up on stage."

Returning to the backstage area, Lyss checked the tuning on her basilka one more time. Speaker Jemson walked to center stage, and Lyss's heart beat faster. Shadow joined her in the wings. Despite his initial reluctance, he didn't seem worried at all.

This has to go well, Lyss thought. Shadow has to find his music again.

Maybe I have to find mine, too. So many important things have been pushed aside by this war.

"And, now, as promised, we have a special treat in store for you—two stellar musicians who trained right here in the Temple School. Two musicians who represent the diversity of our students, onstage together for the first time. Rogan Shadow Dancer and Her Highness Alyssa ana'Raisa, known as Meadowlark in the uplands, the heir to the Gray Wolf throne."

As if in a dream, Lyss followed Shadow onto the stage, keeping her eyes fixed on her feet so she wouldn't stumble. Also so she wouldn't see who was out there, beyond the wizard lights that lined the edge of the stage.

Their entrance was greeted with a roar of approval that

rolled over her like ocean waves. When Lyss raised her eyes enough that she could look over the edge of the stage, she saw that the two front rows were filled with a gaggle of temple students of varying ages. Behind them, her mother, smiling up at her. Captain Byrne, Shilo Trailblazer, Micah Bayar, Aunt Mellony, Finn and Julianna, General Dunedain, and the healer Harriman Vega. Filling the other rows, a quilt of faces of all colors, all ages, and every social class.

Sasha and Cam stood stage left and right, scanning the crowd for signs of trouble. Lyss saw other spots of blue scattered throughout the sanctuary.

As Lyss and Shadow launched into the opening notes of "Upland Dancer," the familiar magic of music calmed her down. When she looked over at Shadow, he had his head back, his eyes closed, as if he were far away, but he never missed a note. As he played, some of the tension in his shoulders eased.

Following "Upland Dancer," the melancholy "Summervale" left people lost in wistful memory, but then the rollicking "Baston Bay" brought the crowd alive, with clapping and impromptu sing-alongs. Lyss and Shadow faced off and sang the call-and-response between the innkeeper's daughter and the ship's captain, bringing cheers and laughter and catcalls. She'd forgotten the simple joy of making music.

It was already time for Shadow's solos. Lyss sat to one side so she could watch both him and the crowd.

"I call this 'Bittersweet.'" Shadow never offered much of an introduction onstage. Either the work delivered, or it didn't. In his case, it always did.

The words and music captured the brilliant anguish of love and loss. It was as if he was reflecting back the shared experience of the queendom. There were few in the audience who had not lost a loved one in this never-ending war. Lyss looked out at the crowd and saw tears running down her mother's face.

When the applause died down, Shadow said, "'Aspen Autumn.'" This one was an instrumental eulogy, the sweet runs of notes calling to mind the glitter of golden aspen leaves in the wind.

And then it was time for Lyss to step out front.

She stood, resting the base of her instrument on the floor. "It has been far too long since Shadow Dancer's music has been heard in the mountain home. I am humbled to be sharing a stage with him. Let's encourage him to keep writing, and to keep sharing it with us."

This was met with noisy enthusiasm.

When it ebbed, Lyss said, "My name is Alyssa ana'Raisa, known as Meadowlark in the uplands. I am the second daughter of Raisa ana'Marianna and Han sul'Alger. I'm going to sing about love and war tonight. First, a song I wrote about people who had no business falling in love. It's called 'The Raven and the Rose.'"

She slung the strap of her basilka over her shoulders, set her feet, and began to play. Trying to ignore the crowd in front of her, she kept her eyes on her fingers as they traveled over the strings. She'd written the song in the style of the timeless ballads sung by traveling minstrels, ballads that were easy to learn, that grew and changed as they passed from hand to hand. It was the story of the clever raven Han Alister, and how he found a home in the Briar Rose's heart, despite her many thorns.

Lyss had hesitated to write it, and then to share it, because she worried that she wasn't the best person to tell this story—both because she wasn't good enough, and because it wasn't her story to tell. By the time she reached the last chorus, Shadow had joined in on the basilka, and everyone in the sanctuary was on their feet, singing along with her.

The song ended to thunderous applause and foot-stomping. Alyssa looked down to see her mother smiling, still dabbing at her eyes—and she wasn't the only one.

It took a deal of time for the audience to settle enough for Lyss to be heard over the ruckus. "I wrote this next song because sometimes love is not enough. Sometimes you have to take the fight to your enemy. It's called 'Children of the North.'" She began with a measure or two of wild upland notes, and then began to sing.

"We are children of the north,
Born among the trees.
We will not take the collar
And we will not bend the knee.
We will fight you in the winter snows

And in the summer mud,
And the slopes of Hanalea
Will be watered with your blood.

"We are children of the north
And we do not fight alone.
Our mothers fight beside us
To protect the mountain home.
From mountain camp to upland vale
You'll hear our battle cry:
You think you've come prepared to fight.
Instead, prepare to die."

Now Lyss advanced to the front of the stage, looked her mother straight in the eye, and sang, each word a blow against their common enemy.

"We will find you in the flatlands
Where there is no place to hide.
We'll drown you in the marshes
Where the Waterwalkers bide.
We'll force you from your strongholds
And we'll drive you to the sea.
We'll burn your golden cities
And we'll set your captives free."

Lyss tossed her head, feeling tendrils of hair coming loose. Kicking off her shoes, she stomped up and down, making eye contact with one person after another, trying to ignore the fabric ripping round her knees. Speaking up wasn't hard when the music freed her. Truth be told, it was a bloody and warlike song to be singing in a temple, but it didn't seem to matter. The entire sanctuary was rocking with the stomping of feet. The students in the front row stared up at her with rapt faces. It didn't feel like a solo when the entire crowd was with her.

> *"We are children of the north.*
> *This time we fight as one.*
> *Wizard, clan, and valefolk,*
> *Our daughters and our sons.*
> *We are not made of flesh and blood,*
> *We're honed of steel and stone.*
> *We will raise another mountain*
> *And we'll build it with your bones."*

The clamor of the crowd reverberated off the stone walls, echoed against the cavernous ceilings, and resonated in her bones. Shadow joined hands with her and they stood side by side. Lyss heard wolfish yips and howling, and looked up to see that almost the entire balcony was taken up by her salvo. It was some time before the crowd quieted enough that they could move on to the finale.

It was "Hanalea's Lament," a traditional ballad of the high country, sung by the full choir, with Shadow and Alyssa on basilka. The audience stood again and sang along. Now tears were streaming down Alyssa's face, too, but she didn't care.

This, she thought. This is what I've been trying to say all along.

When the song was over, nobody seemed to want to leave, but all stood, arms joined, swaying, still singing the refrain, howling, or shouting, "For the queen!" and "For the Gray Wolf!" and "For the Staff and Flash!"—that being the High Wizard's signia.

After the concert, audience members crowded forward, most of them friends and family members of the performers. Lyss ducked backstage to the small room where she'd left her change of clothes. She returned her basilka to its case, kicked off her mincy shoes, and shed her dress, sucking in her first unimpaired breath since before leaving the castle close. Gratefully, she pulled on her leather breeches, softspun shirt, and mourning coat, finishing with a pair of well-broken-in boots. Draping Aunt Mellony's dress over one arm, she picked up her instrument with the other.

"Your Highness?" It was Sasha, just outside the door. "Do you need any help?"

"Coming."

When Lyss emerged, Sasha said, "Well, you look more like yourself. Are you still planning to go out with Finn and the others?"

Lyss nodded. "I know you didn't plan on that originally, so—"

"I talked it over with Captain Byrne, and he's leaving you five more Wolves as escorts. That'll be six of us—plus a wizard, two upland warriors, and a fierce Highlander captain. Think that's enough?"

"That's enough," Lyss said. "We'd better go before they leave without us."

When Lyss and Sasha descended from the stage, the crowd in the sanctuary had thinned considerably. Shadow stood by the first row of seats with his father, Fire Dancer, and Queen Raisa, Aunt Mellony, and Trailblazer.

"Dancer!" Lyss embraced him. "Thanks for coming."

Dancer smiled at her. His face was lined with care, and his blue eyes had faded a little, but his smile was as brilliant as before. "It's not often that so many of my old friends are all in one place."

Shadow looked Lyss up and down, taking in her transformation. "That didn't take long," he said, grinning.

"Alyssa," her mother said, her cheeks pinked up with emotion, her eyes bright with tears. "I had no idea . . . I never imagined that you could . . . That was remarkable. I had forgotten what a pleasure it is to hear you sing and play."

Me too, Lyss thought. "I'm so glad you came," she said. And, then, cheeks burning, she added, "I hope I didn't . . . I hope you didn't feel like I meant to embarrass anyone by making a political statement up there."

The queen smiled. "Alyssa, we won't always agree, but

when you speak, it is always worth hearing. I am so glad that I did not miss it."

"Meadowlark," Trailblazer said, "your anthem reminds me of a Demonai battle dance—it stirs the blood in the same way. Do not be surprised if you hear it echoing through the Spirits this spring."

Captain Byrne appeared, snow dusted over his shoulders and hair. "Well done, both of you," he said, smiling at Lyss and Shadow. He turned to the queen. "Your carriage is outside, Your Majesty."

"Would you like to ride back with me and Aunt Mellony, Alyssa?" her mother asked.

"Well, actually, I—I'm going out with some friends," Lyss said. "We're celebrating Julianna's engagement." Suddenly aware that Aunt Mellony's dress was bundled under one arm, she added, "Thank you for the dress, Aunt Mellony."

"Here. I'll take it," Aunt Mellony said, reaching for it. "It looks like your hands are full."

Her mother came up on her toes and kissed Lyss on the cheek. "I am so very proud of you, Alyssa." She paused. "Don't stay out too late. We have a breakfast meeting tomorrow, early." She hesitated, then couldn't seem to resist adding, "And . . . be careful. It's . . . the dark season, and the wolves are running."

"I will, Mama." Lyss might ride howling into battle elsewhere in the queendom, but here in the capital she was her mother's fifteen-year-old daughter.

The adults moved on, through the temple doors and into the street.

"Your entourage is outside, Meadowlark," Shadow said. "Hadley mentioned something about filthy sea chanteys. She said we should bring our basilkas."

By the time they emerged from the temple, the crowd was nearly gone, and only two or three carriages remained lined up across the street. A light snow was falling, making the cobblestones slick, forming halos around the wizard lights. Lyss drew her mother's shawl closer around her, clutching the handle of her instrument case in her other hand, doubly glad that she'd taken the time to change clothes.

"Bravo, Your Highness, and Shadow Dancer," Finn said, with a little bow. "You've exceeded all of our expectations."

"Which were no doubt low," Shadow said.

"We're going to a place called the Keg and Crown, overlooking the river," Julianna said. "Finn's been there, and he says the food's good."

"I've been there, too," Hadley said. "It's on River Street, which means we'd better walk. You know how narrow that is. I don't think we can bring a carriage through there."

THE WOOING

When Breon returned from his meeting with the client to the high street, traffic had increased considerably. A steady stream of people converged on the bridge, crossing to the temple close.

Now he had time to kill before the concert was over. He could go back to the crib and wait there, out of sight. But he was in no mood to listen to Whacks harping on him, and Goose being miserable, and Aubrey giving him the sly eye. Besides, it was filthy in there and he needed to keep his new clothes clean, at least until after the gig.

He was hungry, but he'd spent the coin that Whacks gave him. Now his purse and his stomach were both empty.

That's when it struck him that there was no reason why

he couldn't attend the concert himself. The banner said it was free, after all, and he was already dressed up. It would give him something to do until it was time to return to his post.

The whole temple courtyard was crowded, and when he got to the front of the line, he could see why. A brace of bluejackets at the door was searching everyone, patting people down, giving everyone a good look-over before they went in. He wondered why. It wasn't hard to get into a temple, as a rule—it was tougher getting out of one. As a precaution, he slid his shiv, his stash, and the locket into the hidey-hole he'd made under the lining of his new jacket.

It took some fast talking to get into the sanctuary with his jafasa. He wasn't about to leave it outside and come back and find it missing. Finally, after a search of his bag and his person, in which they didn't find his stash, his shiv, or the locket, they let him in.

By the time he reached the sanctuary, he didn't see an empty seat anywhere. People were still milling around, the way they do when they think that a seat will magically appear if they go down an aisle for the fifth time. Breon didn't bother. He found a spot next to one of the temple pillars, to the left of the stage. He had to crane his neck to see, and he still couldn't see everything, but he felt lucky to find standing room at all. He could hear muffled voices, and when he put his hand on the stage, he could feel vibrations from people walking around behind the curtain. His heart beat a little faster. He'd spent plenty of time playing gigs in taverns and inns, but never in a venue like this.

The inside was painted up fancy-like—like some place he'd been before that he couldn't remember now. There were greens and winterberry around the windows and along the altars. The stone walls seemed to glow in the light from the candelabra, and the soaring ceilings made it seem like a place where the Maker might want to come and listen to prayers and whatnot.

Maybe, if he had it to do over again, he'd be a dedicate. It seemed like a soft life, except for all the religion.

The temple bells sounded overhead, and a speaker appeared center stage to introduce the first act—a mob of lýtling dancers.

Breon could've counted on the fingers of one hand the times he'd been inside a temple, and then it was usually in a classroom or dining hall, not the sanctuary. He half-expected someone to boot him out, but people scarcely seemed to notice him, intent as they were on the action at the front of the hall.

It was nearly all music and dance—no jugglers or tellers of tales. He couldn't see the dancers so well from an angle, but he could hear well enough. The talent was variable, but enthusiastic, at least, and some of the music was the best he'd ever heard. Nobody played the jafasa, of course—he seemed to have that market cornered.

The final act was a cove and a girlie, both playing

basilkas. The cove looked to be a Southern Islander, but he was dressed in copperhead style, with his hair done up like one of their warriors. The girlie was big-boned, blond, and nervous-looking. They looked like they'd been matched up in the dark.

The songs were standards, their harmonies rough, but nothing a little more practice couldn't fix. Breon was so caught up that they were halfway through their set when he realized it was time to go.

As he began working his way to the back, the haunting notes from a basilka followed him up the aisle, and he had to stop halfway to the back and turn to see who was playing like that.

It was the cove half of the duet, soloing on the basilka. Breon hadn't heard the song before, but it caught hold of his heart just the same.

Breon stood and watched the uplander through another song. Then that player stepped back, and the girlie stepped forward.

She was as long-legged as a colt, and she looked about as comfortable in her slinky gown as Breon was in his new finery. Her hair was a tawny color between brown and blond, like wet sand or pale ale, and the way it was piled up on her head made her neck look even longer.

The audience either knew her, or they wanted her to feel at home, because they all came to their feet and roared a welcome that shook the dust from the rafters. What would it be like to get a greeting like that before you even began to play?

She straightened her shoulders, lifted her chin, and said, "My name is Alyssa ana'Raisa, known as Meadowlark in the uplands. I am the second daughter of Raisa ana'Marianna and Han sul'Alger."

The crowd roared again, even louder.

This stork of a girlie had a shitload of names that seemed to ping in his memory. Where had he heard them before?

"I'm going to sing about love and war tonight. First, a song I wrote about people who had no business falling in love. It's called 'The Raven and the Rose.'"

Her voice wasn't as good as Breon's, and her playing was unskilled next to her companion's, but it was her words that caught his ear. The song was a love ballad, and the lyrics were like nothing he'd heard before—raw and honest, simple and yet true. They told a story of star-crossed lovers who changed the world to make it a place where they could be together.

Breon was cynical about lovers and love songs, but this one put him down on his back with an arrow in his heart. When it was done, the temple exploded in applause. Breon stood like an island with people crying all around him and embracing each other like it was a story they'd all had a part in.

The girl—Alyssa ana'Whatever—stood on the stage, gripping her basilka, spots of color on her cheeks, until the frenzy died down a little. Then she said, in a low, growly voice, "I wrote this next song because sometimes love is not enough. Sometimes you have to take the fight to your enemy."

The song was called "Children of the North," and it was a battle cry.

She sang it in a fierce, proud voice. The melody was catchy, and the chorus easy to remember, and soon Breon was singing along with the rest of the audience, like it was his story, too. Like he belonged here. But he knew he didn't.

Breon knew there was a war going on—there was always a war going on—but it was a war between blue-bloods. His goal was to keep from getting ganged onto a ship or pressed into the army. Now, hearing this song, he was having trouble remembering why it had been so important to survive.

When the song was finished, the room erupted with cheers and applause. Breon felt like a faker, given the sort of life he led. For years, his world hadn't extended farther than a nasty tangle of waterfront streets. It had been forever since he'd looked beyond his next gig, his next meal, or his next hit of leaf. He was always pretending to be someone he wasn't, whatever it took to please the client. He claimed he wasn't a fancy, but he was just putting on airs. A fancy made a more honest living than he did.

Breon lowered his head and bulled his way to the back

of the temple. He slunk past the bluejackets at the door and out into the cold night. Behind him, he heard the singing begin again—this time a faintly familiar upland ballad.

He felt low and wretched, and he knew what would make him feel better.

He left the temple close and crossed the river to the Ragmarket side. Instead of going directly to his assigned position, he turned right, following the river until he could cut down a street farther on. Huddling in the doorway of a closed shop, he dug out the precious sack of leaf and shook a little into his pipe. He stepped back out into the street, reached high, and lit the pipe from the wizard flame in the lantern overhead.

The more he smoked, the more he realized that he'd been right all along. It didn't much matter to him who was in charge—his life wouldn't change, either way. His life was a whole series of todays with no guarantee of tomorrow.

A few minutes later he was on his way back toward the bridge, the magic of leaf rocketing into his fingers and toes, ready to step out of his tawdry skin and into his role.

The concert must have ended while he was otherwise engaged. People streamed past him, mostly families that had walked in from the surrounding neighborhoods. People were buzzing about the music and the dancing and how amazing it all was. Some of the children were in costume, so they must have been up on stage themselves.

Breon set a cup on the ground in front of him, seeding it with a few steelies, then leaned against a building, his foot propped against the stone wall, his jafasa resting comfortably on his knee. Lost in a pleasant euphoria, he adjusted the tuning, the people around him a smear of color and movement. He ran over the set list in his head, one love song after another.

Digging into his pocket, he pulled out the girlie's pendant and dropped the chain over his head, sliding the locket under his fine linen shirt so that it rested on his bare chest. How long had it been since she'd worn this? Closing his eyes, he pressed it against his skin, picking through memories, dreams, and desires, looking for the melody that would resonate with her.

Her music was elusive as a fellsdeer, complex as the sea air, a mingling of love and loss, courage and fear, sorrow and joy and anger. What had been, what was, and what could be. Three notes, with an odd dissonance to them. Three strands, woven together, stronger than any one of them. Raw, unfinished, feral, changeable as a spring day. Maybe it was the leaf—it was probably the leaf—but he fell in love with the girlie's music before he ever set eyes on her.

He wouldn't know if he truly had it until she came, and he played it for her. In the meantime, he launched into his set list of tavern songs and drinking songs and love songs that he no longer believed in.

When he began to play, the coins piled up quickly—they always did. Some people lingered awhile to listen, murmuring softly among themselves like they were still in temple, and others shushing them. Couples, old and young, held hands and smiled.

At first the sidewalks were crowded, but the numbers dwindled gradually and still the girlie with the shawl did not come. Breon felt a prickle of doubt. His client had seemed knowledgeable about what she would be wearing and where she would be walking, but maybe he had been mistaken, or maybe she had changed her mind. Or maybe Breon had lingered too long with his pipe and he'd missed her in the early crowds.

He kept waiting, kept playing and singing, though now the streets were all but empty. Disappointment burned in his throat. He shouldn't have gone off for a hit just as the concert was coming to a close. That was his mistake—the latest of many.

Since he was in no hurry to go back to their crib and face Aubrey and Whacks and Goose with empty pockets, he kept on waiting, looking around to see if he could spot the client lurking nearby. He didn't see him, but as he scanned the area, he thought he saw movement on a nearby roof. When he focused in, he saw nothing, so maybe the leaf was playing tricks on him.

It was snowing harder, and the wind was finding its way through his clothing, and it was more and more difficult to stand in one place and play with his breath coming in clouds and his fingers stinging from the cold. Maybe it was time to accept the fact he'd messed up. Again.

There'll be other gigs, he told himself. Better ones.

Just then, he saw a group emerge from a nearby tavern and head his way. They looked to be about his age, and they were laughing and jostling each other as they came. As they passed in and out of the light from the bridge buttresses, he squinted, trying to get a good look.

It was an odd mingle of people. Two were dressed in clan garb, three wore temple dress-up, and the others were all bluejackets.

Breon guessed bluejackets enjoyed a drink and a bite as much as anyone. But he saw no green-gowned girlie among them.

Something about the group reminded him of the song he'd heard in temple—the one that had made him feel guilty.

We are children of the north.
This time we fight as one.
Wizard, clan, and valefolk,
Our daughters and our sons.

The locket warmed against his skin, drawing his attention. Startled, Breon fingered it and took a second look at the group walking toward him.

That's when he saw her—one of the two in clan garb was carrying an instrument case, and wearing the shawl the client had described to him. She was tall, but she had the shawl up over her head, so he couldn't make out her hair color.

He felt the magic buzz through him like stingo, connecting the locket and the girlie on her way to him. This, then, was his target. Here, then, was his opportunity to make a new start.

He straightened, took a deep breath, found the chords he'd chosen, and launched into her song.

RAGMARKET ENCORE

The Keg and Crown was cozy, with a warm hearth surrounded by winter greens. Lyss pulled the pins from her carefully arranged hair and shook her head, letting her hair fall around her shoulders. That seemed to fit the Keg and Crown better than Aunt Mellony's twist. As did her leathers.

They toasted Finn and Julianna's betrothal, and this time Lyss was able to make a gracious show of it by playing and singing "Lily of the Vale," a traditional love ballad. At the end, Sasha raised a silent toast to Lyss, looking at her over the rim of her tankard.

Lyss and Shadow played the basilka and Hadley sang sailors' songs that were, indeed, so filthy that the entire tavern stared at first, then joined in. They moved on to marching songs and far-away-from-home songs and when-will-this-war-be-over songs. Every so often, they would bang their cups on the table, forcing a kiss from the betrothed couple, who seemed all too willing to comply.

Sometimes, one song leads to another, and one round leads to two. Lyss felt more relaxed and at home than she'd been since she returned to court.

That was when the bonging of the Southbridge Temple bell across the river reminded her of how late it was.

"I have to go," she said, tossing down her napkin. "I never meant to stay this long. I have a meeting at an ungodly hour."

"I'm in that same meeting," Julianna said, pushing back her chair. "We'll all go."

Lyss shook her head. "No, no, stay. I'll take Sasha and Cam and the rest of my Gray Wolves with me. The rest of you don't have a curfew. We'll take one carriage back from Southbridge, and the rest of you can take the other one back."

"Sounds crowded," Shadow said, unfolding to his feet. "I'll go back with you. I'm staying in Kendall House with my father, so it won't be out of the way for me."

In the end, they all left together.

Outside, it was snowing harder, the wind had picked up, and the temperature was dropping as well. Lyss pulled her shawl up over her head to keep her hair from whipping around her face. They walked back toward Bridge Street, Cam in front, Sasha lingering to the rear, swinging her head from side to side, looking for danger. Julianna and Finn walked hand in hand, Lyss and Shadow behind them, talking softly as the snow came down.

They were just turning onto South Bridge when Lyss heard it—a strange, ethereal music that seemed to sink its claws into her soul.

"What *is* that?" She turned and looked back the way they'd come.

"I don't hear anything," Shadow said.

Lyss had no idea what kind of instrument it was, but it sounded exotic, otherworldly. The voice of it was high and clear and pure as the Dyrnnewater, the kind of melody that ensnares the heart on a first hearing, gets the feet moving, and never lets go.

"I'll be right back," she said, and took off running, her instrument case banging against her hip.

"Meadowlark! Wait!" Shadow called, half-laughing. "You're going the wrong way."

The musician stood on a street corner, where South Bridge met the quay, playing a stringed instrument she didn't recognize. He was a slight figure muffled in a thick cloak, the hood pulled close around his face. A busker, it must be, hoping to take advantage of the crowds of music-lovers leaving the concert.

But there were no crowds now, only Lyss.

"Lyss? Hey, Lyss, where are you going?" Now it was Sasha calling after her. Lyss turned back toward the others, spotting them partway across the bridge. Then they disappeared as tendrils of darkness snaked toward her, wrapping around her like a shroud, shutting the rest of the world out. She could hear nothing, see nothing. The shadows filled her mind, so there was only Lyss, the otherworldly music, and the musician.

Lyss couldn't help herself—it was as if the music was tethered to her heart, drawing her forward at a stumbling trot.

The busker lifted his head to look at her, and she could see his eyes glittering within the cowl of the cloak, his breath pluming out in the cold. He flinched back, as if surprised, as if she was not at all what he expected. But then, as she drew closer, he seemed to gather himself. He skipped backward along the riverbank, never missing a note, moving as lightly as a fellsdeer. Though he was moving backward, and she forward, it was all she could do to keep up.

"Sir," she said, digging in her purse for a handful of coins, "what's that you're playing? I've never heard anything like it." He kept retreating, and she followed, her surroundings a soft smudge of shadow so that she wasn't entirely sure where she was. It seemed unimportant next to her desire to follow the music to its source.

He was teasing her with his music, like the piper in

stories. It was as intoxicating as blue ruin. It tugged at her, drawing her on. It was full of promises that she wanted him to keep. Promises meant only for her.

He knows me. He understands. If I keep listening, I'll understand, too.

As they moved down the riverbank, the wind blowing down the river caught his hood and it fell back, displaying a face like that of one of the young gods in the temples, the skin marble-pale, stretched over bone. His hair was the color of upland honey, a deep, rich brown threaded with streaks of red and gold. He smiled, his eyes alive with mischief, as he beckoned her on. He reminded Lyss of one of the faerie folk in stories that lured the unwary into trysts in the high glens—encounters that left a person forever dissatisfied with human lovers.

The busker's head came up, as if he'd heard something. As he looked past her, toward the river, the music dwindled, nearly stopped. The shadows thinned, and Lyss could hear a commotion behind her, the sounds of fighting, shouts of alarm, the twang of bows, and the clamor of weapons. Lyss turned and took a step back toward Bridge Street. But the music started up again, faster than before, frenetic, taking hold of her again, sweeping her away. Up ahead, she saw the busker round a corner and disappear, and she hurried after, trying not to slip on the icy cobblestones.

Turning the corner, she saw him again, standing on a stone bench in a little riverside park, treed like a fox. He stood, his hands still moving over the strings, making that magical music. He'd left his instrument case there, sitting open on the bench.

"Sir," Lyss said, holding up her basilka in its case. "I'm a musician, too, and it's just—I've never heard an instrument like that before."

"It's called a jafasa," he said. She was just a few feet away when he slung his instrument behind him. He bent, scooped something from his instrument case, and extended it toward her.

As soon as the music stopped, her mind cleared of shadow, and she realized that he might be retrieving a weapon. She stumbled several steps backward, groping for her knife. And then she recognized what he was holding.

A bouquet of flowers.

As if in a dream, she took the flowers from him, bringing them to her nose to taste their scent. She recognized red foxflowers, white lilies, and blue trueheart, though there were others she couldn't identify. She was momentarily distracted by an echo of memory—the sense that she'd seen them somewhere before.

"Were you the one I saw onstage?" he said. When she stared at him, he added, impatiently, "Were you the one that sang the song about the northern children?"

"Oh," she said, nodding. "Yes."

"Your performance was brilliant," he said, getting off an awkward bow.

"You were there?"

"I was there. It was . . . it was honest, and honesty is hard to find these days." Then he went back to playing, eyes closed, head tilted back, lips slightly parted, as if the music flowed from some well of magic deep within.

"I might as well be honest," Lyss said, "because I'm not very good at lying."

When he heard her speak, he opened his eyes and smiled. "I know," he said. Then he looked over her shoulder, his eyes went wide, and the music died abruptly. Otherwise she might not have heard the thud of boots on cobblestones, and more shouting behind her.

"Look out, Lyss!" It sounded like Sasha, from too far away.

The busker stood as if frozen, ashen pale, shaking his head, until Lyss heard a familiar *thwack*. It sounded for all the world like a—

The busker leapt from the bench, slamming her flat, onto the cobblestones, sending her basilka flying. He raised his instrument like a shield and another bolt thudded into the soundboard, sending showers of splinters over her face.

Then, suddenly, Cam was there, grabbing the busker by the scruff of the neck, ripping him off her and tossing him aside. He shielded her with his body, pushing her toward a low stone wall along the river walk that would provide a bit of shelter. A bolt sang past Lyss's ear, splashing into the river. And then Cam's body shuddered, and he stumbled.

"Cam?"

They staggered forward a few more steps. He pushed her down behind the wall and collapsed beside her.

"You're hit!"

"Yes, ma'am," he gasped.

Lyss ran her hand over his uniform tunic until she found the arrow shaft embedded in his right lower back. He hadn't lost much blood, but she had to get him to a healer. She came up on her hands and knees, peering over the top of the wall, scanning the buildings huddled along the intersecting streets. The fire seemed to be coming from there. On a nearby roof, she saw a hooded archer calmly reloading his crossbow. He turned, aimed straight at Lyss, and released as she dove back into cover. The bolt whined over her head like an angry insect.

It's me they're after, she thought, her mind beginning to clear from the enchantment of the music. The busker had disappeared, but the bolts were still coming, sending chips of stone flying, so there must be more than one—

"Heads up, ma'am," Cam said, groping desperately for a weapon.

Lyss turned. Another assassin was coming at her from the river, a blade glittering in his hand. She was cornered, with no place to go. He'd be on top of her before she could reach the knife in her boot. She tried to push to her feet, but her boots slid on the icy ground and she fell back, hitting her head, hard, on the wall.

As the assassin lunged at her, she was conscious of Cam rolling so he was half on top of her. The assassin landed, hard, with an odd grunt, and then blood gushed over her and Cam both. Lyss saw a blood-smeared blade protruding from the rusher's back. Cam had found his sword.

Only now he appeared to have passed out. She heard running feet, and a shout: "For the Gray Wolf! For the queen in the north!" It was Sasha.

But there were more blade men incoming. They were like demons, erupting out of the ground. Lyss squirmed out from under Cam, groped blindly and found the handle of her instrument case.

Desperately, she swung the case at the leading blade man. It smashed into his face with all the force she could summon, slamming him onto his back, the dagger in his hand pinwheeling into the street. She slid her hand into her boot as he rolled to his feet and lunged toward her.

He barreled into her and they both fell to the ground, with the assassin on top, his hands wrapped around Lyss's throat. His body flinched as multiple bolts struck him, but he kept hold. His fingers didn't loosen until Lyss's shiv transfixed his throat and blood spilled over her leathers.

I'm glad I changed out of Aunt Mellony's dress, she thought woozily.

Lyss pushed the deadweight of his body off her as more bolts clattered against the courtyard stone. She swung her basilka up, sheltering under it like an umbrella, feeling it shiver as missile after missile struck it, some boring through the soundboard and pricking out the back.

She heard running footsteps, and the street lit up as Hadley raked the rooftops with bolts of wizard flame, clearing them of snow and archers. The bolts quit coming, for the time being anyway. And then Shadow was beside her, shielding her with his body until she was engulfed in a sea of blue uniforms. Finn flamed the riverside, clearing off any remaining assassins. Sasha was still clearing the street.

"Are you able to walk, Meadowlark?" Shadow said, one arm wrapped around her, his face bleak with worry.

"Me? I'm fine. We need to—"

"You're covered in blood," he said gently.

"It's not mine," she said, twisting so she could look around. "Where's Julianna?"

"I sent her on to the temple," Sasha said, suddenly at her side. "Let's go."

"Bring Staunton," Lyss said, planting her feet and pointing to where he lay, still and silent, next to the wall.

Shadow knelt next to Cam, pressing his fingers against his pulse points. "Meadowlark," he said. "I don't know if he—"

"Bring him," Lyss growled. "I'm not going anywhere without him."

Shadow scooped him up and they swarmed toward the bridge, Hadley and Finn providing cover, Lyss in the center of what remained of her guard. They had to pick their way around bodies at the Ragmarket end of the bridge.

"Ambush," Sasha said, stepping over a black-clad body. "They blocked the bridge after we started across. We had to fight our way through. That's why it took us so long to get to you."

They crossed the bridge into the temple courtyard, where two carriages still waited. That's all Lyss saw before Shadow shouldered his way into the temple. Sasha followed, pushing Lyss ahead of her.

Julianna was waiting inside with a young dedicate. "Sweet lady in chains," her cousin whispered, taking in their bloodied appearance.

"Is there a healer on the premises?" Shadow gasped. "This one's hurt bad. They tried to murder the princess heir."

"Of course," the dedicate said, signaling to a young girl who sat next to the hearth, reading a book. The girl took off running.

The dedicate shook back her hood, revealing clan-style beaded-and-braided hair. Reaching behind her desk, she pulled out a longbow and a quiver of arrows.

"That's what I like to see," Shadow said, "a faith with teeth."

"Carry the boy into the sanctuary," the dedicate said. "I'll go upstairs and cover the door in case anyone tries to get in." She ran lightly up the stairs.

As Lyss turned to follow Shadow, she all but ran into Julianna. Her cousin's eyes were red from crying, her lashes clumped together with tears. She stared at Lyss's blood-soaked clothing, looking as if she might faint dead away. "Alyssa," she whispered, her voice breaking. "What have they done to you?"

"They've pissed me off, is what they've done," Lyss said, brushing past her.

Shadow deposited Cam facedown on a wide stone bench. Lyss knelt next to him, slicing his uniform tunic away from the wound. The bolt was all but buried, with only a small bit protruding from his flesh. His skin was icy cold around the wound, and seemed to be getting colder. His pulse was faint and flickering.

"Where's the rest of the Wolves?" Lyss asked, looking around. "Was anyone else hurt?"

"There's one more dead," Shadow said.

"Who?"

"Carew. The rest are hunting down the archers. Hadley and Finn are still out, and we've called in reinforcements from the Southbridge Garrison House. I'm going back out, too." The spark that had been kindled in his eyes during the concert seemed to have been extinguished, leaving them as flat and dead as they had been since he lost Aspen.

This is my fault, Lyss thought. Guilt rose inside her like a full-moon tide. It's Solstice, and Mama said the wolves were running. I should have stayed at home. And now, Shadow . . .

"I don't want anyone else hurt," Lyss said, catching his hand. "Can we call them back until we know what's what?"

Shadow gently pulled free. "If we don't catch them now, they may disappear for good. This is the golden hour, before they have time to go to ground." His eyes met hers, held. "Don't worry. I'll be careful." And then he was gone.

The young girl returned with Ty Gryphon at her heels. He was carrying a remedy bag.

"Ty!" Lyss said, relieved. Ty was Hadley's older brother, and a gifted healer. When Lord Vega wouldn't allow Adrian to work in the healing halls, Ty had taken him on as a kind of unofficial assistant. Adrian always said that Ty was the most skilled healer in Lord Vega's service— including Lord Vega.

Ty spent little time in the capital these days. Lyss hadn't seen him in more than a year—he traveled all over the queendom, wherever the fighting was fiercest.

Ty looked Lyss up and down, taking in her blood-smeared clothing. "Where are you—?"

"It's somebody else's," Lyss said. She pointed to Cam. "He's the patient. He took a crossbow bolt in the back."

Ty glanced at Cam, then back at her. "You're sure you're not wounded? Even a scratch?"

Lyss's head was throbbing, and she could feel a major

lump where it had hit the wall, but it could wait. "I'm all right. See to him first."

As Ty examined Cam, Lyss stroked the blood-matted hair away from Cam's forehead. He didn't respond at all.

"This is someone you know?" Ty asked.

"He's in my personal guard. He's been with me on the battlefields all summer without a scratch, and then he comes home and this happens."

"What's his name?"

"Cam Staunton."

"Could we get some blankets over here?" Ty called to the young acolyte. She brought over an armload, and Lyss put one under Cam's head and one over his hips and legs.

"How long has it been since he was wounded?" Ty asked.

"It's probably coming up on an hour since he was hit," Lyss said.

Ty's lips tightened. "Have you had a look at the bolts they used?"

"There are probably some out there," Lyss said. "I could send someone to—"

"I don't think it will change the treatment plan," Ty said. He pressed one hand against the skin around the wound, gripped his amulet with the other, and closed his eyes, concentrating. Then he moved his hand to Cam's upper back. Then to his forehead—as if he was counting up the damage.

He sighed, sitting back on his heels. "I can try to cut the bolt out," he said, "but it would cause considerable trauma and pain, and it's too late to do any good."

Lyss reared back. "What do you mean, it's too late? He hasn't lost that much blood. I've seen soldiers survive that kind of wound a hundred times."

"It's poison, Lyss," Ty said. "Whoever attacked you, they meant to kill."

"He saved my *life*," Lyss said. "He's just thirteen. That's unacceptable."

"I'm sorry, Your Highness."

No. She would not say good-bye to Cam Staunton. "Can't you suck it out of him with magic?" She'd seen the gifted draw out poison and infection that way. "Or—we could treat it like a snakebite? We could open the wound, so it bleeds the poison out."

"It's been too long. The poison is everywhere now, so I have no hope of drawing it out."

"What kind is it?"

"I'm not sure exactly, though I can probably figure it out once I get hold of one of the bolts."

"I'll get you one," Lyss said, pushing to her feet. "Once we know what it is, we'll find an antidote."

"Lyss," Ty said gently. "Does Cam have a family? We should send for them."

"No!" Lyss said, backing away, angry tears streaming down her face. "I mean, if you don't know what it is, how do you know there isn't an antidote? You should heal him. You're a healer, right?"

It was like Lyss was being sucked into a well of memory, to that day almost exactly four years ago. Her father lying still and cold in the street, and Lord Vega saying it was poison, and there was nothing he could do.

Eleven-year-old Lyss had punched him for it. She wanted to punch somebody now, but she'd grown up enough that she knew Ty wasn't the right person.

"Lyss," Ty said, in the soothing wizard voice Adrian had always used on her. "Could you hold his hands and talk to him? He shouldn't be alone right now."

Lyss blotted at her eyes. She wished Sasha were there—she knew him best. Or anyone else who would know the right thing to say.

"Don't worry," Ty said, as if reading her mind. "Whatever you say will be the right thing."

Lyss would have to do. She sat down next to Cam, took his ice-cold hands between her own, and began to talk. And she talked, rambling on about everything and nothing, recalling the summer's battles, and memories from camp, stories about his mother, and pranks the two of them had played on Sasha. She moved on to the concert, and the songs they'd sung in the tavern, and retold the story of how they'd driven off the rushers together. She even sang to him a little, like she was singing him to sleep.

All at once, Cam's grip tightened, and his eyes flickered

open. "Ma'am?" he whispered.

Lyss leaned in close. "What is it, Staunton?"

"Are you all right, ma'am?" His eyes searched her face anxiously. "Did they get to you?"

"I'm all right," she said. "Thanks to you."

Cam smiled. And closed his eyes.

16

POSTMORTEM

Ty finally persuaded Lyss to let go of Cam's hands.

"We should get you back to the palace, where Lord Vega can do a more thorough—"

"No," Lyss said. "I'm not leaving here until my Wolves come back. I need to know that they're safe, and I want to find out what they've learned."

"They may be out all night, Your Highness," Ty said.

"I'm a soldier, Master Gryphon. I'm used to all-nighters."

"Shall I send word to Lord Vega, and have him attend you here?"

"No!" Lyss said. "Not him." She took a deep breath, released it. She needed to stop taking her frustration out on the wrong people. "You can have a look, if it will set your mind at ease."

"All right." Ty motioned to the acolyte to look after Cam, and led Lyss into one of the side chapels.

It wasn't until Lyss sat down on the steps to the altar that she realized how exhausted she was. Her legs were trembling, and her head ached like fury where it had struck the wall, and she was weighed down with a fresh load of grief. She closed her eyes, wanting more than anything to escape into sleep.

"Your Highness."

She opened her eyes to find Ty studying her with narrowed eyes.

"Not to belabor the point, Your Highness, but—nothing broke the skin? Not even a scrape? A nick? The one that jumped you—did he cut you?"

Lyss shook her head, which set it to spinning so much that for a moment it was touch-and-go whether she might spew into Ty's lap.

"I do have scrapes and cuts," Lyss said, when she'd recovered. "As far as I know, they all came from hitting the wall, flying chips of stone, and the like. To my knowledge, I was not cut by any blade nor hit by any arrows. I hit my head really hard. I'm dizzy and a little sick. Also my neck is badly bruised where he . . . ah . . . tried to strangle me."

The dedicate returned, and set down a large bag beside them.

"Is there snakebite weed, and willow bark?" Ty asked her.

She nodded. "They're in there."

"Could you bring me hot water, then? And cloths to make a poultice?"

With that, Lyss submitted to Ty's careful examination and soothing voice and hands. He eased the pain in her throat and neck and head, then healed her skinned knees, plus multiple scrapes and bruises elsewhere. He covered some of the suspicious nicks and cuts with snakebite weed and spoke charms over them.

"You should leave them," Lyss said, "as a reminder of the price of stupidity."

She didn't really believe that, though. The familiar anger had rekindled inside her, all but replacing the guilt. Some might say that it was foolish to walk out in a city that had claimed the lives of her father and brother.

That is not acceptable, she thought. This is my home. Why should we have to look over our shoulders every single day?

And the busker. It seemed all wrong that she would be betrayed by someone who could play such enchanting music.

Enchanting. Maybe that's the operative word.

He didn't know, said an annoying voice in her head.

What do you mean, he didn't know? How could he not know?

He didn't know there was going to be an attack. He was as surprised as you were. He pushed you down and shielded you with his instrument. Otherwise you would have been hit. Why would he do that if he was in on the plan?

It's not up to me to explain it. I'm still muddleheaded from whatever spell he used on me.

You're the only person in the world who can have an argument with yourself and lose.

Lyss realized that her eyes had drifted shut again. She opened them to find Ty watching her.

"You know the drill," he said, with a sympathetic smile. "You may feel worse tomorrow. If you discover anything we've overlooked, let me know right away."

The acolyte poked her head around the corner.

"Your Highness, your cousin is outside. She wonders if— She would like to see you if she could."

Lyss nodded. "All right."

Julianna all but tiptoed into the room. She had a little more color in her cheeks than she'd had earlier. She looked at Ty, as if for permission. When he nodded, she crossed the room, sat next to Lyss, and took her hands.

"Are you—?"

"I'm all right," Lyss said.

"Finn's being debriefed by Captain Byrne. When he's done, we're going back to the palace. We wondered if you wanted to ride back with us."

Lyss shook her head. "I'm staying a while longer. Until I get more information. If it gets too late, I'll stay in the Southbridge Garrison House."

"Is there anything else you need? Do you want to make any kind of official statement about the attack, or would you rather I wrote up something for your approval?"

"Let's hold off on that," Lyss said wearily. "We'll want to get word to the families of the dead first."

Julianna nodded, shifting on the bench. Finally, she said, in a rush, "I'm so sorry, Lyss. I feel like this is my fault. I never should've insisted that you come out with us. I just . . . felt like we had so much to celebrate."

Lyss shook her head. "Look, it's time to stop blaming ourselves every time King Gerard does something despicable." *It's time to do something completely different.*

"Maybe," Julianna said. She fussed with her new ring, then laced her fingers together. "I don't know how you do what you do," she said, swallowing hard. "When the fighting started, I was useless. I just froze, as if that way I might be overlooked."

Lyss blinked at her, surprised. "Well," she said, "everybody reacts differently in battle. I guess it takes some getting used to."

Julianna stood. "I don't think I'll ever get used to it." She smiled faintly. "I expect I'll see you later today."

Lyss watched her walk away.

By the time Julianna left, some of the other Gray Wolves were trickling back in, among them Sasha. After exchanging a few words with the guards at the door, she came and saluted Lyss. "I thought you'd be long gone by now," she said.

Lyss shook her head. "Sit down, Sasha." She waved her to a spot next to her.

Sasha sat, and peered anxiously into her face. "Are you sure you're all right?"

"Just some bumps and bruises. I've felt worse after a workout with you. I didn't want to leave without getting an update." Lyss paused. "You heard about Cam and Carew?"

Sasha nodded. "When I leave here, I'm going to go talk to Cam's brothers," she said, her voice husky with emotion.

"Wait until morning," Lyss said, "and I'll go with you. There's no point in waking them up for bad news."

"All right," Sasha said. Pulling out a handkerchief, she blew her nose.

"So. What have you found out?"

"Unfortunately, we don't have anyone to question—not yet. We've got three dead ones."

"What about the busker? Did you find him?" If he really wasn't in on the plot, maybe he'd be willing to give up those who had hired him.

"No. But we'll find him. I've sent word up to Captain Byrne for reinforcements so we can do a thorough search of Ragmarket and Southbridge. I'll go back out in the meantime."

"Was there anything on the dead ones that might give us a lead?" *Like a promissory note from King Gerard, or a sack of Ardenine silver?*

"Their pockets were empty," Sasha said. "They were dressed like your usual street rushers. They used crossbows, and those are more common in the south, but they're also good for them who haven't much skill with a bow. Laurent did death mask sketches of them, and we'll show them all around town and see if anyone recognizes them. But it would do us the most good to catch us a live one." She paused. "So, what I want to know is, did you get a good look at any of them?"

"Well, probably the musician is the only one," Lyss said. "The others rushed in, and they were shooting, and—"

"The musician—had you ever seen him before?"

She shook her head. "I don't think so." *Never. I would have remembered.*

"Could you give me a description I can hand off to the Wolves?"

He looked hungry, as if it had been forever since he'd been fed.
No.
He looked like a wood nymph or a young god.
No.
He was the most enchanting boy I've ever seen.
No.

"He . . . he was about our age," Lyss said, "if I had to guess. He was thin, and his eyes—well, you know how the ocean changes color from gray to green when the sunlight hits it?"

"So his eyes were kind of hazel?" Sasha said.

Lyss nodded, though that was a drab kind of description. "Kind of. His hair was mingled gold and red and brown, like aspen, oak, and maple leaves in autumn or flames burning low on the hearth. . . ." Her voice trailed off.

Sasha was taking notes, and now she looked up inquiringly. "So his hair was streaky brown?" She was no poet.

"Right. That's all. And . . . he was well dressed. Fine wool cloak, leather boots, velvet jacket."

Sasha took that down, too. "What was that instrument he was playing? Did you recognize it?"

Lyss shook her head. "I've never seen—or—heard— anything like it. He said it was called a jafasa."

"Jafasa," Sasha repeated. "How do you spell that?"

"I have no idea," Lyss said, "but the music got into my head, like it was written for me. It was like, when he played, everything else was in shadow. Nothing else existed."

"Huh," Sasha said. "He sounds like faerie folk to me. You know how they're always luring people into trouble."

Except I don't believe in faerie folk, Lyss thought. "Looking back, I wonder if the instrument was some kind of flashcraft. Maybe the magic was in it, and not in the busker."

"Maybe," Sasha said. "Well, that's a start. If you could draw a sketch of it, maybe we can make copies and show it around and see if anyone knows of a musician that plays an instrument like that. It may take time, but we'll find him."

"Sasha," Lyss said, "I couldn't help thinking that he didn't know there was to be an attack. It was as if he was as surprised as I was."

Sasha raised a skeptical eyebrow. "Just his bad luck, huh, that he happened to be the one to lure you into an alley?"

Ty had returned and was standing, shifting impatiently. "Do you have your answers, Your Highness? I'd really like to get you back to the palace so you can get some rest."

"There's still Wolves out looking, but I don't think there'll be more news tonight," Sasha said.

"All right," Lyss said. "I am tired."

Just then, one of the Gray Wolves approached them, holding up a fistful of battered flowers. "I was told that you dropped these, Your Highness."

Again, the sight of the flowers struck a chord of memory. "The busker gave them to me."

"You took *flowers* from him?" Sasha stared at her.

"Look, I'm not stupid," Lyss said, her temperature rising. "There was . . . there was something about that music that . . ." She trailed off.

"Hold on," Ty said, stepping between Lyss and the flowers. "I want to take a look at those." Taking hold of his amulet, he fingered them, then spoke some spellwork over them. Finally, he looked up and said, a little sheepishly, "They're just flowers, I guess. Nothing special about them."

But there was. There was something about this mix of flowers, something Lyss should be remembering. . . .

"He must have bought them here in the city," Sasha said. "We'll see if anyone remembers someone buying flowers like these."

Lyss extended her hand and touched one of the foxflowers, sending petals spiraling to the floor. That was when the pieces fell into place. "Hanalea's bones," she cried, shrinking back, beating down hysteria.

The busker was guilty. He was as guilty as he could be, the silver-tongued bastard. And so was King Gerard.

"Your Highness?" Ty looked perplexed. "Is there something—?"

"Those flowers," Lyss said, her voice hoarse. "They're the same as the ones my father bought on the day he was murdered."

FINAL ACT

Breon's gig went south so fast that he didn't have time to think. All of a sudden, bolts were flying fast and furious while his leaf-muddled mind tried to process. The next thing he knew, he'd knocked the girlie flat and was trying to cover both of them with his jafasa until somebody picked him up and flung him aside. He hit the cobblestones hard, and he lay there, stunned, for a moment till he'd got his breath back.

He saw that the archers had focused on a low stone wall the girlie had taken shelter behind in the park. But there were rushers coming up from the river side, too. He watched as the girlie whacked one of them with her instrument case. Then the rusher was on her, and she went down underneath, and Breon knew how that would end if he didn't intervene.

He took one step, then saw a gang of bluejackets swarming toward them and realized he'd be in for hard questioning if he was caught. It seemed like a good time to shove off. It was probably too late to save her, anyway.

He scooped up his bag and his splintered jafasa and took off running, zigzagging through the narrow streets, less concerned about where he was going than where he was coming from. It didn't help that he was in a strange city. A really strange city, as it had turned out.

He heard boots crunching through the snow behind him, and knew he hadn't gotten away clean. He dug deep to put on speed, running blind, hoping he didn't meet up with a dead end.

Dead end—ha! But the joke wasn't all that funny.

He didn't know how long he'd been running when he realized he no longer heard the sounds of pursuit behind him. He slowed to a brisk walk, shaking the snow from his hair and brushing it from his fine coat, unable to quite believe that he'd gotten away.

They'd still be looking for him, though, and he needed to get back to the crib before they found him again. Unfortunately, he was on the wrong side of the river, so he had to get back to the bridge. Using the cathedral spire as a landmark, he worked his way back toward the site of the concert.

But it was no good. The market was boiling with blue-jackets on both sides of the river.

He could see another bridge farther north along the river, so he headed that way. He had to try to get across before the bluejackets spread their nets wider.

When he reached the bridge, he paused in the shadow of a building to scan the area. Seeing nothing alarming, he crossed the promenade along the river and turned onto the bridge.

He was halfway across when he saw someone step onto the bridge at the far end and walk toward him purposefully. His familiar angular shape set Breon's heart to hammering.

It was Darian.

Breon back-walked a few steps, turned, and all but ran into another rusher charging him from behind, his blade glittering in the light from a streetlamp. Breon bent double, hitting him low, and bowling him over like a kingpin.

Breon took off running, back the way he came. He heard the client cursing, shouting to others to join in. He ran up one street, then down another, slid through a crack between buildings too narrow to admit anyone but a cat or a scrawny jafasier. He stood there, gasping, and listened to the herd of pursuers go by. Somehow, he knew there would be a rear guard, and there was. The cloaked figure of Darian stalked by, turning his head right and left as if he could sniff out his prey.

Breon reached up and fingered the magemark on the back of his neck and prayed to whatever gods might listen to a tarnished soul like him. Maybe the gods were listening, or maybe he'd already endured his share of bad luck. All that mattered was that the client passed him by.

Hours later, Breon found a hidey-hole in a stable a few blocks away from the river. Several horses poked their heads out when he slid through the doorway, but the stable hand was dead asleep—Breon could hear snoring from the rear of the building that all but rattled the shingles from the roof.

Once he climbed the chancy ladder into the hayloft, he was tempted to pull it up after him, but he guessed that would point a finger straight at his hiding place. So he left it be and buried himself under the hay in the farthest corner, his shiv in his hand, what was left of his jafasa beside him.

Why he kept dragging that around, he had no idea, unless it was because it was the only thing of value he'd ever owned, and he'd probably never get his hands on another one.

He'd hardly settled in when he heard a banging down below, sleepy curses from the stable hand, the tread of boots, and muffled voices that cleared as the speakers made their way from the back room to the front.

"He'd be wearing fine clothes and carrying a black leather case," a gruff female voice said. Fortunately, that seemed to be about all the description they had.

The stable hand's voice rose. "I already *said*, there an't nobody here 'cept me and the horses. I been on the watch all night."

"You was hardly on the watch when we got here," the newcomer snapped back. "We could hear you snoring clear out in the alley. He could've been sharing your bed and you'd never know it. So we'll take a look around anyway." The ladder shuddered as she began her climb.

Her head poked up above the floorboards, then the rest of her. Breon held his breath and tried not to move a muscle. The bluejacket stalked around the loft, poking into piles of hay with her sword. Once the blade came so close to his eye, it seemed she might have sliced through an eyelash or two. Eventually, the bluejacket disturbed a barn cat, who screeched so loud that Breon all but soiled himself.

Grumbling, the bluejacket disappeared back down the ladder.

"What's this boy supposed to've done?" the stable hand asked.

"Bastard attacked the princess Alyssa," the bluejacket said.

Hang on. Who?

"He and a whole pack of thugs ambushed her."

"Is she all right?" the stable hand asked.

The bluejacket shook her head. "I don't know. I haven't heard. Her father and brother were murdered the same way. Gutter-swiving cowards. I'll gut the lot of them if I get hold of them."

No, Breon thought, offended. I'm a musician, not a killer. I just got mixed up with a bad crowd when I was born.

The voices finally moved away, and he let out his breath in relief. He fingered Her Highness's locket, which still rested against his chest.

Each time he closed his eyes, he saw her face in front of him, her direct brown eyes, her expression when she said "I might as well be honest, because I'm not very good at lying."

He'd known this gig was bad news from the very beginning. Why, then, had he taken it? What was he turning into?

He hoped she wasn't dead.

It took him a long time to fall asleep.

Breon stayed in hiding for two solid days, curled up in his corner, buried in hay to keep warm. Once or twice a day, Clayton, the stable hand, would labor up the ladder into the loft and pitch down hay to the horses. But he was a slow-moving, noisy sort, so Breon was always hidden by the time Clayton stuck his head up through the floor. Breon had to stay still while people were coming and going from the stable, so nobody would hear him moving around overhead. After most of a day spent in one spot, he was so stiff he could barely move.

At night he'd creep out into the stable yard to empty his night soil bucket and have a quick smoke, but the blue-jacket patrols were so thick he never got far before he was driven back inside. He had no prayer of getting across the bridge without being seen, even if he left his jafasa behind, and he had no plans to do that.

By the third day, he was out of leaf and getting desperate. Finally, luck came his way in the form of a wagon that parked in the stable yard long enough to swap out the horses, and also long enough for Breon to slide under the canvas that covered the cargo. He had no idea where the wagon was going, but he figured it must be better than where he was, with blue-coated guards swarming everywhere. If he could get across the river, he'd stop in at the crib and fetch Aubrey and Goose, and they'd be on their way, with or without jingle in his pockets. There was always a way to make a little jingle. Versatility had always been one of his strengths.

The wagon's destination was another market some distance away. When the driver went in to dicker with the merchants, Breon slipped out of the back of the wagon. As he crossed the market, he nicked a carved walking stick from one of the stalls displaying "clan-made" goods and a battered cloak that was stuffed into a basket of rags.

Wrapped in his scroungy cloak, the jafasa underneath so he looked like a hunchback, he hobbled along with his walking stick. That disguise was enough to get him across the bridge.

By then, darkman's hour had come, the temperature was dropping, and the slush in the streets was beginning to freeze again.

He was just turning into the street where the hideout was when he heard someone hiss his name. He looked, and it was Aubrey, motioning from the doorway of a tavern.

Apparently his disguise wasn't as good as he'd thought it was. Taking a quick look around, he ducked inside.

She was huddled at a table to the left of the door, where she could look out of the open window. That must've been how she saw him passing by. A drover's cap was pulled low over her face, and she had big dark circles under her eyes.

"Aubrey!" he said, but she hushed him right away and pushed his jafasa under the table.

"You can't be carrying that around," she growled. "They'll catch you."

"I was on my way back to the crib," Breon said. "I'll stash it there."

She shook her head. "You got to ditch it. I was about to give up," she said. "I figured you was still alive because they're still looking for you. You really stepped in it this time."

"*I* stepped in it?" It sounded like she thought it was his fault. "I can't wait to get my hands on Whacks. He set me up."

"Whacks is dead," Aubrey said, "and so's Goose."

Whacks . . . and Goose. Both dead? Breon felt like he'd been clubbed. Whacks was the kind of person who always landed on his feet, no matter who he had to stomp on to do it. And Goose? He'd cut your throat for a wad of leaf, but other than that he'd always been a harmless sort.

When Breon said nothing, Aubrey pressed on. "And we'd be dead, too, if we'd of been there when they came."

"When who came? The bluejackets?"

She shook her head. "Them that hired you. I guess they didn't want to leave anybody behind to tell tales. The blue-jackets is the least of your worries."

"If it's all right with you, I'll worry about them just the same," Breon said. "Did you see who did it?"

She shook her head. "No, and I don't want to."

"How were they done?"

Aubrey hesitated. "Their throats were cut."

"But you weren't there?"

She shook her head. "Like I said . . ."

"Who told you?"

"What do you mean?"

"Who told you how they were killed?"

"I don't know," she snapped. "I don't remember."

"What do the bluejackets say?"

"I couldn't very well go ask them," Aubrey said. "Anyway, they might not know yet. All I keep hearing about is that blueblood you sung to."

"Is she dead, too?"

Aubrey nodded. "That's the word on the street, anyway."

Guilt welled up inside him, regret for the part he'd played in the murder of the brown-eyed girlie. Her Highness, who wasn't very good at lying.

"Are the bodies still there?"

"What bodies?" she growled. Breon could tell she was rattled, because she was so prickly.

"Goose and Whacks."

"*Probably.* Why are you being like this?"

Why are *you* being like this?

"I want to know," Breon said. "I'm going to go check it out."

"Look, you can't go anywhere near there. I wouldn't be here now, 'cept I was waiting for you. It hasn't been easy staying alive this long, I don't want to ruin it now." She gripped his arm. "C'mon, Bree. Let's get out of this town. Let's go back to Baston Bay, like we said we would. We can start over."

Suspicion flickered through Breon. Aubrey had wanted to leave without Goose and Whacks, and now she was telling him that they had no choice.

Maybe they weren't dead after all. Or maybe she'd been the one that—

No. This was Aubrey. You wouldn't trust Aubrey with your purse, but she wasn't a killer.

Either way, he needed to know.

"You stay here. I'll go myself. When I come back, we'll leave."

"Don't go," Aubrey said, then added, in a rush, "Look, I've got a little leaf. We can smoke it up, then hit the road."

"That's a good plan," Breon said, "for when I get back. Watch my jafasa for me?" He was like a lýtling with one broken toy who keeps dragging it around after him.

"I may not be here when you get back," Aubrey muttered. "I'm making no promises."

"If you're not here when I get back, well . . . good luck," he said, turning away.

He wished he wasn't a stranger in this town. He wished he knew his way around better. He wished he was a pirate sitting on bags of swag. Wishes were free, after all.

The street outside the warehouse was eerily deserted, like everybody outside knew what had happened inside.

Everybody else is smarter than me, he thought. I should just turn right around and go back and smoke some leaf and forget this town and everybody in it. Including her brown-eyed highness.

He paused a moment outside the door, and almost turned away. No. He had to know. He looked up and down the street, saw nobody, and pushed the door open.

He all but stumbled over a body sprawled facedown a few feet away from the door, arms stretched out as if he still hoped to make it out. A faint scent of decay wafted up.

It was Whacks, dressed in his usual tattered finery, his

face mashed into a sticky puddle of blood. Aubrey was right—it looked like his throat had been cut. His hands were swollen, purpling. The killers hadn't even taken his rings.

That, in itself, was terrifying.

Whacks. Running away from trouble, as usual.

Goose hadn't put up much of a fight, either. He lay on his back in the same corner where Breon had last seen him, eyes peeled open so he looked surprised, his pipe lying close to his hand, his throat neatly cut from ear to ear. He was a bit further along in decay than Whacks had been, maybe because it was warmer in his corner. It took everything Breon had not to peer into the bowl of the pipe and see if there was any leaf left.

Goose wouldn't be using it after all.

Telling himself he was looking for clues, Breon searched both bodies. Goose had nothing, of course, except a heel of rock-hard bread in an inside pocket. Whacks, though, had a full purse—the one he kept tied inside the waist of his pants. Mostly girlies, a few steelies. No note signed by the killer or anything.

The fact that the purse was still there signified: one, it wasn't a robbery, and two, nobody else had come in and found the bodies.

Breon tucked the purse away. They had traveling money after all. He searched the rest of the crib but found nothing telltale.

With that, he returned to Goose, thinking he should do something to send him on his way. What was Goose's actual name? Dillon, maybe? It seemed wrong to call him Goose at a time like this.

Breon tried three times to close Dillon's eyes, but it was a no-go; it was like they were glued open. Finally, his own eyes watering, he pulled the threadbare blanket up over Dillon's face. Then he tried to put the pipe back in his hand, but it just kept falling out. Finally, he set it on top of Dillon's chest.

At least he died doing what he enjoyed, Breon thought.

The longer he stayed, the edgier he got. It was time to go.

He was three steps from the door when he heard somebody fumbling with the latch. In an instant panic, Breon looked for a place to hide. Then he realized that no matter where he hid, if they searched the place, they'd find him. In the end, he flattened himself against the wall next to the door, hoping whoever it was would walk past him without noticing. When the door banged open, he ended up behind it.

It was four rushers, all muffled up in coats, all bigger than Breon.

". . . Darian says we gotta search this place and make sure there's no loose ends to tie us to this thing," one of them was saying.

"He should've told us up front what the job was,"

another one whined. "I don't need this kind of trouble. I can't make a move without running into a swiving bluejacket."

"Which is exactly why we need to check this place out," Rusher Number One said. "When these ones begin to stink, they'll be found."

Their attention immediately fastened on Whacks. Breon couldn't help wishing he'd dragged the body farther from the door.

"You two, search this one," Number One said, nudging Whacks with his foot. "You, come with me. Darian said there was another one in the corner. Then we'll sweep the place and be out of here."

When the other two left to have at Dillon, the remaining ones knelt next to Whacks.

"I don't know why this is our job," Number Three whined. "We didn't do 'em. We should be out hunting that scrawny street-rat of a busker."

"You wanna tell Darian you refuse? I don't. Matter of fact, I'm clearing out of this town. Who's to say he won't do us like he done them?"

Breon edged forward so he could peek around the door. They were patting Whacks down. Breon knew he should leave, but still he stayed, hoping he might hear something that would tell him who'd done this thing and who'd given the orders.

And if you do find out? What are you going to do about

it? Hit him with your jafasa? Sing him to death? Send a note to the guard?

He was just so damned tired of working so hard not to think about things.

"Hey! This one's got rings on," Number Three said. He began trying to wrestle the rings from Whacks's swollen fingers.

"Stop that!" Number Four said, looking toward where the other two were searching Dillon.

"Darian don't need to know," Number Three whispered. "Keep your mouth shut and I'll share 'em with you." Leaving off tugging at the rings, he pulled out his knife.

No. Breon didn't want to see this, and then have to try and forget it. In a heartbeat, he'd cleared the door and was back on the street, running for his life. Behind him he heard shouting, but he neither slowed down nor turned around until he burst through the tavern doorway. Once inside, he peered out around the doorframe, but he'd apparently lost them.

To his mild surprise, Aubrey was still there. Her head jerked up at his noisy entrance, and then she smiled in relief.

"I told you I'd be back," he said, dropping into a chair and trying to catch his breath.

Aubrey looked toward the door, maybe wondering what kind of demon was chasing him, then back at Breon. "Well? Did you learn anything?"

Yes. He'd learned that murder had a name, and that name was Darian. Breon wasn't all that sentimental about Whacks, but Goose deserved better. And so did the brown-eyed princess.

"I'm a lover, not a fighter," Whacks liked to say, and Breon had always followed the same philosophy. But just now he wasn't sure what he would do if he met up with Darian.

Best to avoid that meet-up.

"Aye," he said. "I learned that we'd be better off in Baston Bay."

COUNCIL OF WAR

Two days after the concert, Lyss crossed the parade grounds, heading for the barracks. The barracks yard was all but deserted. Normal people were already celebrating the holiday, but Lyss had scheduled a drill for her salvo in late afternoon.

She ought to cancel it. Her soldiers had fought hard all summer. They deserved a rest. Anyway, what good would an extra drill do? It wouldn't prevent attacks like the one at South Bridge.

It had left her more angry than frightened. And grieving and guilty over the two that they'd lost.

Maybe she'd be better off crossing the border on her own—just one gray wolf with a longbow, a sword, and a thirst for vengeance. She'd keep ranging south, taking lesser prey along the way, until she found the king of Arden. And then she would show him what it was like to be hunted.

There hadn't been much progress in finding those responsible for the attack. Though all of Southbridge and Ragmarket were on the watch, in addition to swarms of bluejackets, they'd found no trace of the busker. It was as if the earth had swallowed him up.

Nobody'd seen him busking around Ragmarket before, so he was either new to town or new to busking. Although Lyss had made a detailed drawing of the jafasa, nobody had seen one before, and none of the luthiers in the high street had seen one come in for repair. Shadow had pursued the theory that it might have been flashcraft, but had had no luck. As far as they knew, all flashcraft originated with the upland clans, but none of Shadow's contacts had seen an instrument like that, or heard of one being used in that way.

Speaker Jemson had found a scholar at the Cathedral Temple that was an expert on musical instruments through history. He thought the drawing resembled the *jafasaii*, a type of traditional musical instrument from Carthis. Perhaps it had been brought here by a Carthian pirate.

If the busker's smart, Lyss thought, he'll have dumped it by now.

He had left a bit of a trail in the markets, at least up until the attack. One of the temple dedicates, Samuel Bannock, recalled that a boy who fit the busker's description showed up at the food ministry the morning of the concert. He was dressed shabbily, and looked—and smelled—like he hadn't had a bath in a month. Samuel had mentioned the concert to the boy. Now Bannock was worried that he'd somehow contributed to the attack, especially because one of the guards at the temple door had seen a well-dressed boy with an instrument case come into the sanctuary during the performance.

One of the librarians recalled that that same boy had come into the library the afternoon of the concert. He'd asked for books about sailing ships.

All through the interviews and debriefings, Lyss studied faces and body language, transcripts and reports, alert for the scent of treachery.

Someone in the city was collaborating with Arden. Else how would the busker have known what flowers to buy? How would he have known she'd be walking in the street after the concert? True, her concert appearance had been promoted all over the city. The rushers could have waited outside and followed her to Ragmarket.

But her instincts told her she'd been set up by someone here at court. Could that treachery go back five years? Could it go all the way back to Hana?

Sasha and Captain Byrne kept her up to date on new findings, but Lyss wasn't holding her breath, waiting for an arrest. It would be just like before. Captain Byrne and his Wolves would question everyone and scour the queendom, chasing leads into dead ends as the trail grew colder. And then the wait for the next attack would begin.

When Lyss walked into the duty room, she was surprised to find Hadley standing in front of the map of the realms on the wall, hands clasped behind her back, studying it. On a table against the wall, food and drink were laid out. There were bread and cheese and sausage and cakes, along with two promising-looking kegs. That was rare—unclaimed food never remained unclaimed for very long.

"Hadley! What are you doing here?" Lyss waved a hand, taking in the food. "What's all this?"

"There's a meeting," Hadley said.

"A meeting? Here?"

"We thought that would make it more convenient for you."

Lyss racked her brain, trying to remember if there had been a meeting scheduled that she had forgotten. And came up with nothing.

"You're welcome to use the duty room, if you want," she said, "but I'm supposed to meet with my salvo in half an hour."

"They know about it," Hadley said.

If they know about it, then why didn't I? Lyss thought irritably.

Right at that moment, Sasha walked in, brushing off snow. "I'm here for the meeting," she said, pulling off her gloves and warming her hands by the stove. "It's sure cold around here. I wish we could go someplace warmer."

Then it was Shadow, and Julianna and Finn. Followed by Lyss's lieutenants, Mason, Littlefield, and the newly promoted Demeter Farrow. Ruby Greenholt, another member of her guard. And Ty Gryphon.

"I think we're all here," Finn said, looking around the room.

"It's not my birthday," Lyss said. "So what's going on?"

"We want to plan a wake for Staunton and Carew," Sasha said.

"Oh!" Lyss said, thinking that hardly required an emergency meeting. "That's a great idea. Just let me know when it is, and if you're taking up a collection, I'll—"

"We need your help," Hadley said. "We're hoping you can find us the right place, and help us get the supplies we need—"

"—because you have so much experience at planning this kind of event," Sasha said.

Lyss was lost. "You know I'm glad to help you out in any way I can, but when it comes to parties, I—"

"We're having this party south of the border," Shadow said, with no trace of humor at all. "We want to bring the war to Arden, and we think you know how."

Lyss looked from person to person. Their smiles had

dropped away, leaving them looking fierce, determined, and absolutely serious. Lyss cleared her throat and blotted at her eyes. "I appreciate the gesture," she said. "I really do. It means a lot, coming from all of you."

"This is not a gesture," Littlefield said. "This is real. And if we die in the attempt—" He shrugged his shoulders.

"That's just it," Lyss said. "I don't want you to die in the attempt. If I ever make it to the throne, I want you all at my side. Anyway, there's a limit to what ten people can do."

Someone pounded on the door. Littlefield pulled it open, looked outside, and then swung it wide, motioning to Lyss. "There are some people outside who want to come to the party, too."

Outside, it appeared that Lyss's entire salvo was assembled. As one, they drew their swords, went down on one knee, and set their weapons down in the snow in front of them. "For the Gray Wolf!" they roared. "You have our swords!" And then they howled. It was like a scene from a play or a pageant.

Lyss stood there, speechless, for a long moment. Then brought her fist to her chest in a salute. "Thank you!" she shouted, unsure what else to say. "Now . . . dismissed. The drill is cancelled."

Lyss shut the door and turned to face the co-conspirators. "What did you say to them, anyway, to get them all ginned up?"

Mason shrugged. "It didn't take much, to tell you the truth. Quite a few of them were at the temple concert, and they heard what happened after. We told our squadrons we were planning something difficult and dangerous and highly secret in the fallow season to get back at those who murdered Staunton and Carew and tried to murder Captain Gray. After that, each and every one of the soldiers you saw out there came to us to ask how they could get in on it." She smiled faintly. "I didn't want anybody to feel pressured into joining in. And I didn't want word to get out about what we were doing."

"Staunton was in the field with us all summer," Littlefield said. "Nearly everyone in the Highlanders knew him, and many of us fought alongside his mother, Nance. It'd have been bad enough to lose him on the battlefield, in a fair fight. But to see him ambushed like that—it's just wrong. I'm not the only one that thinks so."

Mason and Farrow nodded agreement.

Lyss turned to Ty. "I don't mean to imply you're not welcome, but why are you here? I know you worked on Cam at Southbridge Temple, but why is a healer planning a military raid?"

"I've been working the battlefields for three years now," Ty said. "I don't know how much longer I can continue to patch soldiers up so they can go back out and fight again, over and over, until they go down for good. I'm more than ready to try something different. As for my role in any . . . undertaking . . . I am a wizard. Though I prefer to assist in my capacity as healer, I'll use my gift for whatever purpose supports the cause."

"Julianna? How do you see yourself contributing to this adventure?" Lyss tried not to sound condescending.

She flushed. "I know that I haven't . . . the kind of experience and skills that most of the rest of you have. I've not been tried on a battlefield, and I'm not sure I'm cut out for it. But I am knowledgeable about the south, and I have connections and agents all over the Seven Realms. I'm hoping I can be of help in other ways."

"What about you, Hadley?" Lyss said. "You haven't had much to say."

"How come we keep talking about the war?" Hadley said, eyes wide and innocent. "I mean, I thought we were here to plan a party."

This was the most motley group of would-be warriors that Lyss had ever seen. "All right, we'll talk," she said. She drew a mug of cider from the keg, clunked it down on the table, and sat. "But, first, the ground rules."

The others ranged themselves around the table and waited, wary and expectant, both.

"This can't be about getting revenge," Lyss said. "I'm not going to squander soldiers' lives to make a point. This has to be a play that changes the game."

"I'm not out for revenge," Julianna said. "For me, it's a matter of policy. I'm in this because I think you're right—we do need a change in strategy. I meant what I said in the small council meeting." She took Finn's hand. "I'm doing this for our children. I don't want them to have to grow up as stepchildren to a war."

"If we take territory, we need to be able to keep it," Lyss went on, ticking her points off on her fingers. "This can't be a skirmish or a hit-and-run. It has to be a target with real strategic value."

"Something the Thane Council can't ignore," Julianna said.

"Can we do all that with a salvo?" Greenholt said.

"It's that or we stay home." Lyss paused. "Since this is your party, do you have any suggestions as to targets?"

"What about Baston Bay?" Hadley said. "That's close to their capital, and it's their most important port. We wouldn't have to march across the flatlands because we could come in by ship."

No, Lyss thought, shuddering. No ships.

"That's pretty far south," Farrow said. "Even if we manage to take it, Arden could come at us from land and sea and we'd be trapped."

"Spiritgate?" Hadley said. "That would have a certain justice to it, since they landed their brigade there when they attacked Queen Court and Fortress Rocks."

"I know that area well," Shadow said. "I've been traveling up and down the coast for the past two years. And it's not out in the middle of the flatlands."

"But it's right on the border, so we'd barely stick a toe into Arden," Lyss said. "That would feel like more of a hit-and-run. And it's not one of their major ports."

"You just don't want to set foot on a ship," Sasha said.

Lyss shrugged. She wasn't going to deny it. "What about a winter attack? That might take them by surprise."

Mason nodded. "It would be unexpected," she said. "But even if we crossed the mountains, we couldn't expect to penetrate very far before having to face their army in the flatlands, where we are at a disadvantage. Arden's cities are mostly far to the south, where it's warm year-round. The farther south we go, the more conditions favor them."

"So we need a target that is important strategically, but close at hand," Julianna said. "And it would have to be something we could reasonably expect to hold." She looked at Lyss. "I know you've been plotting out military campaigns the way anyone else would be planning their dream wedding. Is there anything you know of that would fit those rules?"

Lyss stood, and walked around the table to take a close look at the map on the wall. "What about Delphi?" she said, stabbing her finger into the map. "I've had that on my wish list of targets for a while. It's just on the other side of the mountains." Delphi showed on the map as a dark spot pressed against the mountains to the north.

The others crowded in to see.

"Remind me—what's in Delphi?" Finn said. "Anything we want?"

"Coal mines," Julianna said. "And ironworks and smithies. As far as I know, they're the only ones in the conquered lands. That's why Arden took Delphi over, so they could build the munitions industry close to the source of supply. And so, close to us."

"I've been there," Shadow said, grimacing. "It's always been a gritty industrial center, but now it's become a real hellhole. There's considerable unrest, because of the way they have treated the people there. So Arden maintains a large army presence."

"So not exactly a soft target," Finn murmured.

"More flatlanders to kill," Shadow said, darting a look at Lyss.

"We have eyes and ears in Delphi," Julianna said. "There's an underground resistance movement that might collaborate with us. That would make our small numbers go further."

"How do we get there from here?" Farrow said. "Or can we, in this season?"

Littlefield traced a route on the map with his forefinger. "We could drive straight south through Marisa Pines Pass, but that border crossing is heavily guarded, even in winter." Then he pointed to a spot in the mountains northeast of Delphi and south of Hunter's Camp. "This is Ana Maria Pass. It's a high pass, and already filled with snow this time of year. It wouldn't be easy, but it might be the way to go if we want to surprise them."

"We couldn't bring anything heavy through there," Lyss said. "No catapults or cannons."

"But horses could get through," Shadow said. "And soldiers on foot."

"We're used to traveling light," Littlefield said. "Since we've never invaded the south, we're not really prepared for siege warfare."

"That wouldn't work for us, anyway," Lyss said. "With only a salvo, the key is the element of surprise. We'd have to take the city quickly. If we sit outside the walls waiting for surrender, it gives Arden time to muster a massive response."

"Won't they do that eventually, though, even if we take the city?" Hadley said. "How can we hope to hold it for the long term?"

"Based on what I know about Delphi, it might be difficult to retake from the south, especially if the city could be resupplied through Marisa Pines," Shadow said. "They could never hope to surround us and put us under siege."

"If we can't hold the city, we might have to destroy the mines and munitions factories, cut our losses, and leave," Lyss said.

"It sounds like a lot will depend on how much support we can get from the residents, and if we can pull this off without word leaking out," Julianna said. "Once I reach out to my contacts in Delphi, the sooner we go, the better."

Lyss looked around the table, seeing nothing but excited faces.

"I have something to do first," Lyss said. "The most difficult job of all."

"Which is?" Finn asked.

"I have to speak with the queen," Lyss said.

Excitement turned to confusion and dismay.

Julianna leaned forward. "You mean that you have to come up with a plausible story that explains our absence while we—"

"I mean that we cannot go without my mother's blessing."

That was met with shocked silence. They all looked at one another. Hadley cleared her throat. "Do you really think Queen Raisa will ever agree to this? We might spend a lot of time making a plan, only to have it shot down right away."

"That's possible," Lyss said. "But we still have to ask."

"Have you heard that saying 'Better to ask forgiveness than ask permission'?" Sasha said. "If you ask permission and she says no, then we absolutely can't go."

"You're right, then we absolutely can't go," Lyss said.

Everybody began talking at once, arguing the point, until Lyss slammed her mug down on the table. "Look, nobody is more frustrated about this than me, but my mother is the queen of the realm. If we launch an unauthorized attack across the border, some would call that treason. How could she let that go unpunished?"

"Do you really think she would bring you up on charges?" Mason asked.

"General Dunedain might court-martial the lot of you, for not following the chain of command," Lyss said. Gaaah, she thought, I've been in the army too long.

"If we take the city, though," Finn argued, "if we win a huge victory, don't you think she'll forgive us?"

"What if we don't?" Lyss said. "What if it's a disaster, and we're all captured, or slaughtered? What if we all disappear, never to be heard from again? What if I'm killed, and you all have to answer for it?"

Sasha turned pale. "I'd execute myself, and save Her Majesty the trouble."

"You see? The risk you are taking is far greater than mine." Lyss sighed. "Truth be told, my biggest reason for not proceeding without permission is that I cannot do that to my mother. I'm the only family she has left, except for Aunt Mellony and you, Julianna. If I were to be taken prisoner by Gerard Montaigne, her position would be untenable. It would destroy her and the future of the Line. She might have to step down, or name a new heir."

Now they all looked a little sheepish.

"Bones, Lyss, you sound like the only grown-up in the room," Hadley said.

Lyss laughed sourly. "For once."

"Everything you've said suggests that we shouldn't go ahead with this," Ty said. "Or that, if we do, you should stay at home."

"That's not what I meant," Lyss said. "I absolutely think we should go ahead with this, and it would break my heart to stay behind. I've been dreaming of taking the war to Arden since my father and brother died. But I think my mother deserves the right to say no."

"Do you think she'll want to take it to the small council?" Julianna said. "They won't meet until after the holiday, and we both know what kind of reception you got the last time."

Lyss shook her head. "I don't want to take it to small council. I want my mother to make the decision. I think the fewer people that know about this, the better." She didn't want to say aloud what she suspected—that someone in the city was passing information to Arden.

"All right," Finn said, rubbing the back of his neck. "What do we do now? Just wait until we hear back from you?"

"I intend to speak with her right away," Lyss said. "Meanwhile, we'll need some information from our allies in Delphi, to assess whether this whole thing is feasible." She paused. "Solstice is three weeks away. Do you think we could be ready by then?"

"You're thinking of attacking Delphi on Solstice?" Sasha stared at Lyss.

"I'd like to ruin King Gerard's holiday," Lyss said. "I can't think of a better way to celebrate the return of the light."

IN THE GARDEN
OF QUEENS

The queen wasn't in any of her usual haunts when Lyss went looking for her the next day—not in her small parlor, or her large parlor, or her library, or her audience chamber. Her pony was in the barn, so she hadn't ridden out into the town. General Dunedain hadn't seen her, and she wasn't practicing her sticking on the parade grounds. Her appointment secretary said there was nothing on the books. When Lyss went to her mother's bedchamber, the doors stood open, and the Wolves outside said they hadn't seen her.

And then it came to her—where her mother might be. One of her favorite retreats was the rooftop glass garden where she could visit summer whenever she liked. These days, it was mostly given over to growing fresh fruits and vegetables for the palace and the Briar Rose Ministry.

"I think I know where she is," Lyss told the bluejacket on duty. "I'll just cut through here."

Lyss walked through the sitting room into her mother's bedchamber. She went straight to the closet against the back wall, pushed clothing and shoes aside, and slipped through the secret door in the back panel—a door built by her ancestor, Queen Hanalea, so she could meet her lover, Alger Waterlow, on the sly. Beyond the door lay a small round chamber centered on an iron spiral staircase that led to the roof. When they were little, Lyss, Adrian, and Sasha had used the stairs as a playground, sneaking in and out, playing hare and hounds, and, later, pretending to be soldiers creeping up on Ardenscourt Castle.

They'd quit playing war games when they went to war for real.

Lyss began to climb. It was definitely closer quarters for her now, with her long legs, than it had been when she was little. There was lots of dust, and spiderwebs, as if her mother hadn't been using it much, either. All the way up, Lyss practiced what she would say, the arguments she would make.

What does my mother want?

To keep the queendom safe.

She just had to convince the queen that this was the way to do it.

The staircase led to a hatch in the floor of a small chapel in the garden. Lyss pushed it up and out of the way, then pulled herself up and over, onto the marble floor. That was easier, now that she was taller.

She stood, dusting cobwebs and dirt off her clothes. She could hear voices out in the garden. Her mother and Captain Byrne. When she peeked through the chapel window, she saw that they were seated on a bench by the lily pond.

"Who will you send?" her mother was asking Byrne.

"I'll send my best. All people you know. Garret and Talia—they speak the language and know their way around."

"They did, twenty-five years ago," Raisa said. "You should send someone who's been there more recently."

"Not many younglings go there anymore," Byrne said. "It's a dangerous trip, and most parents don't feel comfortable sending their children."

"It's a shame," her mother said. "I only attended Wien House for a year, but it was still valuable. I think Alyssa would have loved it."

"She's getting considerable practical experience," Byrne said.

"In waging war, anyway."

They're talking about Oden's Ford, Lyss thought. But why would they be sending members of the Queen's Guard down there? The academy had always been ferociously neutral when it came to the war.

"Not that I disagree, but why now, Rai—after all this time? Is there something that makes you think it isn't safe anymore?"

"It's a combination of things—the wolves at solstice, the attack on Alyssa, this feeling I have that I'm overlooking something important. Anyway, it's time. I want to have my children here with me."

Children?

The word seemed to ricochet inside Lyss's head, setting up a clamor of echoes wherever it hit until it seemed like her head would split apart.

Who was at Oden's Ford? *Who?*

Her mother's voice broke into her thoughts again. She was responding to something Byrne had said.

"Look, I know you didn't approve of my keeping it from her, but Alyssa was eleven years old! It was too big a secret for a child to keep, yet so very important that it be kept. We all thought he was dead, remember. We'd held the funerals. We'd already dealt with our grief. And then to hear from Beaugarde out of the blue—I doubted the truth of it. I thought it might be one more ploy from Montaigne—one more attempt to break my heart. We didn't know for sure that he was alive and safe until Lila reported back."

"The princess was eleven then, but she's almost sixteen now. You weren't much older than that when you became queen."

"Alyssa is different," her mother said. "She's more head-strong and impulsive than I ever was."

"You really think so?" Lyss could hear the skepticism in the captain's voice.

She didn't trust me, Lyss thought, her cheeks burning. Maybe I'm just headstrong about different things.

"She would have insisted on marching straight to Oden's Ford and bringing him home."

"No doubt," Byrne said. "Will you tell her now?"

The queen considered this. "It seems too much like tempting the fates to tell her now, before he's home safe."

Adrian. Adrian was alive, and he was at Oden's Ford. And no one had told her these four long years, because they thought she would do something stupid.

With that, the clamor in her brain was replaced by a cold and deadly silence.

The hinges on the chapel door screeched like a demon as she pushed it open. Her mother and Byrne shot to their feet like guilty lovers at a tryst. Byrne pushed the queen behind him, his Lady sword drawn and at the ready. When he saw who it was, he let the tip drop until it pointed at the floor.

"It's just me, Captain Byrne," Lyss said.

"Your Highness," he said, saluting her.

"You are dismissed now, Captain," Lyss said. "I need to speak with my mother alone."

She half-expected him to refuse, or look to her mother

for orders, but he did not. Instead, he returned his sword to its scabbard, saluted her again, and said, "I'll be outside."

When Byrne was gone, they stood looking at each other, queen and princess heir, mother and daughter, dark and light, small and tall.

"I suppose you heard all that," her mother said, chewing on her lower lip.

"Most of it, I think," Lyss said. "Enough."

"Ah." She gestured toward the bench. "Would you like to sit down, Alyssa?"

"I'll stand. I might want to do something headstrong, like impulsively rush from the room and announce Adrian's whereabouts from the tower."

"I deserve that, I suppose," her mother said, with a sigh.

"Yes. You do."

"And you deserve an apology."

"I would prefer an explanation." Cold. Deadly. Numb.

"*I'll* sit down, then." The queen sat down on the edge of the bench as if she, too, might need to spring into action. "Which do you want first—the apology or the explanation?"

"Why don't you begin by telling me what happened the day my father was murdered." Lyss folded her arms.

"Most of what I know, you already know," her mother said. "The rest comes from Taliesin Beaugarde, a Voyageur healer and a dean at Spiritas, the healing school at the academy."

"What about Adrian? What does he say? How could he possibly justify—?"

"We haven't spoken to him," the queen said.

"Adrian has been at Oden's Ford for four years, and you've never *spoken* to him?" Lyss's voice was rising so that she was all but shouting at the end. Cold and numbness were ebbing away.

"Adrian blamed himself for his father's death. He couldn't face us afterward, so he ran. When he met up with Beaugarde in Delphi, he was ill and grief-stricken. He threatened to kill himself if she didn't take him with her to the academy. So she did. Months later, she got in touch with us and let us know that he was alive."

"Why didn't you bring him home right then?" Lyss demanded. "How could you just . . . just leave him there?"

"We thought that leaving him there might be safer than bringing him back here."

This has to be a dream, Lyss thought, like the ones I used to have where Adrian came back and haunted me.

"You thought that leaving him unprotected in the middle of Ardenine territory would be *safer*? Whose idea was that?"

"Just before your father was murdered, someone contacted him, claiming to have more information about Hana's death. He said there was nothing random about it, that it was a targeted attack. Your father was killed before that meeting took place. After that, I thought there must be a spy somewhere close to us. Since Captain Byrne and I were the only ones who knew that Adrian was at Oden's Ford, we decided it was safer to leave him there, and let everyone think he was dead."

"Including me."

"And that is what I need to apologize for. I had my reasons for not telling you as soon as we received Beaugarde's message. What if I got your hopes up, and it turned out not to be true? We didn't know for sure that he was alive and well until Captain Byrne's daughter verified it."

"Captain Byrne has a daughter?"

Her mother nodded. "Lila. She's Adrian's age. After Annamaya died, Captain Byrne sent Lila to Chalk Cliffs, where she was raised by her mother's family. Because she hasn't really been connected to Fellsmarch, we thought it might be safe to have her keep an eye on Adrian."

"So . . . you knew, and Captain Byrne, and Captain Byrne's daughter, what's her name, but I didn't." Lyss felt compelled by hurt to keep driving that blade home.

"We were . . . I was worried that if word got out that Adrian was at the academy, he would be totally vulnerable to agents from Arden. Time passed, and nobody came after him, so it just seemed easier to let things be."

Lyss felt like her head was splitting in two—joy warring with hurt and resentment and the pain of lost opportunity.

For every bitter word that Lyss spoke aloud, a dozen crowded in behind, begging for release. Fortunately, she intercepted most of them.

"And you never contacted him? He doesn't know that you know that he's alive?"

The queen shook her head. "As far as I know, he doesn't. We were afraid that if we reached out to him, our enemies would find him. There was also the chance that he would run. Or worse. Dean Beaugarde was very concerned about his mental health."

"Did you ever intend to tell me the truth?" Lyss said.

"I know I should have done before now." The queen stared down at her hands. "Looking back, I can see that I took the coward's way out. I knew you would feel betrayed, and I just kept putting off this conversation. I thought, perhaps, we would bring Adrian home for your name day this summer." Trying out a smile, she looked up at Lyss. "Now, with any luck, he'll be home just after Solstice."

It was hard to keep flailing at someone who just sat there and took it. Which meant that Lyss could no longer ignore the voice in her head that whispered, *He* wanted *to leave. He* wanted *to go to Oden's Ford. He* wanted *to leave us behind.*

With that, the tears finally spilled over and ran down her face. "How could he? How could Adrian go to Oden's Ford, leaving us thinking he was dead?"

"I think that's a question you will have to ask him," her mother said. "Neither of us knows for sure what he was thinking at the time." She planted her hands on her knees. "Look, I know you're angry and hurt, and I don't blame you. Every parent makes mistakes, Alyssa. When you are a queen, the mistakes are larger and harder to forgive."

"This is exactly why I keep saying that we need to launch an offense," Lyss said. "This is why merely holding our own is unacceptable. This is the kind of trade we are making. I've lost four years with my brother because of this damnable war, and I cannot get them back."

"I've lost four years with my son."

"But that was your choice! And Adrian's choice! I didn't have a choice. When he comes home, we'll be strangers."

"Here." Her mother fished into her neckline and pulled out a locket. She pried it open with her thumbnail and handed it to Lyss. "This is a sketch of him, done by one of the students at the Temple School at Oden's Ford. Lila brought it back to us."

Lyss studied the portrait. There was no doubt it was him, with his auburn hair and blue-green eyes. His face was thinner, his features sharper, as if every bit of baby fat had been rendered away. His eyes were shadowed with painful history. He wasn't smiling.

Lyss blotted away tears. "He looks sad," she whispered, her voice catching.

Her mother's nose was pinked up the way it always was when she was close to crying. "You can keep that," she said, clearing her throat. "I've had a year to memorize it."

Don't let your resentment ruin the joy of hearing this news, Lyss told herself. Adrian was alive—and he was coming home! Whatever had happened, they'd talk through it.

She would find a way to forgive him.

I want to go to Oden's Ford, Lyss thought, gripping the locket in her fist so that it cut into her skin. I want to go bring Adrian back home.

And that's exactly what my mother was afraid of.

Lyss turned away, leaning on the railing around the lily pond, watching the shadows of fishes under the surface.

"Alyssa," her mother said. "I am so very proud of you. You have a raw honesty and courage that I cannot match. Like your father, you have the common touch. Like your grandfather, you are a natural warrior. Soldiers want to follow you. Our enemies look into your eyes and they see their own defeat." She paused. "We are different, you and I. But, sometimes, when our future looks darkest, we are given the queen we need."

Lyss swung around to face her mother. "Do you really mean that?"

Her mother nodded. "I do."

"Then prove it."

"How?"

"If I cannot go to Oden's Ford, then I'm going to Delphi," Lyss said. "I have a team, I have an army, and I have a plan."

The queen extended her hand. "Come. Sit down, and tell me all about it."

SOUTH OF THE BORDER

Lyss sat on her pony at the southern end of Ana Maria Pass, trying to shake off the cold that crept into her fingers and toes and brought tears to her eyes—tears that froze as soon as they emerged. Mincemeat snorted out clouds of vapor that gilded his bridle and encrusted his mane.

It had finally begun—the invasion that Lyss had planned and plotted for so long. When she looked over her shoulder at the moody, snow-shrouded Spirit Mountains, she realized that when she'd crossed the border into Arden that morning, it was the first time she'd ever set foot outside of the queendom. She wondered if the dirt would look different than at home if she dug down through the snow. Even if the king of Arden was buttoned up in his palace, Lyss was still likely nearer to him than she'd ever been. She knew the way. She'd studied maps as closely as another girl might study prospective suitors at her name day party.

Sasha leaned toward her, only her eyes visible between her hat and her thrice-wrapped scarf. "Tell me again why we need a winter campaign?" She resembled a snow-covered mountain herself in her white wool cloak.

The snow was blinding, a swirling and unrelenting white, so it was impossible to tell up from down, or to see more than a few feet in any direction. And although the snow muffled sounds, now and then Lyss heard the creak of leather saddles, brittle in the cold, or the faint jingle of harness. It seemed to come from no direction, and then every direction.

Then the gray shadows would appear, always from the north, moving through the storm like wolves on the hunt. Which they were.

Lyss greeted each new arrival and directed the descending soldiers and horses through a narrow side canyon. The canyon opened into a wide, shallow basin, where they were protected from the wind and snow and not visible to any watchers below. Not that they would have been easy to see, in any event. Like every other soldier, Lyss was wrapped up in a white wool cloak layered and felted so that it could not be penetrated by the wind. Although they varied a little in shade, their sturdy, sure-footed, shaggy-haired mountain ponies were mostly white or pale gray, also. The soldiers streaming through the pass resembled the ancestors who prowled the peaks in the wintertime, walking snow spirits with ghost horses and a deadly touch.

The past three weeks had been a whirlwind. Her mother had convened a very select council of advisers—Captain Byrne, Char Dunedain, Shilo Trailblazer, and Julianna Barrett. They'd pored over the maps, diagrams, and sketches Lyss provided. By the week before Solstice, Lyss had not just one salvo, she had three—all under her command. She had a dozen Demonai warriors, led by Trailblazer. Ty Gryphon was in charge of the medical service. Lyss had supplies, weapons, tents, and other gear for mountain camping.

And her mother's blessing.

Shadow received an urgent message from his father and had to leave for Demonai Camp before they marched. Shadow was heartbroken, but Lyss was secretly relieved. He was just a little too eager to be safe on a battlefield. Hadley wasn't coming, either, since there wasn't much for a ship's captain to do in a mountain assault. So Lyss asked her to go as her representative to Oden's Ford with the others to collect Adrian. That way they could return by land or sea—whatever seemed most practical. She'd given Hadley a personal note to give to him, in case he needed any persuading to come home.

Now, every morning, when she remembered that

Adrian was alive, it was like a small ambush of joy.

For nearly a week, Highlanders and clan warriors had been moving into the mountains, drifting in small groups from wherever they were posted to the staging area on the northern slopes of the Spirits. They regrouped at Hunter's Camp, then entered Ana Maria Pass under cover of a winter storm. Even if the soldiers holding Delphi had considered the possibility of an attack from the north, hopefully no one would expect it to come out of the teeth of the gale.

They'd descended through Ana Maria Pass single file, linked together with a thick rope. The rope had been the key to keeping them all together. Any soldier who let go and stepped a few feet away might never find a way back.

Since there was no way to move wagons through the pass, each soldier—including Lyss—carried a tent, a bedroll, weapons, and several days' worth of food. Some led strings of packhorses with additional weaponry and supplies.

They wouldn't be here long. Lyss had no intention of their spending any precious time bivouacked in the high valley, eating up their meager food supply. The scouts had been out to the south for weeks, and the Demonai had been on the hunt for days, clearing the enemy between the pass and their target.

Lyss fingered her belt dagger, the one her mother had given her on the day she left for Delphi. It was clanwork, the hilt an image of the first Queen Hanalea with her flowing hair.

"Captain Byrne's father gave this to me when I wasn't much older than you," she'd said. "It has served me well. Stay safe and come back to me with a victory." She paused, as if distracted by the wolves she alone could see. Then gripped Lyss's shoulders and repeated, "Come back to me, Alyssa."

Lyss looked to the south, to the flatlands beyond the mountains. Could Montaigne feel her bloodlust through the umbilicus of the road between them? It would be a sweet justice to kill Montaigne with her mother's dagger. A girl's got to have dreams, after all.

But a girl's got to stay alive, because Adrian was coming home.

The crunch of hooves on snow and a rippling of blue shadow under the icy trees broke into her thoughts. Sasha's sword sang as it left its scabbard. Lyss had her bow up and the arrow nocked before she got a good look at the intruder.

A horse and rider detached itself from the forest and moved into the clearing. It was Quill Bosley. He commanded a squadron in one of the added salvos. Unfortunately. It seemed that every time she turned around, he was there.

Dropping his reins, Bosley raised both hands. "Last I heard, Your Highness, we were on the same side."

"Which is why I'd hate to have your untimely death on my conscience," Lyss snapped, rattled by the close call. "What do you want?"

"The lady Barrett asked me to tell you that her contacts from the local resistance are here," Bosley said. "She wonders if it would be convenient to come down to the command tent for a meeting."

"Thank you, Lieutenant," Lyss said. Nodding to Sasha, she put her heels to Mincemeat's sides, and the two of them trotted off after the last of the straggling soldiers.

The valley was already carpeted with white tents, some of them now half-buried in snow, so they were at least well insulated. There were a few small fires burning under canopies to dry wet clothing, but the canopies covered the flames, and the wind snatched and scattered the smoke before it could reveal their location. The horses were penned to one side, against the cliff. Even one of the sharp-eyed mountain hawks, soaring overhead in better weather, would have had difficulty spotting them.

Lyss threaded her pony through the maze of tents, dismounting in front of the command tent. It was unmarked, but it was one of the larger ones, and it stood in a defensible area near the cliff. Several Demonai warriors lounged near the entrance, but she knew they were anything but inattentive. Nodding to them, she pushed through the tent flap and into the relative warmth of the interior, Sasha at her heels.

People were crowded around a table spread with hand-drawn maps and littered with drawing tools. They included Julianna; Finn; Lyss's lieutenants, Littlefield, Mason, and Farrow; Trailblazer for the Demonai; plus Barnes and Kenton, the two captains of the added salvos. And two roughly dressed people Alyssa didn't recognize.

Julianna looked up as Lyss entered. "Here's Captain Gray," she said to the strangers. "She'll be able to speak to whether we can use the cannons on the heights. Captain, meet Brit Fletcher and Yorie Cooper, Patriots of Delphi."

Fletcher was a scruffy middle-aged man with a weather-beaten face and bushy salt-and-pepper hair. Cooper was a stocky, muscular girl with a ragged cap of black hair who might be just a year or two older than Lyss. They were both keeping a weather eye on Finn, the wizard in the room, as if he might burst into flame at any moment. And Trailblazer, in her Demonai warrior garb.

Lyss moved forward to the table, stripping off her heavy gloves and flexing her fingers. It was still so cold in the tent that she could see her breath.

"Did somebody mention cannons?" she said.

"We've got six twenty-four-pounders on the heights above the town," Fletcher said. "They can be yours, if you want them, if you move quick. There's no scouts to the north of there—I mean, who'd be fool enough to be skulking around up there this time of year?" The Patriot snorted laughter at his own joke.

"You're sure of that?" Trailblazer said.

Fletcher nodded. "We've got a lot of hidey-holes up there, so we keep a close eye on the area around the mines."

"They've learned that them that wander around by themselves never make it home," Cooper said, with a wink.

"Anyways, staffing is light," Fletcher said. "They're getting ready for Solstice, and there's already a lot of drinking going on."

"Is there ammunition for the guns?" Lyss asked.

"Tons," Cooper said, grinning. "Stored in armories all along the cliff face. Canister shells and solid shot, both. Because the guns an't rifled, they'll shoot most anything. Nobody's touched 'em since Arden took over on account of the ones they want to shoot at are up the hill instead of down the hill."

Lyss rubbed her hands together as if sitting down to a feast. This was like an extra-special Solstice gift. "Would we need to supply gunners, or are there still Patriots who know how to use them?"

"We an't been under Arden's thumb for that long," Fletcher growled. "We dug the coal, we made the steel, we cast the barrels, and we can sure as hell fire 'em."

"How are conditions between here and there?" Mason asked. "Can we bring our horses through?"

"There's snow, of course, but it an't too deep on the lee side," Cooper said.

Lyss had been studying the maps while they talked.

"The army is here?" She pointed.

Fletcher nodded. "They commandeered a manor house between the mines and the town. That way, they can get a jump on trouble either place. The headquarters an't well fortified. I guess they don't think they need that to defend against a pack of miners."

"I still don't like it," Trailblazer said. "We have to go too far out into the flatlands to get at them."

"That an't the flatlands," Cooper said.

"It is to us," Lyss said. "Out there, their numbers work for them. If we have a choice, we'd prefer to attack from cover."

"We'd just as soon you didn't bring the big fight close to town anyway," Fletcher said. "The people living there don't have much to start with, and I'd hate to see it burnt up or hexed or blown up or whatever." He cast a wary look at Finn, his amulet in plain view over top of his spattercloth.

"You should also know there's some blackbirds been snooping around Delphi," Fletcher went on. "King Gerard's personal guard. There's always some of 'em there, mind you, smacking us down, but these is extras. They've been there for a couple of months."

That caught Lyss's ear. Could it mean that King Gerard was somewhere within reach?

"What are they doing there?" she asked.

"Fighting the plague," Fletcher replied, matter-of-fact.

"The plague!" Julianna said, looking dismayed. "There's

plague in Delphi? I hadn't heard that."

"That's what *they're* saying, anyway," Cooper said. "Some say it's a lie." It was clear from her expression that she fell into the latter camp.

"But why would they claim there is plague if it isn't true?" Lyss asked.

Fletcher shrugged. "About a month after the guard arrived, we was told that some of their mudbacks had caught the plague from women in town."

"So the next thing you know," Cooper said, "there are notices all over town that women have to come in and be inspected and get their hair cut."

"What does their hair have to do with it?" Lyss looked from Fletcher to Cooper.

"They say the women have, uh, vermin in their hair, Captain, ma'am," Fletcher said. "Bugs. And that carries the plague. So they have to have it cut off. Karn and his men have been handling all of that."

Karn!

"You're telling me Marin Karn is up in Delphi cutting women's hair?" Shadow leaned forward, his face sharp with interest.

"Not *General* Karn," Fletcher said. "Lieutenant. Big Karn's son. Young Karn don't seem happy about being here, neither."

"Do you think the king gave him this assignment?" Julianna said. "Is this some kind of punishment?"

Fletcher laughed. "I have no idea. The king and the Lieutenant don't confide in me. All I know is, I've seen no sign of plague in Delphi."

"He's bringing all the women in," Lyss said slowly. "So he's looking for someone?" Who could be hiding here that Arden wanted to find?

"Seems like," Fletcher replied. "I can't imagine who. Hell, maybe it's just one more way to humiliate us. It an't bad enough they force everyone into the mines." He gestured at Lyss. "They've got girls and boys younger 'n you, spending twelve hours a day underground."

"It can't go on too much longer," Cooper said, "'cause they're running out of women. They've begun searching house to house."

"If Marin Karn's son is here," Trailblazer said softly, "then we should find a way to take him alive."

"I don't know how much leverage that would give us," Lyss said. "I'm guessing the general is not the sentimental type." She paused. "Remind me—who commands the mudbacks here in Delphi?"

"A Captain Halston Matelon," Fletcher said. "He's been here a year or thereabouts."

"He's got the reputation of an up-and-comer," Julianna said, as if eager to contribute. "He's risen quickly through the ranks, and his father's on the Thane Council. Though lately Matelon Senior has been on the outs with the king."

"What do the civilians here think of Matelon Junior?"

Lyss directed this to the two Patriots.

Fletcher and Cooper looked at each other. "He an't so bad," Cooper said. "He's a mudback, not a blackbird, and that's in his favor."

"So, we're all agreed that it would be good to draw their troops farther north, away from the town, toward the mountains," Trailblazer said, as if eager to get the conversation back to killing southerners. "Then we could fight from protection, and in conditions they're not fond of."

Lyss brushed her fingers over the faded ink of the map, stopping on the spot labeled "Number 2 Mine." It was snugged up against the southern wall of the mountains. "Who's up at the mines?"

Fletcher blinked at her owlishly. "Well, at any given time there's hundreds of miners underground. But like I said before, only a handful of soldiers to keep the peace."

"But what if there was trouble at the mines?" Lyss persisted. "Maybe a riot of some kind?"

Cooper shrugged. "There's been riots before, but it never really accomplished much in the long run except send a few miners to the gallows. For every southerner we kill, they kill three of us."

"I'm talking something big. Would the army respond to something like that?"

Now Fletcher got it, too. "You know," he said, rubbing the back of his neck, "that could happen. We do like to blow things up."

"That would bring them in range of the cannons, too," Littlefield said.

"I could create some fireworks," Finn said, fingering his amulet.

"No!" Cooper's face reddened, as all eyes turned her way, but she stood her ground. "I mean, if you start off with magecraft, that might tip 'em off," she mumbled. "Our work might not be so . . . uh . . . *fancy*, but we'll get a response, don't worry."

"Maybe not to start," Lyss said to Finn, "but once we get the army up there, I think some fireworks might be just the thing to convince them to surrender."

"One thing that worries me," Julianna said, "is that you mentioned there are children working in the mines. I'd hate for them to get caught up in all this."

"Aye," Fletcher said. "There's lýtlings—and women, too."

Cooper ran her fingers along her jaw. "We can try to keep the lýtlings out of harm's way. It won't be easy, without giving away the plan. As for the women, they have a grudge to settle with the occupiers. You might find many of them have no intention of sitting it out. Women of Delphi are made of steel and iron. They will make their presence felt."

Lyss nodded. "As long as they understand the risk." She moved on to the Highlanders. "Mason, your first arrivals have been resting for several hours. I need fifty ready to ride in an hour."

Mason saluted and left the tent.

"Trailblazer, can I count on the Demonai to handle the soldiers on the heights and take control of the cannons without raising an alarm?"

"Consider it done," Trailblazer said, unfolding to her feet with the grace of a predator.

SOLSTICE IN DELPHI

It was Solstice Eve in Delphi, and Hal was trying to think of something suitably vague and cheerful that he could write to his little sister. He'd been at it an hour, and he was already on his fourth attempt.

Dear Harper,

Another year nearly gone—can you believe it? I wish I could be with you and Mother for the holiday. I'd give a month's pay for one of your Solstice cakes and a basket of sweet oranges. There's lots of ice and snow here, so the gloves you sent are much appreciated. All the other soldiers here are jealous of me.

And some of them are trying to kill me.

Hal slammed down his quill, leaving a large blot of ink on the page. Crumpling it in his fist, he sent it after the others into the flames. He poked at the fire on the hearth until the page was consumed, then fingered the silver thimble that he always wore on a chain around his neck— a gift from Harper, to keep him from harm.

Maybe he should just enclose a signed card with his gift—a beaded leather journal that the vendor in the market said was clan-made. He knew she would love it; he just needed something of himself to go with.

Dear Harper,

Happy Solstice! Thank you for the gloves. Robert and I are spending Solstice together. We can't wait to see you again.

Love,

Your brother Hal

He folded it and tucked it into the dispatch bag with Harper's present and the silver chain he'd bought his lady mother.

Look on the bright side, Halston, his mother liked to say. *Don't be so gloomy.*

Hal tried to think of an upside to his current situation. Well, he *had* gained some survival skills in a place that seemed dedicated to putting him in the ground. These days, he varied his schedule, he never took his meals in his quarters, and he never went anywhere without his small guard of trusted men. He kept his mind sharp and his fighting skills sharper.

Next he'd be hiring a taster, like the king himself.

On the other hand, he was still in Delphi, and his prospects for surviving another year seemed bleak at best.

It had been nearly three months since Hal had led his ragtag band of survivors in a disciplined retreat from Queen Court. At least he'd managed to prevent further casualties. When he rejoined Karn's battalions on the Alyssa Plateau, the general didn't bother to hide his surprise and disappointment. When Karn questioned Hal's decision to call a retreat short of capturing the Vale, Hal looked into Karn's tobacco-spit eyes and reported that all four of his mages had been driven mad by northern sorcery and turned on them, so they'd had to be put down. That had forced their withdrawal from the field.

That ended the conversation, but Hal knew that it wasn't the end of his troubles.

He was right. His younger brother Robert, a corporal, was posted to Delphi in late fall. Hal heard the message loud and clear: *Here's another back to watch. If we can't get to you, your brother will do.* It seemed that Delphi was meant to be the graveyard for Matelons. He wrote to his father, who sent this advice: *Look after Robert, do your duty, and watch your back.*

The problem with looking after Robert was that his

little brother was eager to prove himself, and resisted Hal's attempts to keep him close.

We should engrave that on the Matelon coat of arms, Hal thought. Do your duty and watch your back.

Better watch your back, flatlander.

The girl they called the Gray Wolf still haunted his dreams. Her savage smile, her sun-burnished skin, the fearless way she flung herself, howling, into battle. The way she'd looked at him when his own men turned on him—as if she wanted to know what kind of commander led scrips to a slaughter and inspired a mutiny of mages on the battlefield. He found himself wanting to explain.

It's not what it seems, he would say. It's complicated.

After he returned to Delphi, he'd asked about the Fellsian officer known as the Gray Wolf. All he got was a mixture of scare stories and cautionary tales. None of which were useful.

Maybe she *was* a witch. A sorceress. Isn't that what everyone said, that northern women could steal a man's soul?

She might be a sorceress, but she looked like a soldier to him. Or a shieldmaiden from a story.

Soon after Robert's arrival, Marin Karn's son came to town. He was a lieutenant in the king's blackbird guard. Hal's first thought was that the younger Karn had been sent to spy on him. His second was that little Karn was being punished for something. When Lieutenant Karn began rounding up women and cutting their hair, Hal quit trying to sort him out. Finally, a few days before Solstice, Karn was involved in a brawl in a tavern in town. Marc Clermont, the captain of the King's Guard, was killed, as was the tavern keeper. With that, young Karn took a crew of blackbirds and fled straight back to the capital.

Clermont was gone, and that might be worth celebrating, but Hal guessed he'd better wait until he found out who was chosen to replace him. As bad as things were, they could always get worse.

Look on the bright side, Halston.

Hal didn't have a lot to look forward to, these days, but he *was* looking forward to Solstice. He'd sent Robert south to Temple Church on a trumped-up errand, planning to join him there for the holiday. He and Robert could wash Delphi from their skins and cleanse their souls with good Tamron wine and eat some decent food for a change. It would be a good way to launch the new year.

His reverie was interrupted by a pounding at the door. Hal swore softly. That never brought good news in Delphi.

Dupont, the duty officer, burst in, waving a dispatch. "We've had a bird from Shively, up at the mines," he said. "There's trouble."

Who starts trouble just before Solstice? Hal thought, with a prickle of annoyance. He unrolled the message, flattening it on his desk with his hands.

*Facing large mob of armed miners outside the Number 2
mine. Send help soonest. Suggest a battalion at minimum.*

Hal tapped the dispatch with his forefinger. From what
he had seen during his year in Delphi, Shively was a mean-
spirited bully who'd end up at the bottom of a mine with his
throat cut one day. Like most bullies, he was a coward, too,
and tended to call for help at the least sign of unrest. They
were short-staffed to begin with, because of holiday leaves.

Hal sighed. He had to respond. The mine had to keep
producing. "Sergeant, take a company up to the mine, and
see what—"

A huge blast shook the foundation of the manor house,
sending bits of plaster raining down on their heads. Hal
and Dupont stared at each other, then raced to the door.

To the north, up against the backdrop of the mountains,
flames were shooting high into the air. The mine headquarters was ablaze.

Hal swore softly. Sorry, Robert, he thought. Change
of plans. He bade good-bye to his own holiday plans as he
ruined countless others. "All leaves are cancelled, effective
immediately," he told Dupont. "Sound the officers' call on
the double. It's going to be a long, bloody night."

In the end, Hal took two full battalions to the Delphian
mines, leaving only a skeleton crew behind. He hoped
a show of overwhelming force would put a stop to the

trouble with minimal bloodshed. The ringleaders would have to be executed, of course, but hopefully no more than those. Even his most brutal critics in the capital would support that approach. Arden couldn't afford to slaughter the miners who wrenched coal and iron ore from the ground. He warned his officers to keep a tight rein on their men, since they were already in a mood to teach the snarling dogs of Delphi a lesson.

They climbed the long slope from the army headquarters at a killing pace. As they marched, explosions continued to light up the dark mountains. It seemed that the miners were trying to do the same to the Number Two mine as they had to Number One.

His own men and horses were facing into the storm, and the wind drove the snow into their faces. Ice formed in their hair and mustaches and anything exposed to the weather. Hal worried that by the time they arrived in the hills that enclosed the Delphi mines, they would be as spent as if they had already worked a hard day.

Conditions worsened the farther north they went. Men and horses floundered through waist-high snow. The army of Arden rarely had to move fast through a snowstorm. They did their fighting in the summers. Granted, the weather in Delphi was bad nearly all of the time, but they didn't do too much marching around in it.

One of the scouts reported seeing a small group of white-cloaked figures passing, going the other way. They were moving fast, wearing snowshoes, impossible to catch. Who the hell was that? Hal resisted the temptation to send a company to give chase. The mines had to be his first priority.

They were still a half mile south of their target when the first shell fell among them, toward the rear of the column. It was canister shot, and when it exploded, the flying shrapnel tore men and horses to bits. The troops up front continued marching, unaware that anything was wrong, while those in the vicinity of the hit milled about in wild confusion.

Another shell landed, this time toward the front of the line, and killed or injured a hundred men. All forward progress halted then, with men and horses scattered in all directions, but the snow made it slow going, and three more shells landed with brutal effectiveness before they could spread out enough to limit the damage. By now, those men who were still mounted had their hands full controlling their horses.

By the time the second shell landed, Hal knew what had happened. How it had happened was another matter. He lifted his eyes to the horizon in time to see another missile soar into the sky.

"The cannon!" he shouted to his second-in-command, and anyone else who would listen. "The miners have taken the cannon!" Except the idea that the desperate miners of Delphi could recognize the strategic importance of the

SHADOWCASTER

cannon, seize them from the regulars, and actually use them against his army was hard to believe. Where was the company posted at the mine when all this was going on?

However it happened, the guns on the cliffs were still lobbing missiles into their ranks with deadly accuracy, even though the troops weren't packed so tightly as before. The next shot wasn't a shell, but a load of scrap metal that spread across a wide area, killing men and horses as it fell from the sky. Soon the snow around them was stained red with blood and gore and parts of soldiers. It was a nightmare.

They couldn't stay where they were or they would be decimated. It was either move forward or retreat. "Charge!" Hal shouted, raising his sword above his head and spurring his horse forward. "To me! For the Red Hawk of Arden!" His officers took up the cry, driving their men toward the mines. Only, in the deep snow, "charge" was an exaggeration at best. They managed to prevent a wholesale rout, but as they pushed slowly forward, the deadly rain continued to fall, along with the snow. By the time they were close enough to the mountains to be out of range of the guns, their numbers were reduced by nearly half.

For the second time in six months, I'm presiding over a slaughter, Hal thought. What am I doing wrong?

For one gut-wrenching moment, he wondered if he'd been set up again.

They were forced through a narrow ravine on the

approach to the mine, and spears and lances and arrows showered down on them from both sides. Miners shooting arrows? Where did they learn to fire with such accuracy? It was almost impossible to spot the attackers in the snow; they seemed to blend in, somehow, white shadows only, constantly moving. It was like running a deadly gauntlet, death coming out of nowhere, men falling all around.

Some of the men fled, all in a panic, shouting, "It's the spirits! The demon spirits have come out of the mountains!" Most were seasoned fighters, veterans of campaigns in the Fells, who'd encountered deadly northern tactics in the Spirits.

But the others pressed on, though fewer and fewer of them, and their attackers appeared in the flesh, wielding swords and lances and wearing white cloaks. They were like no miners Hal had ever seen, but like no soldiers, either. At first they were silent, and then they began howling, more and more of them, like a gale roaring through the mountains. And shouting, "For the Queen in the North! For the Gray Wolf!"

These were not miners at all. Hal had miscalculated, seriously miscalculated, and now he and his men would pay for it.

Hal pulled out the dispatch Shively had sent earlier, flipped it over, and scribbled a note on the back. He thrust it into Dupont's hands. "Take this back to the garrison house and send it on to Temple Court."

Dupont blinked at him. "But, Captain . . . ?"

"Go *now*, and that's an order." With that, Hal turned back to his decimated army.

By the time the army of Arden stood before the mines, there were only a few hundred of them left. They were surrounded, fighting for their lives, and Hal saw no one who looked like a miner. Hal was standing back-to-back with another soldier, fighting three attackers hand to hand, when the soldier's body jerked, then slumped to the ground, leaving Hal's back unprotected. As he turned, something struck him on the back of the head, knocking him flat on his face in the snow. He rolled onto his back and opened his eyes in time to see a white-clad soldier standing over him, raising his staff for the killing blow.

Hal twisted, trying to avoid the blow, but it still landed, and he didn't remember anything after that.

IN THE DEEP MIDWINTER

When Hal awoke, he was lying in a stone chamber, on a hard pallet on the floor. His sword was gone, his wrists and ankles were manacled together, and his head hurt like fury. There were torches stuck into the walls at intervals, and as he lifted his head, he could see other bodies on other pallets around the room. None of the others wore the red hawk. He was the only one.

The last thing he remembered was that he was fighting for his life in front of the Number Two mine and somebody clubbed him in the head. Why, then, was he still alive?

Shadowy figures moved among the injured in the make-shift hospital, tending to them. The healers were dressed in nondescript clothing, and he didn't recognize any of them, but then he wasn't sure he would recognize any miner of Delphi, anyway.

One of the attendants noticed he was awake, left the room, and returned with a weatherbeaten woman in torn and bloodstained copperhead garb, her hair a mass of trophy braids. She wore a wicked-looking dagger at her waist.

What would a copperhead be doing here? Other than serving as just one more embellishment to Hal's living nightmare. He eyed the dagger, weighing his chances of grabbing hold of it. When he looked up at the copperhead's face, the challenge in her eyes was plain to read: *Try me.*

Maybe later, Hal thought. He needed to find out where he was now in order to plan an escape.

"Get up, flatlander," the copperhead said in Common.

Hal planted his feet and attempted to rise, but apparently took a little too long, because the warrior gripped his arm and jerked him to his feet, none too gently. Hal tried to pull free. That set his head spinning, and he braced himself against the wall to keep from toppling over or spewing on the floor.

"Where am I?" he asked, playing for enough time to regain his balance.

From the copperhead's expression, Hal might have been a cockroach she'd squashed under her boot. "I'll let Captain Gray tell you anything she wants you to know," she said, giving Hal a shove toward the door. "She's the one that spared your life, though I don't know why."

Glad it wasn't up to you, Hal thought. And then: Who the hell is Captain Gray?

They threaded their way between the pallets and out of the room and into a narrow tunnel, black rock on either side. A fine black dust lay over everything.

Still in Delphi, after all. Hal's muddled brain finally matched up the dots and he realized he must be underground, inside one of the mines. He had never been down one before. The air was rank, oppressive, almost too thick to breathe. The length of chain between his ankles allowed him just enough room to shuffle along quickly. He had to pay close attention or risk falling on his face on the rocky floor.

They came to a side tunnel, guarded by two stone-faced, spattercloth-clad soldiers. Highlanders. What were they doing here?

And then he remembered. There had been northerners at the mines, fighting alongside the miners.

His escort conferred with the Highlanders, and Hal was ushered into another chamber hewn out of the rock. A woman dressed in brown-and-green spattercloth was seated behind a makeshift desk made out of ammunition crates, scrawling something onto a page. Her coloring was different than that of Hal's escort, and her honey-colored hair was woven into one fat braid, beaded and feathered as well. She wore a scarf—the kind used by northern officers to distinguish rank. A captain's scarf. This must be Captain Gray.

Just behind her stood another woman in the same colors who could make three of most men. She was all muscle, and her head nearly brushed the roof of the cave. Something told him that this was the captain's bodyguard.

Lately, it seemed that he could use one himself.

Hal stood awkwardly, just inside the door, his escort next to him, for what seemed an eternity, while everyone in the room ignored him.

When the captain finally set aside her paperwork and looked up at him, Hal's heart almost stopped. It was the officer from Queen Court Vale with the raptor eyes—the one who'd handed him his ass and then saved it by killing his own mages.

Hal could tell by her amused expression that she remembered him, too. "Happy Solstice, Captain Matelon," she said. "May the sun come again."

Solstice? Hal had forgotten all about the holiday. He should have known by the bits of evergreen tacked up on the walls.

"Thank you, ma'am," Hal said. Personally, he'd have to say that it wasn't off to a very good start. "If you know who I am, you have the advantage of me." He'd thought that was a fine turn of phrase, but the northerners seemed to find it funny.

"Yes, Captain," the officer said. "I *do* have the advantage

of you." Everybody laughed. Even the fierce-faced copperhead smiled. When the merriment died down, she added,
"I'm Captain Gray, of the queen's Highlander army."

Captain Gray. The Gray Wolf. It all made sense now,
except—

"But the Highlanders never come south of the Spirit
Mountains."

"Surprise." Gray's smile grew wider, toothier, almost . . .
wolfish.

There were two other people sitting on crates nearby.
One was a scruffy-looking man with torn, bloodstained
clothing and a bristle of beard. The other was a tall, slender girl in finely made civilian trekking gear, her midnight
hair done up into an elegant knot. She looked like she
would be more at home in one of the salons at court than
in the Number Two mine. Maybe it was because she was
the only one not wearing somebody else's blood.

She noticed him looking at her, because she said, "Captain Matelon, I am Julianna Barrett, the queen's liaison to
the Patriots of Delphi." She gestured toward the scruffy
man. "Perhaps you know Fletcher, here. He's one of our
local partners."

Hal studied the man, then shook his head. "Forgive
me," he said. "Perhaps we've met, but—"

"I've been out of the mines a few years now," Fletcher
said. "I run the leather shop in town. I made some boots
for you once. Other than that, I always went out of my way

to avoid you." He grinned, exposing highly variable teeth. "Welcome to the free city of Delphi."

"Our newest friend and ally," Barrett added.

"Your newest . . ." Hal stopped and organized his thoughts. "You'll never hold Delphi. Our armies will come north again in the spring. You know they will."

"And we'll be ready for 'em next time," Fletcher said. "We won't be caught napping again."

Gray didn't look particularly worried, either. "Perhaps we have more surprises in store for Arden. Perhaps if this place were defended properly, it wouldn't be so easy to take. Perhaps, the Maker willing, your despicable king will be dead by then." That last part she said with considerable venom.

It's personal, Hal thought. I wonder why.

"Well," Hal said into the charged silence. "It seems that a lot can happen in a day." He paused. "What about my men?" he asked. "Where are they?"

"Your troops here at the mines fought bravely," Gray said. "Unfortunately, very few of them survived. At present, a few hundred of your men are huddled in your indefensible headquarters, trapped between us and the militia in town, trying to decide who to surrender to. So far, the miners have taken the town from the Ardenine blackbirds, killed most of them, and driven the rest out of town. As I understand it, not many got away. People are truly angry in this city of Delphi. Perhaps you can explain it?" Gray raised an eyebrow. When Hal said nothing, she added, "If you ask me, I think your men would be better off surrendering to us than to the Patriots."

Hal had to agree. But he still couldn't quite put this puzzle together, how a miners' riot turned into an invasion.

"Your father is Lord Matelon, correct?" Barrett said.

"Aye," Hal said, seeing no purpose in denying it.

"It was Captain Gray who recognized you and intervened to save your life," Barrett said.

Hal glanced at Gray, then away. "If you're thinking about demanding a ransom from my father, he won't pay it."

"Why not?" Captain Gray again. "He doesn't want you back?"

"I'm going to assume he wants me back," Hal said. "But he doesn't believe in paying ransoms or meeting the demands of hostage takers. Though he might use my death as a means to rally his bannermen."

"Well," Barrett said, with a wry smile, "from what I've heard about your father, that doesn't surprise me at all."

"Whatever you decide to do with me, I'd ask you to show mercy to my soldiers. They are good men, mostly, and here under orders."

Captain Gray fingered her braid. "Shall we show them the same mercy afforded our captured troops by the king of Arden?" she said in a voice as hard and cold as tempered steel.

"Hopefully not," Hal said, startled into honesty.

The two of them stared at each other for a long moment.

Finally, Gray settled back in her seat. "If your remaining troops surrender," she said, "we will treat them as humanely as we can, as prisoners of war."

"Thank you," Hal said.

"If . . ."

Here it comes, Hal thought, my opportunity to prove what kind of man I am. "If?"

"If you write a message to the duty officer at your headquarters, giving permission for their surrender under those conditions," Gray said. "I also want you to write to your father, and tell him what has happened."

Hal waited for the rest, and when it didn't come, said, "That's it? No demands?"

"No demands," Gray said. "We just want him to know. Nobody should have to wait and wonder about a loved one gone missing." Again, there was an unexplained edge to her voice.

"It would probably be best to send it via my brother Robert at Temple Church," Hal said. "That would be the surest way to get it to my father these days." Without its being intercepted.

"We'll see that it gets to him," Barrett said.

Gray tapped her pen against paper. "I wondered if you could help me with something. We've been looking for someone we understand is currently in Delphi, but we've been unable to locate him. Perhaps you can help. A Lieutenant Karn?"

"Karn?" Hal shouldn't have been surprised. Northern spies were everywhere. "He was here, but he's gone now. He left a few weeks ago."

"Too bad. Do you know what he was doing here?"

"Fighting the plague," Hal said. "That's what we were told."

"And is there plague in Delphi?"

Hal hesitated, unsure what he could say without betraying his command. "Lieutenant Karn said there was plague in Delphi, so there must have been. I never saw it, myself."

Gray came to her feet and dusted off the seat of her breeches. She was a tall one, too—she almost matched him in height. "The miners say they haven't seen any plague, either. So why do you think Karn was here?"

Hal met the captain's eyes, and for some reason found himself telling the truth. "This is just a guess, but I believe he was looking for a particular girl."

Gray studied Hal, then nodded, as if she'd decided to believe him. "Why did he leave, then?"

"I believe he found her," Hal said.

FLAMECASTER

The saddlery in Middlesea was a busy place, and the tanners and jorimers should have been used to custom orders from the multinational clientele who came and went through the port. Still, the clerk behind the counter raised his eyebrows when Jenna Bandelow gave him the sketch of what she wanted made.

He turned the drawing this way and that, as if thinking that he had it upside down. "What's this for again?"

Jenna had her story ready. "I'm a performer in a traveling show," she said. "I ride the elyphants and gryphons. Our gryphon's grown out of his tack again."

"Gryphon?" The man's jaw set stubbornly. "There's no such thing."

"Come out and see," Jenna said. "Only five steelies for standing room. We're here all week."

"Five steelies! Not likely," the clerk snapped. "I got little enough money and I'll not be wasting it on the likes of you."

Jenna shook her bag of coin. "If you've got so little coin, I'd think you'd be eager for the business. Can you do it or not? Elsewise I'll spend *my* little bit of money someplace else."

The clerk studied the drawing some more, then looked up with a crafty expression. "This here's going to be pricey, 'cause it takes a lot of leather to make it adjustable. Do you really need this much tolerance in a—?"

"This gryphon's growing fast," Jenna said. "I want to be able to use this for a year, at least."

"Hmm. Does it need to be brain-tanned steer hide? And brass fittings? That gets to be—"

"Let's pretend we already had this conversation, and at the end, I stood with what I had," Jenna said. "I know what I want. Now, can you do it? Otherwise I'll move along."

The clerk scratched his belly and hitched up his breeches. "What about this other thing? I don't usually do clothing." He tapped the other sheet she'd given him—drawings of a helmet, gauntlets, and a breastplate. Plus a jacket and a split riding skirt.

"Right," Jenna said. "It's armor, and—and a sort of a

costume. You know, for the show. Now how much and how long?"

"It'll take a couple weeks," the clerk said, and then named a price.

Jenna returned her purse to her bodice and turned to go.

"Wait!" he said.

She turned back.

"What's the problem? The time or the price?"

"Both," Jenna said. "I expect to meet robbers in the borderlands, but not on the high street."

"My goods are clan-made, and custom," the clerk whined. "They don't come cheap, and there's a lot of demand, so it takes time."

"I don't care how many orders you have, just move mine up front, and we can do business."

"Well," the shopkeep said, grinning greasily, "it *would* speed things up if you would come in for a—you know— private fitting after the shop is closed. I can't make any promises, but—hey!" he shouted after her as she banged through the door. "You're with the circus, right? Don't be getting up on your high horse, now."

"Asshole," Jenna muttered as she strode down the street, dodging the contents of a slopjar being thrown from an upper window and wishing her sense of smell wasn't quite so acute. She'd been avoiding towns and cities as she worked her way north along the coast, but the Fellsian border was only a few miles away and she'd hoped to replenish her supplies and procure some custom equipment before she crossed over.

What she really wanted to do was turn around and go back to Ardenscourt, and find Adam Wolf. Or at least pick up his trail.

You don't know that he's still there. You don't even know if he's still alive. If he's left, you'll have a devil of a time finding him, because you don't know his real name, or where he's from. He said he was from the north, but even that might be a lie. Back at Ardenscourt, being together was enough. There was no point in planning for a future when death was just a step away.

She imagined wandering from place to place, asking everyone she met if they'd seen a red-haired mage healer who looked rather wolfish.

Next time, I won't be in such a rush to fall for a stranger, she thought. Next time, I'll get more information. And then: There won't be a next time. The healer had tried to save her, and it might have cost him his life. If Adam Wolf still lived, the very best way to show her love was to stay the hell away from him.

Once, Jenna had been foolish enough to dismiss her grandmother's warning—that the magemark on the back of her neck had made her a target. Once, she'd been foolish enough to think that she could hide from her fate in a remote border town. Now, the knowledge that she was being hunted gave her a prickly feeling that made her want to dive into cover and stay there. If she could be found in

Delphi, she could be found anywhere.

Jenna was *not* the kind of person to dive in a hole and stay there. Back in Delphi, when King Gerard murdered Riley and Maggi, she'd refused to heed her father's advice to hide in an upstairs room. She'd made the Ardenine garrison bleed.

Now King Gerard was dead, but Strangward and the empress were still out there.

She touched the magemark on the back of her neck, recalling the reckless words she'd said to Riley the day he died. *We are chosen, you and I. We'll write our own story.*

She would not write a story about a mole or a rat, living underground. My realm is the skies, she thought. Even if it's only for a little while.

So. Jenna's other choice was to enlist Flamecaster if he was willing, and with him learn to fight as a team. By the time Celestine hunted them down, they would be ready, and they would find a way to win. Jenna swore that neither one of them would ever be caged up again.

Strangward would have the answers she needed. She would hunt *him* down—and force him to reveal the meaning of the magemark and uncover the secrets in her past.

Where would he be now? If he'd survived Flamecaster's attack on the tower at Ardenscourt, would he have returned to Carthis, or would he still be prowling the empire, looking for her?

The emissary had said that the empress was coming

soon. She could be here already. When Jenna closed her eyes and thought of the empress, looking for a future truth, all she saw were ships, stretching to the horizon.

That lent an urgency to Jenna's mission. She'd hoped that the roomy, desolate north would be a good place for flight training, but she didn't want to fly into the mountains without a better seat and better control over her steed. Even then, with the storms that raced south over the Spirits in winter, she would be taking a huge risk. So they had been traveling north, following the coast, hoping to find a break in the unforgiving terrain.

Which had led her to the saddlery. But there was no way she would pay the tanner's price. She was beginning to think she'd have to go back to being Lyle. Or Toby or Jack or Riley.

She stopped at the market, but there were no leatherworkers there. She did buy a loose shirt and trousers from a rag merchant, and a longbow from a clan trader.

She'd heard stories about the upland clans, famous for making a living from an inhospitable land. They were hunters, gatherers, jewelers, weavers, known for their beading and leatherwork. Their work was prized throughout the empire, and clan traders were known to drive a hard bargain for all kinds of goods.

The woman measured Jenna's height and the spread of her arms with a knotted string and pinched her bicep. She chose a bow from the display, strung it, and invited Jenna to try it. Even given her years of hard work, in the mines and out, it was surprisingly hard for Jenna to draw. Still, she left with the bow and a quiver of arrows.

She was passing by a livery stable and it occurred to her that she might be able to get a line on a saddlery in town. Another clan trader was standing outside the stable, chatting with the stable boy in Common.

Jenna studied the man with interest. This trader was dressed in deerskin leggings and high boots, a fur-trimmed winter parka over top. And he was young, from his looks, no older than she was. His features and complexion, though, more closely resembled those of a Southern Islander than an uplander. Here and there, his wavy hair had been forced into clan-style braids and decorated with feathers and beads, as was their custom.

The trader gave the stable boy a handful of coins, lifted a saddle off a rack, and carried it into the stable.

"Hello," Jenna said to the stable boy when the trader had gone. "I'm looking for someone who can do custom leatherwork. Do you know anyone like that?"

The boy glanced toward the stable door. "Rogan can probably help you. He knows where to get just about anything you want—at a price."

"I was hoping to work directly with the harness-maker," Jenna said. "It's a highly specialized job."

The boy shrugged. "There's Darol's Leather, up on the—"

"I've already been there," Jenna said, shaking her head. "Well. I'll see what this Rogan has to say."

It took Jenna's eyes a few minutes to adjust to the darkness of the barn after the brilliance of the midday outside. It was also much warmer inside, where the raw wind off the Indio couldn't find her.

The trader had his pony cross-tied in the aisle. She was one of the shaggy, sturdy breed favored by uplanders. He was rubbing her down, examining her hooves, and murmuring sweet nothings to her. Still, somehow, he heard Jenna coming. He turned around, his back to the pony, his hand closing on the hilt of a knife at his waist. His casual stance was contradicted by his narrowed eyes and the tension in his posture.

"Excuse me," Jenna said. "I didn't mean to startle you. I'm Riley."

He looked her up and down, as if trying and failing to match the name and its owner. "I'm Rogan." His hand stayed on his knife.

"I understand you're a trader?"

"I am," he said. He was testy for a trader—most were charmers adept at parting you from your money. He didn't seem to care whether he did any business or not.

"I need some custom leatherwork done," Jenna said. "Do you know anyone who can do that?"

"Did you try the leather shop up on the—?"

"I did," Jenna said. "That's why I'm asking you."

Amusement flickered across the trader's face. He circled around his pony so he was facing her over the animal's back, and continued the rubdown.

"All of my sources are north of the border," he said.

"I see," Jenna said. "I happen to be going north. Could you give me a name of someone I can look up when I get there?"

"They only deal through me," Rogan said, spreading a colorful clan blanket over the pony's back. He followed with the saddle. It was plain he was getting ready to leave.

Jenna's temper snapped. She was cold, and hungry, and had spent too much time away from Flamecaster already. Who knew what kind of mischief he'd gotten up to in her absence? Worse, he might be coming to find her.

"Fine," she said, clenching her jaw. "Thank you for your time. I'll try to find someone that'll take my coin once I cross the border."

As she turned away, the trader said, "Wait."

She turned back to face him. *"What?"*

"What is it, exactly, you are looking for?"

Rolling her eyes, Jenna handed him the drawing she'd made.

He studied it, frowning, then looked up and said, "Are you sure this is right?"

"Never mind," Jenna said, sticking her hand out again. "I can see that I'm wasting my time."

"Talking to me is never a waste of time," Rogan said.

"Where are you going, once you cross the border?"

"Well, Spiritgate, for a start," Jenna said, unwilling to give too much information away.

"That's a dangerous place, right now," Rogan said.

"Every place is dangerous," Jenna said.

He nodded his agreement. "What about after that?"

"I haven't decided," Jenna said.

"Well, if you haven't decided," Rogan said, "you could go to Fortress Rocks."

Jenna folded her arms, awaiting yet another proposition. "Why would I want to go there?"

He grinned, his teeth flashing white in the darkness. "Because that's where I'm going, after I make a couple of stops."

"I'm not really looking for a traveling companion," Jenna said, thinking, I already have one, and that's more than enough.

"Good, because I'm not, either," Rogan said. "But I know a clan leatherworker that lives near Fortress Rocks who could make this, and she's amazingly fast."

"That's good to know," Jenna said. "But that's out of my way. I would prefer to stay close to the coast. If I haven't found what I want by the time I get to Spiritgate, maybe I'll come west."

"You'll want to go to her," Rogan said. "If you're look-ing for quality, that is." He waved the paper at her. "I'll probably get there before you."

Not unless you're riding a dragon, Jenna thought.

"I'll put the order in, and it will be ready when you get there." Tucking the drawing in his pocket, the trader mounted his pony. "See you at Fortress Rocks."

"Hey, give that back!" Jenna sprinted toward him, but the pony was already moving. "I never said yes."

"Ask for me at the Cold Moon Tavern at Fortress Rocks," Rogan called over his shoulder. "They'll know where to find me."

THE ROAD TO NOWHERE

Once Breon agreed to go back to Baston Bay, Aubrey insisted that they travel straight east to the coast and take ship from Chalk Cliffs. She argued that would be safer than traveling on the main road through the high passes to Delphi and then east to the sea. No doubt those borders would be watched.

Maybe it was safer, maybe not. It meant traveling through the Fells, where Breon felt like he had a huge target on his back.

Besides, it was a hard road they'd chosen. People called it a road, but that was putting a bright polish on it. It was more of a trail that went straight through the mountains. He and Aubrey were city bred, not accustomed to roughing it in the countryside.

It had taken four days to travel from Baston Bay north and west to Fellsmarch in the fishwagon. Though Chalk Cliffs was closer, as the crow flies, it took a lot longer to get there. Or maybe it just seemed longer because Breon had passed much of the first trip in a pleasant haze of leaf. Now that he was hoarding and conserving, and walking most of the way, it was an ordeal.

He fingered Her Highness's locket. It still hung from a chain around his neck, next to the pendant his father had left him. He knew he should pitch it over a cliff along the road, but he didn't. He told himself maybe he'd find a way to send it back to her family.

Now and then, he wondered what it would sell for, and how much leaf that would buy. And how quick that would bring the bluejackets down on him.

The road between Fellsmarch and Chalk Cliffs offered few chances for a lift. There was little traffic this time of year save soldiers and bluejackets riding to and from. He guessed they'd be glad to pick him up, but they probably wouldn't take him where he wanted to go.

At first, Breon and Aubrey stayed at inns, but at the last two, he'd seen his image posted up over the bar, on a poster offering a reward for his capture alive and warning that he was desperate and dangerous.

The sketch didn't do him justice—it made him look like a shifty-eyed backstreet rusher—but the drawing of his jafasa was amazingly detailed and true to life. Aubrey had tried to make him dump the jafasa then and there. Aubrey could usually talk him into anything, but not this. It had belonged to his da, though how he knew that, he couldn't have said. That and a broken pendant were all he had to remember him by. Not that he remembered him.

Breon had traded his fancy clothes to a sheepherder who needed something posh for the holiday. In return, he got a thick wool jacket and breeches and cap that were better suited for winter travel but made him look like a farmer who'd lost his herd on the way to market. He still gimped along with the walking stick, hoping that would get them more rides.

What worked best was when Aubrey stood out at the roadside alone. Once somebody stopped, Breon would pop up and climb on, too.

Most everyone they saw on the road or in the taverns seemed to be going the wrong way. The rides they did get were for short distances, and sometimes they'd be let out in the middle of nowhere.

If he'd been better at slide-hand, he'd have tried to lift something that would help him find the driver's song. Otherwise his voice wasn't enough to get them where they wanted to go.

So they traveled in fits and starts, part of the time on foot, Breon diving into cover whenever they heard traffic approaching on the road. As they climbed toward the eastern pass, the wind grew colder and the snow deeper and Breon realized that walking all the way to Chalk Cliffs might not be such a good idea.

Their latest ride dumped them out at a little crossroads, nestled in a gorge between two mountain ranges.

"Are you really going to leave us here, in the middle of nowhere?" Aubrey said, batting her eyelashes at the teamster.

"Fortress Rocks is just down there," the man said, pointing left down the side road. "Maybe somebody there can give you a ride the rest of the way." He turned right and was soon out of sight. So they began to walk the unknown distance to town.

Breon didn't look forward to making the climb through the next set of passes. Since he had a little coin in his pocket, he was thinking maybe they should hire a wagon to take them the rest of the way. This might be their last chance to do that. From what everyone said, it was all mountains until they reached the sea.

He hoped there was a wagon-worthy road through the mountains that lay ahead of them.

"Do you know how to drive a wagon?" Breon asked Aubrey.

That was like lancing a boil.

"How would I know how to drive a wagon?" she snapped. "Do I look like someone who ever owned a horse? And where would we hire one if I did? And why are you still carrying around that bag of splinters? Any-body sees that, you'll be locked up for sure."

"I already told you, I can get it fixed. Otherwise, how are we supposed to make a living once we get to Baston Bay?"

She took a deep breath, then let it out, as if releasing her anger along with. "We'll be fine," she said. "I'll get my game going as soon's we get to Baston Bay."

Like usual, she was vague about what that game might be. Breon didn't want to get dragged into anything that might draw the attention of the bluejackets.

"I'm thinking we ought to stay low for a while, until this blows over."

"You murdered a princess, Bree," Aubrey hissed. "This is not going to blow over."

"I never did," Breon said hotly. Why did she keep say-ing that?

"And you think a good way to lay low is to go out and busk the streets? Which is what you were doing when you got into trouble in the first place?"

"You got any better ideas?" Breon shot back.

"Yes," she said. And walked on.

Maybe, Breon thought, but she'd be the first to com-plain about an empty belly. Aubrey had been prickly and irritable ever since they left Fellsmarch, but it was a prickly and irritable kind of situation, so it was understandable. Sort of. It was as if she blamed him for what happened to Whacks and Goose, when none of it was his idea.

Up ahead, Aubrey rounded a bend and stopped in her tracks. "Blood of the martyrs," she muttered.

Breon came up beside her. Blocking the road was a gate, and next to it a guardhouse. Both looked raw enough to be newly built. Breon took a step back, but they'd been seen, because spattercloth soldiers came boiling out. He'd learned a long time ago that running makes a person look guilty of something. He gripped Aubrey's hand and kept walking forward.

When they reached the gate, one of the soldiers barked, "What's your name and your business at Fortress Rocks?"

Aubrey began to cry.

"Hey, now, sis," Breon said, patting her on the shoulder. "Don't worry. These ones won't hurt us."

Aubrey just cried harder. She was the prettiest crier Breon had ever seen. Not like some, who got all puffy-eyed and snot-nosed.

"What's wrong with her?" one of the soldiers said, pointing. A burly, bearded soldier with a flattened nose pulled out a handkerchief and gave it to her.

"My sister and I are from Spiritgate, down on the border," Breon said, looking Flatnose in the eyes. "Some mudbacks came through and they —they—" He stopped and blotted away tears with his sleeve. "Our house is burnt and the rest of our family is dead. So we're on our way to Chalk Cliffs—we've got family there."

The soldiers all looked at each other. "I wonder if they're

the same bastards who came here," one of them said.

"There were mudbacks here?" Breon looked from face to face. "When was that?"

"Back in late summer," Flatnose said.

"I think it was around then," Breon said. He looked at Aubrey, who nodded, sniffling.

"All we have is the clothes on our backs," Aubrey said. "Do you think we can get work in town? We need to make some money so we can hire space in a wagon to take us to the coast."

"There's construction work to be had," Flatnose said, eyeing Breon's bony build skeptically. "They're having to rebuild most of the town. But it won't be easy to find a ride. With the holiday just over, there's not much traffic on the road this time of year."

At the end of it, the soldiers took up a collection for them before they sent them on their way.

Breon slid a look at Aubrey as they left the gate behind. She smirked back at him and whispered, "Didn't I tell you, Bree? Didn't I tell you we was good together?"

That warmed him up inside. Though he couldn't help wondering if he should be worried that lying seemed to come as easily as breathing to him.

It was good they'd had the warning at the gate, because when they finally rounded the last bend and saw the town, they were stunned.

"Holy saints," Breon whispered.

A good part of the town was in ruins, nearly everything burnt or broken, the scent of woodsmoke still lingering. The keep had been largely knocked down, only its tower left standing as a jagged tooth against the mountains behind it. Was that the fortress the town was named for?

Mourning colors were draped over railings and twined with pine roping. Rosettes were tacked to some of the doors alongside Solstice greens. As Flatnose had said, several buildings were under construction.

Along the way into town, they'd passed a newly built temple, its churchyard prickled with new remembrance stones.

If a person could overlook the damage to the town, the valley was pleasant—peppered with hot springs and geysers. It was almost balmy there, compared to the high passes they'd been through.

One of the buildings that had been repaired and restored was a place called the Cold Moon Tavern. They took a chance and booked a room there, guessing that there wouldn't be many visitors, carrying tales from the capital. They had a decent meal, and Breon managed to score a small amount of low-quality leaf. Aubrey was friendlier and more cheerful than she'd been since the night of the street concert. Everything taken together, he was beginning to feel a bit more optimistic.

Until he began trying to find a ride to Chalk Cliffs.

It wasn't for lack of charm—between the two of them, Breon and Aubrey could charm the skin off a dog. The problem was that few people came through town, and none of them seemed to be going their way. Either they were staying in Fortress Rocks until spring, or they were heading back west to Fellsmarch, or they had no room.

It was good the inn was cheap, because they ended up spending two weeks there. Breon wanted to try his hand at singing in the evenings and passing a hat, but Aubrey talked him out of it.

Their luck finally changed when they met up with a clan trader at the inn. At least he was dressed like a clan trader. He was also as serious as the pox, his eyes like windows into a place you didn't want to go to. Breon thought there was something familiar about him, but the world seems to be full of people who look like other people, and fool you. Besides, Aubrey said she'd never laid eyes on him before.

The only thing that mattered was that he said he was driving a wagon all the way to Chalk Cliffs.

Traders were usually fast-talking sharpsters—always eager to make a deal—but not this one. He wanted nothing to do with them until Breon showed him some coin, and that got him interested enough to let them make their case. He finally agreed to take them, but there was a large condition attached to that.

"I'm waiting for someone," he said. "And I can't leave until she comes."

"Why? Is she riding along?"

"No." He seemed to feel no pressure to elaborate.

"When is she supposed to arrive?"

The trader shrugged. "Probably not for a few days or a week."

So there was nothing to do but wait another week, spending their coin on bed and board, using up Breon's supply of leaf again. If they ran out, it wouldn't be the end of the world. He could take it or leave it, but this was, after all, a stressful situation. Not a good time to be without.

FORTRESS ROCKS

Jenna awoke to the sound of crunching bones and ripping flesh. She pressed her hands over her ears and cursed her dragon-sharp hearing. Resisting the temptation to stay where she was, muffled up in her bedroll, she crawled forward and stuck her head out of the tent to be met by the metallic scent of raw meat.

Flamecaster looked up from a half-eaten carcass, shreds of meat hanging from his jaws, blood smeared all around his mouth. He lay in the center of a large patch of melted snow, his scales glittering in the morning sun. He looked pleased with himself.

He lifted one foreleg, as if to judge how much was left, then peered up at Jenna. *Share?*

"That depends on what it is." Jenna stood, stamping her feet in the snow to get her blood moving, rubbing her backside. She crossed to where the dragon lay just as he spit out a wad of wool.

From the looks of things, breakfast was a sheep, of the rangy, mountain kind. It had a leather tag in its ear.

"That's some farmer's livelihood, you know," Jenna said, in a halfhearted scold. Better a sheep than somebody's child.

Live-li-hood? Flamecaster looked back at the carcass. *Looks like goat.* He nudged a choice shoulder joint toward her. *For you.*

Jenna's mouth watered. After weeks traveling with a dragon, she'd developed an appetite for rare meat. That was on a fairly long list of things she didn't want to think about. Like Adam Wolf. And the glittering scales that kept coming and going on her skin. And the fact that shooting with a longbow is harder than it looks. Maybe she should try shooting flames out of her mouth.

"I don't have time to roast meat, Cas," she said, using the nickname she'd devised when "Flamecaster" seemed too formal and too awkward. She chewed on a stale chunk of waybread.

Flamecaster snorted. In his opinion, waybread did not count as food, and cooking ruined perfectly good meat. He pinned the joint of mutton with one foreleg and swept it with a gout of flame so that it was charred on the outside.

He looked up brightly. *Now ruined.* He nudged it toward her and smiled in the way only a dragon can smile, and Jenna's heart melted, as it always did.

The irresistible scent of roasted meat wafted up, and Jenna took the time to rip off a fist-sized hunk and wrap it in her waybread. "I have to go to town."

Cas's head came up, the forest of horns on his head rattling as he laid them back.

"Don't worry," Jenna said. "I'm coming back."

He cocked his head suspiciously.

Two weeks ago, in a sudden fit of conscience, she'd decided it was best to part ways with Flamecaster. She'd begun to realize that she was putting the sun dragon at risk by allowing the bond to grow between them. Those hunting her would have to kill him to get to her. She had no doubt that they would do just that.

But a dragon is not so easily dismissed. When she'd "set him free," Cas had treated it like a joke (though an embarrassingly bad one). She'd sternly sent him away, but he kept creeping back, bringing gifts of dead rabbits and chickens and shiny stones as peace offerings, begging forgiveness for whatever he'd done to deserve banishment. She'd tried to sneak away, and he'd played it like a game of hide-and-seek. The longest she managed to evade him was half a day. By the time he found her, they were both half-crazy with misery, and she spent the whole next day promising never to do that again.

"I'll see you soon," she said brightly, getting to her feet.

The dragon's head drooped, almost comically. He peered up at her with his golden eyes. *Give Jenna ride?*

Jenna shook her head. "They're not used to dragons here. If anyone sees you, it will just cause trouble. Please please please stay right here. Take a nap or something, all right?"

Go hunting in town?

Jenna spent one delicious moment imagining bringing Cas the dragon to town, and introducing him to Rogan the arrogant trader.

But no. A dragon was like a big, impressive sword that she could never hope to wield.

"No. I'm buying some . . . some glitterbits for you and me. A surprise. But only if you stay here."

That did the trick. The dragon flopped down on his belly, lifting his head enough to peer winningly through his eyelashes.

Flamecaster, she'd learned, was very fond of both glitterbits and surprises. The combination was the one reward beyond food and Jenna's company that seemed to work with him. The dragon's loyalty to her was unquestioned. The notion of obedience was very questioned.

"When I get back, we'll fly to the coast," she said. She felt the heat of his attention until she rounded a turn in the trail.

A dragon is not a dog, she kept telling herself. And he

wasn't a horse, either, and so she found herself making her way to town on foot, following a steep, icy trail out of the heights and into town.

Fortress Rocks was a strategic spot where the Firehole River roared through a deep gorge on its way to the sea. The road between Fellsmarch and Chalk Cliffs passed through here, and if a person wanted to stop an army, this would be the place. It appeared that it had once been an important military checkpoint, but now most of the man-made fortifications were in ruins.

As Jenna descended into the gorge, it became noticeably warmer. The ice disappeared, the ground grew muddy, and moss and lichen and plants she didn't recognize clothed the rocks along the trail. As she neared the bottom of the gorge, she began to catch glimpses of the river. Plumes of steam rose where water from the hot springs discharged into the colder water flowing out of the mountains. It was like a warm oasis in a frozen world.

As she got closer, she realized that there had been trouble in the oasis. Most of the main buildings were damaged and burned, with just a few left standing or restored enough for use. The whole town smelled of blood and woodsmoke. Would the leatherworker Rogan recommended still be there? Would the trader show up at all? Had it all been a cruel joke he'd played on her?

Still, she'd come all this way, so she had to follow through. *If I've come all this way and the trader isn't here,*

Jenna swore, I'm going to track him down and make a saddle and harness out of his hide.

Any oasis draws a mix of creatures, and this one was no exception. It had been days since Jenna had seen another person, but the main street here was bustling with horses and wagons and a stew of walkers—traders and teamsters, soldiers and travelers probably waiting for a break in the weather outside the bubble of the gorge. Flowers—watered by the thick mist—spilled from baskets hanging from porches.

Fortress Rocks? The name didn't fit, somehow. Jenna wondered how long she could hide here unnoticed. Probably not very long, with an impatient dragon waiting for her in the hills. If she didn't get back soon, he might come looking for her.

She'd visited some temple libraries, trying to gather more information on dragons, but there was little to be found. She could find no history of dragons living in the Seven Realms. The only references she could find mentioned Carthis. It seemed dragons were relatively common in remote areas of Carthis, preying on sheep, cattle, and people, and in general making life more miserable than it already was.

There was nothing on Dealing with Dragons or like topics.

The Cold Moon Tavern wasn't hard to find. It seemed to be the center of activity on the main street, patrons overflowing onto the porch and into the street. They were a rough lot, but that was nothing new to anyone who grew up in Delphi.

Jenna couldn't help thinking of her father's inn, the Lady of Grace, back in Delphi, her refuge and home for so many years. Was it still an inn, or had the northerners taken it over after the city fell? It didn't matter. It wouldn't be the same without her father standing behind the bar.

Inside the Cold Moon Tavern, all the tables were occupied. Jenna scanned the patrons, looking for Rogan, and didn't see him. She took another look, this time to identify trouble that might come her way. A handful of soldiers shared a table, apparently deep in their cups though it was just after midday. They wore the browns and greens of the northern army. Which was something she would have to get used to, now that she'd crossed the border.

A clan family shared another table—dressed in furs, deerskins, feathers, and fine boots, even the lýtlings. Probably traders on the road from one camp to another.

A young couple shared a table in the back. They seemed to be arguing about something, from the hand-waving that was going on. The girl was pretty and plush, but she had a stormy expression on her face. The boy had red-gold hair that glittered in the light from the hearth, and his face was fine-planed and handsome. He was so thin, though, that Jenna wondered if he had the lung fever.

Ask for me at the Cold Moon Tavern at Fortress Rocks. So Jenna squeezed in at the bar and ordered an ale.

The tavern keeper clunked a tankard on the wood in front of her and said, "You're new to town, aren't you?"

Damn. It's one of those places where they notice any newcomer.

"Just passing through," Jenna said. "I was hoping to meet up with a trader, name of Rogan."

For a moment, the bartender looked puzzled, then his confusion cleared. "Oh. You mean Shadow. He goes by Shadow Dancer here in the north."

So he has an alias, Jenna thought. That doesn't surprise me at all.

Some of that must have shown on her face, because the innkeeper added, "That's his clan name. He doesn't use it in the south."

Fine. When it came to aliases, Jenna was queen of the world. "Do you know if he's in town?"

At that, the bartender's expression turned wary. "I don't know. I'll send my boy to ask after him. Who should I say is looking for him?"

"He probably won't remember my name," Jenna said, "but it's Riley."

A spot at a table opened up while she was waiting, so Jenna sat with her back to the wall.

It wasn't long before Rogan/Shadow Dancer swept through the door. He caught her eye, but put up a finger, signaling her to wait a minute while he spoke with the couple at the next table.

"All right," he said to them. "The person I was waiting for is here now, so I'll be leaving for the coast tomorrow morning. You can come with me if you shut it and follow my rules."

The girl looked like she was going to argue, but the boy nodded quickly and said, "Done. Thank you."

Then the trader came and sat down at Jenna's table. "Welcome to Fortress Rocks," he said. "I'm called Shadow in the north."

"So I hear."

"You're here sooner than I expected."

"Does that mean that my commission isn't finished?" Jenna raised an eyebrow.

"I didn't say that."

Jenna waited, but he didn't elaborate. "So it's ready?" she pressed.

He nodded. "It is. I told you she could get it done."

"What would you have done if I didn't show up?"

"I knew you would, sooner or later."

Jenna clenched her teeth. She was peeved with the high-handed trader, but she reined herself in. She needed to do the deal and be gone.

"Could I see it, then?" she said. "I'm in a bit of a hurry."

"Of course." He stood. "Sparrow's on her way into town. She's going to meet us at the stable down the street."

Jenna followed the trader out of the inn and down the sidewalk, wondering if she was being led into some kind of a trap.

"Is this leatherworker one of your regular suppliers?" Jenna asked.

"She is getting to be," he said. "I worked with her sister for several years, and now Sparrow is stepping into her shoes."

The stable seemed to be nothing more or less than what he'd claimed it was, and just a little ramshackle.

"Wait here," Shadow said, and disappeared inside.

Jenna moved close to the window so that she could use her dragon-sharp ears to eavesdrop on the conversation.

"She's here?" It was a female voice, quite young, a little panicky. "I thought it was going to be another week."

"She made really good time," the trader said. "Let me see what you've done."

Jenna heard footsteps, and when the girl spoke again, it was from farther away. "I used the measurements you gave, but I kept thinking I was somehow getting it wrong."

"Sparrow!" Shadow said, a hint of awe in his voice—something Jenna wouldn't have expected. "This is amazing work. If I didn't know better, I would think that Aspen—"

"No," the girl said flatly. "There will never be anyone as skilled as she was."

"How are the lýtlings doing?" he asked.

"Mags still cries a lot, but the twins are beginning to

forget. They were so young when she was killed. I'm keeping them all really busy."

"So you're getting enough work? You have enough to eat?" Shadow was like a different Rogan, one with a heart.

"Too much work, the lýtlings say." The girl laughed. "Even though I'm young, everyone knows I trained with Aspen, and so many of our best craftspeople have been killed. I don't have much time for hunting, but Fern keeps us well fed."

"Good," Shadow said. They were walking again, their voices moving closer. "The buyer is outside. We shouldn't keep her waiting any longer."

Jenna moved away from the window just in time as Rogan walked out into the stable yard with a young clan girl, probably twelve or thirteen.

"I'm Sparrow," the girl said gravely.

"I'm Riley," Jenna said. "Ah . . . are you the harness-maker?"

"I am," she said. "Do not worry, I know what I am doing. I worked with my sister since I was three." Her formal use of Common told Jenna she didn't often speak it.

"That's not what I . . ." Jenna trailed off, because that was exactly what she was worried about.

"I have your order ready. Let me show you." Sparrow led Jenna toward the back of the line of stalls, to where a large box stall had been made over into a kind of shop displaying bridles, belts, bags, and other leatherwork. It smelled of leather, which brought back memories of Fletcher's Tack and Harness.

A large bundle wrapped in leather lay on the bench. Beside it lay the most exquisite saddle Jenna had ever seen. Lightweight, yet with enough structure to give her a good seat in flight, and lined with sheepswool.

"I used the dimensions you gave me, and rigged it up the way you said," Sparrow said. "Shadow said this was for a—a gryphon."

"Right," Jenna lied. "The only one in captivity. I'm with the circus."

Sparrow kept her face blank and her voice neutral, displaying no trace of skepticism, as if she received orders to trick out gryphons every day.

She unwrapped the leather bundle. "And, here—here's the rest of the rigging, the bridle, plus the jacket and skirt you ordered."

It was a short jacket, lined in sheepskin, and cured to shed water. It wasn't armor, exactly, but Jenna hoped it would turn away the cold and wind, and yet give her the freedom of movement she needed. And a split skirt, almost like chaps, that would keep her legs warm and offer them some protection. She hoped.

"I always measure twice," Sparrow said, "but you'll still want to try those on. As for the tack, I like to have a try-on, so I can make any adjustments you need before you—"

"That won't be necessary," Jenna said. "I left Griff back on the coast with the rest of the circus. You can't bring a circus through the gorge."

"Couldn't you just fly here? On the gryphon?" Shadow asked.

"Ah, no," Jenna said. "I didn't want to chance it until I got my new tack. That's why I didn't want to travel all the way here. Plus, he's on a special diet." *Just stop now*, Jenna told herself. *Don't get too fancy.*

"Then how are you going to get this lot back to the coast?" Shadow asked.

Jenna was stumped for a minute. "Well, I . . . I thought I'd hire a wagon, and—"

"It happens that I'm heading for Chalk Cliffs now," Shadow said. "Would you like to ride along? We can haul your equipment, too."

The trader was being too damned helpful. Jenna was a pretty fair liar, but she was used to lying about every-day things, not gryphons and dragons and the like. She resolved to stick to basics in the future.

"How about we'll just settle up and I'll work that out on my own?" she said. "What do I owe you?"

Sparrow looked at Shadow, and he nodded, his dark, suspicious eyes fixed on Jenna. Sparrow named her price and Jenna counted out the money.

I hope this is all worth it, Jenna thought, as she toiled back up the trail toward her camping spot, her new purchases draped across her back. I hope I'll be able to be more than a passenger when I don't have to worry so much about holding on.

When it comes to fighting back against the empress, I have a feeling we're going to need every edge we can get.

A HARD ROAD TO
THE COAST

Travels with the trader got off to a rocky start. Breon had hoped to ride in the back of the wagon with the cargo so he'd be less visible, but their driver was having none of that.

"You'll sit up here with me or get down and walk," the trader said.

"Could I at least put my rucksack in the—?"

"No."

Either he had a briar up his bunghole, or there was goods in that wagon that he didn't want them to see. It might be leaf, though leaf usually went the other way, from the coast to the midlands. Breon was keen to take a peek. But something about the trader's eyes made Breon reluctant to tangle with him.

You don't want to get off on the wrong foot, he told himself. It's hard enough to get a ride.

So Breon sat with his bag containing his jafasa between his knees. Aubrey snuggled up against him and fell immediately asleep. It was as if, when asleep, she forgot that she was mad at him. She seemed friendlier, now, than she had been. Maybe it was because they were finally on the next-to-last leg of their journey.

Breon tried to start up a conversation with the trader. "They call me Bree," he said.

The trader grunted.

"And you are—?"

"Shadow."

"Where are you from?"

"Marisa Pines Camp." It must have been plain that Breon had no idea where that was, because he added, grudgingly, "In the uplands."

"What's your cargo?"

"Trade goods."

"You planning to sell that lot in Chalk Cliffs?"

"Maybe," the trader said.

"Do you ever have trouble getting across the border?"

"No." Shadow showed his teeth in a dangersome, shark-like smile, which at least was more of an answer than he'd volunteered so far.

"We'll be looking for passage on a ship from Chalk

Cliffs to Baston Bay," Breon said, changing the subject. "Do you think it'll be a problem finding a berth this time of year?"

"I don't know," the trader said. And then maybe nosiness was catching, because he poked at the instrument case. "What is in the bag?"

Breon was in no hurry to show off the broken jafasa. Traders were usually in on the latest news, and maybe he'd heard about the murder in Southbridge and maybe he'd seen the drawing of the jafasa, and maybe he'd like to collect a reward.

Breon was prepared with a story, at least. "I'm selling the finest clan-made walking staffs," he said. "Hand-carved and magicked for strength so they'll never break, warp, or rot." He extended the walking stick he'd nicked at the market. "See? Give this a try. When you hold this in your hand, you'll know you're holding quality."

The trader made no move to take the staff. "If you paid a clan-made price for that, you were robbed," he said, snorting.

"You're wrong," Breon said, conjuring up a wounded expression. "This is the genuine article. I got it direct from a copperhead."

"Who got it direct from a Tamric sweatshop."

"Hang on." Breon began fumbling with the fasteners on his jafasa case. "If you don't fancy this one, I've got plenty more in my—"

"Never mind," the trader said, dismissing him.

With that small victory, Breon quit pressing his luck. He settled back, closed his eyes, and let the movement of the wagon lull him to sleep.

It didn't take long for him to realize that it was a stroke of luck that matched them up with the trader, since it was likely they wouldn't have made it through the eastern passes without him. He might look like a Southern Islander, but he proved he was at home in the mountains in a dozen ways. He provided clan waybread and dried venison that could keep you going on an all-day trek. He found game where it seemed like nothing could possibly survive. He could build a fire in a snowdrift, and it didn't smoke at all. He found them shelter from a storm under a tree with branches that swooped all the way to the ground.

When the snows grew too deep to plow through with the wheels, he brought out runners from a compartment under the bed of the wagon. The kind of compartment that smugglers use. The trader positioned his body so Breon couldn't see down inside while he helped attach them to the wagon so they could forge on.

It was hard to help and keep up his gimpy guise, but the trader probably assumed Breon was a slacker anyhow, so he didn't ask questions.

Until they got closer to Chalk Cliffs. Then he got real nosy. "What was your name again? Bree?"

Breon nodded.

"Where are you from? I can't place your accent."

Breon had no idea where he was from, but he wasn't going to start that conversation. "I'm from the coast, farther south. Baston Bay. Where it's a lot warmer than this."

Shadow eyed him, as if judging the weight of his purse. "If you've got some coin for passage, I know some masters and factors who might be able to help you."

"For real?" Breon said. "That'd be—"

"We have our own contacts," Aubrey said. "Our own plans. Thanks anyway."

Breon gave her a *What's up with you?* kind of look. "C'mon, now, it can't do any harm to hear what they have to say. Maybe we can get a better price."

"I'm just saying, it's a waste of time, because—"

"And if your contact an't there? What then?" Breon turned to Shadow. "I'll talk to your friends and see what's on offer. Then we'll decide."

The trader shrugged, as if he didn't care one way or the other. "Fair enough. But I have a stop to make first."

Being close to the border between Arden and the Fells, Chalk Cliffs was more like a fortress than a typical harbor town. It was surrounded by massive stone walls and perched high on the cliffs overlooking the harbor below.

The bluejackets at the gate questioned Shadow long and hard, then escorted him into the little guardhouse next to the gate for more talk. Breon kept his hat pulled low and slumped down in his seat, glad it was the trader and not him who was being questioned in the guardhouse.

Still, the siren scent of the sea was in his nose and his heart beat a little faster and the blood sang in his veins. Almost there.

Wide awake now, Aubrey took his arm. "Let's just go," she said. "We'll find us a place to stay and go down to the harbor on our own. There's a captain I know who's likely in port right now. If not now, he soon will be."

Breon stared at her. As far as he knew, Aubrey had never been to Chalk Cliffs. How would she know a captain who would be in port? Was that part of the game she had going?

"We haven't paid Shadow yet," Breon said, "and he's given us good value for what we agreed on. I an't going to stiff him."

"I don't know," Aubrey said. "I've just got this bad feeling."

And then it was too late, because the trader had emerged from the guardhouse.

"We're good," he said, climbing up into the seat again. "There's a couple of ship's captains who stay at this place I know of down by the waterfront when they're in port. We'll go there now." So there was nothing to do but ride along.

They pulled up in front of a seedy-looking tavern two streets away from the harbor front. "I'll be just a minute," he said, swinging down from the driver's seat. "I'll see if they're there." He disappeared into the dim interior.

As soon as he was gone, Aubrey slid down onto the street. "Keep watch for him coming back. I'm going to see what he's hiding in the back."

"I'm in enough trouble as is," Breon hissed.

"*You're* in trouble," Aubrey said. "I'm not."

"Look, he's done us a kindness, and that's not the way to repay it," Breon said.

"I just want a quick look. It's not like I'm planning to *steal* anything." She winked, then sidled along the side of the wagon and lifted the tarp that covered the wagon bed so she could crawl underneath.

With growing misgivings, Breon watched the door of the tavern for the trader's return. Several people came and went, but not Shadow. He could hear Aubrey rummaging around in the back of the wagon, the boards creaking under her weight.

"Blood and bones," she muttered. "Will you looka that?"

"Come on out of there," Breon hissed. "Whatever he's got, it an't worth it." That's when he heard the tavern door bang open and looked up to see Shadow striding toward the wagon.

"Aubrey!" Breon hissed. He heard her quick intake of breath, then the thud as her feet hit the cobblestones. Then her voice. "Meet me at the Gray Goose." Then she was gone.

Breon slid down off the seat and met Shadow halfway between, hoping to draw his attention away from the wagon. "Well?" he said. "Did you see anyone you know?"

Shadow's big hand settled onto Breon's shoulder. "This is your lucky day," he said, with a tight smile. "There's people in there I want you to meet." His eyes swept over the wagon. "Where'd your friend go?"

"I went to the privy behind the inn, and when I come back, she was gone. I know there was a ship's master she wanted to go see. Maybe that's where she went."

Shadow took another good look around the inn yard. "Why would she leave without telling you?"

Breon shrugged. "Why does she do most of the things she does?" he said, making it clear he wasn't her nanny. "Anyway, I think she's mad at me."

"Well, let's go on in and see what we can find out," the trader said, scooping up the bag with Breon's instrument and handing it to him. "You don't want anybody running off with this while we're inside," the trader said, by way of explanation. "There's a lot of slide-handers around here."

By now, alarm bells were ringing inside Bree's head. It didn't help that Shadow kept one hand on Breon's shoulder all the way to the inn door.

"You know what?" Breon said. "I think I need to go back to the privy. I'll meet you inside." He tried unsuccessfully to pull free.

Shadow's hand tightened on his shoulder. "You can

shortcut it straight through the inn," he said, hauling open the door and pushing him inside so he all but fell on his face.

Breon knew he was in trouble when a pair of ham-like hands grabbed him and slammed him up against the wall. They patted him down, none too gently, searching for weapons, ignoring his protests. They took away the little shiv he kept for emergencies, and his pouch of leaf.

Turning his head, he saw that there was just the three of them in the room—Shadow, Breon, and a bluejacket the size of a large tree. He took a second look, and was astonished to see that it was a girlie.

She was familiar, somehow, like maybe she'd slammed him up against a wall before.

"He's got to be the one," the Tree said. "He looks familiar, and he fits the description." She pulled a folded paper from her pocket. It was a smaller version of the posters Breon had seen.

They both looked from the drawing to Breon and back again while Breon tried to look as little like the picture as he could, which wasn't hard, since it wasn't even a good likeness.

"Where's that instrument you said he had with him?"

Shadow set Breon's bag on the table and unfastened the catches. He lifted out the splintered jafasa and held it up for the other one to see. Even though it was broken, it matched the drawing just fine.

"Be careful with that," Breon said. "I got that from my father."

"Well, looks to me like *you* didn't take very good care of it," the bluejacket said.

Breon thought of telling her he wasn't the one that broke it, but guessed it wouldn't do him any good.

She went right back to searching him, taking her time on this round. Shadow seemed to be studying the broken jafasa, as if trying to figure out how to work it.

"Give it here, and I'll show you how to play it," Breon said, figuring it couldn't hurt to ask.

Shadow just snorted and went on with his examination.

It was then that the Tree found Breon's shine—Her Highness's locket and the pendant he'd got from his father.

Uttering an oath that any tannery-hand would be proud of, she ripped them off over Breon's head. She thrust the locket into his face.

"Explain that, you goat-strumming lowlife."

That's what he got for trying to hold on to anything.

"I bought it off a picaroon in the capital," Breon lied. "He was starving, so I did him a favor. He said it was his grandmother's."

"So—you admit you were recently in the capital?"

"Ask your friend Shadow. He's the one gave me a ride along the road."

Now the Tree dangled Breon's pendant in front of

him. "Who'd you steal this from?"

"I didn't steal it. It belonged to my father, too."

The Tree eyed it suspiciously. "It looks like it's broken. Where's the rest of it?"

"It's always been like that, far as I know," Breon said.

"What does it do? Is it a compass or what?"

"I don't know what it does. It's never done anything for me but lend me a little extra shine."

Words surfaced in his head, like bodies on the water.

Keep this with you and you can always find your way home.

Breon, hoping she'd give it back, stuck out his hand, but she tucked it away in her pocket.

She kept on patting him down, and eventually she discovered the magemark on the back of his neck. "What the bloody hell is this?" First she poked at it, and when nothing happened she began prying at it, trying to pull it loose. Finally, she pulled out her shiv and tried to slide it underneath until Breon could feel blood running down under his shirt.

"Blood and bones!" he said, trying to twist away. "It don't come off. I should know, I've had it all my life. It would've been sold off by now if it did."

"It might be some kind of flashcraft," Shadow said, getting his own poke in. "What is this blue stone? Is this a sapphire? Aquamarine?"

I wouldn't know a sapphire from a hunk of glass, Breon thought. "I don't know. I've never even seen it."

"Is this platinum?" Shadow tapped the metal framing with his finger.

"I don't know," Breon said. "If it was anything valuable, somebody would've slit my throat for it by now."

The trader closed his hand over it, as if trying to read it through his fingers. At least *he* didn't try to rip it off. "What does it do?" he asked Breon.

"Nothing, far as I know," Breon said, though he'd always wondered if it had something to do with his vast personal charm and extraordinary talent.

"Maybe it's some kind of a permanent amulet?" Shadow sat back on his heels.

"You think he's a wizard?" The bluejacket backed off a little, then tried to pretend she hadn't.

"Damn right I am," Breon said. "You'd better be nice to me or I'll turn you both into carbuncles on a pig's ass."

That earned Breon a punch in the nose. Shadow had to step in to prevent the bluejacket from going on with smashing his head into the oak bar.

"Talbot!" Shadow grabbed the bluejacket's arm. "I know that you're angry about Lyss. Which is all the more reason we need him alive and well enough for questioning. He hasn't been convicted of anything. Yet." His expression said that it was just a matter of time.

For a mixed-blood smuggler, Shadow seemed very tight with this bluejacket. In no time, they had his hands shackled together and his ankles, too.

"I'll send a bird to Fellsmarch and find out what Captain Byrne wants done with him," Talbot the Tree growled. "Maybe they'll send a wizard to check out his tattoo or brooch or whatever it is. In the meantime, we'll keep him nice and cozy in the guardhouse." Her glare said that it wouldn't be all that cozy, and not nice, either, if she had anything to do with it.

"I think it's best if we keep this quiet until they come from the capital to claim him," Shadow said. "Whoever hired him won't want him talking to us. If they hear that we've got him, they'll try to either kill him or spring him. Let's take him over to the lockup now and get him out of sight. I have some business to handle tonight, but I'll ask him a few questions tomorrow before I leave for the down realms.

"His partner might come here looking for him," Shadow added. "She's Ardenine, brown hair, broken nose, about fifteen, sixteen years old, and her name is Aubrey." He did that thing with his hands that people do to depict a curvy woman. "Tell your guards to be on the lookout for her. We'll want to question her, too."

"What made you suspect him?" Talbot asked Shadow as she hauled Breon to his feet, nearly wrenching his arm out of its socket.

"I was curious about his bag," Shadow said. "He didn't seem to want anybody else to touch it, and I wondered why he was so jumpy. So I took a look the first night."

So Rogan swiving Shadow Dancer's known all along, Breon thought. And here I was sticking up for him. I hope Aubrey robbed him blind.

Sorry, Aubrey, he thought. I won't be meeting you at the Gray Goose anytime soon.

CLASH OF SWORDS

In the days that followed the liberation of Delphi, Lyss kept having to remind herself that they were the ones who had won. Sometimes she felt like the victim of a cruel joke. She'd never realized that the end of any battle is just a prelude to more politics.

Her mother had sent warm congratulations. She ordered that Delphi be welcomed as an ally, and ruled with a light hand. The plan was to put the territory under martial law until it could be transitioned to self-rule. Then, in a nasty move, she named Lyss to represent the queendom in the negotiations.

I want you to own this, and not because I want you to get the blame if it goes wrong. I want you to know how it

*feels to make a decision and live with the consequences, good
or bad.*

In other words, every victory has its price. When you
win, you have to quit fighting, and rule.

So here she was, sitting in meeting after dreary meeting, discussing coal production targets, road building, food
distribution, and medical services. She might as well be at
home. At least there, she knew where the broken stones
were in the castle wall. At home, if someone stabbed her in
the back, she at least might have a guess who it was.

Dealing with the Delphians was like herding angry
cats. As long as Arden held the city in its iron grip, that
common enemy united the people. Now that the occupiers were gone, the realm seemed destined to descend into
internecine squabbling. Old disputes rose up like fester-
ing boils on the civic skin. The population had a massive
grudge against Arden, its blackbird guard, and its mudback
army, with some left over for anyone perceived to have
cooperated with them.

The former mayor was found dead in an alley, his throat
cut, his body wrapped in an Ardenine flag. The mine
supervisor was found buried under several tons of coal. It
got to the point that Delphian collaborators begged to be
taken into custody for their own protection, but the city
jails were already bulging. That required attention, too—
sorting out who should stay and who should be released.

To Lyss's surprise, Julianna was a major help. She seemed to thrive on all the jobs that Lyss detested. She remembered every name, and she managed mind-numbing details with cool efficiency, pushing people until they discovered common ground. Her natural charm seemed to grease every wheel that squeaked.

Lyss missed Sasha. Sparring with her might work off some tension. At least she'd listen to her complaints without trying to fix them. But first Sasha, and later, Finn had been dispatched on to Chalk Cliffs to join the garrison there in case Arden tried to bring reinforcements in by sea, as they had before. So these days Lyss had to wear herself out with long patrols, slogging through deep snow, and sparring matches with less challenging opponents.

When I am queen, she thought, I'll keep my friends close, and my enemies closer.

She caught her breath. *When I am queen?* When had she started thinking of that as something she might actually look forward to?

One clear, cold morning, Lyss and a triple of Gray Wolves rode up to the army headquarters. It was in a manor house north of town, now occupied by the Fellsian Highlanders. The survivors of the Ardenine army were being held up there, both because it offered the only guardhouse large enough to hold them, and to protect them from the angry population. General Dunedain's staff and Julianna's eyes and ears had been debriefing the Ardenine prisoners, gathering what intelligence they could about troop strength and weaponry. Lyss often sat in.

Maybe I can't ride into Arden and kill King Gerard, but I can find out as much about the enemy as possible, she thought. With the added bonus that it got her out of the city and its endless meetings.

When they reached the stable yard, Lyss handed off her pony and strode toward the manor house. Before she reached it, she was distracted by the clatter of sword on sword and the shouts of onlookers. Following the noise, she came upon Halston Matelon and a Highlander, going at it with heavy wooden longswords. A mixed crowd of soldiers stood watching, the mudbacks cheering on their commander, and the Highlanders shouting encouragement to their own man.

Despite the cold weather, they were both steaming in the cold air and breathing hard, so they'd been at it for a while. There was an intensity to the bout that said it was more than a casual match. Matelon's raven-wing hair was plastered to his forehead and sweat ran down his face and under his uniform collar.

Just then the Highlander turned, and Lyss saw his face. Blood and bones, she thought. It's Bosley. Clearly, Matelon had found a way to get under the young officer's admittedly thin skin.

"That's it," Matelon was saying, like a teacher to a pupil. "Don't fix on what I'm doing now, think about what I'm going to do, and keep moving to counter. That way you—"

"Shut the hell up! I'm here to school you, not the other way around. I don't need some slime-bellied mudback to tell me how to use a sword."

What's this all about, anyway? Why are these two sparring with each other? Lyss edged forward for a better view. When the Highlanders saw who it was, they hastily stepped aside to let her through.

Bosley tried a quick jab inside Matelon's reach. Matelon leapt backward and even Lyss could tell the tip was inches short, but Bosley crowed, "Hit!"

The mudbacks exploded into shouts and catcalls, but Matelon just shrugged. "All right. If you say so."

Bosley thrust his chin forward. "Are you questioning my call?"

If he's not, I am, Lyss thought.

"I would never insult a man by questioning his call," Matelon said. He resumed his ready stance. "Shall we?"

This time, Matelon's sword was everywhere, cutting and thrusting, a blur of motion. He called out three hits in as many minutes in a flat, almost bored voice.

The Ardenine was damned good. It made Lyss wonder if he'd been holding back before.

"That wasn't a hit," Bosley said, after the third was called. "That was a miss." A low rumble of disapproval rolled through the southerners.

Matelon raised an eyebrow. "I see," he said, eyes

narrowed, spots of temper blooming on his cheeks. "I stand corrected."

Lyss scowled in disgust. She wanted to root for her own man, but Bosley was making it difficult.

The next time Bosley tried for a hit, Matelon countered with a fierce blow, and the Highlander's sword went flying.

Bosley retrieved his weapon and tried again, with the same result. "Bloody bones!" Bosley swore, when it happened a third time. "That's not proper swordsmanship. Are you a mind reader or what?"

Matelon picked up the fallen sword and handed it back to Bosley. "I'm no mind reader," he said. "But you signal what you're going to do before you do it, every single time."

"I do not!" Bosley said, sticking out his chin.

Yes, you do, Lyss thought, embarrassed at Bosley's bad showing and poor sportsmanship.

"Very well, Lieutenant," Matelon said. "You are correct. I *can* see inside your head, and likely so can all of your opponents. Perhaps you should talk the copperheads into making you a magical helmet."

The mudbacks doubled up laughing and the lieutenant's face went purple with rage. Bosley charged forward, swinging the flat of his blade at Matelon's head. The southerner sidestepped nimbly but stuck out his foot, and this time it was Bosley himself who went flying, skidding some distance through the snow on his face until he came up against the stable wall.

Bosley rose onto his knees. "Pin his arms!" he growled, reaching for his sword.

Lyss planted her boot on it. "Stand down, Lieutenant," she said. "You're done here."

Bosley looked up, his face contorted into a snarl that drained away in an almost comical fashion when he saw who was standing over him.

"Captain! I didn't realize that you were here."

"Obviously," Lyss said.

Bosley scrambled to his feet, leaving his practice blade in the snow, and got off a combined bow and salute. His lieutenant's scarf was layered in slush and his face scraped and reddened by his face-first slide.

"Does Captain Barnes know that you are sparring with Captain Matelon?"

"He doesn't *specifically* know it," Bosley said.

"Meaning he doesn't know it at all?"

"We—Matelon and I—we were just giving the troops a skills demonstration," Bosley said, shooting a warning look at Matelon as if daring him to disagree. The Ardenine tightened his jaw and said nothing, but his body was as taut as a drawn bowstring.

"Indeed you were, Bosley, but I don't know what exactly it was you were trying to demonstrate," Lyss said. "Were you aware that Captain Matelon is the son of an

Ardenine thane and a prisoner of war? Had you considered the strategic cost to us if he were to be injured or killed?"

Bosley stared at her for a long moment, as if considering and discarding several possible responses. Finally, he gathered his wits and said, "That's why I held back, Your Highness, so as not to hurt him. Had I known that the captain was such a fragile bit of crockery, I would have found a sturdier opponent."

Too late, Lyss realized that she'd handed the lieutenant a weapon and an excuse. When she looked into Matelon's gray-green eyes, she was reminded of the expression "if looks could kill."

Unable to undo the damage or conjure up a suitable reply, she said, "You are dismissed, Bosley."

He bowed again, with more grace this time, collected both swords, and strutted off like the cock of the walk, leaving Lyss, her guard, Captain Matelon, and a dozen gawking soldiers.

"The rest of you as well. Go on." She waved the audience away.

Matelon bowed curtly. "By your leave, Captain," and went to turn away.

"I didn't mean you, Matelon," she said. When he turned back, his face stony, she added, "I want to hear what you have to say."

"About?" He cocked his head.

"I want to hear your side of the story."

Matelon dabbed at a cut on his chin that he had acquired along the way. "I have no 'side.' Lieutenant Bosley told you what happened. It would be inappropriate for me to comment." It was like he chewed on each word before he spit it out.

"I apologize for Bosley's behavior," Lyss said.

Matelon shifted his weight from foot to foot, obviously eager to be on his way. "Forgive me, ma'am, but if you think Bosley's behavior was improper, you should be speaking to him and not to me."

With that, Lyss's temper snapped. "Follow me, Captain, and that is an order." Turning to her Wolves, she said, "Drag him if he doesn't come on his own." Lyss stalked toward the manor house without looking to see if he was behind her. Eventually, she heard his boots crunching through the snow, following after.

CLASH OF WORDS

Hal, his heart sinking like a stone, followed after Captain Gray. He should have better managed his temper, but it wasn't easy. Idleness drove him mad. He was not a happy captive.

It didn't make much sense for Gray to be leading the way, since Hal knew the garrison headquarters a lot better than she did—he'd lived there for nearly a year.

If she'd just tell him where she wanted to go, he could get them there. But as it was, he followed after her like an obedient dog going to be put down.

As they walked, Hal ran his eyes over the damage done to his former headquarters. He'd been so proud of the improvements he'd made since his arrival in Delphi. Now his palisade was a charred ruin, which demonstrated the power of wizard's flame against walls of wood.

The northerners were rebuilding with stone. There was plenty of that around.

Stone next time, he thought. He couldn't help himself, couldn't believe that there wouldn't be a next time. He'd never been good at losing.

Now he'd made things worse by drawing Gray's attention again. She'd made it plain the day they'd met that she bore a giant grudge against Arden. He didn't want her to be taking an interest in him. His duty as a prisoner of war was to protect his men and escape if he could.

She'd saved his life—twice now. Why? His biggest worry was that she intended to use him in a way that would dishonor his family name. Would the northern witches fashion him into a weapon that could be wielded against his homeland? The thought made his skin crawl.

I'll kill myself before I betray my command, he told himself. The church frowned on suicide, but Hal had never been all that well churched, anyway. A church that burned people to save their souls would surely understand the difficult choice before him.

After the brilliant, brittle cold of the grounds, the interior of the mansion seemed oppressive, the air too thick with heat and magic to breathe. Gray shed clothes as she walked—her gloves, hat, scarf, and, finally, her thick outer coat, draping it over her arm. Water dripped onto the stone floor as the frozen bits layering her coat melted.

Underneath, she wore copperhead-style clothing—leather trousers that fit her long legs closely and a loose overshirt of embroidered wool. Hal liked the way she walked, with long strides so a man didn't have to mince along in her wake.

He'd thought maybe they would go to the great hall, where the northerners had established their military command. She did pause briefly and speak to the soldiers standing guard at the entrance, but then she walked on past, into a corridor that led toward the back of the house. Her usual small escort followed along behind. Hal glanced back at them, feeling more comforted than dismayed by their presence.

That's when Hal realized that they were heading for the library, where he'd spent a lot of time during his residence here. He'd done considerable reading, trying to learn more about mining and iron-making so he wouldn't have to rely on the corrupt officials in charge of production to make good decisions.

Even if the job you're assigned is not to your liking, a Matelon will see it done. His father had drilled that into him from a young age.

The library was deserted; the only light was what leaked in around the heavy shutters. Gray walked around the room, throwing the shutters open to spill in light and fresh air.

Hal stood ramrod straight in the middle of the room, fists clenched. *Why did you bring me here?* he thought. Though he'd had a taste of ruthless politics at the Ardenine court, he was, like his father, a soldier at heart.

When the captain had the room lit to her liking, she waved her guard to the other side of the room and gestured to a pair of chairs under the window.

"Sit, Captain," she said.

"If you don't mind, ma'am, I prefer to—"

"I intend to sit, and I won't have you standing over me." She claimed the chair closest to the window, so that the light poured over her. Closing her eyes, she basked in the sunlight like a cat. Without opening her eyes, she said, "Your gutter-swiving king has taught me to dread the dark days of midwinter."

What does she mean? We never march north in midwinter.

Also, Hal couldn't remember ever hearing a lady use the term "gutter-swiving."

He sat in the other chair, taking advantage of the opportunity to take another good look at her. Her fawn-colored hair was sun-streaked from long days spent outdoors. Now it was done up copperhead style, the multiple braids decorated with beads and feathers. One braid per kill—wasn't that the rule?

Hal couldn't help himself. He began to count.

Right then, the princess opened her eyes to catch him leaning forward from the edge of his chair, looking at her.

He reared back in his chair and shifted his eyes away.

Saints and martyrs, he thought.

"Would you like something to drink, Captain?" Gray said. "You must be thirsty after your bout."

Hal knew better than to accept that kind of offer.

"I prefer to drink from the common well, Captain," he said. "I've advised my men to do the same."

Gray looked perplexed for a moment, then apparently worked it out, because she scowled.

Damn! He should have just said he wasn't thirsty. He wasn't here to yank anyone's tail, not if he hoped to survive.

"Do you really think we would feed and house you for a week, and *then* poison you? That would be damned inefficient."

Hal didn't look at her—he was worried he might reveal too much if he met her gaze. "Perhaps not a potion to kill, but one to . . . to turn us into something we're not."

"You mean . . . like a toad or—or—a billy goat?" Her lips twitched, as if it was all she could do not to burst out laughing. "I know! A flock of chickens. We could use some fresh eggs around here."

Hal stared at her. Did she really not understand what he was talking about? "We've heard stories of spells and potions that steal a man's courage or his strength. That cause him to turn against his fellow soldiers and kill them. That give him such a massive case of the itches that—"

"Believe me, Captain, if I had that power, I would have

sent you all home with the itches a long time ago," Gray said, wiping at her eyes.

With that, she made one of her abrupt turns. "Now, tell me about you and Bosley." She tilted her head back and looked down her nose at him.

Hal sighed. He had no desire to entangle himself in this. He'd overheard Bosley bragging to his fellow soldiers that he and Gray were lovers. Bosley had described a series of recent trysts with her in embarrassingly graphic detail. Maybe customs were different here in the north, but it seemed crude and dishonorable to share that.

He couldn't fathom what Gray saw in Bosley, but it was none of his business, after all.

Then why did he spend so much time thinking about it?

"Captain?" Gray said, bringing him out of the bed-chamber and back to the library.

Hal cleared his throat. "I'd organized some tourna-ments for my men, to keep them occupied and to give them something to look forward to," he said. "It started with practice swords and quarterstaves, but later we added footraces and wrestling, stone slinging—whatever they wanted to do with what we had available." He wiped his damp palms on his breeches. "I put up a standings board, and passed out ribbons to the winners.

"The first day, it was just a handful, but the next day more turned out, and then still more. Soon they were orga-nizing events on their own, and coming up with prizes that they—" Hal stopped, took a breath. He was proud of what he'd done, but that didn't mean Gray was interested.

Yet she nodded thoughtfully. "So you improved both the morale and the physical conditioning of your soldiers," she said. "Smart."

"Then, one day, during the games, some Highlanders approached and asked if I could include them in our bouts. I wasn't keen on the idea, but they persisted, saying that they . . . ah . . . could use more training than they were getting. As it turned out, they were in Bosley's command." He looked up at Gray. "Don't get me wrong, ma'am, I'm not criticizing anyone, I just—"

"Stipulated," she said, sitting back and resting her hands, palms up, on the arms of her chair. He couldn't help noticing how callused her hands were from the use of weapons. He'd never met a highborn woman with hands like that. He wondered what it would be like to have a go in the practice yard with—

"I said *stipulated*, Captain. Do go on."

He looked up, blinking, then realized that he'd been staring. "So Bosley's soldiers began participating in some of the tournaments. Having a larger group was good, because I could switch off the matchups and—"

"It seems you have no problem sleeping with the enemy."

Hal's face heated, his mouth went dry, and he shifted in his chair. "Ma'am?" he said hoarsely.

"You *know* what I mean. What would your father say if he saw you training Fellsian soldiers?"

She'd chosen those words on purpose. She was toying with him. Hal tried to control his temper. "My father would approve of my learning more about Fellsian training methods and military practices. He would be glad I wasn't sitting on my ass, getting soft. To summarize, ma'am, my father would have no problem with it, but Lieutenant Bosley apparently did."

"What makes you think that?"

Damn again! He'd meant to keep his report totally neutral. If Bosley was sleeping with his commanding officer, the last thing Hal wanted was to get caught in *that* cross fire.

Too late. He was too far in to take it back, but maybe he could regain some ground. "Somehow, the lieutenant got word of what was going on. So he came to the session this morning and suggested that the two of us have a go to . . . ah . . . demonstrate proper form."

"Hmm." She worried at one of her nails with her teeth. "Why do you think that Lieutenant Bosley disapproved of your sessions with his soldiers?"

Hal hesitated. "Maybe you should ask the—"

"I'm asking you."

Hal tried to think of a way to put a more positive face on it. "I guess he thought I was interfering with his way of doing things or poking in where I had no business."

"Did you readily agree to the . . . demonstration?"

"Ma'am?"

"Did Bosley give you a choice?"

Sweat trickled between Hal's shoulder blades. Captain Gray had a way of cutting all the way to the bone.

"You can tell the truth, Captain," she said softly, looking straight into his eyes. "This is between us."

And, somehow, he found himself saying, "I didn't think it was a good idea for us to have a go. I told him I wouldn't include his soldiers anymore if he didn't like it. I tried to get out of it, but the lieutenant was . . . He insisted."

"He wanted to show you up?"

"You should ask—" When Gray scowled at him, he gave in. "I suspect so, ma'am. If I was a smarter man, I would have found a way to lose to him." He paused. "I don't like losing."

"Me neither, Captain. But you'd better get used to it."

"Ma'am?"

"I'm going to drive your armies into the sea." It was as if they'd been sparring, and then all of a sudden she went for the throat.

"Why? Because you have more magic on your side?" he said, drawn in despite his determination not to be. "If I had my way, it would be a fair fight, men against men, with no . . ." He mimicked a spellcasting gesture.

"Men against men? Oh. Right. I keep forgetting. You don't have women in your army."

Hal couldn't seem to open his mouth without hitting a nerve. He darted a look at her. "No. We don't, ma'am." He tried to think of something to add, to explain it. "Our women are not like you. They are not well suited for battle."

"You might find out that they are more capable than you know."

"I'm not saying that women are incapable, I am saying that they are capable of . . . different things."

Captain Gray snorted. "It's no wonder you're losing."

Hal could feel the hot blood rising in him. She seemed to know just where to poke him. "We lost a battle, because we were outplayed. Not the war. Your soldiers, both the copperheads—"

"Clans," she corrected.

"—both the clans and the Highlanders fight hard, and they are some of the bravest soldiers I've ever met. No bit of ground is easily won. But face the facts. You are starving up here. At first, I thought my men were being given lean prisoner rations. Then I realized they were getting the same as your own soldiers."

"We've managed," she said. "Maybe it isn't fancy, but—"

"You cannot grow enough food to support yourselves, and now that we've deployed a navy you won't be able to bring in foodstuffs by sea. We draw troops from every part of the empire—"

"Troops that really don't care whether you win or lose.

Troops that just want to survive the war and go home. Many of whom are unwilling conscripts. Is that why your own mages tried to kill you? Would *you* like to go to war with a flashcraft collar around your neck?"

It's a little more complicated than that, Hal thought. But he wasn't going to tell this northern captain that his own king was gunning for him.

"And yet we've won control of the entire continent, except for a few outliers," he said. "Our granaries are bulging, and we control the sources of iron, and steel, and gunpowder. What do you intend to fight with?"

"We recently acquired some new coal mines and iron furnaces," she countered. "Were you aware of that, Captain?"

"Aye. You did. But you won't hold them for long. You are surrounded by enemies, and you can only live on courage for so long. You are going to lose, Captain. Time—and everything else—is on our side. Best to plan for it."

Now she rose, and paced back and forth, punctuating her speech by slamming her fist into her other palm. "What would you have us do, Captain? Bend the knee after twenty-five years of war? Watch them slaughter the Spirit Clans and burn and collar our wizards? Turn our rivers into cesspools and build a Delphi in the middle of the Vale?" She swiveled, her braids flying, and came and glared down at him.

He tried to think of something encouraging to say.

"Ma'am. We are soldiers, you and I. There is always a need for soldiers. It might be that our lives wouldn't change much, no matter who sits on the throne." Even as he said it, he didn't believe it.

Her expression said that he was impossibly naive. "I am not a soldier in the eyes of your king, your church, and your commanders. Do you really think my life wouldn't change if Arden wins this war? What do you suppose would happen to our queen and our princess heir? You've been demonizing them for years, calling them witches and whores and sorceresses and accusing them of all manner of foul deeds. Is there any way your war-weary people and your bloodthirsty church would allow them to live?"

She really cares about them, Hal thought. She loves her queen—that's plain to see. This is not just a job for her. Hal had always been a loyal soldier, but his relationship with King Gerard had nothing to do with love. It was duty. He'd never bought the church's argument that his king was anointed by the gods.

Hal groped for a reply. How had they moved on to politics and religion, topics he was never comfortable with?

In truth, he had no idea what would happen to the Fellsian royals, but he wasn't optimistic, based on past experience. He had a duty to try to encourage the northerners to surrender, but he couldn't bring himself to make any assurances about their safety.

"The church doesn't speak for everyone in Arden,"

Hal said, which was about as positive as he could make it. "After the war, King Gerard will want to pacify the northern realms as quickly as possible. The thanes—my father included—are weary of war as well, and more and more reluctant to contribute money and men to the cause."

Captain Gray was nodding encouragingly. Hal stopped abruptly, realizing that he'd been ensnared into revealing too much.

The northerners didn't need to know how much pressure there had been in the south for an end to the war. But it was so hard to remember that she was his enemy, and not just a brave girl—a soldier—faced with an impossible choice.

"So. Anyway. It might be that an advantageous marriage could be arranged that would bring the kingdom of the Fells into the fold."

From the look on her face, he might have just asked her to bite into a turd.

"*Queendom*, Captain," she spat. "This is a queendom. Your king made that offer to our queen more than twenty-five years ago. She refused him then, and he invaded, launching this war. Since then, Arden has murdered her husband, and her daughter, and"—she stumbled a bit—"and tried to kill her son."

"This is war," Hal said. "People die—even innocents die, unfortunately." It sounded weak, even to him, even though it was true.

"I'm not talking about killing enemy soldiers in battle," Gray said. "I'm not even talking about civilians caught in the cross fire. I'm talking about Ardenine assassins sneaking into our cities and ambushing us on the street and in our beds."

Hal had no idea what she was talking about, though it wouldn't surprise him to find out that King Gerard had employed that kind of tactic abroad as well as at home. This was the king who had won the throne by killing off his older brothers. This was the king who had sent Hal and his battalion of younglings on a suicide mission.

Hal had signed on as a soldier, but he'd never signed on for the job of defending Gerard Montaigne. He found himself stumbling badly.

"I don't know what you—are you sure that they were attacked by agents of Arden? Isn't it possible that—?"

"When Princess Hanalea was murdered, your king sent her head to her mother in a golden casket with a note, in case she didn't give credit where credit was due," Gray said. "This campaign of assassination has been going on for more than four years." She fixed him with a pair of brown eyes hard as agates. "Frankly, Captain, I'd rather die than marry any son of Arden."

29

INN LOCKUP

They took Breon's jafasa, and his leaf, and his shepherd's clothes, and put him in mud-colored breeches and a shirt. They left his hands and feet loosely shackled so he could shuffle all around his little cell. They even brought him some books about ships when he asked for them. Encouraged, he asked for wood, and tools for carving, but they didn't go for it.

If he was going to survive this latest setback, if he was going to charm his way out of this, he was going to need an instrument to channel through. His voice wouldn't be enough to put a dent in these hard-hearted captors. And, so far, he'd not been able to pinch anything from them that he could use to link to their music.

To be fair, the lockup at Chalk Cliffs keep wasn't bad, as lockups go. Not that Breon'd had a wide experience, being mostly law-abiding, but he'd been in gaol in Arden and Bruinswallow and Tamron—well, twice in Tamron—and this was top-shelf in comparison. For one thing, it wasn't underground, it was in a tower, and he could hear the sea through his tiny, barred window. The wind off the Indio was cold, but he didn't close his shutters, because he wanted to smell and hear the sea during what might be his last days.

Even the food was decent, that first night—fish stew and bread to sop it up and a leftover Solstice cake. Breon ate it all, not knowing what plans they had for him, aware that this might be his last meal. Also because he was starving. Also because he had a special fondness for cake.

They seemed to be having trouble rounding up important people to talk to him—ones that could be trusted, anyway. Maybe they were all at some blueblood meeting. Still, he had a steady stream of visitors. First came a whole posse of bluejackets to empty his chamber pot, during which they eyed him like he might jump them at any moment.

How many bluejackets does it take to empty a chamber pot? he wanted to ask, but thought better of it.

A copperhead healer arrived with her own escort of bluejackets to treat his black eye and bruised cheekbone. Breon asked if she'd ever thought of trying razorleaf to relieve pain and she said no.

Finally, Rogan "the Rat" Shadow Dancer barged in with his bluejacket mate, Talbot the Tree, and a handsome young mage with striking silver hair, icy blue eyes, and a distinctive glow of magic.

Breon eyed the new mage nervously. Why was he here?

Breon happened to be sitting cross-legged on what passed for a bed, trying to fashion a whistle out of a piece of cork with the tip of a spoon.

"What are you doing?" the trader demanded.

"Just passing the time," Breon said, like any dolt who might occupy his time by whittling a cork.

"Give it here," Shadow said, sticking out his hand. Breon handed it over, and Shadow put it into his pocket.

Breon rolled his eyes. "Leave a man with a cork and he might poke you with it."

Talbot rested her hand on the hilt of her sword. "Poke me, and I'll poke you back, you scaly, scum-sucking sneaksby."

Breon cocked his head, nodded grudgingly. "Impressive."

She scowled. "What?"

"Your use of alliteration. Can you say that again? That scum-sucking thing?"

"What in the bloody hell—?"

"No, no, no," Breon said, shaking his head. "I'm looking for S-words." Opening his journal, he pretended to scan down a list. "I've got 'slug-strumming strammel' and 'spoony sap-sculled simpleton.'" He looked up brightly. "Which do you prefer?"

Talbot lunged at him, but somehow Shadow got between them before she landed a blow. He gave her a talking-to in a low voice, probably saying, *Don't break it before we squeeze it dry.*

Breon couldn't say why he kept provoking her. He was like a lýtling who set things on fire just to watch them burn.

Talbot finally settled herself. Still, she gripped the front of Breon's shirt and pulled him to his feet so they were eye-to-eye and nose-to-nose. "I don't like you," she growled.

"I like you," he said, which might have been a bit of a stretch. Then again . . .

"Let me be clear with you, flatlander," Shadow said, in a voice as cold as the northern sea. "For years, your kind has been slithering into my homeland and murdering the people I care about. It's one thing to meet enemies on the battlefield. It's another to attack them on the streets or in their beds, to lure them with a pretty face and bewitching music. So. Before this night is over, I will know everything you know about who hired you to lure the princess heir into an ambush. How quickly you tell me will determine your condition by the time we finish."

Shadow hadn't been all that personable on the road, but now he'd shed whatever vestige of charm he'd shown before.

He's lost someone in the war, some particular person,

Breon thought. And you're the handy target who's going to end up dead if you can't keep your smart mouth shut. But it was hard to open his mouth and answer questions and keep the wrong thing from leaking out.

Talbot pushed Breon down into a chair and darbied his hands to the arms.

Breon was used to working an audience, and he was beginning to realize that being a smart-ass wasn't the right play here. He was beginning to realize that this might be his most important performance ever.

"I'll tell you what I know," he said. "I've got nothing to hide, and nobody to protect. But what happens if I'm telling the truth and you think I'm lying?"

"That won't happen," the new mage said, gazing at Breon like he was a nasty problem that needed solving. "I'll use persuasion to make sure of it."

Cold sweat trickled between Breon's shoulder blades. What did he mean by *persuasion*? Magic? Torture? Hypnosis? Could this mage really make him tell the truth? How much of the truth would he have to tell? Somehow the truth always made him look bad. Sometimes a bit of a spin helped to—

"I don't believe we've met," he said to the mage.

"I'm Finn sul'Mander," the mage said. "What's your name, busker?"

"It's Breon, but I sometimes go by Bree."

"Breon what?" Talbot sat forward, feet planted, like she was ready to pounce when Breon slipped up.

"Breon d'Tarvos," Breon said.

"Does that mean you're from Tarvos?" Shadow asked.

Breon knew it wouldn't play well to tell them he had no idea where he was from. So he said, "Yes. I mean, I assume so. Hence the name."

"Where is Tarvos?" Shadow said.

Bloody bones. Who knew there'd be a geography question?

"It's on the seashore," he said. "A harbor. I don't remember much about it."

Warm brown sandstone. A sea so blue it hurt the eyes. Brilliant sunshine and cool shadow.

"Let me see this magemark I've been hearing about," sul'Mander said, scooting his stool closer.

Breon leaned forward, the image of cooperation. The mage ran his fingers over the magemark, but at least he didn't try to pry it off the way Talbot had done. "What do you know about this?" sul'Mander said, tapping at it with his finger. "Did somebody fasten this onto you?"

"It's a birthmark, far as I know," Breon said. "I've had it as long as I can remember. I know that it's fancier than most."

"Is anyone else in your family marked like this?"

"I don't know. I seem to be—I assume I'm an orphan. The first memories I have are running the streets in Baston Bay, trying to stay alive."

"Have you ever met anyone else with this mark?" the mage persisted. "In Arden or elsewhere?"

"Not that I know of. I mean, people don't usually go around showing off their necks."

"Could it be some kind of built-in amulet?"

"I don't know," Breon said. "No matter how many times you ask me, it's the truth."

Now Breon felt a burning sensation, as if sul'Mander were heating the metal, and he tried to shift away. "Ow!" he said finally. "Are you trying to melt it or what?"

"Finn?" Shadow said. "Could we move on to the attack on Princess Alyssa?"

"Finn" reached out and pressed his right hand over Breon's, cradling his amulet with the other. Heat poured in through the mage's fingers, shooting through Breon like blue ruin, but at the end of it, he felt no different. It was like it came and went and left nothing behind.

That wasn't so bad, Breon thought. Maybe magic is vastly overrated, like so many other things.

Finn frowned, as if puzzled.

"Well?" Talbot said, leaning forward.

"It's not working," Finn said. "He's resisting it."

"I'm not resisting," Breon said, stung. "I'm an open book. Ask me a question." Turning his head from side to side, he mimicked both sides of an interrogation.

"Young man, tell us what happened the night the princess was attacked."

"I'd be glad to, Your Honor. I was—"

"I don't have to ask you a question to know that it's not

working," Finn said flatly. "And your answers mean nothing if we don't know that you're telling the truth."

The only thing worse than lying and getting caught was telling the truth and being called a liar.

"Did you search him?" Finn said. "Could he be wearing or carrying a talisman against high magic?"

"We took a pendant off him," Talbot said. "That was all." She patted him down again, just to make sure. "Unless it's that thing on his neck that's interfering." She made it sound like the magemark was an ugly wart or a tumor. Pulling out a wicked knife, she said, "I could try to pry it off him again."

Breon pulled in his head like a turtle and strained at the darbies fastening his wrists to the chair. "I told you—it doesn't come off."

"It's too risky," Shadow said. "We don't want to kill him before we get some answers."

What about after, Breon thought as Talbot put the blade away.

"Let me try again," Finn said, opening the magical floodgates once more. "I'm trying to break through the barriers, but I don't want to injure him."

No, Breon thought. You don't.

Breon felt the burn again, scouring out his insides so that he felt like he did after suffering through a bad case of the trots. But, at the end of it, he felt no more likely to tell the truth than usual.

Finn sat back, rubbing his chin and frowning. "Strange."

"What's strange?" Talbot eyed Breon like he was, indeed, something strange.

"It doesn't seem like I'm connecting with him."

We've only just met, Breon thought. These things take time.

Seriously, though, he had no idea why Finn's magic wouldn't work on him. And why he wouldn't at least try to ask a question.

"If we're not connecting, then how do you know I'm lying?" he said out loud.

"Shut up, busker," Talbot said.

"Make up your mind. Do you want me to shut up, or do you want me to talk?" Breon said. Then immediately regretted it when Talbot backhanded him across the face.

"Sasha!" Shadow shook his head, frowning at her.

Talbot hung her head. "I'm sorry," she mumbled, staring at her boots. "I shouldn't have done that. He just gets to me, you know?"

Breon could feel the blood trickling down from his cut lip. The leaf is making you reckless, he thought. You can't afford that now. He was beginning to wish the mage's truth-spell *would* work—that way he'd be believed. But maybe connection and persuasion was a two-way street. On impulse, he leaned forward, looked into Finn's eyes, and attempted to catch the thread of his music. Even if he couldn't give it back to him, he'd have more information than he did before.

But Finn's eyes were like iced-over pools that he couldn't penetrate. Breon could hear no song at all.

Was it because Finn was a wizard? Had he ever tried to charm a wizard before? Maybe not.

That was when Breon's chair burst into flame. Breon screamed, twisting and turning, unable to get free. Quick as thought, Talbot snatched the quilt from Breon's bed and tried to smother the flames with it, but the chair kept burning. Finally, Talbot cut through his bonds with her knife and freed him from it. Then Finn put it out with some kind of charm.

"What was that all about?" Finn demanded, kicking at the heap of charred wood. "What purpose did that serve? If you were trying to kill yourself, there are easier ways."

"Me?" Breon gasped, tears leaking from his eyes. His arm was blistered from wrist to elbow. "I don't know what the hell happened, but it wasn't me that did it. Do you think I'm s-stupid enough to set myself on fire?"

"We have no idea how stupid you are," Finn said.

Breon didn't even try to respond. He was in a sea of agony that rolled over him in waves. Even adding up all the painful experiences he'd ever had, nothing compared with this. If he'd ever had any plans to set himself on fire, this experience had set him straight. Just kill me, he thought. Or cut off my arm, which has to be less painful than what I'm feeling now.

Finn looked up at Shadow and Talbot. "Shall we continue with—?"

"No," Talbot said. This was so unexpected that everyone turned and gaped at her.

"Can't you see how much pain he's in?" she said, looking stricken. "We have to take care of his arm."

"Look, why don't I come back and try again on my own," Finn said. "As soon as he's feeling better."

"Let's hold off for now," Shadow said. "We've sent word to Captain Byrne and the queen. I'm sure Princess Alyssa will want to question him herself."

With his mind in a fog of pain, it took Breon a moment to process what he'd just said. "Wait—what? She's alive?" Breon looked from face to face, sure this was some kind of ruse, or trick, or ugly joke. "The princess is alive?"

"Aye. She is," Talbot said. "Lucky for you. But two of her escorts was killed in the attack. That ought to be enough to hang you."

From Good Charley to Bad in a twinkling, but Breon didn't care. He hardly noticed when the healer came in. Having that guilt over the girlie's murder lifted from his shoulders was almost worth the pain.

GOOD NEWS AND
BAD NEWS

After the disaster of his interview with Captain Gray, Hal continued his tournaments, but once again restricted them to his own soldiers. Gray came and watched the workouts two days in a row. Hal assumed it was to make sure they weren't stockpiling weapons or planning an escape or playing with the other team. On the third day, Gray called him in after the competitions were over and suggested that they organize a series of meets between volunteers from both the Highlanders and the Ardenine army.

Hal tried to see a trap in that. Were they looking for a sporting way to finish them off? Food was in short supply, after all. It must be costing them to feed the remnants of his squadron. "You're not worried that either side might forget that it's a game?" he said.

"We'll still use rebated and wooden weapons," Gray said. "I'm thinking we could field mixed teams, designated by color, so it's not northerners fighting southerners. We'll start with competitions that don't involve one-on-one fighting."

"No mages?"

She nodded readily. "No mages."

"What about women?"

"What about them?"

"Would they be participating?"

"If they volunteer," Gray said, lifting her chin, that familiar flame of warning lighting in her eyes. "Why do you ask?"

"I just . . . wondered," Hal said, shifting from foot to foot.

"As long as your soldiers know the risks, and as long as they volunteer, I can't imagine there would be a problem," Gray said, stuffing her hands in her jacket pockets.

From her expression, she'd scored a point on him, but it took Hal a moment to work it out. His upbringing had given him no skills to deal with this.

"Why are you doing this?" he blurted.

She looked at him as if it must be obvious. "I'm impressed with your program, Captain. I'm hoping that we'll all learn something."

Again, some of Hal's men were wary of the matchups after their previous experience, but others clearly looked forward to demonstrating their skill with martial arts.

Generally speaking, the northerners were not highly skilled in classical longsword fighting of the sort Hal had been brought up on. That made sense, since they did most of their fighting from cover and from horseback, in a hit-and-run fashion. When they did fight with swords, the match was not always decided at the end of a blade. They cunningly combined grappling and footwork with sword-play and could often gain the advantage over a stronger arm.

That came to be called "northern rules" in their bouts, and it leveled the field between men and women more than Hal had expected. Most men were stronger, and taller, with a longer reach, but that didn't mean that they would win every single time.

Hal had to admit that, in a real battle situation, there *were* no rules.

The clans did not deign to participate in most of the contests, since they used few of the weapons Hal's men employed. The exceptions were knife-throwing and wres-tling, skills they excelled in. Time and again, Hal ended up pinned to the ground. Some of Hal's men grumbled at that, but the bouts were, after all, voluntary.

One afternoon, Hal found himself facing off with Captain Gray at the longsword. He'd been matched with her twice before. He'd won both of those matches, but it hadn't been a walk in the park. She was tall and strong for a woman, and she had a long reach as well. And it seemed like she'd watched every one of his matches since.

They came up face-to-face and bowed to each other, and Captain Gray said, "Northern rules?"

Which, to Hal's mind, meant no rules at all. "Northern rules," he said, with a shrug.

"Go to," the matchmaster said, and they went at it with a will.

It seemed Gray had learned something from her study of his previous matches. Almost immediately, she drove in close, so they were all but nose-to-nose. Hal couldn't recall fighting so close-in before, where his size and reach did little good.

Not only that, her scent filled his nose—a musky mix of sweat, and sunlight on skin, and lanolin. She thrust out a foot, entangled his ankles, and he went down hard on his back, the air exploding from his lungs. Laughter rained down on him from all sides, even from his own men.

"Point to Captain Gray," the master bawled.

She's been spending time with the Demonai, Hal thought crossly, as Gray extended a hand and helped him up.

The next match ended about the same as that one, though it did take longer.

"Match to Captain Gray," the onlookers shouted in

unison. There followed scattered howling.

There was nothing witchy about her tactics—she used speed and agility and focus, just like any other soldier.

But she wasn't like any other soldier. Not like any he'd encountered, anyhow.

Despite the cold, she shed her jacket and rolled back her sleeves, revealing corded biceps gleaming with sweat, and a puffy scar that ran the length of her left forearm.

Her top two shirt buttons were undone, and Hal could see a pendant glittering at her neckline and a tattoo on her collarbone—a gray wolf.

Don't get distracted, he thought. Focus. In the next match, she slipped past his sword and drove in low, plowing into his middle, but this time he grabbed onto her so they both went down, with Hal on top. He found himself pressed flat against her from chest to knees, their faces again just inches apart. Some devil spirit seized him, and it took everything that was in him not to finish their match with a kiss.

He could guess how *that* would be received.

Overhead, he heard the boutmaster call, "Match to Captain Matelon." But he scarcely noticed.

Gray squirmed under him, trying to flip him off her, and to his mortification his traitorous body reacted to this with great and obvious enthusiasm.

Captain Gray noticed, of course. She didn't pretend not to, like any southern lady would do. She didn't seem embarrassed at all. Instead, she lifted her head so her breath warmed his ear, and said, "Sword in your pocket, Captain?"

Hal pitched himself to one side, landing face-first in the snow, afraid to roll onto his back. Fortunately, the snow melting underneath him put an end to his dilemma rather quickly. When he thought it was safe to do so, he propped up on his hands and knees and looked up. Gray was grinning and extending a hand to help him up.

He accepted, because it would have been childish not to, but when he was on his feet, he pulled free immediately.

"No harm done," she said, looking highly amused. "Good match, Captain." She looked around. "It seems we have lost our audience."

A commotion in the manor yard had drawn the attention of the match spectators, who had lined up along the wall and were gawking at a crowd of newcomers gathered in front of the door. Hal heard shouting and cheering and general merriment. Then the bells in the manor chapel began to ring—not the familiar, measured cadence he associated with loss, but the pealing sound of good news.

His present worries were replaced by new worries. Good news for the Fells was likely to be bad news for his homeland. When fireworks began going off, he was certain.

Bad news or good news, Hal thought. It's all a matter of perspective.

"Well," Gray said, "either somebody got married, the queen's delivered demon twins, or we've won the war."

She seemed to be waiting for a reaction to this latest poke, but Hal declined to play. He'd had enough schooling for the day. "Which of those possibilities do you think is most likely, ma'am?" he said stiffly.

Her smile faded. "Maybe we should go see what's happened." She picked up her jacket and shrugged into it, smoothing her hair with both hands.

Matelon straightened his shirt, following with his uniform jacket. It was in bad shape, torn in places and stained with blood and dirt. He'd attempted to rinse out the stains, and he'd done his best to darn the rips with his careful stitches, but it wasn't much of an improvement. At home, he would have replaced it long ago.

She studied him critically as they walked toward the crowd. "Your jacket looks like it's seen hard use. We could probably get you something else to wear."

"This serves," he said gruffly. "It helps me remember who I am."

In the entry of the manor house stood a slender, dark-haired woman dressed in traveling garb—wool trousers, a heavy wool coat, and boots. Next to her stood a tall, weathered bluejacket with an elaborate sword, and two other women. One wore a Highlander uniform. The other was Lady Barrett, who'd interviewed Hal several times since he'd been taken prisoner. She'd returned to the capital a week ago. Now she was back, with some companions.

Captain Gray seemed exceptionally glad to see them, because she charged forward, leaving Hal behind. Before she reached them, though, she seemed to remember herself, skidded to a halt, and saluted, bringing her fist to her chest. "Your Majesty," she said to the woman in traveling garb. "Welcome to Delphi."

"Thank you, Captain Gray," the newcomer said, with a warm smile.

Your Majesty! Hal stared at her, trying to reconcile the woman in front of him with the bloodthirsty demon-riding witch he'd heard about all his life. His first thought was that she looked thin, and weary, and yet bursting with good news.

"General Dunedain," Gray said, saluting the other woman, who answered in kind. Now Hal was close enough to see that the woman wore a green officer's scarf. A general's scarf, it must be.

"Welcome back, Julianna," Gray said to Lady Barrett. "I'm so glad to see you—all of you. Why didn't anyone tell me you were coming?"

"I didn't know myself, until day before yesterday," the queen said. "That's when I heard some good news, Captain, that I just had to share in person."

"Arden surrendered?" Gray guessed.

"Almost as good," the queen said. "The monster is dead."

Gray frowned, looking puzzled. "The monster?"

"Gerard Montaigne. We just received word from our agents in the south. He's dead."

Gray took a step forward, staring at the queen, her face alight with mingled joy and disbelief. "Dead?" she whispered, as if this news was a bright, shiny package she was afraid to open.

Dead? The word echoed in Hal's head. King Gerard is dead? What would that mean for his family? Might it mean that he could finally go home?

Well. He looked around the headquarters, at the bluejackets and Highlanders all around him. There were definitely some obstacles in his way.

"We don't know exactly how and when it happened," the queen was saying. "We surmise that it was just after Solstice. It seems that there was some kind of attack on the palace at Ardenscourt—an attack that is being blamed on me." She shrugged, as if wearing that blame wasn't too burdensome.

"Something smashed the palace tower to bits," Lady Barrett said. "They're claiming it was a demon—this magical creature that nobody can find now." She rolled her eyes. "Every time the southerners lose, they blame it on demons. Supposedly Montaigne wasn't killed in the attack, but was so despondent afterward that he threw himself from the tower." She shook her head. "I haven't found a single person who believes that. Whenever Montaigne got a little down, he just murdered a few people, and that set him to rights."

That much is true, Hal thought. But, if there was an attack . . . who else was hurt? It was the winter season, after all, when his family was likely to be at court. He edged forward, unable to contain himself. "Was anyone else killed or injured?"

They all turned round and looked at him.

"Have we been introduced?" the queen said, cocking her head, fixing him with green eyes that seemed to look right through him.

Gray jumped in to explain. "Your Majesty, this is Captain Halston Matelon, the former commander of the Ardenine forces here in Delphi. Captain Matelon, meet Queen Raisa ana'Marianna."

"Captain Matelon," Queen Raisa said. "I met your father once or twice when I was a little girl. An impressive man and far too good a soldier to be fighting on the wrong side. I've heard that you are highly capable on the battlefield as well."

"Thank you, ma'am," Hal said, keeping his eyes fixed on the ground. "But if I were highly capable, I would not be standing here a captive. I would have won."

"Don't be too hard on yourself, Captain," the queen said. "Captain Gray is one of our most well-respected commanders." She winked at Gray, who looked as if the queen had just handed her a bouquet.

Queen Raisa put her hand on Barrett's shoulder. "Lady Barrett may be able to answer your question about casualties. She's read all of the dispatches in full."

Barrett nodded. "There were some casualties in the attack, but we don't have names. From all accounts, Queen Marina and the two children survived. Prince Jarat has been crowned king."

Hal had met Prince Jarat a few times. He hadn't come away impressed, but it was hard to imagine that the prince could be worse than his father.

The queen kept studying Hal, as if working out what manner of a man he was. "Captain Matelon, Lady Barrett has heard other news that you, in particular, should know," she said.

Barrett took a second look at the queen, as if to verify that she really wanted her sharing anything with Hal. Then she shrugged, and said, "Apparently there's been considerable grumbling among the thanes following the loss of Delphi. Some have refused to offer more men and more money to the war effort."

"I see," Hal said, in what he hoped was a neutral way. This was nothing new. He recalled his conversation with his father just after his reassignment to Delphi. Lord Matelon had blamed it on his own outspoken criticism of the war. The Matelons had long resisted funding King Gerard's obsession with the frozen north.

"Now I'm told that several of the most powerful thanes,

including your father, have publicly broken with the king over the issue. Before the king . . . died, of course."

Hal straightened, his stomach churning. After twenty-five years, was the civil war starting up again? Could the rebellious thanes be responsible for the king's death?

Civilian casualties had been catastrophic when Gerard was battling his brothers for the throne. *A civil war has no winners, only losers, and is to be avoided at all costs.* That was another truth that had been drilled into him since he was small.

"If that is true, I'm sorry that my failure played a part in that."

"Think of it not as your failure, but our success," Gray said, drawing a grin from Dunedain.

"In response, Montaigne imprisoned the families of members of the Thane Council, including your mother and sister. Apparently he intended to keep them as hostages against the thanes' good behavior."

This was going from bad to worse. His father had warned him to stay out of the king's gaol at all costs. Now Harper and their lady mother had taken his place. Harper had inherited their father's temper and stubborn streak. Who knew how she would respond in this situation?

He cleared his throat. "That's difficult to believe," he lied. "The king must have known that my father would never surrender to pressure of that kind."

"Keep in mind that I have no way to verify that story,"

Barrett said. "I'm told that the king's behavior was . . . erratic prior to his death. Thanelee Matelon and her daughter have not been seen since Delphi fell, but they may be in hiding for safety's sake. However, I do have it on good authority that your father has called in his banners."

Hal felt pounded by bad news, outnumbered by his enemies, with no way to confirm or disprove what he'd been told. But he had to ask. "Have you . . . have you heard news of my brother Robert?"

"We believe he's at White Oaks, with your father," General Dunedain said.

That, at least, was good news. White Oaks was the seat of the Matelon holdings, and its keep would be a formidable nut to crack.

"It may be that we're wrong about your family," Barrett said. "Or that, under a new king, a general pardon might be issued."

"I'm wondering if the death of your king might signal a new relationship between our realms, Captain," the northern queen said. "What do you think?"

"Forgive me, ma'am," Hal said, his mind swimming with worry. "I'm not much for politics."

"Spoken like a true soldier," the queen said, glancing at Gray. "Still, I look forward to hearing your opinions."

Something's going on, Hal thought, looking from Barrett to the queen. Something I don't know about yet that's caused them to allow me to listen in while they discussed developments in Arden. How much of what they've told me is true? What is it they are wanting me to do?

Now, apparently, that had ended, because Captain Byrne motioned to his bluejackets. "We're going to spend some time briefing Captain Gray on recent developments. Escort Captain Matelon back to his quarters."

BAD NEWS AND GOOD NEWS

When Matelon had gone, Lyss led the way to the privacy of the library. Once they were there, her mother opened her arms, and Lyss flew into them, all but lifting her mother from the floor in a savage dance of victory.

We will raise another mountain
And we'll build it with your bones.

"I only wish I could have killed the bastard myself," Lyss said. "But I'll take it, just the same." She poured steaming mugs of wassail for everyone and they took seats around the hearth.

"Ah, sweetheart," her mother murmured. "I have waited so very long for this day. I just wish that we could all be together, so we could celebrate properly."

Lyss knew she was thinking of her grandfather and her father, her sister, and Adrian, too. "They're here in spirit, Mama. And soon Adrian will be here in the flesh." She paused, eager to share in the celebration at home, even if it was secondhand. "Are the bonfires burning in the Spirits?"

"They are," her mother said, smiling. She looked around. "You've made yourself at home here, I see."

"We have more good news, Your Highness," Captain Byrne said. "We believe we have captured the busker that lured you into that ambush."

That drove everything else from Lyss's mind. "Really? Are you sure it's him?"

Byrne nodded. "He was carrying the ruins of that . . . instrument you drew for us. He claims to be a traveling musician. He admits he was hired to play for you, but denies any knowledge of what they were planning to do."

"What's his name?" Lyss asked.

"He says it's Breon d'Tarvos," Byrne said.

"Where's Tarvos?"

"It's a port in Carthis," Byrne said. "I don't know anyone who's ever been there, but it's supposed to be a nest of pirates. He claims he isn't magical, but he has some kind of strange emblem on the back of his neck."

Lyss couldn't help fingering the back of her own neck. "Emblem?"

"It's raised, metallic, but embedded in the skin and impossible to remove," Byrne said. "It resembles white gold or platinum with a faceted blue stone. Shadow wasn't familiar with it, and he's knowledgeable about flashcraft and magic. Finn doesn't know what to make of it, either. Maybe it's some kind of pirate badge."

"Or maybe Arden is controlling its mages with embedded amulets instead of collars," Lyss said.

"There's one more thing," Julianna said. "A year or so ago we received a message from Carthis, from someone who called herself the Empress in the East. She was offering a reward for anyone with a badge or brooch embedded in their skin. The message came via a pirate, and we'd never heard of this empress, and we'd never seen anything like that anyway, so we pretty much ignored it. Now I'm thinking we should try to get in touch with this empress and see what she can tell us."

Lyss nodded. "Was the busker taken in Fellsmarch, or—?"

Byrne shook his head. "No, he was captured in Chalk Cliffs, and he's being kept in the guardhouse there. It seems that he intended to take ship for Arden, which counts against him. Shadow and Talbot and sul'Mander have been interrogating him, but he's sticking with his story."

"I want to go to Chalk Cliffs and talk to him," Lyss said, remembering the boy with the haunting eyes and the ethereal music. "I might catch him in a lie or persuade him to confess. Besides, I need to find out what it was about him that turned me into a fool." And cost two good Wolves their lives.

Her mother nodded, as if she'd expected that. "I agree. I don't blame you for wanting to unearth the whole story. Although I have hopes that, with Montaigne dead, his grudge died with him. Perhaps we've seen the end of these murders."

Lyss's breath caught. That hadn't even occurred to her. Was it possible? Did this mean that she would no longer have to worry every time her mother walked out the door? Could Lyss really walk the streets of the capital without listening for the sound of crossbows?

"I want you to take a squadron of Highlanders with you," the queen said. "Captain Byrne will send two triples of Wolves along. I want some strength in numbers, especially if they might be bringing the boy back to Fellsmarch. I don't want this fish slipping through our fingers."

It would be good to get out of Delphi, briefly, anyway, and see Sasha and Shadow—and Finn—again.

"I'm curious about Captain Matelon." General Dunedain turned her cup between her hands. "He has an excellent reputation as a field commander, and yet you've defeated him on the battlefield twice in a row. Now that he's been your prisoner for several weeks, what do you think of him?"

"Matelon?" Lyss considered this. "He is a soldier's

officer. His men are intensely loyal, with good reason. As far as our face-offs, you already know that Matelon was dealt a very bad hand at Queen Court."

"Interesting that Karn would put an officer like Matelon in that position," Julianna said. "Has he said anything about that? Complained about it?"

Lyss shook her head. "As you might have noticed, he's very closemouthed when it comes to offering opinions. He doesn't trust us."

"I would be surprised if he trusts anyone, after being raised in Arden," Raisa said.

"What about here in Delphi?" Dunedain persisted. "How did he fare here?"

"Here at Delphi, Matelon made mistakes," Lyss said. "He allowed himself to be drawn into a battle on our field, on our terms. He was outsmarted. It happens." Lyss paused. "Since we're on the topic of Matelon, what was that show in the yard all about?"

"Show?" Julianna raised an eyebrow.

"I had the feeling that you were playing him," Lyss said. "That there was a purpose to spilling all that."

"There was," Julianna said, looking over the rim of her mug at Lyss.

"What Julianna means is that we're still trying to figure out whether Montaigne's death is bad news or good news for us," her mother said.

"How could it possibly be bad news?" Lyss stared at her

mother in astonishment. "I mean, you already said—"

"We don't know much about the prince," Julianna said. "Up to now Gerard's been making all the decisions. As his brothers found out, relatives who didn't go along with Gerard's agenda paid a blood price. Now King Jarat will be in a position to make policy. Being sixteen, he's hard to predict. Queen Marina is regent, but she's never had much agency, as far as we can tell."

"Maybe," the queen murmured, looking unconvinced. "She is a Tomlin, after all. She might surprise you."

"Before Gerard's death, there was chatter about some mysterious new ally who would help Arden win the war once and for all," Julianna said. "We don't know if Gerard was blowing smoke, or if the deal is still on the table. Meanwhile, the thanes will likely see this as an opportunity to regain some of the power they lost under King Gerard. He'd been systematically stripping them of lands and incomes since he ascended the throne. And any one of them—Matelon Senior, for instance—might decide he'd like to be king himself."

"Sounds like a political mess," Lyss muttered.

"It is," Julianna said, with a kind of peculiar delight. Unlike Lyss, she seemed to thrive on political messes. "We can sit up here and watch, *or* we can try to shape things to our advantage."

"How would we do that?" Lyss said, intrigued in spite of herself.

"There are several possibilities," her mother said. "If the

civil war continues, we'll back the side that wants to make peace with us."

"The thanes are likely to want peace," Julianna said, "because they've been the ones paying for the war in men and treasure. They've been complaining about it for years. That was at the root of the falling-out between Thane Matelon and Gerard."

"If the thanes want peace and King Jarat wants war," Lyss's mother said, "then we strike an agreement with the thanes and we send Captain Matelon back to fight alongside his father."

"What are the other possibilities?" Lyss said warily.

"It may be that King Jarat and the thanes will reconcile immediately, now that Gerard is out of the way," Julianna said. "If that happens, the question is, will they want to continue this war, or sue for peace?"

"In other words, was this damnable war really all about King Gerard's hurt feelings, or is there more support for the war than we think?" Lyss said.

All around, heads nodded.

"The Church of Malthus might favor carrying on with the war, since they've sold it as a battle between good and evil," Julianna said. "But they have a history of standing down when confronted with the power of kings and princes."

"If they choose peace, then prisoners will be repatriated," the queen said. "Matelon goes home."

Julianna and the queen must have worked all this out

between them before they came, Lyss thought, with a flicker of irritation.

Julianna was good at this, she was so damned good at it, and yet . . .

"And if it's war . . . ?"

"If everyone's in the war party, then we don't want to send young Matelon back to them," the queen said. "Not only is he a capable military strategist and commander, but we would lose whatever leverage he gives us."

"You heard what he said about his father," Lyss said. "That he wouldn't—"

"I know what he said. From what I know of Matelon Senior, the captain may be right. But sometimes, when the money's on the table, we make a different choice."

When the money's on the table? What the hell did that mean? Lyss's temper flared. "What happens if they refuse to deal?" she said. "Do we cut off his head and send it to his father in a box?"

This was met with shocked silence.

"No, Alyssa, we do not," her mother said, her voice thick with disapproval. "Nor do we throw him into a dungeon. You should know better than that. He'll be kept in comfortable quarters, suitable to his rank. He is a prisoner of war, after all."

"What if he doesn't go along with your plan?" Lyss said, looking from Julianna to her mother. "What if he tries to escape?" She gestured at their surroundings. "This was never intended to be a prison. It's right on the border, and it's not very secure."

"We know that," her mother said. "That is why we're going to move him to a more secure location." She paused. "I want you to take him with you to Chalk Cliffs."

Lyss's mind was already racing, divided between travel plans and the tactical conversation. Now it screeched to a halt. "Matelon? Why would I take him along?"

"I'd like to get him out of Delphi and into the Fells. As you pointed out, this location is not all that secure. There's a keep at Chalk Cliffs that's suitable."

So I shot my own self in the foot, Lyss thought. She didn't like any plan that used Matelon as a game piece, and now she would be helping to move it forward. Plus, the last thing she needed was to babysit a prisoner all the way to the coast.

Let Julianna escort Matelon to prison, if she's so keen on the plan.

"That's not a good idea," Lyss said, after discarding *That's a terrible idea* and *That's a stupid idea.*

"Why not?"

"He'll try to escape the first chance he gets, and that's going to be even harder to prevent while we're traveling. He's going to be hot to get back to Arden and see what's what with his family."

Her mother rubbed the back of her neck. "We can hardly blame him for that."

"If he tries to escape, do we shoot him?" Lyss's voice was rising, and both her cousin and her mother were staring at her as if baffled.

"You must make sure that doesn't happen," the queen said.

Lyss was a little baffled herself. Why was she standing up so strongly for Matelon? What, exactly, did she want done with him? Did she have a sense of ownership because she had been the one to spare his life in the first place?

Does it mean that you're actually growing fond of him?

No. You're just trying to make sure he gets a fair deal.

Lyss disliked the whole notion of interfering in Arden's affairs or using Matelon to gather information or make their case. It smacked too much of southern tactics in the past. *What makes us different from them?*

The queen leaned forward. "Try to win him over, Alyssa. It seems to me that you have a lot in common. I'm hoping that once he understands that we're not all witches and demons, he'll be an ambassador for us once he goes home."

"*If* he goes home," Lyss said. "If you're going to take him hostage, it seems to me that it would be better to take him back to Fellsmarch, where there's a stronger keep."

"If we make a deal with the thanes, it will be easier to send him back to his father by ship," Julianna said. "It's too risky to send him overland through Arden."

Matelon's a soldier, Lyss thought. A good soldier. He's

done nothing wrong. Leave him be.

"I know this doesn't sit well with you, Alyssa," the queen said, twisting her wolf ring, "but the stakes are very high. This is war, and we have to fight it on every battle-field. As you know, we've been struggling. Your capture of Delphi and Montaigne's death are the first bits of good news we've had in a long time. If we play our cards right in Arden, we could end this bloody war and have an ally to the south for the first time in my lifetime. We might even regain some influence over the other realms. If we back the losing horse, we could be paying for it for years." She paused, and when Lyss said nothing, added, "This is not a negotiation. These are my terms. Otherwise, you can stay here or return to Fellsmarch with me."

"If those are my choices, then I accept your terms," Lyss said, looking her in the eye.

"Good. Now," the queen said, raising her glass, "I would like to raise a toast to the brightest winter solstice in a very long time. The sun has come again, thank the Maker. It may be that our Solstice curse has finally broken."

They all drank deeply and Byrne poured more. But Lyss couldn't help worrying that the fates were listening. And making their own plans.

ON THE ROAD TO CHALK CLIFFS

Just a day after the queen of the Fells arrived, Hal was playing nicks and bones by the fire with Bernard and Littlefield. They'd set up a regular game in the afternoons when the weather was bad, which was nearly all the time.

Bernard was one of the survivors of the Ardenine garrison. Littlefield commanded one of the Fellsian squadrons, and reported directly to Captain Gray. Others sat in as they came available. Hal had made a point of getting to know as many northerners as possible. He reasoned that he could use all the friends he could get.

Captain Gray appeared at the guardhouse door wearing a scowl. "Matelon. Pack your things and be ready to ride out early in the morning."

There wouldn't be much packing up to do. All he had was the clothes on his back, his cold-weather gear, and two changes of smallclothes.

"Where am I going?" he asked.

"You'll find out."

When Gray went to turn away, Matelon said, "Ma'am?" When she turned back, he said, "Shall I tell my men to get ready as well?"

"No," she said. "Just you." And she was gone.

Hal turned back to his companions. "Does either of you know what this is about?" He was mainly directing this at Littlefield, who was, after all, Captain Gray's direct report.

Littlefield shook his head. "I'll see what I can find out."

That evening Littlefield found Hal in the practice yard. "It's all hush-hush, but I heard that one of Captain Barnes's squadrons is riding out tomorrow, too." He shrugged. "I couldn't see the harm in telling you that much."

Was this good news or bad news?

"Thank you, Littlefield," he said lightly. "I appreciate it. And if I never see you again, I'll forgive you the five crowns you owe me."

"And I'll forget the seventeen crowns *you* owe *me*," Littlefield said. Growing serious, he clasped Hal's hand. "Good luck to you, Matelon."

After Littlefield left, Hal leaned against the palisade, thinking. He didn't like the idea of being separated from what remained of his command. It wasn't that he had illusions that he could protect them against whatever harm might come their way, but at least he would have been there as their advocate. It was one of the reasons he'd stalled on planning an escape from the compound. And now it might be too late.

Whatever the plan was, Captain Gray didn't seem happy with it.

What did that mean? Did it mean that the queen and her party would be escorting him back to Fellsmarch for safekeeping? Would Captain Gray be riding along? He found himself hoping that she would be. In the time they'd spent together, he'd become convinced that she was not a witch—only a soldier like himself. They'd come to an understanding, a relationship of mutual respect. He'd learned a lot, and had realized that she had a lot more to teach him. He hoped that she was learning something, too.

She fascinated him, challenged him, sometimes enraged him—but she was never boring.

Don't lose your head, Matelon. Don't let her distract you from your mission.

It didn't matter where they were taking him. He had his own plans.

It turned out that Captain Gray *was* in the party that left the Delphian army headquarters before dawn the next morning. To Hal's dismay, Lieutenant Bosley was, too. It seemed that he was the commander of the squadron of Highlanders Littlefield had mentioned. There was also a swarm of bluejackets, who seemed to be assigned to watch over Hal. He saw their colors peeking out from under their white woolen cloaks.

Hal's mount was one of the shaggy mountain ponies his captors favored, which was just one more sign they were heading north. He was grateful for the thick wool cloak, tent, and bedroll the quartermaster gave him. Those would be helpful when he struck out on his own.

He was less grateful for the shackles Bosley brought.

"What's this?" Hal said, eyeing them unhappily. That would complicate things.

"Captain's orders," Bosley said, with a smirk. "Give me your wrists, flatlander."

Hal thrust them toward Bosley. "Do you really think I'm stupid enough to try to escape into the mountains in the winter?"

"It doesn't matter what I think," Bosley said. "It's what Captain Gray thinks that matters."

Bosley always said "Captain Gray" like it was some kind of secret joke. What the hell, Hal thought. Does he think it's amusing to be using such a formal term for his lover? I wonder what he calls her when they're alone?

Not your business, Matelon.

At least the little pony was easy for Hal to mount, even

with his hands bound, but he felt a little foolish sitting atop her.

As Hal had expected, they put their backs to Arden and rode into the mountains. After studying the map he'd taken from a drawer in the duty room, he'd guessed they might take the main road north through two clan camps to the capital of Fellsmarch. Instead, they took a path that was little more than a hunting trail that seemed to be heading north and east.

In places, the snow was drifted so high that a horse and rider might completely disappear if he made a misstep. Vast portions of the country they were traveling into appeared completely empty of roads or trails. He was beginning to question his ability to find his way back. If he planned to escape, it made sense to do it sooner rather than later, so there would be less chance of getting lost and less distance to cover on his way back south.

As they climbed, Hal began to appreciate the merits of these shaggy, stocky ponies. They were strong and sure-footed, with no delicate long legs to slide and break in this icy terrain. They had incredible stamina, seeming unfazed by a daylong, uphill climb.

Maybe he should introduce a breeding line of ponies into the empire horse lines. Though it would be a job to persuade any of his fellow officers to climb aboard one.

He'd hoped to talk to Gray during the day and see if he could tease more information out of her, but he never had the chance. The trail was so narrow that there was little movement up and down the line. He was surrounded by bluejackets, while she must have been riding in the rear with the Highlanders. With Bosley. He tried to put that thought from his mind, but it remained there, like a burr in his boot.

They stopped for the night on the lee side of a massive rock formation that provided some shelter from the wind. Once Hal had dismounted, Bosley came and removed the chains from his hands so he could tend to his horse. "Best behave," the lieutenant said, resting his hand on the pommel of his sword and smirking at him.

He's hoping I make a break for it, Hal thought. Which means I need to get away clean.

His bluejacket nannies chose his campsite for him, well within the perimeter, then set up their tents all around him. Hal methodically pitched his tent and arranged his bedroll to his liking. He saw Bosley pitching a large, rather more elaborate tent nearby—was it Captain Gray's?—and a smaller, plainer one next to it.

To Hal's disappointment, his escorts picketed all of the horses together and set a guard on them. Hal took his supper of hard bread and cheese surrounded by bluejackets—none of whom he'd met before. When he tried to start a conversation, they had little to say. The witch queen was taking no chances that her prize would slip away.

The Highlanders were bunched around several other

campfires, and Gray was with them. He could hear them talking and laughing and showing off the way men—and women, apparently—will do around the fire. Now and then he heard Bosley's voice above the rest. That did not improve his mood.

It was almost as if Gray was avoiding him.

What's wrong with me? Hal thought crossly. I'm the prisoner of the upland queen. Gray has no reason to avoid me or spend time with me or think about me at all.

He couldn't help himself. She was unlike any woman he'd met before. Granted, he'd never spent much time with women other than family, because he'd been a soldier in his father's command since he was eleven years old, and, as the captain relentlessly pointed out, there were no women in the Ardenine army.

During the winter social season, he dutifully attended the parties he was invited to and danced with the girls who were matched up with him and kissed the ones who were willing. He enjoyed dancing and kissing well enough, but when it came to talking to them, he had little to say. They were not interested in the same things as he was, and he'd find himself fleeing to the billiards room or the cards room as soon as politeness would allow. Just like his father before him.

He'd never worried about wooing, because he knew he'd have little say in a final match, anyway. That would be dictated by family, and politics, and dowries, and holdings. When it happened, he would make it work.

Even if the job you're assigned is not to your liking, a Matelon will see it done.

Gray was different. She was interested in all of the same things as he was, even though they agreed on practically nothing. She would debate any point into the dust, allowing no compromise—not even an agreement to disagree. Truth be told, he'd rather argue with Gray than make small talk with anyone else.

Was he drawn to her because she was more like a man than other women he'd known? Was it because he was more comfortable with his own kind?

No. She made him uncomfortable in all kinds of ways.

Hal crawled into his tent, weighed down by the realization that he wasn't going anywhere—not tonight, anyway.

Sometime during the night, he awoke to loud voices nearby, some kind of an argument. Lifting his tent flap, he peered out and saw that it was Gray and Bosley, standing in front of the two tents Bosley had pitched earlier. Gray was in Bosley's face, flinging her hands around in that way she had. Bosley had both hands up, as if to ward her off, and he was talking fast and persuasively. The next thing Hal knew, Gray was waving a dagger under Bosley's nose.

With that, she turned and crawled into the smaller tent. Bosley stood glaring at the tent, hands fisted. After taking a quick look around, he crawled into the larger tent.

Lovers' quarrel? *It's not your business, Matelon.* Still, he went to sleep smiling.

IN THE RUINS

Two days later, they were still traveling northeast, and Hal still hadn't made his move. When the weather was clear enough, he could see the massive peak of the Harlot to his right, so he knew they had traveled quite a distance to the east. Toward midday, they entered a broad, flat valley, and he realized they were at the western end of Queen Court, the scene of his late-summer humiliation at the hands of Captain Gray.

Look on the bright side, Halston. At least this way, he would get to see the vale that had been his target. He'd never made it that far on his earlier visit.

Though they were walled in by mountains, and the fields were snow-covered, the fertile valley reminded Hal of home, with its farmsteads and hedgerows. Here and there, plumes of steam signaled where the hot blood of the uplands broke through a thin skin of rock and soil. *This is what we were supposed to burn and destroy, had we made it through the pass,* he thought. *Now, I'm just as glad we didn't.*

Unfortunately, he was seeing a lot more of Bosley than he was of Captain Gray. Each day, before they mounted up, Bosley shackled his hands, taking his time, enjoying the moment. Each night, when they stopped, Bosley removed the bonds, taunting him, daring him to try to escape. Hal envisioned himself wrapping the chain around Bosley's neck until his smirk disappeared. And *then* escaping.

What could Captain Gray possibly see in him? Bosley's speech and attitude said that he was highborn. But Gray didn't strike him as a soldier of fortune, someone who would marry for money.

How do you know that? What do you really know about her, anyway? Where was she born? Did she always know she wanted to be a soldier? What did she like to do when she wasn't in the field? Does she share your aversion to smoked snails?

It's not your business, Matelon. That was becoming his new motto. He needed to leave, and leave soon.

They camped for the night beside the remains of the Queen Court keep. Hal had always been fascinated by castle architecture as it related to defense and offense. Before the winter dark came down, he walked around the outer perimeter, assessing strengths and weaknesses.

His guard didn't even bother to follow him. Without a horse, he wouldn't get far with mountains all around.

This keep lacked the thick stone skin Hal associated with northern castles. Even when newly built, this would not have been hard to crack.

Now, if he occupied this keep, how would he go about defending it? Hal honored the crumbling wall by entering through the ruins of the old gate instead of climbing up and over.

There wasn't much left of buildings inside the wall, either. It appeared that the original structure was built largely of wood, and centuries of punishing weather had returned it to the earth. All in all, to call it a "keep" was being generous. This reminded him more of manors and hunting lodges in the gentle south of Arden, built for beauty, not for strength.

Hal stood, hands on hips, studying on it. The best way to defend this place was to prevent the enemy from reaching the walls in the first place. He'd clear away the trees that had crept in, all around, then position bowmen at the corners with—

"I'd dig a moat," somebody said, "and fill it with watergators."

Hal spun around, groping for a sword that wasn't there. It was Gray. She was perched in a niche in the wall, one knee bent, the other leg extended, a sketchpad on her lap.

"That would be a start," he said. "But it wouldn't keep them out for long."

"At least I'd get to see some of them eaten," Gray said, displaying her fierce smile.

"It puzzles me," Hal said, picking up a loose stone and tossing it over the truncated wall. "How did they ever expect to defend it?"

"It never had to be defended. This is a relic from a different time. It was once the council house for representatives from all of the Seven Realms. The Gray Wolf queen convened them here once a year, at the summer solstice. The entire vale would be carpeted in pavilions flying banners from the different realms. It was like a massive fair, with people wearing their ceremonial garb. They held tournaments. . . ." Her voice trailed off.

"I've never heard about that, ma'am," Hal said honestly. It was difficult to imagine a time when Arden and the Fells had a shared history. "That must have been a long time ago."

"It was. Before the Wizard Wars. Before the Breaking. Before the New Line of queens. I'm sure the scholars in the empire like to downplay that history. I'll wager that Gerard knew about it, though. That's why he sent you here this summer to destroy it."

Running her hand over the stones, she said wistfully, "According to the old manuscripts, the interior was like a woodland cathedral. At midsummer, the sun never quite dipped below the horizon, so they would dance all night in the twilight."

"You know your history," Hal said.

"The upland clans say that it's important to remember the old stories," Gray said. "As soon as you forget a story, it comes around again, and you have to relive it."

Gray was obviously proud of her homeland's past glory. Hal found himself feeling a bit guilty about Arden's role in its decline.

Empires come and go, he thought. Dynasties rise and fall. It's the way the world is made. It's nobody's fault.

His father had said that the never-ending war against the north was rooted in King Gerard's personal grudge against the witch queen. Captain Gray claimed it was because Queen Raisa had spurned Gerard's offer of marriage.

It's not worth it, he thought. From what he'd seen, there was nothing up here to justify the spending of more lives and treasure. We should leave the north alone and consolidate and manage the territory we have. Let the thanes tend their farms and rebuild their livelihoods. If we reestablished trade with the north, everyone would prosper, north and south.

He hoped this change of heart wasn't a result of the fact that he was falling hard for his gaoler.

He tried to tell himself that it was simply a recognition of her natural talent for command. She clearly had the respect of her soldiers, and made sure they were taken care of. Even better, she seemed to have even less interest in politics and social niceties than he did. He loved the way she gave no quarter in the practice yard, fighting each match with grim determination, as if it were a life-and-death struggle.

He loved the way she threw back her head and laughed until tears leaked from her eyes. The way she tracked down Bosley and confronted him when he treated her like something less than a real soldier.

He loved those long legs and her tightly muscled—

No.

She is an enemy soldier, he repeated to himself for the thousandth time. He might be attracted to her, but she had no interest in him, except, perhaps, as a sparring partner. She was brusque, abrupt, openly hostile at times. They'd be having a conversation, and they'd seem to be getting on well, and then it was as if she suddenly remembered who he was, and that was the end of detente.

Hal looked up and Gray was looking down at him, her hands on her knees, studying him with the intensity she brought to every task. He realized he'd fallen silent for too long.

"What are you drawing?" he said, eager to change the subject. He was always needing to change the subject with her.

She held the sketchpad out to him. He took it and studied what she'd drawn. It was clearly a rough sketch, but the structural detail was amazing. She'd rendered the ruins as they were, but she'd extended them with smoky lines to create a ghostly image of the building as it had once been.

"You are . . . I am . . . I had no idea you were an artist," Hal said.

"You don't have to sound so surprised, Captain," she said. "Anyway, how would you know? I don't have much time for art these days. I think my legacy will be written in blood, not in oils and watercolors."

"This war won't last forever," Hal said.

"The question is whether I'll survive the peace." She slid a look at him. "Maybe the key is to live in the moment. It's not like we can control the future anyway."

A year ago, he might have disagreed. He'd been raised to believe that if a man worked hard, played by the rules, and kept his word, he could make a good life for himself. It was that kind of thinking that had brought him here.

Arden always needs capable officers, he thought. They recruited talent from every subject realm. Gray was clearly devoted to her homeland, but she seemed like a practical sort. Maybe he could put in a word once the war was over and find her a command somewhere, maybe in the down realms.

Gray began gathering up her drawing supplies and sliding them into her carry bag. "You sure spend a lot of time thinking, Captain Matelon," she said. "That's unusual in a southerner."

"Don't quit working," Hal said. "I didn't mean to interrupt you. I'll go, and leave you to it."

"It's getting too dark to see now, anyway." Gray leapt nimbly down from her seat on the wall, setting her carry bag at her feet. She leaned against the wall next to him, her shoulder just touching his, seeming in no hurry to go back. As the wind sent eddies of snow swirling from the tops of the walls, Hal was suddenly aware of how alone they were, in the ruins of the old council house at the dying of the day. Although he could still hear the faint sound of voices from the campsite, it felt like a million miles away. He wavered, pondering what to do.

The truth was, he wanted to kiss this northern girl, and go on from there. He wanted her more than any woman he'd ever known. It had started back in Delphi, and it had only gotten worse. At the same time, every element of his upbringing, every rational bone in his body said that it would be a big mistake. Probably the mistake of a lifetime.

This wasn't like him—it wasn't like him at all. Maybe it was the mountain air, or the witchery all around him, but he needed to leave this place before he did or said something dishonorable or unforgivable or suicidal.

He couldn't say why Captain Gray got under his skin the way she did. Though strong and well made, she was no great beauty, compared to the women he'd been introduced to at court. Yet, when they were together, she elbowed everything else out of his mind.

"Matelon?"

He looked up, and she was studying him with her amber eyes. Did she know that she had this effect on him? He prayed to all the gods she did not.

"Would you like to kiss me?"

This came as such a surprise—more of an ambush, really—that it took a while for Hal to organize a response. It didn't help that the blood had deserted his brain and redeployed to other regions.

Was this a trick question? The best response he could manage was a hoarse "Why do you ask?"

She huffed her breath out. "Because you keep staring at my lips."

Hal's cheeks burned. "Oh. Ah. I'm sorry if I gave the impression that I—"

"Was I mistaken, then?"

Hal opened his mouth to lie, and then stopped, and shook his head. "No. You're not mistaken."

"Oh." Other girls he'd known might blush and flutter, but not Gray. He waited for her to punch him instead, or laugh, or tell him how stupid and arrogant he was.

Instead, she said, "Well, then. Go ahead, I don't mind."

"You don't mind?" This was totally outside Hal's admittedly limited wooing experience.

"No. I don't mind," she said with a shrug.

"Oh. Well, do you *want* to?"

"Forget it," she growled, spots of pink coloring her

cheeks. "Let's walk back. I've spent less time dickering over a horse."

Hal's father always said that a good soldier adapts to a changing battlefield.

"Wait."

When she turned back, he cradled her chin with his gloved hands and kissed her. Her lips were warm and rough and perfect. Encouraged, he slid his arms around her and pulled her close, extending the kiss. They were of nearly equal height, and they fit together like the two halves of—of something fine. Even through several thick layers of clothing he noticed the way her breasts pressed into him—he'd thought she was all muscle—and the tidy way she curved down to her waist. She smelled like fresh air and sweat, metal and horse—perfect.

When they finally broke apart, she studied him a moment, then took his face between her warm hands and kissed him again, long and deep, their hearts thumping between them.

With a kind of growl, Hal pinned her to the wall and answered her with a longer, deeper kiss of his own. And then it was like a kind of madness took them, a frenzy of kissing, a sudden frustration with the layers of cold-weather clothes that separated them.

Hal wasn't a total novice, but he wasn't a deft hand at this, either. He should have made a better job of it, since she wore men's clothes, after all. Finally, he yanked her shirt free of her breeches and thrust his hands underneath. His hands were rough with calluses and they must have been cold, but she didn't seem to mind. Instead, she slid down the wall, pulling him down with her, then rolled on top so she sat astride him, pawing at his clothing, fumbling with his shirt buttons, trying to find a way in. When she ripped his shirt open, he heard buttons plopping into the snow all around them. And then she was kissing and nipping at every bit of bare flesh she could get at. Though still fully clothed, they were somehow belly to belly, skin to skin.

He was beginning to regret not being the sort of man who carried a sheath around. Besides, how could he possibly go about asking whether she might be willing to—?

"Captain Gray!" someone shouted, frighteningly near at hand. "Where are you?"

"Matelon!" somebody else shouted.

They sprang apart like bolts shot from a bow. Gray's cheeks were flushed, and her braid was all but pulled apart. There followed a frenzy of buttoning and fastening and tying and tidying. Hal buttoned his coat over his buttonless shirt just as a mob of bluejackets boiled around the corner of the gate, Bosley in the lead.

"There you are!" Bosley's eyes swept the scene inside the perimeter. By now it was all but too dark to see. Which was a blessing, since it made the spot where the snow was packed down less obvious. Hal planted his foot over two dark spots in the snow. Buttons.

Bosley's glare fastened on Hal. "What are you two doing out here in the dark?" he demanded. He sounded more like somebody's enraged father than like a betrayed lover.

Hal decided he'd better let Captain Gray answer that question. When he didn't respond, Bosley turned on Gray. "You shouldn't be out here alone with him! What's the matter with you? If the queen were to see you like this, she—" With that, he stopped on his own, as if unable to find a path forward.

Gray slowly turned her head, as if she couldn't believe her ears. "Are you addressing *me*, Lieutenant?"

"*Somebody* needs to speak up, for safety's sake," Bosley said, looking to the bluejackets for support and getting none.

"And you're thinking that someone is *you*?" Captain Gray cocked her head, as if she was just now figuring that part out. "You are out of line, Lieutenant. How and where I choose to interrogate a prisoner of the crown is none of your concern."

Of all the terrifying stories Hal had heard about northern torture tactics, this particular interrogation technique had never been mentioned.

"You expect us to believe that you were *interrogating* him?"

"I have absolutely no expectations of you, Bosley, except

that you return to your tent and stay there. While there, I suggest that you study the Officer's Rules of Good Order. Pay special attention to the chapter on the chain of command." She waved her hand, dismissing him.

Bosley stood frozen for a long moment, fists clenched. Then got off a salute and stalked away. As he passed Hal, he delivered a look so venomous that Hal all but made the sign of Malthus.

Bosley means to kill me before we get wherever we're going, Hal thought. I need to be gone before that happens.

AT CROSS-PURPOSES

Lyss crawled into her tent, her heart still pounding, the blood still raging through her veins. Her lips felt slightly bruised from kissing, her skin sanded and sensitive from Matelon's touch. Desire was still burning so hot inside her it seemed she would never put it out.

Should I go out and roll in the snow? Would that help?

Her mind was a battleground of conflict—the memory of her guard's shocked and worried faces, embarrassment at being surprised like that, the eerie sense that she'd been possessed by the kind of romping jilt who would take advantage of a prisoner of war. She wanted to do things with Matelon that she'd never contemplated before.

This was mingled with an intense desire to push Bosley over a cliff.

When my mother told me to win Matelon over, this is probably not what she had in mind, Lyss thought. But she'd given Lyss an impossible task: keep the thaneling prisoner, but make friends with him.

What must Matelon be thinking? Did this confirm everything he'd heard about the women in the north? He'd seemed enthusiastic enough, but maybe he felt like he had to go along. Was he worried about what might happen next or was he cynically looking forward to it?

Her answer came two days later when Matelon bolted. Lyss had called a halt for the midday. Matelon went off for a piss, and never came back. He'd staked his pony a short distance away, and so it was some time before he was missed. His hands were still shackled, but that didn't stop him.

It took the best part of that day to track him down. He was smart. Instead of retracing their trail back south, he'd continued east, apparently planning to round Alyssa Peak and cross the plateau to Spiritgate. He knew the territory, after all—he'd come that way in the fall with Karn's army. But one rider is easy to spot on the expanse of a snowy plain. When they ran him down, it took four soldiers to subdue him, and all parties ended up bruised and bloody. When he was finally pinned, Lyss had to intervene personally to prevent Bosley from pounding him to a pulp.

When the healers were done with him, Lyss went to see him in the makeshift tent they'd put up for the purpose.

He was sitting on a trunk, his manacled hands dangling between his knees. They'd stripped him to the waist so they could wrap his broken ribs and get at his many cuts and bruises. Around his neck, he wore a silver thimble on a chain—an odd ornament for a soldier.

The muscles that layered his shoulders and arms were inscribed with the remnants of past battles overlaid with the fresh wounds of today. Lyss longed to trace that history with her fingers so she could read the man beneath.

Haven't you done enough damage?

Matelon looked up, and caught her staring. "My sword-master used to say that the scars a man carries are the evidence that he let someone get too close."

"He was right," Lyss said. "But that's how we fight in the north—in close." She paused, and when he didn't respond, said, "You shouldn't have run."

"You should have let me go." He looked away.

"I can't do that. The queen forbade me to . . . The queen made it clear how important it was to keep you from escaping."

"What do you—what does your queen intend to do with me?"

"I don't think she knows. It depends on what happens between your father and the new king."

"So I'm to be imprisoned until that's sorted out? That could take years."

"This war won't last forever," she said, echoing Matelon's

words in the ruins of the old castle. She paused, and, then, in a rush, said, "Captain, I'm sorry about the other night."

His eyes met hers. Steady, honest eyes that made her feel worse than ever. "I'm not."

"That should never have happened. It was wrong to put you in that position."

"I rather liked that position while it lasted," he said, without a trace of a smile. If he'd smirked, she would have had to kill him. "I didn't run because of what happened in the ruins. In fact, that was the one thing that might have persuaded me to stay."

"I should not have misled you about what can happen between us," Lyss said, the words all but catching in her throat. Why was it so damned hard to do the right thing?

"Didn't you say that the key is to live in the moment?" Matelon said.

"That's the excuse people use for foolish behavior."

"I am not a giddy person," Matelon said, and the whole notion was so ludicrous that Lyss might have laughed if she hadn't had this big aching hole inside. "But I've never met anyone like you. We have so much in common, and yet you've made me question everything I thought I knew. It's . . ." He looked down at his hands. "It's painful, but I want to keep on with it. I'm teachable, and I think we could be good together in whatever way makes sense to you."

Matelon was no poet, either, but he got the job done.

"And yet you ran?"

"Aye," he said. "I ran. My family is in danger. My sister . . . she's just thirteen. If what your queen says is true, she's in the gaol at Ardenscourt. I've seen it." His face was a mask of worry.

"Our lives are at cross-purposes," Lyss said. "It's time we recognized that. But I hope that we can still be friends." For once, she took no joy in scoring a point on Matelon.

"Is this how you treat your friends in the north?"

"This is war," Lyss said. "We are soldiers. I wish things could be different." She wondered if this new pain in her gut was her heart breaking.

Matelon gripped both her hands. "We *are* soldiers," he said. "We are not game pieces on a board. Don't let them play us. Give this thing a chance."

Lyss gently pulled free. "You're wrong, Captain," she said. "We never had a chance. At the end of the day, that is all that we are—game pieces. If you don't know that by now, you soon will."

The rest of the way to Chalk Cliffs, Lyss put Matelon's pony on a lead line, where he could be towed along amid a group of Wolves. Every night, she ordered Matelon shackled to a tree. She'd already decided that there would be no more private conversations. She'd always been as easy to read as any book, and she didn't want to offer him any encouragement. Her life was complicated enough as it was.

Then why did she feel this desperate sense of loss?

She also ordered Bosley to have no direct contact with Matelon. He didn't take it well.

"What do you mean, no contact? I am the commander of this squadron, and, as such—"

"And, as such, you report to me," Lyss said. "My only regret is that I didn't act on this sooner."

"Is this about when we had to subdue him? Did he lodge some kind of complaint against me? If so, he—"

"I have eyes, Bosley. As a prisoner of the crown, Captain Matelon is under the charge of the queen's Gray Wolf guard. I've already spoken with Corporal Greenholt and instructed her to that effect."

"But—"

"Further, if anything happens to my prisoner between here and Chalk Cliffs—if he falls off a cliff, or dies in his sleep, or mysteriously disappears—I'll see you brought up on charges."

"How do you expect me to—?"

"You're done, Lieutenant. Now, go."

All through the rest of the trip, Lyss imagined that she felt the captain's eyes on her. But it was probably swiving Bosley. If he kept on the way he was going, *he* was going to end up falling off a cliff.

Everything taken together, she was relieved to descend the long slope to the stark white cliffs of the northern coastline and to see the angry gray Indio beyond. She looked forward to seeing Sasha again, someone she could actually talk to.

The plan was to stash Matelon away in the keep and send word via Julianna's operatives in the south to see if contact could be established with the thane his father. Otherwise, they'd keep his presence quiet in order to prevent any possible attacks on the city in an effort to free him. That was diplomacy—a mixture of friendly faces and veiled threats.

Lyss had visited Chalk Cliffs several times in the past. The town had once been a bustling, prosperous port— but it was hard to believe it now. Blockades by Ardenine warships and attacks by Carthian pirates had reduced commerce to a trickle. Warehouses stood empty, since little to nothing was coming in, and clan crafters and vale farmers were forced to find other routes for their trade goods. The high street was lined with taverns and bawdy houses and little else.

The keep was perched on a cliff-faced bluff that thrust out into the ocean. The waves crashing on three sides meant that Lyss never slept well under that roof. But, except for the fact it was on the coast and so vulnerable to attack from the sea, it was as secure a place as any in the queendom. To meet the seaward threat, large cannon had been mounted on the clifftops overlooking the harbor.

Lyss knew Matelon would try to escape again, the first chance he got. She didn't blame him, given the situation with his family, but she couldn't let that happen, not after she and her mother had argued over it.

She didn't want to throw him in the dungeon, either. When she explained the situation to the duty officer, he recommended that the Ardenine captain be quartered in a suite of rooms isolated on the seaward side.

"If you don't want to put him in lockup, that's the best place," he said. "Put a brace of bluejackets outside of the door, and he's not going anywhere, and nobody's getting to him, either."

Lyss ordered a fire laid on the hearth, refilled the lamps with oil, and had a variety of books brought in. Warm clan-woven blankets were piled on the bed. There was a desk with writing materials, and a small table for private dining. French doors led to a balcony overlooking the sea.

Do you think Matelon's going to be any happier if he's kept in a gilded cage?

Would *she* be content in any Ardenine prison, even if it were plush?

Or is this supposed to make you feel less guilty?

When Lyss showed Matelon into his new quarters, he paused just inside the door and took a good look around. He's doing the same as he did at Queen Court, Lyss thought. The same as I would do—surveying the defenses and how to break through them. The southerner had said little since his escape attempt, but she was under no illusion that he'd given up.

He walked farther into the room, setting down his

bag with his belongings. He'd been forced to give up his ruined mudback uniform coat after his escape attempt. Rather than put him into Queen's Guard blue or Highlander spattercloth, Lyss had found him a warm sheepskin coat and a linen shirt, both clan-made.

That would likely set tongues to wagging.

She handed him a bundle of clothing. "Since the ones you're wearing seem to fit, I brought you two more shirts and a pair of breeches in the same size. I'm thinking you'll want to get into a hot bath before dinner."

"Dinner?" he said, glancing at the table and chairs.

"Dinner's at seven in the dining hall," she said. "I'll have you escorted down when it's time."

At first, he looked as if he might refuse, but then he nodded. "All right," he said.

"I have some business to attend to now. Is there anything else you need, Captain?"

When he looked at her, it was like a sword rammed through her gut. "No, ma'am."

"When you're ready for your bath, just knock. The guards are right outside." She left him standing alone in the center of the room, the bundle of clothing in his hands, the sound of the crashing waves all around.

35

THE BUSKER

Lyss found Sasha in the garrison house, where she was helping the new arrivals settle in. Most of the Highlanders who had been stationed there had been deployed to help with the attack on Delphi. Now Bosley's squadron would stay to reinforce the garrison here.

Lyss embraced her friend—reassured by the solid feel of her in the quicksand of her life. "What's the news?" she said. "Have you wrung any more information from the busker?"

Sasha shook her head. "If you ask me, it's a waste of time, your coming all the way out here," she said. "Finn used wizard persuasion to try and get the truth out of him, but it didn't work. Then he set himself on fire, and—"

"Finn?"

"No. The busker."

"What?" Lyss stared at her. "Was he badly hurt?"

"It burned his arm pretty bad before we could put it out. It's looking a lot better now."

"Was he trying to kill himself?"

Sasha shook her head. "I don't know what he was thinking. But we stripped everything out of his room that we thought he could harm himself with, and he hasn't tried it again, so maybe he learned his lesson. He keeps begging for a mouth harp, a drum, a set of pipes—something he can play music with. It's like he's starving for it."

There had been a time when being without music would have broken Lyss's spirit. But that was a long time ago. "Or he's playing you," Lyss said. "You haven't given him anything, have you? Anything to play, I mean?"

Sasha shook her head. "That seemed like a bad idea after what happened in Ragmarket. He fancies himself to be a charmer, but it's all a big show. Now he's pretending to be sick." Sasha snorted in disgust.

Lyss squeezed Sasha's shoulder. She knew that much of her anger stemmed from Lyss's close call the night of the concert, the fact that Sasha hadn't been able to prevent it, and the fact that nobody had been held accountable for Staunton and Carew. Yet.

Still, it almost seemed like Sasha was trying to convince herself.

"Have you heard any news from Arden? Any signs that they might come after the busker?"

Sasha hesitated. "All's quiet as far as Arden is concerned. But people in town are on edge. They say they're seeing a lot of strangers on the streets. Me, I'm thinking, it's a port town, what do you expect?"

Lyss laughed, but she couldn't help feeling a prickle of unease. Chalk Cliffs didn't see near the shipping traffic that it once did. Why would there be a sudden influx of strangers?

The guardhouse wasn't exactly a dungeon by castle standards, but it was relatively secure, being built of stone and lodged within the stone walls of the keep.

Maybe we should move the busker into the cliffside tower with Matelon, Lyss thought, since that's the most impregnable part of the keep. Most of the cells they passed by were empty, save those occupied by a few local thieves and street fighters. With less commerce, there were fewer sailors getting into the kind of mischief that happens in port.

As they neared the end of the hall, Lyss could hear a faint sound—like moaning—that grew louder until they stood before a heavy cell door.

"Well, he's still at it," Sasha said. Then she banged open the door. "You, there! Wake up. Someone's here to see you."

Lyss followed Sasha into the cell and scanned the room.

A washbasin on a stand; a chamber pot; a narrow pallet on the floor, piled with blankets, someone huddled underneath. That was it.

Sasha marched over to the bed and shook its occupant roughly. "I said get *up!*"

"I'm getting ready to get up," the person muttered. "Just give me a minute. It's just so bloody cold here that it's hard to get out from under the blankets."

The bed's occupant sat up, shivering, shoulders hunched. It was the busker, but he'd changed for the worse since he'd charmed her in the street. His face had gone from finely etched to hollow-cheeked and haggard. Though he'd claimed to be cold, his face was shiny with sweat and his damp hair was plastered to his forehead. He scratched himself in a rude place. "What time is it, anyway?"

"Time to get up."

"Time to take a piss, you mean." Walking on his knees to the edge of the pallet, he was fumbling with the buttons on his breeches when he looked up and spotted Lyss. Swearing, he dove back under the covers.

"You should of told me somebody was here," he said, his voice muffled by blankets.

"Who'm I, nobody?" Sasha shook her head in disgust, giving her an *I told you so* look.

"Busker!" Lyss said sharply. "Don't waste any more of our time. Take a piss if you need to and let's talk."

He sat up again, the blanket draped over his head like

a Voyageur's cowl, and blinked at her like an owl in day-light. And, then, somehow, he slipped over the edge of the bed and down on one knee on the floor, arms spread gracefully, head bowed—a genuflection worthy of any up-and-comer at court.

"Your Munificence," he said. "Please forgive me. My p-p-piss and I are at your command."

Lyss tried to think of what she should command his piss to do.

But then she took a second look. He was so bloody thin, and the outstretched hands were trembling, and when his eyes met hers, the bottomless hunger in them broke her heart.

Sasha was not amused. Grabbing the busker's out-stretched arms, she twisted them behind his back and shoved him flat on his face on the floor. Planting a knee at the base of his spine, she growled, "Do you think this is some kind of joke? The princess doesn't have time for your nonsense."

"Hang on," Lyss said. "Let him go, Sasha."

Sasha looked up at her, a warning in her eyes. "He's a chameleon, Your Highness. He knows how to play you."

"I know that," Lyss said. "And you may be right, but, still."

Reluctantly, Sasha released the busker and sat back on her heels, hands on her thighs, waiting.

Pale as eggshells, the boy lay on the cell floor, gasping

for breath. Then he rolled over, tried to sit up, then doubled over again.

Lyss knelt next to him.

Sasha put her hand on Lyss's arm. "Your Highness. Don't get too close to him. If he's really sick, it might be something catching. And if he's not, he might witch you. At least wait until we can have a wizard in here with us."

Lyss had no gift for healing, no instinct for diagnosis, but she couldn't help thinking the boy's distress wasn't a sham. Not entirely, anyway.

"What's the matter with you?" she said.

This time, the busker came up onto his knees. "I'm sorry, Your Highness, to be in such a state. I—" He retched, then threw up onto the stone floor, spattering Lyss's knees.

"I—I'm sorry." Taking hold of his shirttail, he tried to swipe the sick from her trousers.

"Leave off," Sasha growled. "Don't touch her, you mur-derous, gutter-swiving—"

"I'm all right," Lyss said. "I've been smeared with worse. Never mind."

The busker licked cracked lips. "I'm sorry about the mess. I'm just not at my best in the morning, is all. Perhaps, if you . . . came back later . . ."

Behind her, Sasha snorted in derision. "You'd think he was coming off a binge, wouldn't you? I guarantee, he hasn't been drinking in here."

Lyss stared at the busker, who lay, sucking in shallow

breaths. "How long has he been like this?"

"He looked pretty good when he arrived," Sasha said. "It's only been today that he's been complaining that he's sick. Maybe he heard you were coming and knew the jig was up."

"Call in a healer," Lyss said.

"With all due respect—"

"Do it," Lyss said wearily. "He may be faking, but we can't take the chance that it's something serious, or something catching. He needs to stay alive."

The healer, Grace, looked too young to have much experience, but she'd practiced under Willo Watersong at Marisa Pines Camp, so she must have had some chops.

She studied the busker, her eyes narrowed. Then checked his pulse, brushed the backs of her fingers across his clammy skin, and peeled back his eyelid to have a look, ignoring his weak protests and a series of vile oaths, followed by the usual litany of apologies.

She leaned in toward him and said, "Did you take something, boy?"

"No," he said quickly, as if he'd anticipated the question.

"No?" She raised an eyebrow.

"Well, not for a long time."

"What do you call a long time?"

The busker didn't respond, only lay there in a heap of misery.

"We can't help you if you don't tell the truth," Lyss said.

"You're not here . . . to help me," the busker said.

"Maybe we can help each other," Lyss said.

The busker rolled onto his back, shading his eyes against the light with his forearm. "All right. I do use the leaf, now and then," he said. "But I can take or leave."

"How long's it been?" the healer asked.

"This morning."

"This *morning*?" Sasha would have said more, but Grace raised her hand to hush her.

"So you've used it in here?"

He nodded. Then twitched as tremors rolled through him.

"There's no way you smuggled anything in here," Sasha said, looking personally offended. "Or smoked it if you did. I don't believe you."

The boy cracked a smile. "Maybe," he said, "I outsmarted you. Maybe *some* people aren't as hard-hearted as you are." He gasped and doubled up, clutching at his middle. "Only this seems to be . . . unusually . . . ." He didn't seem to know how to finish the sentence.

Sasha began tearing the cell apart, pawing through the busker's meager belongings. "Where is it?" she demanded. "Where'd you hide the rest of it?"

"There wasn't much," he said. "It's all gone. I wouldn't—aaahhhhh!" His face twisted, squeezing out tears, and he rolled into a ball.

"I think you might have smoked some bad leaf," Grace said. "It would help if I could have a look at any that's left."

For a long moment, the busker didn't respond. Then he reached into his breeches and pulled out a small pouch. "Here." He swallowed hard. "But I hope you'll . . . see your way clear to . . . give it back . . . when you're done looking."

Grace didn't reply. She yanked open the drawstring neck and shook a dark wad out onto her palm. She rubbed it between her fingers and took a sniff. Her eyes widened, and she took another. Then she dumped the leaf back into the bag, crossed to the washstand, and scrubbed her hands thoroughly.

"Whoever sold you that leaf was no friend," she said. "It's been soaked in oil of moonflower."

"I've never . . . heard of that," the busker gasped.

"That's because it's a poison," Grace said.

For a long moment, nobody said anything. Sasha in particular looked like she'd been run over by a cart.

"Well," the busker said, with a hollow laugh, "that explains a lot."

Lyss dropped to her knees beside him. "Busker," she said, "this is important. Where did you get this razorleaf?"

He looked up at her with muddled eyes. Then he shrank back, batting at something invisible. "Get away!"

Lyss leaned back to avoid his flailing arms. Sasha moved in on his other side, doing her best to pin his arms.

The busker quieted a bit. His eyes cleared and focused in on Lyss. "I—I didn't know. Your Highness, you have to believe me. I didn't know they were going to try and kill you."

"I believe you," Lyss said, gripping his hand. "Now, where did you get the leaf?"

"Somebody must've slid it through the bars last night while I was asleep," he said. "I woke up and found it. I thought it was . . . a Good Samaritan."

He went rigid and began to tremble uncontrollably.

"He's having a seizure," Grace said. "Roll him onto his left side, put a pillow behind him, and make sure he can breathe. You." She motioned to Sasha. "Keep an eye out. If he vomits, clear it out so it doesn't go into his lungs. His lips are pink and his nails are, too, so he's getting air. Hopefully his lungs aren't too damaged."

"Is there any treatment we can give him?"

"Just support. If he'd *swallowed* it, we could dilute it with water or use charcoal or force vomiting, but it's in his bloodstream already."

"This is my fault," Sasha said, her face gray. "I should have known I couldn't keep this quiet. I should have been more careful. Now somebody's got to him on my watch."

Anger and frustration knifed through Lyss. "What are his odds, Grace?"

The healer rocked her hand back and forth. "I'd like his chances better if he was healthy. From the looks of things, he's been using a lot of leaf. If you keep on using, you just burn yourself up. A lower body weight makes any poison more potent."

Lyss looked across at Sasha. "Who has access to the cell block?"

"Just . . . the Queen's Guard," Sasha said. "Some in the Highlanders. Nobody from outside."

Lyss stood. "We need him alive, and well enough to interview. Clearly, somebody doesn't want that to happen. I don't want him to have any visitors without my approval, and no unvetted guards on him. I'm putting the two of you in charge of his care. I want both of you in here around the clock until he recovers."

"Me?" Sasha said, looking horrified. "I thought that with you back here, I'd be assigned to—"

"This is the most important thing you can do right now to keep me safe. If he dies, we'll lose the one connection we have to whoever ordered the attack."

Lyss could hear the boy's raspy breathing from where she stood. *Don't you dare die on me, busker. If you do, I'll make a special trip to hunt you in hell.*

36

BY LAND AND BY SEA

It had been two weeks since Jenna collected her leatherwork from Sparrow, but she and Cas hadn't traveled far.
They had decided that Fortress Rocks was a good location for flying practice. It was remote enough that they
could fly for miles without being seen, and the terrain was
variable—craggy mountains and high plateaus and coastline within a few hours as the dragon flies.

She hesitated to travel too far from the coast until she
and Cas got a few things sorted out between them. Like
the many differences between people and dragons—their
priorities and their physical limits. Cas was high-spirited,
headstrong, and growing at what seemed to be an impossible rate.

The clothing and armor Sparrow had made for her fit well, so now she looked like a real warrior, but that didn't really make her one. She was woefully short on the kinds of skills she would need to confront Strangward or the empress. She didn't exactly know what she would be up against, but she had a feeling that a sharp pair of ears, a keen eye, and a layer of scales wouldn't be enough.

As a working-class city girl, she'd never had any reason to learn to use a bow, even for hunting. She'd had no practice with a sword. The closest she'd come was when she'd killed Marco with her mother's jeweled dagger. She *was* good at setting fire to things and blowing things up on the ground. She guessed she could drop boulders or bombs on an enemy. Still, she felt like the weak link.

Cas had armor and weapons built in. He seemed to look on Jenna as a small, rather feeble dragon who'd somehow misplaced her wings yet showed no sign of growing a new pair. They practiced incinerating dead trees and sharpening Cas's aim even when flying at high speed, and flying the zigzag patterns that would allow them to evade enemy fire. Sometimes they played games in the sky, writing words with smoke and flame, because that took precision flying. Sometimes they engaged in mock aerial battles with eagles and hawks.

The tack Sparrow had made worked spectacularly well, especially considering that the leatherworker had never seen a dragon. Jenna had to make some adjustments to get it to the right size, and then continually refit it to accommodate Cas's growth. She'd always been good with her hands.

Flamecaster scarcely seemed to notice the harness and saddle once Jenna strapped it on, but it gave Jenna a lot more confidence when the young dragon got creative with aerobatics. Now she clung to his back like a briar in wool, no matter how many twists and turns he made.

For now, the best strategy seemed to be avoiding people altogether. The sudden appearance of a dragon in any populated area would end badly for Cas or the people or both. Once they landed, Jenna wouldn't be much help unless her opponent agreed to hold still long enough to be blown up. She resolved to change that.

I can't hide out forever, Jenna thought. Sooner or later I'm going to have to go hunting for bigger game.

She didn't know much about foraging, either. Flamecaster brought fresh meat on a regular basis, and Jenna was able to rig up a fishing line and catch a few fish, and she found some mussels in the streams, plus watercress and cattail shoots and frozen cranberries in the marshes. Most everything else was buried in snow, or if it wasn't, she was afraid to eat it.

Cas made no secret of his disdain for the vegetables she found (*not food; food for food*), though he did have a bit of a sweet tooth. But Jenna could gather berries all day and it wouldn't even be a mouthful for the dragon.

She wanted to get familiar with the harbors and inlets along the coast, places where a pirate might be found. She'd also promised Cas they would go fishing. So, one morning, they headed for the coast. They left before the sun was even a glow on the horizon, hoping that by the time it was light, they would be far to the north, where, Jenna hoped, it would be less populated and they would be less likely to be seen.

They soared over snow-covered peaks, then turned straight north toward an inlet called Invaders Bay on the map. The mountains formed a dark wall to their left, and the distant Indio was somewhere out there in the dark to their right.

The peninsula they were crossing was relatively flat, and snow-covered. Midway across, Jenna could see a large, dark shadow below, moving south toward them.

"What's that?" Jenna muttered.

Herd of fellsdeer? Flamecaster said hopefully. *Fat sheep?*

"Not at night," Jenna muttered. "Let's go see."

As they drew closer, Jenna could see that it was a swarm of riders, pushing hard to cross that flat span of land. Now and then they glittered as the setting moon reflected off the weapons they carried. An army.

As they flew over the horse troops, Cas stayed high, which was his usual practice when they encountered the rare person on their flights. Hopefully, in a land unfamiliar with dragons, they'd be taken for some sort of large bird.

Was this the northern Highlander army on the move, riding hard to meet some sort of threat from the south? If so, they weren't wearing their usual camouflage clothing, the greens and browns of the forest or the white of the winter landscape. Could Arden be moving to retake Delphi or attack Fortress Rocks again? They weren't wearing the dirtback tan of Arden, either. In fact, their clothing varied dramatically—so much so that they didn't look like an army at all. But they moved like an army under orders for a forced march. Could they be a band of mercenaries hired by Arden?

Were these more of Strangward's lot—what was it King Gerard had called them—horse savages? Had they come here from Carthis to close the jaws of a trap around her from a different direction?

It's not always about you, she told herself. But she needed to know.

"Cas! Can you go a little lower?" By now, the moon had been swallowed by the clouds shrouding the western peaks, so at least they wouldn't cast a shadow on the ground. Jenna had to hope that her eyes were sharper than those of the horse warriors.

Flamecaster came around and crossed the peninsula again, dropping much lower than he usually did so she could take a closer look. Though the riders were bundled up warmly, there was something about their dress and appearance that reminded Jenna of Strangward's guard—the Stormborn, he'd called them. Then her breath seemed to catch in her throat. They were mages—most of them—mages who displayed an odd, tinted glow like the one she associated with Strangward's companions. Strangward's mages had glowed red. The wizards she'd seen in Delphi—the only kind she'd seen until recently—glowed with a blue-white light.

These glowed purple, like a shadow, or a deep bruise. Almost as if they were sucking up light rather than giving it off.

Why would they send so many, to hunt one girl? They didn't know about Cas, did they? Or were they on some other mission?

Should she warn someone? Who? If they were looking for her, the last thing she needed was to draw attention to herself. Riding in on a dragon would be a good way to do that. She didn't know enough even to take sides. Anyway, maybe mages in the north came in all sorts of colors.

This northern country that had seemed so empty was getting too crowded.

"Let's get out of here," Jenna said, nudging the dragon with her knees. "Let's try our luck farther south this time."

Cas turned, making a wide, shallow arc to head back toward the shelter of the mountains.

They approached the coast again, this time aiming between the town of Chalk Cliffs and the border port of Spiritgate. As they neared the ocean, the terrain plateaued until it ended in a series of white cliffs along the water. Those were easy to pick out, even in the gray dawn, for sharp-eyed flyers. A harbor town hugged the tops of the cliffs. This would be Chalk Cliffs.

Fish? Flamecaster prompted her, in case she'd forgotten.

"Remember? First we're going to fly along the coast and look for ships. Then we'll fish."

Fishing was the carrot that had enticed Cas to agree to this plan. After his experience with Strangward, he was still wary of ships.

The dragon ascended rapidly as they passed over the harbor and the few ships anchored there. Higher and higher they flew, and Jenna knew that the dragon meant to come down in one of his steep dives that left her stomach far behind. But as they reached the top of the climb, she looked out to sea—far out to sea—and saw three tall ships anchored a few miles offshore, silhouetted against the brightening eastern horizon.

What are they doing out there? Jenna thought.

Flamecaster saw them just about the same time, and put on the brakes so abruptly that if not for her improved seat in the saddle, Jenna would have been pitched over the dragon's head.

Dark place. Chains. Collar hurts.

Making a tight turn, the dragon made a beeline for shore, his neck stretched forward as if that would get him there sooner.

"Hang on! Wait! It's all right, Cas. I won't let that happen to you again."

It made no difference. The dragon didn't slow down until they were back over land again. She could feel his heart thumping in his throat, and every now and then he whimpered.

Jenna thought about it. She'd never gotten a good look at Strangward's ship, except when they'd soared over it just before it exploded. Her vision was good, but the dragon's eyes were even better. "Do those ships look like the one you came here in, Cas?"

Maybe. His hide quivered under her fingers. *No fish today.*

Had Strangward returned so soon, with three ships this time, to try his luck again? Had the empress joined the hunt? How would they know if she was here in the north?

They could be Ardenine vessels, ready to swoop in on ships entering or leaving the harbor. Or pirates after other goods that had nothing to do with her.

Mountains? Cas had been subtly shifting course, flying more and more westerly, away from the coast. She understood his desire to flee back into the mountains. But if they were going to go after Strangward or the empress, Cas would have to make his peace with ships.

They both had demons to fight. Maybe, with a little shared courage, they could do it.

"Not every ship is after us," she said, resting her cheek on Flamecaster's shoulder and stroking him between his stubby horns. "Let's find some fish."

She'd been working on teaching the dragon directions, and now he swerved south, following the coast, just off-shore. They'd gone just a short distance when another tremor ran through him.

More ships. Cas was trying to sound nonchalant. *Not after us. Maybe.*

Jenna looked down and saw what seemed to be a race going on. Two northbound ships were running parallel to the cliffs, zigzagging back and forth to catch the wind. The ship in the lead was a smaller vessel, broad of beam, with two masts. It wallowed a bit through the waves, slow to turn and maneuver.

The other was a sleek tall ship, with multiple sails. This one closely resembled the ship she and Adam Wolf had destroyed at Ardenscourt, and the ships they'd just seen lurking offshore. Jenna didn't know much about ships, but even she could tell that this was the faster of the two. It seemed like it was only a matter of time before the one overtook the other.

Was the smaller ship a Fellsian vessel, under attack by Arden or the empress? If so, should they help?

This is not your fight, she told herself.

If it's not, then how do you know when it is *your fight?*

A memory came back to her, of her father pleading with

her to quit blowing up things.

I wish you wouldn't . . . do the things that you do. That's surely a job for someone else. Nobody takes the risks that you take.

And her response.

I'm not going to huddle in a garret while others do my fighting for me.

If that's Strangward's ship, or Strangward's allies, then it's my fight.

Jenna sighed. "Cas, can you go down a little closer so I can make out the colors?"

Making a shallow turn over the land, Cas came around again, swooping lower over the two ships. The smaller ship flew a banner with a yellow star on a blue field. Was that the Fellsian flag? She had no idea. The larger ship flew a black flag, which seemed to name it the villain.

As if to underline that thought, the larger ship launched a ball of fire at the ship in the lead. It landed a short distance off their bow. It was not cannon fire; it was some kind of magery.

Pirates miss. Cas curled his lip in scorn, exposing sword-sharp teeth. *No good.*

"I think they're missing on purpose," Jenna said. "They don't want to sink them, they want them to surrender."

Now the larger ship ran another flag up its mast. It was a purple death's-head on a black background. The same colors Strangward's ship had flown. Pirate colors. Did that mean it was Strangward? How could he have found another ship so quickly?

Was it the empress herself?

Suddenly, Cas pitched and rolled sideways, flapping madly to regain his equilibrium and avoid smashing into the cliff. By the time he righted himself, they were some distance inland. For a moment, Jenna thought that she might lose her breakfast.

Jenna sick? Cas sounded worried. She couldn't blame him. She'd thrown up on him before.

"It was just . . . I guess I wasn't expecting that," Jenna said. "What happened?"

Wind changed.

That stirred something in Jenna's memory, but she couldn't pin it down.

By the time they made it back to the coastline, the smaller ship was lying just offshore, the bigger ship blocking the way out to sea. They could see people moving on the decks, and she could hear shouting between the two ships. The pirates seemed to be demanding that the smaller ship surrender, and the crew of the smaller ship seemed to be refusing.

Now the small ship raised a different flag, a stylized dragon (not Fellsian, then), and returned fire, destroying the pirate ship's tallest mast. The dragon-flagged ship plowed north again, hugging the shoreline. After some momentary confusion, the pirates gave chase, lobbing bolts of flame at their quarry that came close, but never hit. Cas followed, skimming the clifftop so hopefully they wouldn't be seen.

Should they intervene? Set fire to the pirate ship? Drop a block of granite onto its deck and put a hole in it? It would be easier to pick sides if they knew for sure who was down there. Since they didn't, it was hard to justify risking themselves.

Does he really think he can outrun them? Jenna thought.

Not running, Flamecaster said. *No feet.*

Jenna rolled her eyes. Dragon jokes.

As it turned out, the little ship didn't need their help. Just as the bigger ship seemed close to overtaking them again, it appeared to slam into an unseen barrier. With an awful crunching, grinding sound, the bow of the pirate ship lifted a little, then settled back as the ship shuddered to a stop, listing. The smaller ship sailed on. Jenna could hear faint cheering from the decks. Now she could see the shadowy shapes under the water, extending out from the shoreline. A reef.

It took a moment for her to figure it out. The smaller, shore-hugging boat had a shallower draft than the sleek pirate. She could glide over an obstacle that stopped the blue-water ship in its tracks.

In other words, the crew of the little ship had out-smarted the pirates.

The pirates had figured that out, too, because now a storm of flame arced from the larger ship, hissing into the water all around the other ship, which was rapidly putting distance between them. One blast of flame finally hit home, cracking one of the masts in two. But the little ship kept moving, the crew manipulating two smaller sails, until it was out of range.

Jenna was torn between following after the smaller ship and taking a closer look at the pirates, who were swarming over the decks, trying to put out the flames in the mast and rigging. She could see someone standing on a small, raised deck behind the tallest mast, shouting orders to the others. Someone who glowed so brightly that Jenna had to squint.

"Can you get down a little closer?" *I'm sure those are someone's last words*, she thought.

Jenna could sense the dragon's bone-deep terror. *Not after us. Not after us.* He slowly spiraled down toward the water's surface, his muscles bunched with tension.

Maybe it was catching, because, as they drew closer, a dull dread took root in her and grew. The magemark on her neck seethed and burned as if it might burst into flame. Every fiber of her being screamed *danger.*

Jenna? Cas gave her a mental nudge.

"One quick look, then we'll go," she said.

The first surprise was that the figure on the deck was a young woman, not much older than Jenna. Locks of metallic silver hair twisted around her head like a nest of snakes in a scary story. She wore a leather waistcoat over a snowy linen shirt with a divided skirt. The dagger belted at her side—

Jenna's heart quivered and almost stopped. It was a jeweled, curved dagger—like the one left to her by her mother. The one her father had kept hidden in a box under her bed until they came for her.

This must be the empress that she'd been warned about. That had been hunting her. That she was hunting now. *Celestine*. Surely she was too young to be an empress.

It was as if the empress heard her name. She stiffened, then looked up and saw them.

A rush of emotion all but foundered them.

"You!"

Jenna wasn't sure whether the empress spoke aloud, or inside her head, but the message was clear—mingled triumph, joy, and unbridled lust. The empress extended her arms greedily, reaching for them.

"Cas!"

The dragon was already climbing, his neck extended, his muscles bunching and releasing as he sliced through the air. Jenna clung to his back, shaking, and no use to anyone.

When they were high in the sky, Jenna took one quick look back. The empress still stood on her ship's deck, hands on hips, watching them go, ignoring her crew, who were still frantically fighting the fire.

When they were out of sight of the pirate ship, Cas

slowed his frantic wingbeats and flattened his climb a bit.

What now? It was a measure of his agitation that fishing wasn't even mentioned.

"We need to find that smaller ship the pirates were attacking," Jenna said. "It seems like they might have some of the answers we want."

37

A SECOND
INTERVIEW

Breon didn't remember much about the days immediately after he smoked the bad leaf. Most of it, he didn't *want* to remember, being the kind of person who tries to move on from misery. He didn't know how much of it was from the poisoned leaf, and how much from withdrawal, but it wasn't something he cared to relive in his mind or elsewhere.

But there *were* a couple of high points. For instance, Talbot scrubbing the muck off him with this wonderful rough, hot washcloth, which left his skin tingling. And feeding him thick soups and rich puddings once he stopped hurling. She might have even massaged his back when it was tied up in knots, but he might have made that up.

There was this other thing that was probably a dream, but he enjoyed it anyway. He heard this wonderful music, and thought it might be choirs of angels, which didn't make sense, given the way he'd lived his life up to now. It turned out to be the princess, playing her basilka for him.

Now I can die happy, he thought. He'd thought he was on his way to doing that before he got executed. They likely had special methods for those who try to hush a princess, and he'd just as soon sit that out.

But now he was actually feeling better, so he had to act fast. Dying seemed easier than escaping. Breon closed his eyes and folded his hands and tried to let go of his body, but he kept on breathing, and, before long, he got hungry and thirsty and had to take a piss. Why is it that a person is always dying when he doesn't plan on it, but when it's in his best interest, he has no luck at all?

The next time Talbot came in, Breon asked for pen and paper, and she brought some. "I hope you're planning to write out your confession, scumbag," she said, but he could tell that her heart wasn't in it. Breon was pretty sure he was winning Talbot over; as time went on she seemed less and less likely to cut off body parts. That had been his goal—to remain intact during his incarceration. A man has to have goals, and now that he was off the leaf, he was doing better at remembering them.

Besides, Breon wasn't used to being hated. He didn't like being packed in with somebody who looked like they wanted to yank his guts out through his eyes. Or some other aperture.

Another good word, *aperture*. He wondered where he'd picked that up. Words were like the Tamric itch—all of the sudden you had it, and don't know where you got it.

"Well?" Talbot said. "What are you planning to write?"

Breon hadn't realized that she actually wanted an answer. "I'm going to write my eulogy," he said.

"What's that?" Talbot said suspiciously.

"It's kind of a tribute speech they give after a person is dead," Breon said.

"Why do you need one of those?" Talbot took a quick look around. "You aren't planning to—?"

"You're the one that said I'd be hung for the two that died in Ragmarket."

"Oh. Right. You will be." Only this time she wasn't gloating, like before. "You're going to write your own?"

"Nobody else is going to do it."

"You've got that right," she said, with a snort. But still, she stood, rubbing the back of her neck, frowning at him. "You don't have anyone? There's nobody we should send a message to?"

"No," he said.

Aubrey had cared about him—he was sure of it. But he wasn't going to send them out hunting for her. He imagined himself going to the block, and her out in the audience somewhere in a long black veil. He liked everything about that story except the going-to-the-block part.

Then he had an inspiration. He looked up at Talbot and said, "If I write something down, would *you* read it?"

"Me?" Talbot took two steps back. "You don't want *me* reading it." She paused. "Do you?"

"I do," Breon said. "I feel like you've been a big part of the story of the end of my life. I've probably spent more time with you than anybody else that's—that could do it."

"What are you going to write?" Talbot asked suspiciously.

"You'll see. If you look it over, and you don't want to read it, you don't have to. I'll be dead, anyway."

"All right," she said. "Fair enough." She cleared her throat. "My name is Sasha."

"Call me Breon. If you want."

It wasn't easy to come up with anything to write. Half of his life had been blotted from his memory, and he didn't really want to write the other half down. Now that his mind was clear, he was remembering things he'd done that he'd just as soon leave buried. It was like when you find something promising lying in the street and you rinse it off and it's just a hunk of broken glass.

It's all in the presentation, he thought, looking over his page of scratched-out lines.

He tried to look out for his friends.
He knew how to have a good time.
He told stories.
He loved sunrises and puppies and walks by the ocean.
Sometimes, he made people forget their worries for a little while.

Then again, you could say pretty much the same for leaf. Speaking of leaf . . . he wondered if he would be granted any last requests.

When he wasn't struggling to put words together, he spent his time reading and sleeping and eating.

It wasn't a bad way to spend his final days. He was just grateful that he wasn't spending them sweating and shaking and cramping and heaving. He was mortified at the display he'd put on when the princess came to see him. He would offer a sincere apology if he ever saw her again, which he probably wouldn't. Which was probably just as well.

A few days later, Breon was sitting under the window, where the light was best, struggling with his eulogy. Sasha had called him a charmcaster, but that didn't seem to project the right image. He'd decided he should go with something more dramatic. Like Shadowcaster.

They called him Shadowcaster, because he came out of
the shadows, and stole the minds and hearts of men. Also
women.

They called him Shadowcaster, because he cast a great shadow over the events of the day. People called him a murderer, but it just wasn't true.
They called him Shadowcaster, because his music was like a torrent of light amid the shadows.

No. Actually, it was the other way around.

That was the problem. He was trying to write a story about a hero, but the truth kept elbowing in and ruining it. *This story isn't about you. This is about the person you wish you were.*

Just then, the door banged open, and in came Her Highness with Sasha Talbot, a moblet of bluejackets, and, to his surprise, Rogan Shadow Dancer—Shadow in the north. The trader must be back from wherever he'd gone off to. To Breon's relief, the young mage, Finn, wasn't with them this time. Breon brushed his fingers over his nearly healed arm. He still wasn't exactly sure what had happened. But he wanted to avoid a repeat.

The princess arrived with an entourage.

Entourage. That was a good word.

Shadowcaster always traveled with an entourage. His friends were many, and his enemies few.

Maybe in his next life.

Breon wrote the line down before he put his scribbling

aside. He rose and crossed the room to where they stood. The bluejackets leapt to get between him and the princess.

He made what he hoped was a graceful bow. "Your Highness," he said. "I apologize for my appearance and my behavior the last time we met."

"Are you talking about the time you lured me into an ambush, or the time you threw up on me?" the princess said.

"I apologize for both," Breon said, bowing still lower. When he straightened, she was studying him, her head cocked, eyes narrowed.

So he studied her back. The night of the concert, he'd seen her first on the stage in her fancy dress and later on the street in her tribal garb. Now she was dressed like a soldier, in the spattery colors the northerners wore. It was like she was three different girlies in one. He'd sensed some of that in her song.

You're not the only one that's a chameleon, he thought. Only, in my case, it's more like I don't really know who I am.

"You're looking amazingly well," the princess said. "It's hard to believe you're the same person."

Breon fussed with the cuffs of his prison shirt. He'd rolled them a bit and turned up his collar for a casual, jaunty look. "I am not the same person, Your Highness," he said. "I am transformed, thanks to Corporal Talbot here, and Grace, and your team of healers. I would be happy to answer any questions you have. I can't tell you how relieved I was to find out that you survived the attack the night of the concert."

"Especially since you were caught," Sasha said.

The princess looked him up and down, head to toe. "Are you getting enough to eat?"

"Yes," Breon said, embarrassed. He knew he looked like a street urchin in a famine. He patted his stomach. Or where it should have been, if he'd had one. "The food's good, and there's plenty. I've probably already gained a few pounds."

"You could use a few more," the princess said bluntly. She motioned for the guards to bring up some chairs. Three chairs facing one. "Sit down," she said.

Breon took the single chair, and the princess sat opposite, with Sasha to her left, Shadow to her right. That was when Breon noticed that Shadow was carrying his jafasa. Not only that, it had been repaired. It looked to be as good as new.

Shadow set the jafasa on the floor, the neck resting against his thigh, and curled one arm protectively around it.

Breon stared at it. It was like it crowded everything else out of his mind. It was the first time in a long time that he'd felt a bone-deep ache for anything other than leaf.

"What do you like to be called, busker?" the princess asked.

"Breon," he said. He licked his lips and took a chance. "I can't help but notice that you've repaired my jafasa."

Shadow nodded. "I believe I have restored your musical instrument to playing condition."

"Shall I try it and see?" Breon said, reaching for it.

Shadow pulled the jafasa back, out of reach. "You'll have to take my word for it, for now," he said.

For now. Did that mean that, eventually . . . ? "I didn't realize that you were a luthier," Breon said.

"I make flashcraft," Shadow said.

Breon shifted his hungry gaze from the jafasa to the trader. "Flashcraft? What do you mean?"

"We are assuming that there is magic in this device, that it functions like an amulet to channel power," the princess said. "So we decided to repair it and see if it would help us understand your magic."

"Has it?"

The trader shrugged. "We're all eager to hear what *you* have to say."

It had been a long time since Breon had thought of much aside from making it to his next hit. He'd not thought of his talent for connection as magery. That would be a dangerous play in Arden or any of the down realms.

"I don't know, I just—I'm just a musician. I don't know how it works. I mean, I know how to play it, is all." He paused. "I can play the flute, too, and the basilka, and the harpsichord, in a pinch."

"Do they all . . . charm people . . . the way the jafasa does?" Shadow stroked the fretboard gently. Like he was taunting him.

"Musical instruments are simply tools that allow nuanced musical expression in the hands of the right person," Breon said.

They all gaped at him.

He was a little surprised himself. He sure was discovering a big stash of words now that he'd quit the leaf.

"The magemark on your neck says that you're more than a simple musician."

"I said I was a musician. I didn't say I was simple." He thought a moment. "Like I said, any instrument helps, even my voice. It's just that the jafasa, or the basilka— really, any stringed instrument—can deliver a complexity that my voice can't. People are chords, not single notes. So unless somebody is a very simple person, my voice doesn't capture them exactly."

Her Highness nodded. "When I heard you playing, it was like— it was like I *knew* the song before I ever heard it."

"I've never, you know, been on the receiving end, so all I can tell you is what it's like from my end." He thought a moment. "I connect to people," he said. "I read them, and I hear their music, and play it back to them. Everyone is different. Everyone has a different song."

"I don't understand," Shadow said.

"You see, that's what's so seductive," Breon said.

Everybody flinched at the word *seductive*, but he soldiered on. "We come into this world alone, and we go out of it the same way. Even our partner, our lover, our best friend—they can only know a part of us, and that knowledge is imperfect. Imagine hearing *your* song, *your* truth, reflected back to you. It resonates here." He pressed his fist against his chest.

"I don't have to imagine it," the princess whispered, putting her hand over her own heart.

"Are you saying that you're a mind reader?" Sasha looked a little panicky, like she wanted to race from the room. Like she had thoughts she didn't want to share.

Breon shook his head. "It's more like a current that runs between me and the listener. It's like, all your life, you've been looking for someone who understands. And now you do."

"It seemed like it shuts out everything else, too," the princess said. "It was like everything else was thrown into shadow."

Exactly, Breon thought, pleased. Shadowcaster.

"The question is, busker, are you casting light or casting shadow?" Shadow said.

That was a very good question. Breon wished that he had a very good answer. He just shrugged.

"Who hired you to lay in wait for the princess heir and lure her away from her friends?" Sasha said, as if eager to get onto a more solid footing.

"I didn't do the deal myself," Breon said. "It was my manager."

"Your manager?" The princess sat forward. "Who is that?"

"He went by 'Whacks' but I think his real name was Crosby, or Crowley, maybe."

"Whacks?" Talbot butted in.

"Right. You know." From the blank looks on their faces, they didn't know. "Like shares. Everybody gets a whack of the pie. But Whacks always got the biggest slice."

"Where can we find him?" Shadow said.

"He's dead. He was murdered in a warehouse back in Fellsmarch along with one of my—ah—colleagues."

Princess Alyssa's eyes narrowed, and Breon got the idea that she already knew about the bodies in Southbridge.

"I was—I think it went down when I—during the street concert," Breon said. "If I'd of been there, I'd be dead, too." He scanned their faces, looking for sympathy, but got none.

"And you were the *only* one that escaped?" Shadow wasn't buying.

"Well. Me and Aubrey," Breon said. "You know, the girlie that traveled with us."

"So Aubrey was in on it?" Shadow leaned forward, as if eager to suck down this new knowledge.

"What do you mean, 'in on it'?" Breon was getting a little prickly himself. "She knew about the gig, that's all. We're musicians. There were four of us that traveled together, including Whacks."

"Where is Aubrey now?" Shadow asked.

Maybe he and Aubrey had been at odds lately, but Breon wasn't going to give her up. "Like I said, I don't know. All I can figure is, she saw through you before I did and ran." He paused. Something had just occurred to him. "Hang on. She wasn't the one who outed me, was she?"

"No," Shadow said. "I figured it out on my own. So this Whacks was the one who gave you the orders? You're claiming you never met the client?"

They all three leaned forward.

"Actually, I did meet the client on the street before the concert." Breon explained about the meeting with the supposed star-crossed suitor, the instructions he'd been given. "He was the one that gave me the locket and the flowers."

"*He* gave you the flowers?" Shadow looked at Talbot, as if that was a major clue.

"Aye, he did. I thought it was peculiar at the time, that he didn't want to give them to her himself. I mean, wouldn't you want to get the credit?"

Sasha pulled out the princess's locket, pried it open, and studied the images inside. "Why would this client give you her locket? There's no picture of her in here."

"Why would she carry a picture of herself, when she could always look in the mirror?" Breon said, then cursed himself for a smart-ass.

"What Talbot means is, why was the locket important?" Shadow said.

"It . . . it sometimes helps me to connect if I have something that belongs to them," Breon said. "It helps me get to know them better."

"I knew it," Talbot said, slapping her thigh, as if he'd just signed a full confession. "Maybe you're not a regular wizard, but you're some kind of charmcaster, just the same."

The way she said *charmcaster*, it sounded filthy.

"I'm a *musician*," Breon said stubbornly. "It was supposed to be a street concert. I had no idea what was going down."

"You didn't think that was an odd request?"

Breon hesitated, then decided to continue on with the truth, since it hadn't cost him so far. "Aye, I did think it was an odd request, but no odder than some others I've heard. As soon as some hear 'private performance,' they get all kinds of ideas. But I'm a musician—that's all. Not a killer."

Although the client *had* asked him to lead the girlie along the riverbank to a secluded place where he'd be waiting. And Breon *had* questioned it at the time, but went ahead anyway.

Anybody with a brain in his head would have known something bad was going down, this annoying voice in his head said.

"What was the money?" Shadow asked.

When Breon didn't answer right away, Sasha said, "What did you get paid to deliver a girl into the hands of assassins?"

"What did *I* get paid? Nothing. Well, I *did* get a suit of clothes and a bath, but—"

"Lives go cheap these days, don't they?"

"No!" Breon said. "According to Whacks, the client was offering forty girlies. I was supposed to be paid after the wooing."

"The . . . wooing? Is that what you call it?" The princess glared at him.

Breon's cheeks burned. "Since the client told me he was a . . . a suitor, I used music to put the—the"—he didn't want to use *target*, since he was in enough trouble already—"the *audience* into a willing mood."

"Willing to do . . . what?" Sasha had the kind of look on her face that said she might just come through the table at him.

Breon groped desperately for something to say that wouldn't be too incriminating. "Willing to . . . uh . . . listen to what my client had to say. That's all."

Talbot shook her head, her face twisted in disgust.

Breon sighed inwardly. I'm losing ground again, he thought. She'll be back to hating me before long.

"What did he look like?" Princess Alyssa said.

"I didn't get a good look at him. He was all wrapped up in a cloak, with a scarf muffling his face." Breon paused.

"He was tall—taller than me. And . . . I'm not sure, but I think he was a mage."

Shadow sat forward. "What makes you think so?"

"He had a mage-ish glow."

"Now we're getting somewhere," Sasha said, with mock enthusiasm. "We'll just question all the tall wizards in the queendom and see if we can turn up any leads."

"That helps, though," the princess said. "Anything that narrows the search. Was there anything else? Even something minor?"

"Well . . . he clanked."

"He *clanked*?" The princess raised an eyebrow.

"Yeah. It was like something jangled when he moved."

"He clanked and he jangled, and he glowed," Sasha said. "We'll nail him for sure."

"Did the client give you a name?" Shadow asked, not looking especially hopeful.

Did he? Breon tried to remember. "I don't think so," he said slowly. And then it came to him, like sunlight breaking through cloud. "It was Darian," he said. "He said his name was Darian. His rushers called him that, too."

"His rushers?" Her highness cocked her head. "You heard them talking? How, exactly, did that happen?"

It seemed like every question Breon answered only birthed another question. Yet he was finding that if he told the truth, he didn't have to remember what lies he'd told before.

"A couple of days after the concert, I went back to the

warehouse where I'd been staying. When I got there . . ." His voice faltered. "When I got there, Whacks and Goose were dead. They'd been murdered."

"How were they killed?" Sasha asked. Again, Breon had the feeling that she knew the answer, and was testing him.

"Their throats were cut. While I was there, I heard somebody coming, and it turned out it was Darian's rushers, come back to make sure there was no clues left. I heard them talking then."

"And, once again, you escaped," Shadow said, raising an eyebrow.

Breon looked him in the eye. "I escaped."

"What else did they say about this 'Darian'?"

"From what they said, he sent them back there to make sure there were no clues left behind," Breon said. "They seemed scared of him."

They all looked at each other. "Was there any mention of Arden, or the war, or why they would target me?" Princess Alyssa asked.

Breon thought about it, then shook his head. "They all seemed afraid to ask questions."

"I'm told you got this musical instrument from your father," Her Highness said. "Was he a musician, too? Was he the one who taught you how to play?"

"Maybe. I think so. I'm not sure." When Sasha huffed at him, he said, "Look, you always think I'm lying, but

I'm telling the truth here. I don't remember anything from before I was about ten years old. I remember wandering the streets of Baston Bay, dragging the jafasa behind. So I started busking, even back then—it was one way for a ten-year to make a little coin. Still, I'd probably be dead if Whacks hadn't taken me in and added me to his traveling show." Breon looked from face to face. He'd done his best, but they still looked disappointed.

"I must admit, Breon, that I am running out of patience," Her Highness said. "You are the single thread that might allow us to track down those responsible for a series of cowardly murders. I need more from you."

"I have told the truth, Your Highness," Breon said. "It's so bloody rare that I suppose I shouldn't expect everyone to recognize it when they hear it."

The princess leaned forward, hands on her knees. "I need a lead. I need to find out who is feeding information to those who mean to do us harm. I need something we can use." She gestured toward the others in the room. "Everyone here has suffered losses—grievous losses. What am I supposed to tell them?"

For once, Breon had nothing to say.

"Many in my position would feel justified in resorting to torture," Princess Alyssa said, with harrowing frankness.

Gods and martyrs, Breon thought. Why couldn't I be the prisoner of a sweet, fairy-tale princess instead of this fierce, warlike one?

"If you torture me," Breon said, "I will talk. I will sing like any bird. I will tell you the most marvelous, detailed stories. I will name names at the highest levels. In fact, one of my accomplices may be right here in this room." He paused, letting that sink in. "And it will all be a lie. Because I already told you the truth, and that wasn't good enough."

His eyes met the princess's. He was all in, knowing that his play could either: one, prompt them to pull out the torture tools right away, or two, convince them that torture was a waste of time. Naturally, he was hoping for two.

Princess Alyssa sighed. "It's only my belief that torture doesn't produce actionable information that stays my hand in this case," she said.

Breon's breath whooshed out, leaving him a little weak and giddy. "If I may say so, Your Highness, you are truly an example for others when it comes to—"

"However," she said, setting his heart to hammering again. "We have other ways to exert pressure." She picked up the jafasa with one hand and strode to the hearth, dangling the instrument over the flames. "I'll give you a week to think about it. After that, this goes into the fire." She handed it back to Shadow. "Think on that, busker. Maybe you would like a chance to play this one last time before we carry out your sentence."

You are truly an example for others when it comes to hardheartedness. That's what I meant to say. He was already writing a tragic ending to this story.

As she turned away, Breon said, "What is the custom here in the north? Am I to be hung, beheaded, or burnt alive?"

She turned back, and smiled a crooked smile. "Maybe all three."

REUNION

Jenna found that she preferred the role of hunter to that of prey for a change. Still, even from the air, the fugitive ship wasn't easy to find. The sun was setting again when they finally found it hidden in one of the inlets that sliced the shoreline. The ship was nudged up next to the high cliff, and camouflaged with branches and leaves. If not for their two pairs of dragon-sharp eyes and a fairly small footprint of land to search, they might not have found it. The crew of this ship, whoever they were, seemed to be skilled at lurking along the shore unseen. Was it because of previous encounters with the empress, or did they, too, have something to hide? The fact that they hadn't fled back into a major port raised some important questions.

Such as: If they were not northerners, then who were they? Had Jenna and Cas come upon pirates attacking each other?

They landed on top of the cliff that hemmed in the inlet, and crept forward until they could peek over the edge. Down below, they could see a small, hot fire sheltered under the cliff overhang. The enticing smell of roasting meat wafted up to them.

But the closer they got to the ship and its crew, the edgier Cas became. *Saw ship. Now go.* When Jenna didn't respond, he nudged her, practically knocking her over. *Go!*

"I need to talk to them," Jenna said stubbornly. "You stay here. I'm going down there."

If there is such a thing as a dragon pitching a fit, Cas came close, complete with a flaming display. He rose up on his hind legs, and Jenna was startled at how big he had become. *No! Bad ship. Bad men. Enough. Go find sheep.*

"Shhh. They'll see you."

Collar. Dark. Chains.

"I know you don't like ships, but—"

Collar. Dark. Chains.

"I have to go."

The dragon's armor glittered as tremors ran through him. *Cas come with Jenna.*

She knew he was scared, and it touched her that he wanted to come with her anyway.

"If you come down with me, you'll scare them."

Yes.

"I want to talk with them, not fight with them. Anyway, you can't maneuver down there. It's too narrow, and you're too big. I don't want you to get hurt."

Cas folded his wings tightly against his body and curled his tail around his feet. *Small now.*

In the end, Jenna descended the steep, treacherous trail alone, following the rocky bed of a small stream. All the way down, the dragon's disapproval clamored in her head.

He'd promised to stay on top, but dragon promises are as lasting as a late-spring snowfall.

She inventoried her weapons. She had her bow, but she wasn't yet an accurate shot. She had her knives. She had her wits. That would have to do.

When she reached the bottom, she followed the narrow, rocky beach toward the sound of voices and the flickering light of the campfire. The crew spoke an unfamiliar language, but they were laughing and boisterous, so Jenna got the idea that they were celebrating their narrow escape.

Easing forward on hands and knees, Jenna peered around a shoulder of rock. Night had effectively fallen down in the ravine. Seven men and women sat cross-legged around the fire, their faces illuminated by the flickering flames. It seemed they had just finished their meal. Jenna would have thought they'd be passing around a bottle, but instead they were gathered around a small iron stand where they seemed to be brewing . . . tea.

Pirates having a tea party? Not possible.

Then a man on the near side of the fire stood, his back to Jenna, his fair hair glittering in the light from the fire. He stripped back his sleeve, exposing his muscular fore-arm. Drawing a blade, he ran its tip along his arm, leaving a dark line of blood in its wake. While the others watched raptly, he held his arm over the pot simmering over the fire and allowed his blood to drip into it. He followed with a fistful of leaves.

After the brew had steeped for a few minutes, he poured it into small cups and passed them around. Each person murmured something and drank.

Was this some kind of pirate religion? A bizarre blood rite? Was the fair-haired man a priest or a sacrifice? Jenna's vision rippled as she sought to find the truth in him. Something about his stance, the lithe way he moved, even his clothing was familiar.

Then it came to her, like a punch in the gut. It was Strangward. Strangward and his gang, still clinging like a tick to the coast of the Indio.

Why, then, had the empress fired on him? He was her emissary, right? Maybe Jenna should have recognized him sooner, but it had never occurred to her that Celestine would be firing on her own man.

Then again, he *had* failed in his mission to collect Jenna. Was he paying a blood price for that? With every fiber of her being, Jenna hoped so. This man, and his mistress, had destroyed her life.

She'd never expected to find her quarry so easily, and

she didn't like these odds. She needed more firepower. Rising into a crouch, Jenna took one step back, then another. That's when the scent of danger filled her nose. Hearing a slight sound behind her, she grabbed for her knife, began to turn. Someone seized hold of her, two massive arms lifting her so that her feet left the ground. She struggled, but her arms were pinned so tightly that they were going numb. Her captor carried her forward, into the firelight.

The others scrambled to their feet, drawing a variety of weapons. Everyone but Strangward. Balancing lightly on his feet, fingering his amulet with one hand, head cocked, he studied Jenna and her captor. The light of recognition kindled in his eyes, and his eyebrows rose in surprise.

"Hello, Jenna," he said in Common, as if he'd run into her in the market. "This is . . . an unexpected pleasure." His crew shifted and murmured, but still did not stow their weapons.

Jenna sorted through several possible replies. In the end, she said nothing, letting her scowl do the talking.

Strangward looked over her shoulder. "Put her down, Teza," he said. "Also, please disarm her so that we can have a civil conversation."

The pressure on her arms eased, leaving her hands tingling as the blood returned. Teza carefully set her down on her feet, took the knife from her hand, and patted her down for other weapons. Her skin grew oddly numb, and she knew her scales were surfacing, as they always did in times of danger.

When he was nearly finished, Teza stopped and stared at her, the puzzlement on his face almost comical. Then he reached out a dirty finger and ran it over her cheek.

"Lord Strangward!" he said, standing to one side and pointing. He added something in their own language.

Strangward studied her, then brushed his fingers lightly over her face and the skin on her forearm. He didn't seem nearly as surprised as Teza. "Dazzling," he murmured. He took a step back and looked her up and down, taking in her riding skirt and sheepskin jacket.

"It seems that you have been transformed," he said.

"It seems that you and your empress are not getting along," Jenna said. "Why is that?"

Surprise flickered across his face. Taking her elbow, he drew her closer to the fire. "Please," he said. "Sit down."

Well, Jenna thought, you did want to talk to somebody who could tell you more about the empress. She sat in the same cross-legged style as the others had.

He gestured toward the teapot. "Would you like some—?"

"No," Jenna said flatly.

He grinned. "It's an acquired taste. But I can make a fresh pot, if you like, without . . . spiking it."

"No, thank you."

He sat down opposite her. "We have some roasted wild

turkey and flatbread, if you'd like some."

Jenna wavered. It had been forever since she'd tasted bread. And turkey had always been one of her favorites. And she needed to keep her strength up. "How is the turkey cooked?" she asked.

Strangward laughed, a genuine, hearty laugh that seemed to come from deep within. "You are a demanding guest," he said. "When someone gives you a sweet cake, do you poke holes in it to check the filling before you take a bite?"

"If I thought it might be filled with blood, I might."

He laughed again. "I promise that any blood you see belonged to the turkey." Strangward whacked off a slice of meat with his knife, folded it into a piece of bread, and handed it to her.

Jenna took a big bite, blotting at the juice that ran down her chin. It was perfect. She took another bite.

"I believe we got off on the wrong foot the last time we met," Strangward said. "I'd hoped to pull off a rescue, but King Gerard got in the way."

"*That* was a rescue?" Jenna lifted an eyebrow. "If so, it was a pretty poor one."

Strangward grimaced. "I failed. Clearly. It was hastily planned, and badly executed, but when I got word that the empress had found a girl with a magemark, I had to act fast, before she collected you."

"So you really don't work for her?"

"No," Strangward said. "I really don't."

"What do you care what happens between me and the empress? We'd never even met before you came swaggering into Ardenscourt."

"Because she is hunting me too." He paused long enough to let that penetrate, then said, "Here, I'll show you." He bowed his head low, took her hand, and pressed it against the back of his neck. She could feel the cobwebbing of metal, the cool hardness of the jewels set into his skin.

She pushed forward onto her knees, brushing his hair aside so that she could take a closer look. She guessed it must resemble her own magemark, though she'd never seen her own. It was an intricate design with wavelets, jagged bolts of lightning, and towering thunderclouds.

"What does this signify? What is your gift?"

"I have many gifts," he said, tipping up his chin. "One of them is the ability to influence the wind and weather." Sliding his hand under his shirt, he pulled out an object on a chain and extended it toward her. "Does this look familiar?"

Jenna stared at it, then reached out a finger to touch it. It was a piece of a broken pendant, a mariner's compass like her own. She nodded. "I had one, too, and I'll bet that it fits together with yours. But we'll never know that, because I haven't seen mine since Ardenscourt."

His face fell. "Oh. I'd hoped it might offer some clue."

Tears prickled in Jenna's eyes. She wasn't alone. She wasn't alone after all. But—but—

"What does it mean? Why are we marked like this? And why is—what does she want with us?" Jenna couldn't help looking out toward the sea.

Strangward shook his head. "I don't know. I wish I did. That would help me figure out what to do about it."

It came back to her, that last night in the tower, Strangward asking her, over and over, why the empress was hunting her. And she'd thought it was peculiar that *he* was asking *her*, because if anyone would know, he should.

"How old are you, anyway?" she asked him.

"I believe I'm about seventeen," he said. "So we're of similar age, but neither of us knows, exactly."

"Do you know of any others like us?"

"There were two others that I know of," Strangward said. "They were—"

"—about our age, I'm guessing."

He nodded. "Cele tracked them down and took them back with her to the Northern Islands, and they haven't been seen since." He shrugged. "Now it's *possible* that they are living lives of leisure as guests at the empress's court, but—"

"But you don't believe that."

He shook his head. "No, I don't. Each time she finds one of us, she grows markedly stronger. It was after she lured one of us to the Northern Islands that she grew strong enough to break out of there. We cannot afford for her to get any more powerful." Strangward spoke lightly, but Jenna could read the bone-deep fear in him. She also sensed that he knew a lot more than he was saying.

"Is that why you planned to kill me?" Jenna demanded, her voice echoing against the cliffs.

The pirate flinched, and he and Teza exchanged glances.

He doesn't realize that I overheard their conversation in my room, when Teza offered to step in and kill me so that Strangward wouldn't have to, Jenna thought. Strangward had refused, saying that he would do it himself.

For all I know, he hasn't changed his plans.

"My Lord," Teza said quickly. "You don't have to—"

"No," Strangward said. "You cannot step in and save me every single time." He looked directly at Jenna. "The empress has had several opportunities to kill me, but she hasn't. I believe that, whatever her purpose is, she needs us alive. So. I planned to kill you if I couldn't rescue you, because sometimes, when a person is desperate, he does desperate things."

Right. Of course. Jenna stood, dusting off the seat of her skirt. "Thank you, Strangward. This has been very informative. I wish you luck staying out of the empress's way."

Strangward blinked at her. "Where are you going?"

"I have business of my own," Jenna said.

"But . . . you need to . . . we need to stay together," the

pirate said, "so we can work out a way to defeat Celestine. We need to partner up."

"Maybe I don't want you as a partner," Jenna said. "Maybe I don't trust you."

"I was wrong—I realize that now. I apologize. I can see why you would find it . . . off-putting."

"When people ruin my life and then try to kill me, yes, I do find that off-putting," Jenna said.

"Don't you see? If we don't work together, Cele will win," Strangward said.

"I think I'd rather take that chance than take my chances with you," Jenna said.

"I cannot take the risk that you will fall into her hands."

"It's not your risk," Jenna said. "It's my risk. I'll decide whether to take it."

Strangward's face hardened. "I'm sorry, Jenna. I can't let you go." He nodded to his crew, and they moved quickly, encircling her to block her escape. "I hope that, over time, you'll see that—"

Jenna looked past them, down the inlet. "*There* you are," she said brightly. She gestured, pointing. "Have I introduced you to my friend Cas?"

Strangward shook his head, as if impatient with her attempt at trickery. "I promise you, I don't intend you any harm."

"I wouldn't worry about convincing *me*," Jenna said. She pointed. "Convince *him*."

The wide-eyed reaction of his crew finally made Strangward turn to see.

Filling the entire ravine from wall to wall was an enormous, pissed-off dragon. Flame swam over his hide, and his amber eyes were filled with menace. He drew back his lips, exposing swordlike teeth.

Strangward actually did a double take. His eyes widened and he gripped his amulet, taking two steps back.

"I would advise you to drop your hand, Strangward," Jenna said. "Cas is carrying a major grudge against you, and you don't want to give him an excuse to indulge it."

Slowly, the pirate dropped his hand. The look on his face was mingled disbelief and admiration. "Is that . . . is that the sun dragon that I—?" He leapt back again as the leaves at his feet exploded into flame.

"I really *don't intend you any harm*," Jenna said, "but I'm finding that dragons are not always that easy to reason with." With a bit of a swagger, she walked toward Cas. The pirates silently stepped aside and let her go. They stared as she gently stroked Cas's side.

"It seems I have underestimated you," Strangward said.

"I get that a lot."

"We could be powerful allies."

"Except for the part about watching my back all the time." Fitting her foot into the stirrup, she leapt nimbly into the saddle and looked down at their gaping faces. "Now, as I said, I—"

"Jenna, please," Strangward said, speaking low and persuasively. "Give me two minutes. This is important."

"All right," she said. "Talk to me."

"The fact remains that Celestine is here," Strangward said. "Believe me, she is here for us, and any others of our kind. Think of all the trouble she went to in order to track you down in Delphi. She will never stop hunting us. She has ships off the coast as we speak, and an army marching toward Chalk Cliffs. Once she wins the deepwater port, she'll begin to offload her army. She means to conquer these realms so that she can destroy our last refuge. It's that important to her."

Jenna thought of the army she'd seen, crossing the plateau, and couldn't help shivering.

"Her soldiers are bloodsworn slaves—physically enhanced and all but impossible to kill." Strangward paused, and his crew shifted and murmured. "We're going to have to help these wetlanders fight back."

"*We?*"

"Starting now. The garrison at Chalk Cliffs won't be expecting an attack from landward. We need to warn them. That's where I was heading when Cele drove me into hiding. There's no way I can get there in time. But you"—he pointed at Cas—"you can. It's still going to be really lopsided, but maybe, with a little warning—?"

He's telling the truth, Jenna thought. This time.

"All right," Jenna said. "We'll see what we can do."

Cas was still eyeing the pirates longingly.

Fry the bastards?

"No, Cas."

Please?

"No, Cas."

Burn ship?

"If you insist." Jenna smiled at Strangward and his crew and said, "Better move aside. We'll need a running start."

Strangward and his crew pressed themselves to the cliff face under the overhang. Cas barreled across the sand, then launched into the air. As he passed over the hidden ship, he flamed it from bow to stern.

Oops.

The foliage piled on top of the ship caught fire readily. Soon flames were pluming high in the air.

Looks like you're going to need another ship, Jenna thought.

Cas completed two barrel rolls before they turned south and flew toward Chalk Cliffs.

LIVING ON THE EDGE

Lyss picked her way up the rocky trail, avoiding the wet and slippery spots where the spray from the Indio had made the footing treacherous. Matelon walked behind, a measured distance away. Four of her Wolves trailed along behind them. They'd been several miles around the bay, and now they were climbing to the top of the cliffs overlooking the straits.

In the week since the interview with the busker, she'd been taking Matelon out walking nearly every day. She knew he'd want to stay in shape, and he deserved to get some fresh air. They both needed to burn off energy. And it was something they could do together with little risk of kissing.

It wasn't that she was worried about what *he* might do. He was too damned honorable. She was worried that *she* would be the one to succumb to temptation. That would only reinforce the southern notion that northern women were witches and harlots.

Not that she cared what southerners in general thought, but, more and more she found herself caring what this particular southerner thought.

There was nothing she could do about the vivid memories of their previous kisses that seemed to bubble up continuously.

Didn't you say that the key is to live in the moment?

That's the excuse people use for foolish behavior.

It wasn't a great day for a walk. All the way around the bay, the wind drove sleet into their faces. By now Matelon knew better than to take her elbow to help her over rough ground or offer his cloak if the wind-whipped rain and sleet threatened to drive them inside.

"If I'm too stupid to bring my cloak, then I deserve to get wet," Lyss had told him. "That is how we learn not to be stupid."

"That is also a good way to catch cold," Matelon said.

"Would you expect me to give you my cloak if you forgot yours?" she asked. And that was the end of it. He was teachable.

Lyss set a killing pace, but the Ardenine seemed scarcely winded. Eventually, they reached the top of the cliff and walked along the edge. Far below, the ocean slammed into the broken rocks as the tide came in.

The keep was perched on a rocky promontory that thrust far out into the Indio, guarding the narrows that led into the harbor. Across the straits, the cliffs were fortified and lined with cannon that could fire down on any ships that entered the roads uninvited.

At the end of the point overlooking the harbor, a stone wall ran along the edge of the cliff. Lyss pointed across the narrow strip of water. "See? That's what I'm talking about."

Matelon greeted the sight with a low whistle. "Are those Comptons?"

Lyss shook her head. "Demis. That gets us faster turnaround on reloading. They're more efficient than yours, too, since we use a closer tolerance to reduce the windage."

"Isn't that risky?"

"Not if you know what you're doing. And we do."

Matelon stared out at the guns for a long while, as if he was either admiring them or memorizing their positions. Then he turned and leaned back against the wall. His hair was a tousle of icy clumps; his cheeks were pinked up from the cold. "Why are you showing me this? Aren't you afraid you're giving away secrets?"

"Oh, I have no doubt that General Karn knows about these," Lyss said. "He probably has the blueprints tacked up on his wall. That's probably why your navy hasn't tried a frontal assault through the straits." She paused. "Anyway, I knew you'd be interested. And it might convince you that we know what we're doing, whether we end up allies or enemies."

"Thank you for showing me." He hunched his shoulders and swiped ice from under his collar. "How do you keep your powder dry up here?"

Lyss laughed. "I'm not going to tell you all our secrets, flatlander. I will say that it involves black magic."

Matelon looked out to sea, resting his gloved hands on the wall, squinting against the sleet. Then he shifted his stance, turning his back to the wind and looking south.

"A copper for your thoughts," Lyss said. When he flinched, she knew that he was thinking of home, and how to get there.

"I was thinking that it isn't a good day to be on a ship," Matelon said, still looking into the distance, where Spiritgate must be.

"It's never a good day to be on a ship," Lyss said, with enough heat that the Ardenine turned back toward her and raised an eyebrow. "I don't like ships, or the ocean," she said. When he said nothing, she added, "I hope we'll have word from your father soon."

He grunted a response. The silence grew, heavy and thick and totally self-conscious, the memory of Queen Court hanging between them like overripe fruit. Lyss could hear the soft voices of the Wolves from across the pavilion. Out of the corner of her eye, she could see the shadow of stubble along Matelon's jaw, the smudge of a bruise overlaying his cheekbone, the narrow strip of skin between the top of his collar and his earlobe. All of it— every bit of exposed flesh—seemed to badly need kissing. Lyss dug her fingers into the ice and tried to think about cannon.

Matelon shifted his shoulders, stamped his feet, stuffed his hands into the pockets of his sheepskin coat, licked his lips, and looked everywhere but at her. "Well. Maybe we should—"

"Hang on." A flicker of movement had caught Lyss's eye. To the northeast, just above the horizon, something was soaring. It looked to be a bird. A very large bird, swooping and diving in and out of the clouds. It seemed almost . . . illuminated.

Matelon followed her gaze, squinting. "What is it?"

Lyss pulled out her glass and trained it on the horizon. "I don't know," she muttered, handing the glass to Matelon. "Are your eyes better than mine?"

The creature plunged toward the ocean like a stooping bird, skimmed the waves, and beat its way skyward with a very large fish in its grip. It glittered once in the low sun before it disappeared into the clouds.

Matelon handed the glass back. "You would know better than me, ma'am. Whatever it is, we don't have those in Arden."

"We don't have them here, either." Lyss peered through

the glass again, but the winged creature, whatever it was, had disappeared.

"It reflected the light like it was jeweled, or armored, or something," Matelon said. "Does that help?"

She shook her head. As she stowed the glass away, she heard a loud bonging, and realized it was the bell that signaled the arrival of a ship.

Lyss looked out to sea, which extended, gray and choppy, to the horizon. Empty. When she looked back toward the harbor, she saw that the ship had already slipped through the straits and dropped sails as it headed toward the docks.

"It's one of yours," Hal said, with a trace of disappointment. "A gray wolf on a field of white."

Could it be Hadley, returning with Adrian? Lyss's heart beat a little faster. "Let's head back," she said.

Lyss took the twisty path down from the point, descending at breakneck speed, flying around the turns, with Matelon doing his best to keep up with her. There was no reason to be in such a hurry. She knew it would take a while for the ship to settle in at the dock and off-load passengers and cargo.

At the bottom of the path, she handed Matelon off to their Gray Wolf escort and hurried down the quay to where the ship had tied up. It was a three-masted vessel with a snarling wolf as the figurehead. That, along with the banner, told her everything she needed to know. Hadley's ship was the *Sea Wolf*.

Now her heart hammered in her ears, and she broke

out in a cold sweat. She looked down at herself, at her winter cloak, rimed with ice and smelling of wet wool. She tucked stray bits of hair behind her ears. Her brother's approval had been so important to her when she was little. What would he think of her now? Would he even recognize her?

What would she think of him? Their mother had suggested that he was so damaged by what he'd seen and experienced that he had to run away. That she worried he might take his own life.

It didn't matter. They'd always been close. They would find a way to fix it together.

Lyss looked for his head poking up above the others, his mop of red-brown hair. She didn't see him. She began walking toward them, slowly, picking out the people she knew. There was Hadley, directing the crew off-loading a small amount of cargo and luggage. She recognized Garret Fry, who was a colonel in the Highlanders, and the Gray Wolf Talia Abbott. Both were old friends of her parents. There were several others with them, none of whom she recognized.

Could he have changed so much? Lyss pulled out the small portrait her mother had given her. And studied it. No. She would know him if she saw him.

Was he still aboard the ship? Maybe he had a lot of belongings to get together. Couldn't somebody help him? Then she saw that they were taking down the gangway.

Dread fisted her in the gut. Where was Adrian? Had he refused to come after all? Had they been unable to find him? She accelerated into a run.

That was when Hadley turned and saw her. Hadley's eyes widened, her mouth pinched shut, and she turned pale as rough-water ice. She looked as if she'd like to turn and run right off the end of the dock in order to avoid facing her.

But she didn't. Instead, she broadened her stance, pushed her shoulders back, and waited until Lyss all but skidded to a stop in front of her.

"Lyss," Hadley said. She stopped, cleared her throat. "I didn't know you would be here."

"Where is Adrian? He didn't come back with you?" Lyss looked from face to face. Their faces looked like they'd been hammered flat.

Hadley gripped both her hands. "Lyss," she said, her face crumpling a little. "Let's go inside where we can talk."

"Why?" Lyss set her feet. "Just answer my question."

No one answered her question, not out loud, anyway.

"Something's happened to Adrian," Lyss said. Though she sucked in breath after breath, she still felt starved for air.

"We will tell you what we know," Hadley said, squeezing her hands. "But I'm not going to tell you this story standing on the dock. We are going to go somewhere private and sit."

Lyss ripped her hands free, turned on her heel, and

walked landward. Whatever had happened, it wasn't Hadley's fault, she thought. You don't have to kill the messenger.

The keep was a bare-bones kind of place where privacy was hard to find. Lyss led the way into the armory, since it was usually deserted at this time of day, except for the weapons master, and she booted him out. She sat down on a bench and rested her hands on her knees, her heart thumping in her throat.

The three of them, Hadley, Abbott, and Fry, sat side by side on a bench opposite hers like students called to account.

"Well?" Lyss said, when nobody spoke up.

"So," Hadley said, "we sailed down the coast to Baston Bay and traveled inland from there. But when we arrived at Oden's Ford, we learned that there had been an attack on Adrian's dormitory a few months ago. Several people died—five priests, two provosts, and two dorm masters." She stopped, her voice catching in her throat.

"Two students disappeared," Fry finished for her. "Adrian was one of the two students."

"The attack seemed to be centered on Adrian's room," Hadley said, as if to kill any flicker of hope Lyss might harbor. "We spoke with Joniah Balthus, the dean of Mystwerk. He said that Adrian's bed was soaked in blood. Two of the dead priests were found in his room."

That word penetrated Lyss's bleakly chaotic thoughts. "Priests? Why priests?"

"Balthus says they were a radical splinter group within the Church of Malthus that goes around killing wizards and . . . and . . ." Hadley's voice trailed off.

They waited, then, as if Lyss might say something back. But she didn't. If she opened her mouth, if she moved a muscle, if she broke out of her frozen state, she might start screaming and flailing. And that she wouldn't do.

Of course Adrian wasn't coming back. Of course. She was like a young plebe who kept falling for the same prank.

Finally, Lyss looked at Fry. "They didn't find Adrian's body?"

The Gray Wolf shook his head. "I'm sorry, Your Highness."

"Captain Gray," Lyss corrected him automatically. "Who was the other student?"

"Her name was Lila Byrne," Hadley said. "Captain Byrne's daughter."

"Ah. Of course." Lyss picked at a scab on her arm, raked at it with her broken fingernails until the blood flowed again. She watched it trickle down her arm.

Her gut told her that Adrian was dead—that, surely, he was dead—but maybe it was because she couldn't stand another empty siege of wondering, waiting, and hoping. Of spotting his face in every crowd, of hearing his voice around corners, of treasuring up everything she would say to him when they were together again.

I've done this, she thought. I'm not doing it again.

Lyss couldn't shut down the voice in her head that kept

repeating, *You could have been together. You could have had these four years, and now he's gone, because our own mother knew where he was all along and left him there until our enemies tracked him down and killed him.*

This is why Mama wanted to keep this secret until Adrian came home. Somehow she knew that this would happen.

It was as if Gerard Montaigne had reached his dead hand out of the grave and broken Lyss's heart one last time.

"One thing you have to say for Captain Byrne," Lyss said finally. "He never hesitates to sacrifice a child for the cause. He should have had more children. My mother, too."

"I'm sorry, Your—Captain," Fry said softly. "This is not the way we saw this operation ending."

Hadley cleared her throat. "We are traveling on from here to the capital, to let the queen and Captain Byrne know what we . . . what we found. You should come with us. You and your mother should be together right now."

"No," Lyss said. "I mourned for my brother four years ago. I'm not going through all that again. I'll just try to forget that—that any of this happened. When I finish up here, I'll go back to Delphi."

"Please," Hadley said. "You should talk to her. I'm sure she and Captain Byrne could answer many of your questions if you give them—"

"No." Lyss shook her head. "I'd rather pretend that

Adrian died in his home city, beside our father, and not far away, among strangers."

Tears were streaming down Hadley's face now. "What do you want me to tell your mother?"

Lyss patted her hand, finding herself in the odd position of consoling her. "I just can't go back there right now. The risk is too high that one of us will say something unforgivable. Tell her . . . tell her I'll need a little time."

Hadley stared at her, searching her face, as if the Lyss she knew had been swapped out for a stranger.

"We'll be here a day or two before we leave for the capital," Abbott said. "So you can still change your mind. In the meantime, we brought back a small crate of Adrian's personal effects. I thought you might want to go through it."

"Thank you," Lyss said. "I'd like that."

Hadley slid an arm around her. "Let's go find Sasha," she said.

DUEL

Hal, unable to sleep, lay on his back, his fingers laced behind his head, his brain rattling like a runaway cart from one problem to another. It had been some time since he'd heard the bell in the tower overhead bong one, but frustration was keeping him awake despite his long walk through the wind and sleet with Captain Gray.

He couldn't complain about his treatment. If he was a prisoner, he was being cradled in an open hand. He knew that hand would close into a fist with another escape attempt. So it wasn't enough to escape the keep. In Delphi, he'd been close to the border, at least. Here, there was lots of open space to cover before he reached friendly territory.

If it was even still friendly to Matelons.

He left his locked quarters only for meals, and for his walks with Captain Gray, which inflicted their own kind of torment. Speaking of which, what or who was she expecting to arrive by ship? Why had she barreled down the steps like there were demons at her heels?

He should have a plan by now. Time was wasting, while events in the south went on without him. His father might already be marching on the capital. His mother and sister might be dead. Or worse. He had so many reasons to want to get home. And one reason in particular to stay.

He recalled what he'd said to Gray after his bout with Bosley. *Our women are not like you.*

Nobody was like her. And now, maybe, he was ruined for anyone else. Meanwhile, she'd made it plain they had no future together.

His king had sent him north to die. So far, he'd managed to stay alive, but the experience had changed him. Would he even fit in when he went home?

I need to get out of the witchy north, he thought, before I lose myself. If it wasn't already too late.

A noise outside his door made him sit upright. The guards in the corridor seemed to be arguing with someone. A voice rose above the others, shutting the discussion down. "I *will* see him, I don't care what time it is. Now get out of my way."

It was Captain Gray.

Hal groped for his breeches, yanking them on hastily.

He was just buckling them when the door banged open, and there she was, a bottle in one hand, the other propped against the doorframe. Her shirt was untucked, hanging midway to her knees. She was in her stocking feet, and long strands of hair hung down around her face. Her eyes were deep wells of pain and grief.

"Captain Gray," Hal said warily. "It's late."

"It is late," she said, her voice a low growl. "It's late. It's too bloody late." Her gaze traveled over his chest and shoulders, lingered there a moment, then seemed to focus. "Where's your shirt?"

"Forgive me," Hal murmured. Snatching it up, he pulled it over his head without unbuttoning it. Looking past her, he saw bluejackets milling in the corridor behind her as if unsure what to do. Gray set the bottle in a corner with exaggerated care. Then she turned and threw her shoulder against the door, slamming it in their faces. As Hal watched in amazement, she dragged a massive breakfront over until it blocked the door. She studied it a moment, hands on hips, then spun around to face him.

"Now," she said, grabbing up the bottle and thrusting it toward him. "We are going to play a game."

Hal eyed the bottle. "A game?"

"A riddle game."

Hal looked down at the bottle, then back up at Gray, and realized from her slow, deliberate speech that she had been drinking. A lot. "I was just going to sleep," he said.

"Could we play tomorrow?"

She wagged the bottle in his face. "We're doing this now."

He took a step back. "Let's wait until tomorrow."

"What's the matter? Are you scared?"

"Yes," Hal said honestly. "You're scaring the shit out of me." He took the bottle, tipped his head back, and took a careful swig. Blue ruin. It all but lifted the top of his head off.

"Hey! We're not playing yet." She grabbed the bottle back and drank, her throat jumping with each swallow. She thumped it down on Hal's little table and slumped into one of the chairs. "You. Sit," she commanded, pointing at the other chair.

Hal sat across from her, resting his hands on the tabletop.

"Here's the rules," Gray said. "I'm going to ask you riddles, and if you can't answer, you have to take a drink."

"Ma'am, I'm really not much for—"

"And every time you say 'ma'am' you have to take a drink."

Hal pressed his lips together and waited.

"Now, then," Gray said. "First question: Why are southerners such assholes?"

"That's not a riddle," Hal said.

"Answer the question."

"Why are you trying to pick a fight with me?"

"You're the only flatlander within reach."

Hal studied her haggard face. In truth, she looked like she'd been run over by a team of horses. He'd seen that expression before, on some of the men in his command. Ambushed by grief, they had taken to drink in an effort to drown it.

It was the face of heartbreak. Did it have to do with the ship that had arrived that afternoon?

"What's happened?" he said. "Tell me what's wrong."

"That's not an answer." She pushed the bottle toward him, and it rocked dangerously. "Drink up."

"I'm not going to do this," he said, shoving his chair back. "I'm going to call for the guards." Crossing to the door, he took hold of the breakfront and tried to drag it aside. A flicker of motion caught the corner of his eye before Gray bulled into him.

This time, Hal was smart enough to mind his feet, shifting them out of danger at the last minute so she was unable to sweep them out from under him. Even drunk as she was, she came close to rolling him over her shoulder. He wrapped his arms around her in a kind of bear hug, and wrestled her to the floor so he could pin down her flailing arms and legs. It took the full weight of his body to keep her down. She was yelling something at him, over and over.

"Why did you do it? Why did you bastards murder my brother? He was a healer! He never did anyone any harm."

Bewildered, Hal tried to remember what she'd told him

about her family. If he remembered right, her brother had died years ago.

Sometimes drink will surface long-buried hurts, like corpses floating out of a flooded graveyard. Hal had seen it before, in taverns and inns, when the hour was late and the ale had been flowing.

"I'm sorry about your brother," Hal said. "Too many people have died in this war—people we can't afford to lose."

"Sorry doesn't bring him back," Gray said, her voice hitching. She'd stopped struggling, and now lay on the stone floor, limp and weeping.

"I know," he murmured. "I know." He didn't know, exactly, but he could imagine how he would feel if the war took Harper and Robert from him. Though, just now, they seemed more at risk from his own king than from the enemy they were supposed to be fighting.

Taking a chance, Hal slid his arms under Gray, leaned his back against the wall, and scooped her onto his lap. She buried her face in his shirt and kept crying, clutching a fistful of the fabric. Gently, he rocked her, smoothing back her hair and kissing her forehead, murmuring whatever came to mind. Eventually, she slept, lips slightly parted, tears still leaking from under her eyelashes.

He recalled the glib words he'd said to her, the excuse used through history by soldiers standing up for the killing trade.

This is war. People die—even innocents die, unfortunately.

He thought about carrying her to the bed, but that was risky in a hundred ways. So he sat, cradling her in his arms, thinking that he never wanted to let her go.

He heard new voices in the hallway. Someone hit the door, hard, and it shifted the breakfront a little. Three more body hits, and the door had slid open enough to let them squeeze through, Talbot in the lead, still rubbing her shoulder. She froze, scanning the scene, the bottle on the table, Hal propped against the wall with Gray snuggled in against him, her fingers tangled in his hair.

Talbot raised both hands, palms up, the universal sign for *What the hell?*

Hal motioned Talbot over, and she squatted in front of them. He eased Gray into Talbot's arms. Talbot stood, nodded at Hal, as if acknowledging their partnership, and carried Gray from the room. The other bluejackets moved the furniture back into place and left, closing the door behind them.

Happily, they left the bottle of blue ruin behind, and it helped Hal into sleep.

DRAGON

Being from Delphi, Jenna was no stranger to cold, nasty conditions. But flying along the frozen coastline to the north was brutal. The wind off the Indio was bone-chilling, and the shore was layered in ice where the waves splashed up.

Urgency lent them speed, which drove the cold wind through Jenna's new clothes. The knowledge that she might be too late to save Chalk Cliffs thrummed in her veins.

She didn't trust Evan Strangward, but when she closed her eyes, she could see the town in ruins, overrun by the army she'd seen crossing the snowy moor. She believed him when he said that if Celestine won a foothold on these shores, it was bad news for both of them.

She was grateful for the heat that constantly seethed beneath Flamecaster's scales. Riding Cas in these conditions was like bellying up to Brit Fletcher's stove in the dead of a Delphian winter—roasting in front, freezing behind.

Ordinarily, Jenna loved night flying, soaring over sleeping villages shrouded in snow, their lights like small beacons in the darkness. She and Cas had to be careful not to fly too near the clan lodges. Dogs always seemed to sense their presence and would run along, barking, in their wake.

Food?

"You can't possibly be hungry. You had an entire sheep for breakfast."

Sheep mostly wool, not much meat.

Tonight, to avoid being spotted, they flew so low that at times it felt like swimming, with walls of foam-flecked waves all around them. In their early days of flying, Cas had sometimes miscalculated, and they would end up plunging into freezing seawater. These days, that was rare.

As they flew south, they began to hear an irregular booming sound, and Cas's flight slowed perceptibly.

Guns. Go home, find sheep?

Jenna tightened her knees along the dragon's spine. "We need to warn them."

When she and Cas argued, it was like having a debate

with herself. Sometimes it was hard to sort out who was on which side. When they agreed, they were of one mind.

Now they could see flashes of light along the escarpment as they approached the white cliffs of the harbor they had seen earlier. Just outside the harbor mouth, a small flotilla was firing back.

They flew high, high, higher so they would be only a speck in the darkness to anyone below, then swept back and forth across the battle scene several times. The ships were showing no sign of making a run in, but simply hovered there, just out of range of the cannon on the cliffs. Almost as if they had no intention of risking an attack by sea.

It's a diversion, Jenna thought, so they don't notice trouble coming from the other direction.

"Let's fly west."

Cas banked, turned, and they soared back over the shoreline, following the road that led toward the interior. Below, they could see movement, the occasional flash of light off metal, and hear the tread of hooves in the snow that meant that a large company of riders was approaching the town from landward, staying off the road and within the cover of the forest. They must be the ones she'd seen crossing the frozen wastes on the peninsula. Now there could be no doubt about their destination.

Strangward had told the truth.

What to do?

She had to find a way to help—to warn them about the oncoming army. But she couldn't very well land a dragon in the middle of town. By the time it all got sorted out, somebody would be dead. If Cas landed somewhere and Jenna tried to enter the city on foot, she might be too late, or, worse, get caught up in the fighting.

But how could they send a clear message to the town without putting themselves at risk?

DREAMS TO NIGHTMARES

Hadley and the others left for Fellsmarch the next morning. Lyss stayed behind, nursing an awful hangover. This is why I don't drink, she thought. Not much, anyway. From now on, I'm sticking to cider. And maybe ale. Except for special occasions, like when we win the war.

She resisted the temptation to send Matelon to Fellsmarch with the travelers. She couldn't remember much about what happened in his quarters. The bits she did remember were a mixture of mortifying and inexplicably tender.

The way he talked to her, his voice a low rumble of calm. The kisses he planted along her hairline, each perfect in its own right. The thud of his heart against her back.

His eyes, the color of lichen after a rain, fringed with lashes that matched his raven-wing hair.

For the first time in a long time, she'd felt safe, nestled in Matelon's arms. It wasn't that she was looking for protection. It was more that she could trust that she could close her eyes knowing he would watch her back. And if they swapped places, she would watch his.

But every time she tried to savor the compassionate, tender moments, she'd stumble into something mortifying.

And how did she end up in the arms of a southerner, when she'd gone there to—what was it he'd said? Pick a fight? That was the thing about Matelon—he seemed steady, and easy, almost boring . . . and then he'd make her do something she never intended to do.

He made *you do it? Who attacked who?* the voice in her head said. *I'll bet none of his frail southern flowers has challenged him to a drinking game.*

Yet, on any given night, all over the realm, people were drinking a little too much and saying and doing things they would regret the next day. She wished she could afford to do that, and laugh it off.

Lyss didn't even remember deciding to go to Matelon's room. Hadley and Sasha had sat with her for most of the day in sort of a three-person wake. The last her friends knew, she'd gone to bed. She knew they blamed themselves now for her excursion the night before.

Lyss had little to no appetite, and no desire for anything

more challenging than a piece of toast and a bowl of porridge—foods she ordinarily refused to eat.

Toward the end of the day, she finally fell asleep, fully clothed, lying on top of her bed, but awoke to a persistent pounding at her door.

"Go away!" she said groggily.

"Lyss! Open up! We're under attack!"

Then tell *them* to go away, Lyss thought, before she came fully awake. She rolled out of bed, crossed to the door, and wrenched it open.

It was Sasha, her hair disheveled, her shirttail hanging out from under her uniform tunic, looking like she'd just rolled out of bed, too.

"*Who's* attacking us?" Lyss said, leaning on the doorframe.

"We don't know for sure. There're three ships, out beyond the harbor mouth, firing at the gun emplacements."

"Have they hit anything?"

"I don't know."

"Unless their guns are a lot better than ours, it won't be easy, shooting up at them like that." Lyss sat down on her bed and pulled on her boots. A good fight could be the cure for embarrassment and heartbreak.

As they hurried down the hallway, Lyss could hear the boom of cannon fire. "Who's the duty officer?"

"Graves. He's up on the batteries, directing fire."

With Sasha at her heels, Lyss climbed the steep staircase

to the batteries overlooking the straits. As she neared the top, she breathed in the acrid scent of gunpowder and felt the shudder of percussion under her feet.

The wind off the Indio lashed Lyss's face as soon as she emerged from the staircase. Gouts of flame illuminated the faces of the gunnery crew as they fired the matches. There were two fully crewed twenty-four-pounders on this side of the straits, and two on the other, which should be plenty, Lyss thought, to hold off three ships. She peered out to sea, but the weather made it difficult to see anything until the flare of the shipboard guns pinpointed them. Their shots arced harmlessly into the sea, or smashed into the cliffs far below the batteries.

Munroe Graves was already hoarse from shouting orders to the gunnery crew across the straits.

"What's the news?" Lyss asked, struggling to make herself heard over the thunder of the cannon and the howling of the wind.

"It didn't take long for them to figure out our range, and they've stayed just outside of it," Graves said. "Which means they can't hit us, we can't hit them. So what's the point? We all should of stayed in bed."

"Who's across the way?" Lyss nodded at the south-side batteries.

"Bosley."

"Have they shown their colors?"

He shook his head. "Nah. There's not much point, with them out so far."

"But why would they do this? They might as well dump their ordnance into the sea."

"Target practice?" Graves suggested.

"Hmm. Well, tell your gunners that we don't have to answer every barrage. Maybe they've got shot to waste, but we never do."

"We'll just keep 'em honest, that's all."

A thought struck Lyss. "Do you have sentries deployed to make sure small craft aren't landing down below, while we're distracted?"

"Already handled, Captain," Graves said.

Lyss leaned her arms on the parapet, watching the bombardment and their halfhearted response. Worry nagged at her. What were they overlooking? It would help if they knew for sure who was out there.

"Do you have anything that might give us a little light out there so we could get a better look at those ships?"

"We have some incendiaries," Graves said. "Even if the ships are out of range, we can shoot 'em high and they might go off close enough to light them up."

"Let's do that. But wait for my go-ahead."

Lyss found Sasha among the soldiers at the cliffside. "Sasha—where's Matelon? Is he in his quarters?"

"As far as I know," Sasha said, giving her a narrow-eyed look. "Do you want me to check?"

"Take a triple to his quarters and escort him up here. I want him to take a look at those ships."

"Right away," Sasha said, bringing her fist to her chest.

Hal dreamed that he'd somehow returned home to White Oaks—the White Oaks of his boyhood, when it was more of a manor and less of a fortress. He was walking through the gardens with his little sister Harper, telling her about his adventures in the north.

"Is it true that the witches in the north ride demons through the skies, looking for wayward children?"

"If they do, I never saw it," Hal said. "They mainly look for wayward grown-ups."

"No they *don't*," Harper said, lifting her chin. "Grown-ups never get in trouble for anything."

"Sometimes they do," Hal said.

"So is that just a story parents tell to make their children behave?" Harper persisted, glancing over her shoulder to make sure Lady Matelon was nowhere near.

"Maybe some do, but I think others truly believe it," Hal said. "It's a lot easier to fight monsters than flesh-and-blood people."

"No, it's not," Harper said. "Everybody knows that monsters are bigger and fiercer than people."

Hal laughed. "Did you know that there are people in the north that say *we are* monsters?"

"Really?" Harper looked up at him, wide-eyed. "Well, they're wrong!"

"Maybe," Hal said.

Harper grabbed his sleeve. "Do you think it's possible

that we are wrong about the northerners, too?"

"Maybe," Hal said.

A clamor of metal on metal yanked him out of his well of dreams.

"Flatlander!" Somebody shook him roughly. "Wake up!"

Hal opened his eyes, squinting against the lantern thrust into his face. He couldn't see who stood behind the lantern. "What?"

"Captain Gray wants to see you, on the double."

Now he recognized the voice. It was Corporal Talbot, Gray's bluejacket shadow.

Hal sat up. "What time is it?"

Talbot thrust his sheepskin coat toward him. "Put this on, or go half-naked, I don't care. I *said* on the double."

Hal slid into his shirt, and the heavy jacket she gave him, and the hat and gloves. She was dressed for the weather, too.

"I take it we're going outside," he said.

Talbot grunted in reply.

Hal followed Talbot down out of the tower and crossed the drawbridge to the fortifications along the cliffs that gave the port its name.

"How is she?" Hal asked.

"Who?"

"Captain Gray."

Talbot looked him up and down, then shook her head. "You'll see."

"Did something happen to her brother?" he asked, as they climbed the treacherous staircase.

"I don't know what you're talking about," Talbot said, then gave him a look that said she did know, but she wasn't going to answer him.

Finally, they emerged onto the clifftop just in time to meet the roar of a twenty-four-pounder.

"Who are you shooting at?" he asked, ears still ringing.

Talbot pointed. "Ask the captain."

"Matelon," Captain Gray said, motioning him to join her at the wall, her manner brisk and businesslike, her eyes fixed out to sea.

When he came up beside her, he saw the lines of weariness in her face, the purple shadows under her eyes. She looked like someone grieving and hungover and still doing her job.

She looked like a hero to him.

"I'm going to give you some light, and I want you to take a look at some ships out here and tell me if you can identify them." She signaled the crew on the nearest cannon and they lit the match on it.

Boom! The shell arced high, high, higher, then exploded far offshore, flooding the ocean with brilliant light.

Squinting against the wind, Hal studied the three ships silhouetted against the horizon.

"Well?" Gray said, gracious as always. "Are those yours?"

Hal watched until the brilliance died and the ships were

lost in darkness again. "They're too far away to be certain," he said, "but I would say they are not empire ships. At least not ships in the regular navy." Something else caught his eye as he peered into the darkness, something bright streaking across the sky. Another shell? A shooting star?

"What's that?" He pointed.

"Blood of the martyrs," Gray muttered, suddenly beside him at the wall. "I have no idea."

It swooped down like a flaming arrow until it appeared to pass among the masts of the mysterious ships. A faint cracking sound carried across the water, as if it had run into one of the masts. The object turned, growing larger and larger until Hal realized it was flying directly toward them.

"Take cover!" he shouted, pulling Gray down, next to the wall, covering her with his body. He was aware of a searing heat and the scent of burning wood as something huge passed close overhead, and then a dull *thunk* as something dropped onto the pavers.

Demons, he thought, sweat trickling down his back despite the cold. Flying demons. I knew it. Hal didn't really believe that, but was having trouble coming up with another explanation.

He covered his head with his arms, waiting for an explosion, wondering if he'd end his life here at Chalk Cliffs as bits of shark bait in the sea. But nothing happened, and after a moment he cautiously propped up and looked at what had fallen onto the clifftop.

It appeared to be the mast from a ship, ripped loose and trailing broken rigging.

Hal scrambled to his feet and lunged toward the mast, but Captain Gray beat him to it, pawing through the debris and coming up with a banner bearing a death's-head on it.

"Pirates?" Talbot said, running her finger over the emblem Gray displayed.

"It's coming back!" somebody shouted. Hal spun around to see the flying creature bearing down on them from landward this time, clutching something in its claws. As it flew over the batteries, it let go, and again something hit the ground with a sickening thud.

This time, it was a man. Hal could tell from the way the body was splayed on the pavement that he wasn't going to get back up.

They gathered close around the body. It looked to be that of a soldier, bristling with weapons, dressed for the cold. As Hal watched, Talbot pulled a curved blade from a scabbard at the man's belt and held it up for them to see.

"Pirate?" Talbot said again, but Hal knelt beside the broken body and saw that the man wore boots that had spurs attached and he smelled strongly of horse and dried sweat.

"Whoever he is, he came by horse," Hal said. "But where would he have come from? And is the flying beast on their side or ours?"

"Look!" Gray pointed skyward. The winged creature was flying in a tight maneuver, spitting flame and smoke, leaving a trail in the sky. Some kind of emblem . . .

"It's an arrow," Talbot said.

"Pointing west," Gray said, swiveling to look in the direction it pointed. Hal followed her gaze, looking over the town to the western wall. Beyond that, darkness.

"Graves!" Captain Gray shouted. "Sound the alarms. I want as many soldiers as possible on the city walls to land-ward. I think this bombardment is a diversion from the real attack."

"Yes, Captain." Graves left at a dead run.

Somewhere below, alarm bells began to clamor. When Hal scanned the sky, the flaming beast had disappeared.

Gray turned toward Talbot and Hal. "Talbot, I want you to take Matelon to the cell block in the tower. Post a triple guard on him. If it turns out that our visitors are coming after him, I'm not going to make it easy."

"But Captain . . . I could help," Hal said, frustration boiling up in him. "I told you. Those aren't empire ships. Give me a weapon and I'll—"

"Not this time, Captain," Gray said, turning away.

43

TOO LITTLE, TOO LATE

It was clear from the beginning that this battle would be different from any Lyss had fought before. She'd always fought in the field, where she used the terrain to her advantage and mobility was a major part of her battle strategy. Advances, retreats, flanking movements, ambushes—they were all tactics she employed. While she was grateful for the protection of the keep, it was also a trap. There were no advances—only retreats.

This enemy was different, too. Lyss was used to fighting Arden's mercenaries and unwilling recruits, most of them already in a lather about going up against demons and witches. These were fierce, hardened warriors with curved blades who were all but impossible to kill. When Lyss cut off the head of one of them, he kept coming until she took off his legs as well. It was as if they were possessed—as if they didn't feel pain and embraced death with a will.

The soldiers were not Ardenine, though they could be mercenaries hired by Arden. These didn't fight like mercenaries, though.

If they were pirates, they were like none Lyss had ever heard of before. She thought of pirates as masters of the hit-and-run, the claiming of soft targets. As Hadley had said, pirates don't like targets that shoot back.

Chalk Cliffs was not a soft target, but these pirates kept coming. Whatever drove them, it was scary as hell.

The warning they'd received gave them time to close and secure the gate before the first wave of enemy horsemen penetrated the town wall. It soon became clear that some of the enemy were already inside—maybe the strangers the garrison had worried about. They erupted from hiding, often killing dozens before they were put down.

The town's strongest fortifications faced the ocean, not the landward side, and the high ground to the west allowed the attackers to rain arrows and incendiaries down on their heads. Lyss put the townspeople to work putting out fires and wetting down the buildings.

The keep's big guns were placed to fire down on ships attacking from the sea. But the enemy ships remained far outside the harbor, no doubt waiting for the land attack to soften up the defenses and disable the cannon before they ventured in.

Eventually, the Highlanders were able to rotate the

cannon in their emplacements and fire across the city, and so take out some of the enemy weapons.

Wizard flame might have been effective against them, but they'd never know, because the gifted were elsewhere, mainly in Delphi, where they'd helped take the city. Lyss dearly wished she could have them back again.

She ordered birds sent to Fortress Rocks and Fellsmarch, even though she knew that any response would be too late to save the town. Sasha was beside herself, because she couldn't keep Lyss off the walls and out of the fight, and because she couldn't come up with a foolproof escape plan, either.

With pitched battles filling the streets, and fires raging in many of the buildings, Sasha finally managed to force Lyss into the keep.

"You need to get out, Your Highness," she said. "You need to leave while you still can."

"I don't think that was ever possible," Lyss said. "By the time we knew what was happening, we were surrounded."

"Why are you working so hard to protect Captain Matelon while you put yourself at risk? Who do you think is more important to the future of the queendom—him or you?"

"I'd rather go down fighting than be killed sneaking out of the back gate."

"What about the front gate?" Sasha said. "Leave by boat."

No. Not possible. Out of the question.

"Did you see those ships out there? How far do you think we would get?"

"They're staying out of range of our cannon," Sasha said. "The weather's dark and miserable. Take a small boat, go out through the straits, hug the shoreline, and follow along until you reach a safe place to land."

"No," Lyss said briskly. "Now, if there's nothing else, I'd better get to—"

"I know you don't like boats, but—"

"I'll die on dry land, thank you," Lyss said. Already, her bowels were turning to water, and she tasted metallic panic on her tongue. Once again, she saw the water closing over her head, felt the smothering pressure of it, her lungs screaming for relief.

"What would be worse—going out on a boat or being captured by Arden?"

"I don't mean to be captured," Lyss said grimly.

"You owe it to your mother the queen to survive!" Sasha shouted at her.

You mean the mother who lied to me? Who betrayed me? Who let me think my brother was dead all these years when I could have been with him or at least said good-bye?

Lyss thought all that, but she didn't say any of it, because she knew in her heart of hearts that it was unfair. So all she said was, "No." It was a triumph that she kept her voice from trembling.

Sasha gripped her shoulders and shook her. "What about your father? What would he want you to do? Would he want you to sacrifice yourself and leave your mother all alone? Or would he want to protect the Gray Wolf line? Do you want him and your brother and sister to have died for nothing?"

"That's not fair," Lyss muttered. "That is totally not fair."

"What's the old saying about love and war? If you're gone, then so's his line. Now, come on. We'll go down to the cellar dock. You can slip right out of the keep and into the boat with nobody the wiser."

"No."

"Don't make me knock you on the head and load you in the boat like a barrel of salt fish," Sasha warned.

Lyss had no doubt that she would do that if she could. She sighed, a long exhale of surrender.

"You win," Lyss said. "I'll try the boat, but you're coming with me."

"No!" Sasha blurted. "I mean, you go ahead, and I'll follow a little later. I just need to kill a few more mudbacks, or whatever they are, and then I'll—"

"I'm not going if you're not going. I'll need your help. We're taking Matelon and the busker."

"What? Have you lost your mind?" Sasha's expression said that she probably had. "The two of them'll cut our throats and push us over the side."

"I'm counting on you to prevent that," Lyss said. "I still think the busker can help us figure out who's behind these killings. And I'm not giving up Matelon, if he might help bring some of the southern thanes over to us." Lyss paused. "Since you like quoting my da so much, here's another of his favorite sayings—take or leave."

Breon wasn't sure how long he'd been hearing the sound of cannon fire. For a while, it came fast and furious, but then it dwindled to an occasional vibration in his breastbone. Maybe the battle was still going on, but it was hard to tell, locked in a dungeon.

He'd never been in a battle before, so that was interesting. Especially since, at the moment, he was out of the line of fire.

Still, it was lonely, down here in the cell block, where there were no other prisoners, and even the guards hadn't been very sociable. They made sure he was fed and watered, and they emptied his chamber pot, but that was all.

He needed something to take his mind off his worries. He was a very creative worrier. Unless Aubrey had brought an army to save him, it really didn't matter to him, personally, who won. Prisoners didn't usually fare well in wartime. They were a complication nobody needed.

He tried to sleep. But he couldn't, what with the cannon fire and distant shouting and worrying and the faint, nagging craving for a hit of leaf.

No. He was going to die clean, if it came to that.

At least this gaol was different from others he'd been in. Not that he was an expert. Most cells were like cold, damp, dark closets with thick wooden doors and little peepholes. These were built of stone, but the fronts were a grid of iron bars that let the light and air in. If he craned his neck, he could see all the way up and down the hall. There'd been nothing to see for a good long time.

After a while, he heard somebody coming—footsteps and the rattle of keys. He sat up. Long shadows preceded the newcomers down the corridor between the cells. They seemed to be arguing.

"Put a sword in my hand and let me fight," one of them was saying. "You need every able-bodied man on the walls. I'm not any good to anyone down here."

"No offense, but nobody wants to be fighting next to a slimy-assed southerner."

No offense? Breon thought. Even the most thick-skinned person might—

"It doesn't matter who they are," the first man persisted. "They are no friends of mine. I can help."

Let him help, Breon thought. If he's crazy enough to want to.

"Save your breath," one of the gaolers said. "I'd be glad to make that trade with you, Matelon, but Captain Gray ordered us to lock you down here, and that's what we're going to do." They unlocked the cell across the way from

Breon's, pushed the prisoner inside, and locked the door behind him.

"I hope you rot down here," the chatty one said. Then they both trooped back through the corridor and up the stairs.

Breon's new neighbor swore at their backs and then paced around his cell a bit as if he hoped that he might find a tunnel out or an extra set of keys.

"Hey," Breon said. The man spun around and groped at his hip as if he was used to finding a sword there. "If it was up to me, I'd of let you fight. You look like you'd be good at it."

The other man gripped the bars of his cage and peered across at him. He was tall and muscular, the kind that would be called well made if you were going for a military look.

"Unfortunately," the man said in Ardenine-accented Common, "you are not in charge."

"I'm Breon d'Tarvos," Breon said. "I'm a musician wrongly imprisoned for a crime I didn't commit." Maybe it was early to be bringing that up, but he didn't want his new neighbor to get the wrong idea—that he was a criminal or something. "Call me Breon."

The soldier eyed him as if trying to guess what crime he'd been accused of. "Halston Matelon, prisoner of war. I go by Hal."

"What's going on out there?" Breon asked. "Who're we

fighting, and are we winning or losing?"

Hal's jaw tightened. "The horsemen wear no uniform or signia, but the ships besieging us carry a death's-head banner."

"Pirates, then," Breon said, feeling an odd quiver deep in his belly.

"Or line soldiers pretending to be pirates."

Breon hated to push his second question, but he did. "So . . . how is it going?"

Hal shook his head. "Short of a miracle, I'd say we're done for. I'm going to be on the losing end of my second battle in a month."

"If they won't let you fight, they can't blame you, can they?" Breon thought that was a reasonable deduction, but Hal just shook his head and kept prowling, examining the places where the bars met stone, maybe hoping for a gap he could wriggle through. With those shoulders, though . . .

"They're pretty well built, these are," Breon said, slapping his palm against the bars. "Not that I'm an expert, being law-abiding and all."

After pacing and muttering a while longer, Hal finally seemed to give up, and he sat down, slumping against the wall. "What is it you're accused of that you didn't do?" he said.

Breon guessed that Hal really didn't care, that he was just being polite, but it was nice of him to ask.

"They think I conspired to kill the princess Alyssa," he said.

Hal turned his head to look at him. *"You?"*

Breon nodded, unoffended. "Hard to believe, isn't it?"

"Why do they think it was you?"

"Well, it's true that I was there when it all went down," Breon said. "But I had no idea what was going to happen. The princess keeps coming down here and trying to get me to finger the people behind it, but I can't tell her what I don't know."

That got Hal's attention. "The princess Alyssa . . . was *here*?"

Breon nodded. "Still is, as far as I know."

"She couldn't be here," Hal said, with conviction. "We're all going to be slaughtered."

Breon was finding out that Hal was a pessimistic sort.

"She's a tough, military kind of princess. She's probably out there in the thick of the fighting." Breon paused, and when Hal kept frowning and studying on it, added, "I mean, it's possible she left. Last I saw her was dinnertime yesterday."

"Yesterday? But . . . why haven't *I* seen her, then?"

Breon shrugged. "Don't feel bad. She's a busy person, and I guess she has to focus on the important prisoners. Maybe there's nothing she wants to pry out of you."

Hal chewed on this awhile, then straightened a little and said, "This princess—what does she look like?"

"Well, she's very tall and long-shanked, with hair the color of pale caramel. Lately, she's had it done up in a fat braid, with—"

"Saints and martyrs," Hal swore, glaring up at the ceiling. "Why didn't I see it?"

"So you *have* met her?"

Hal nodded. He had the stricken face of a man who's looked back along the path he's on and discovered he's been walking on very thin ice, with no way to go back.

"You know what always helps when I . . . ?" Breon's sentence trailed away as he heard quick footsteps approaching and the rattle of keys. He stood, craned his neck, and peered down the hallway.

It was Her Highness, with Sasha, grim looks on their faces, bags slung over their shoulders, and armed to the teeth.

Sasha unlocked the door to Breon's cage and tossed the keys to Her Highness so she could do the honors for Hal. Hal kept staring at the princess like she might strip off a mask and turn into somebody else right in front of him.

"Let's go, busker," Sasha said, handing him the kind of warm waterproof coat that fishermen and sailors wear. "Put that on and bring your belongings."

"Where are we going?" Breon said, sliding into the coat.

"The enemy is inside the keep, so we're going for a boat ride."

SHIPS IN THE NIGHT

You're a fool, Halston Matelon, Hal told himself, as "Captain Gray" and Corporal Talbot ushered him and Breon down two more flights of stairs. *You'd better stick to fighting, where at least you have a little skill.*

The Gray Wolf, they called her. Hal had been hearing that name for years. She was a legend on both sides of the border, known as a fierce and savvy fighter.

The Gray Wolf was Captain Gray. Of course she was. Also Alyssa ana'Raisa, the heir to the Gray Wolf throne. Also Lyss.

As he thought on it, as fragments of conversation came back to him, his mortification grew. Hal blithely assuring her that, as soldiers, their lives wouldn't change much, no matter who sat on the throne. Hal suggesting that a royal marriage might put a big fat bow on the peace accord.

How could he ever look her in the eye again?

How much of what had happened between them was real? Had she been laughing at him behind a façade of eager kisses and embraces?

No. For someone who'd been lying to him from the day they met, she was the most honest person he knew.

Hal peered sideways at Lyss, looking for some evidence of royalty that he'd missed before. He saw none of that. In fact, she looked as pale and wretched as he'd ever seen her. She looked like she might faint dead away at any moment.

His heart went out to her, despite the fact that she'd made a fool of him. "Are you well, Captain?" he said, resisting the temptation to take her arm.

"Fine," she whispered, unconvincingly. "Couldn't be better."

The farther they descended, the damper it was. Hal could smell the sea and hear the crash of waves against the walls of the keep. On the lowest level was a small dock, protected from the weather, likely meant to allow the off-loading of people and supplies without the risk of being smashed against the cliffs. Several small boats were tied up there, rocking in the waves that found their way inside.

Talbot tossed their kit bags into the largest of the boats, carefully distributing the weight. "You sit up front, Captain," she said, putting out a hand to help her into the boat.

"Could I . . . could I sit in the middle?"

"I thought we'd put these two midships, to handle the oars. I'll sit in the back and keep an eye on them. That leaves the bow."

"Oh," Gray said miserably. She put out a foot, as if to step into the boat, then yanked it back. "What if we barred the doors and hid down here? If they're pirates, they'll likely just steal what they can and leave again."

"Get into the boat, Lyss," Talbot growled. "Now."

She's frightened, Hal thought. She's absolutely terrified. That was when he remembered what she'd said. *I don't like ships—or the ocean.*

Gray edged forward again, and this time Talbot half-lifted her into the boat. She crawled toward the front and huddled in the bow. Hal followed her in, and then Breon did, each claiming a thwart and a pair of oars. Talbot cast off, and climbed in last, shoving the craft away from the dock.

It was tricky, navigating out through the water gate, rounding the corner, and putting their backs into it to open space between the boat and the cliffs so they wouldn't risk smashing up before they even got started. This coastline was treacherous under the best of conditions, but now it seemed like a gale was coming out of the northeast. It didn't help that they were in such a tiny boat. They'd go down into the trough and then up over the crests like a cork. The good news was that in these seas there was little risk they could be spotted from the ships lurking offshore.

To Hal's surprise, Breon was a capable oarsman—better than Hal, in fact. Clearly he'd done rowing before. But where would a street musician get that kind of experience?

Breon kept shooting looks over his shoulder at Gray. When Hal stole a look, he saw that she had her head down, eyes closed, keeping a white-knuckled grip on the gunwales as if that way she could pretend she was somewhere else.

"Do you think she's going to hurl?" Breon whispered to Hal, nodding toward Gray. "We're not even into the bay."

Shaking his head vigorously, Hal mouthed *no* to the busker. Maybe she would, and maybe she wouldn't, but Hal didn't want to give her any ideas.

Fortunately, the tide was in their favor, and they had very little rowing to do on their way through the straits, just what was required to keep them off the cliffs to either side. He could still hear the boom of cannon from the cliffside batteries, and see the ruddy flashes on the horizon that he knew was answering fire from the enemy ships. Hal tried to look up to the top of the cliffs, slitting his eyes against the rain and sleet to see whether anyone was still fighting up top. He couldn't tell. Already his shoulders were burning, protesting against the unusual strain after weeks of idleness.

They were close to the exit into the open bay, and now

Hal could hear waves crashing against the cliffs ahead. Talbot stood in the stern, guiding them by screeching when they seemed likely to ram into the rocks. Finally, they were around the corner and pulling, pulling, pulling against the force of the flowing tide. Their little craft rocked wildly in the currents, and he could hear something rolling on the floor under his feet, and Gray whimpering behind him.

Eventually, as they left the straits behind them, the rocking eased. It was still rough, even in the bay, but manageable, between him and Breon. They followed the coast to the northeast, hoping they could get out of the bay without venturing close enough to the enemy ships to be spotted.

It was, all in all, a long, miserable night. They almost capsized when they left the bay for the open sea, but managed to ease around a point of land and into the shelter of the shoreline again. Hal transitioned from burning pain to a kind of numb acceptance, his body reacting automatically to the demands of the oars while his mind strayed to the possibility of escape.

If he could get away from the others, he would still be in the Fells, but he ought to be able to blend in well enough to make his way south eventually. Assuming they landed someplace close enough to civilization that he didn't die of exposure before he found shelter.

At some point during the night, Breon slumped from his seat and into the bottom of the boat, overcome by exhaustion. Without a word, Captain Gray scrambled back, seized his shoulders, and pulled him forward, draping him over the thwart so he wouldn't drown in the water sloshing in the bottom of the boat. Draping an oilskin over him, she replaced him on the forward set of oars.

For a princess, she's not much of a complainer, Hal thought. This was somehow reassuring, that the fierce Fellsian captain he'd fallen for was still there.

At least this way, it'll keep her blood moving so she doesn't freeze to death.

Finally, toward morning, the storm abated and they found a little inlet to shelter in. Hal and Talbot and Gray bailed out as much water as they could, huddled together for warmth, and unrolled the sail over top. Despite the cold and all his aches and pains, Hal slept like a dead person.

45

CASTAWAYS

When Hal awoke, the brief winter's day was well under way. He realized that Gray was snuggled up against him, her face buried in his chest, her breath warming him through his wool tunic. One long leg was thrown over his hip, and . . . anyway. There was no more sleeping after that.

The princess slept restlessly, muttering under her breath, her limbs twitching violently like she was still fighting her personal war in her sleep. Every time she moved, Hal's treacherous body reacted.

When he could stand it no longer, Hal eased away from her and sat up. Now something was jabbing him in the backside. He reached down and found a long object carved from ivory, decorated with sea monsters and dragons. The finger holes along its length told him that it was a sailor's flute. It was beautiful work, and he wondered who might have left it there. His sister Harper would love it, he knew, if he ever had a chance to give it to her.

Don't think like that. You will.

Sliding the flute into his coat, he poked his head out from under the canvas.

Talbot was ashore, having cleared the ice from a patch of sand and built a fire. She'd hung wet clothing over branches to dry and was drinking from a steaming mug. Breon was up, too, sitting on a boulder, cradling something in his arms, mourning over it like it was a dead child.

"Will you get over it, busker?" Talbot growled. "Put that thing down, or give it a decent burial. You're alive. You should be thanking the Maker for that instead of complaining."

"It was my father's," Breon said. "It's all I had of his. It was just repaired, and now it's ruined again. It got soaked, and the joints are coming apart."

"Come on, now," Talbot said gruffly. "It's a new day. I've some hot tea for you and you can soak your hardtack in it, and I've got an end of cheese. You worked real hard rowing that boat last night, and you must be hungry."

Breon shook his head. "I'm not hungry." He rubbed the back of his neck and winced. "I don't feel so well, and my neck hurts something fierce."

"You probably pulled a muscle or something," Talbot said.

"It's more like it's burning," Breon said. He fingered it again. "Something's wrong, I can feel it."

Talbot levered herself to her feet. "Here, you want me to take a look at it?"

Now he clapped both hands over the back of his neck. "No!" he said. "Never mind."

"Suit yourself," Talbot said, shrugging. "I'll be back in a little while."

"Where are you going?" Breon asked.

"The latrine, since you had to know." And she disappeared into the woods.

Hal climbed out of the boat. "What's ruined, Breon?" he said.

"My jafasa," he said, turning his attention back to the object on his lap, stroking it gently. "Talbot took it on the boat, and now it's ruined."

Hal squatted next to him. He was no expert, but it looked beyond repair. "I never heard of that—a jafasa."

"It's a musical instrument, from Carthis," Breon said, blotting his eyes with his sleeve. "My father taught me to play."

"Your father's gone now, I take it," Hal said.

Breon nodded.

Talbot was right. What with everything else, it didn't make sense to be mourning over a broken musical instrument. But the busker's pain was obviously real. Hal cast about for something to say, but he'd never been all that good with words. Groping in his pocket, he brought out the carved flute.

I'll probably never get home anyway, he thought.

"Here," he said, thrusting it toward Breon. "It's not the same, I know, but maybe this can be a reminder, somehow, of this conversation about your father."

For a moment, he thought the busker would refuse. Then Breon reached out and took the flute from his hands. "Thank you," he said, stroking the fantastical carving. "I've always been partial to the flute. My father played the sailor's pipes sometimes." Looking a little brighter, he tucked it away in his bedraggled coat and took a trip to the woods himself.

Even though it looked hopeless, Hal rewrapped the jafasa in its oilskin and found a spot for it in the boat. He didn't want to get the busker's hopes up, but maybe something could be done with it when they reached safety.

"It's late! Why didn't anyone wake me up?" Gray clambered out of the boat, all but tipping it over, and waded to the shore. She scanned the beach and, apparently seeing that they were unsupervised, said, "Where's the busker? And Talbot?"

"I'm right here," Talbot said, emerging from the trees, followed by Breon. "Nobody's going anywhere. You can't walk more'n a hundred paces in any direction without running into a cliff. The only way out of here is the way we came in."

"Then we'd better be on our way," Gray said, scanning the clifftops above them. "We'll find a place to put in where we can find a path inland." She didn't look happy about putting out to sea again, but she seemed resigned to it, anyway.

Hal rolled his aching shoulders, hoping this leg of the journey would be a little easier.

"Have a seat," Breon said, gesturing toward the boulder he'd vacated. "I'll have a look at the sailing rig. Once we reach open water again, we'll make better time if we can find the wind." Stepping into the boat, he began wrestling with the lines.

"Need any help, busker?" Talbot said.

Within the hour, they were on their way again. Once they'd eased out into the bay, Breon hoisted the sails. Hooking his feet under a center cleat, he held the tiller in one hand and the lines in the other, ducking under the boom as if he'd spent his whole life lashed to a mast.

Why would a busker seem so at home in a sailboat?

The sun broke out of the clouds, and the winds freshened out of the south, so they made good progress. Even Gray had a little more color in her cheeks. But Breon kept fingering his neck and scanning the horizon, his face clouded with worry.

They were an hour out when Talbot said, "We've got company."

It was a good-sized ship, running parallel to the shore, and it was rapidly closing the distance between them.

"Maybe," Talbot said, "it's one of ours." But she didn't sound hopeful.

From the looks of the ship, Hal guessed she was one of the vessels they'd seen outside the harbor at Chalk Cliffs.

"How did they find us so quickly?" Hal muttered. "It should have taken them a day or two at least."

"What I don't get is why they would leave off sacking the city to come after us," Gray said, studying the busker narrow-eyed, as if he might have the answer.

Breon just stared at the ship with a bleak expression, as if he was looking death in the face. The boy was a puzzle, but it wasn't Hal's to solve. When he looked toward land, he saw that they'd left the high cliffs behind, so the shoreline here was a little more accessible. Still, he wasn't optimistic. They had no gear, no horses, no food. It was likely they'd be hunted down before they could get any distance from the shore.

"Let's find a place to land," Talbot said. "Once we're ashore, hopefully we can find a hidey-hole and they'll give up."

"They won't give up," Breon said, adjusting the mainsail in order to capture a little more wind, and scrambling from one side of the boat to the other as they came about.

"Well, you're Mr. Cheerful, aren't you?" Talbot said, forcing a laugh.

"Can everyone swim?" the busker asked abruptly.

Everyone nodded but Gray, who turned the color of green foam.

"Don't worry," he said. "You won't have to swim far." He leaned forward, talking fast and persuasively. "If we land, they'll know right where we are. So here's what we'll do. See that rocky point up ahead? I'm going to bring us as tight into there as I can. When I give the word, the rest of you are going to slide out of the boat and swim for shore, and I'm going to sail her on a little farther before I abandon ship. Hopefully, they'll follow the boat."

"But then they'll catch *you*," Talbot said.

"Maybe he *wants* to be captured," Gray said.

They all turned and looked at her.

"Maybe our pirates are in league with the busker," she said, nodding toward the enemy ship. "Maybe the attack on the keep was an effort to free him."

Breon stared at her, momentarily losing track of the sails, which spilled air and began flapping. He jerked a thumb seaward. "You think I've got an army and a ship-load of pirates at my beck and call?"

Gray rolled her eyes. "Doesn't anyone else think it's odd that a busker climbs into a jolly boat and magically turns into a sailor?"

Breon laughed bitterly. "I'll tell you right now, nobody's got my back. I landed in Fellsmarch with three friends, and now two are dead and the third disappeared. These days, if I got all my friends together, they'd be lucky to fill a privy."

"Really? I used to have a family, busker, and now it's down to my mother and me."

"Fine," Breon said. "I confess, you nailed me. It's just an elaborate scheme to escape."

"Could we talk about this later?" Hal said. "They'll be on top of us before we know it. If we're going to do something other than surrender, we'd better do it now."

Breon lunged across the boat, grabbed the lines, shoved the tiller, and they came about so they were slanting toward the point. "Do whatever you want. I'm going on in before they get close enough to count heads. I'll say the word when we're as close as we're going to get, and that's when you jump." He glanced back at Gray. "I promise that if I survive, I'll turn myself in and submit to the queen's justice."

"Matelon," Gray said.

Hal leaned toward her. "What is it?"

To his surprise, she gripped his shoulders and kissed him, hard and thoroughly, while everyone else in the boat gaped at them.

"In case this is good-bye," she said. "I'm sorry about a lot of things, but I'm not sorry that we met. I've learned a lot, and—and—" She swallowed hard, and tears spilled down her cheeks. "I'm just sorry that we had to meet as enemies."

"It's not good-bye," Hal said stubbornly.

By now it was shallow enough that Hal could see rocks

coming up under the wind-ruffled surface. The busker loosed the sails, dumping out air, slowing their forward progress.

"Everybody ready?" When just a few yards of turbulent water separated their boat from the point, he shouted, "Now!"

Hal rolled over the side and into the stunningly cold water. He kept his head underwater as he took a few strong strokes toward shore. The next thing he knew, he was running up against the rocks in the shallows. Though he wanted nothing more than to haul himself out onto dry land, he came up for a breath, then submerged again, holding his breath so as not to be spotted before the jolly boat got well away.

Finally he broke the surface, gasping, and looked seaward.

Their little boat was already far to the north, racing along the shoreline under full sail. The enemy ship had turned north with it, following along parallel in the deeper water.

Hal crawled out of the water and onto the shore, scraping his hands and knees on the rocks. He spotted Talbot a short distance away on hands and knees, coughing out seawater. He looked up and down the point.

"Where's Captain Gray?" he said.

"I haven't seen her since I jumped out of the boat," Talbot said. "I all but drowned in these currents." The

bluejacket pushed to her feet, shaded her eyes, and sur-
veyed the shoreline. Then scanned the waves that smashed
diagonally into the rocks. "Lyss!" she cried. "Lyss! Where
are you? Answer back so I can get a fix on your location!"

But there was no response. Hal looked down the
shoreline in the direction the current was running, but
saw nothing. Breon d'Tarvos and the pursuing ship had
rounded a bend and were out of sight.

"I should have kept a hold on her," Talbot said, a quiver
in her voice. "Or we should have stayed with the boat.
This is my fault. I know she's afraid of the water."

"Maybe she just got swept farther down the beach. Let's
follow the shore and maybe we'll find her."

"But what if she comes here looking for us, and we're
gone?" Talbot said.

"We could split up," Hal suggested. When Talbot glared
at him, he added, "Would it help if I gave you my word of
honor that I won't try to escape?"

"We stay together," Talbot said. "Let's go."

46

BEACH MUSIC

"You were supposed to jump off the boat," Breon said, looking over his shoulder to where Her Highness cowered in the stern.

"I was going to," she said, teeth chattering. "I really was, but I changed my mind." With that, she finally let loose and spewed over the side. Then hung there, arms draped around the oarlocks, head down.

They were speeding along, faster than it seemed possible to go in such a small boat. It should have taken every ounce of Breon's concentration to keep the boat moving and avoid a miscalculation that would leave them in splinters up on the rocks. And yet . . . in a way, handling the sails and managing the boat was like breathing. The scent of the salt spray was intoxicating—it went to his head like a hit of leaf. He wondered if he'd been using the leaf as a poor replacement for . . . *this*.

"You're really good at this," Her Highness said, as if reading his thoughts.

"I know," he said. It wasn't bragging, it was the truth. It was just the latest in a long line of surprises—good and bad. On the other side of the ledger, the magemark on the back of his neck. Right now, it burned like fury. He didn't remember it ever doing that before.

"How did you learn to sail?"

"I don't know," he said. "But you should've jumped when you had the chance."

"I didn't want you to get away." She smiled weakly.

Dread rose in his throat like black bile, and he swallowed it down. He'd never been one to barf aboard ship and he wasn't going to start now.

"In fact, you *did* want me to get away," he said. "As far away as possible. They'll murder you." He nodded toward the ship.

"Your friends?"

He shuddered. "They're not my friends."

"Who are they?"

"I don't know."

"You really should have given up the leaf a long time ago," she said, regaining some of her usual know-it-all prickliness.

"That's not the problem," he said. "I didn't lose my memory because of using leaf. I used leaf because of the things I can't remember."

For instance, he didn't know why the woman on the ship was looking for him, but he knew now that he didn't want her to find him.

By now, the black ship had outpaced them and turned in toward the shore so she lay to the leeward side of them. As he watched, the ship began dropping a litter of jolly boats.

"Should we turn around?" Her Highness said, strapping on her baldric and methodically arming herself with all manner of weapons.

"Won't do any good, strong as this sea is running. It's time to go ashore and hope we can give them the slip. Can you get on the oars again?"

Without a murmur of protest, she edged forward to the rearmost thwart and began pulling with a will. As if anything that got her onto dry land quicker was worth the sweat.

"Now," he said, "as soon as we run aground, jump out and run, and don't look back. If we split up, maybe one of us will get away."

She grunted, which left him in the dark as to what she'd actually do.

But when they hit the shallows, she vaulted over the side of the boat and took off running, disappearing into the jumble of broken rock that lay between the beach and the mountains beyond.

Good, he thought. That was one worry off his plate. Maybe she hated him, but he didn't hate her. He felt bad about what had happened to her family. Who could blame her for wanting justice?

I'm a lover, not a hater, he thought.

Two boats were pulling hard for the shore, closing in on him. Now what?

He took off in a different direction than the princess had gone, threading his way into a labyrinth of rock so that he couldn't be spotted from the water. He got to a point where he had to begin climbing, trying to find toeholds, reaching, gripping stone, pulling himself up. Eventually, he came to an overhang, and he could go no farther. So he settled onto his perch, huddling deep in his coat, and waited.

Soon, he heard voices from the beach, so he knew the boats must have landed. After another little while, he heard the voices moving closer, felt the magemark on the back of his neck burning, burning, burning. Something about the lay of the land funneled voices up to him.

He heard a woman's voice, as warm and intoxicating as hot buttered rum. "It's this way. We're getting close now." He could hear the excitement in her voice.

And then another voice, one he recognized, high and anxious. "You won't hurt him, right? You said you wouldn't hurt him. You're just going to take him back home on your ship."

It was Aubrey.

And then the first voice, larded with sorcery. "Of course," she said. "That was the bargain, wasn't it? I am going to take very good care of your magemarked friend."

For one hopeful moment, Breon wondered if the story he'd made up was true—if Aubrey was bringing an army to save him.

But no. He knew in his heart of hearts that wasn't Aubrey's style. That she could never pull that off.

In his heart of hearts, he knew that it meant that she'd betrayed him.

Just for a moment, then, he put his head down and surrendered to despair.

"We'll be fine," she'd said. "I'll get my game going as soon's we get to Baston Bay." Was this why she'd talked him into returning to Baston Bay? Was he the prize in the new game she had going?

I was loyal to you, Aubrey. I wouldn't give you up to Her Highness and her crew, even when they threatened to torture me.

Point of correction, Your Highness, he added. *Actually, I have no friends at all.*

He slid forward on the ledge so he could peer over and look down on the way he'd come. Eventually, they came into view—a crowd of pirates or warriors with purple-blue auras. At the head of the band, a tall woman in glittering armor, her silver hair snaking around her head, one hand clamped around Aubrey's arm. Her aura was blue-white, so brilliant that he had to squint against it. She was young, though—younger than he'd expected.

Aubrey wasn't small, but she seemed very small in that company. She was dressed in the clothes she'd been wearing when he'd last seen her. So maybe she hadn't cashed in yet.

When they reached the bottom of the steepest climb, the mage looked straight up at where Breon lay hidden. His magemark rekindled like a flame against his skin. Now that she was closer, he could see that her silver hair had two broad streaks in it—one gold, the other blue.

"He's up there," the mage murmured to Aubrey. "Call him down."

"Breon!" Aubrey called, looking in his general direction and waving her hand. "Hey, Breon! It's Aubrey. Come down here. I've brought help."

Breon said nothing. Maybe the mage suspected he was up there, but he wasn't going to open his mouth and leave no doubt.

"I was crazy worried when you was in prison," Aubrey said. "I couldn't figure out a way to get you out. And here you got out on your own. I can't wait to hear how you done it."

Breon said nothing.

"I thought you said the boy was a friend of yours," the mage hissed.

"He is," Aubrey said. "You sure he's up there?"

"He's up there," the mage said flatly. Pulling Aubrey closer, she murmured something in her ear, then pushed her toward the foot of the trail.

"Bree!" Aubrey said, looking paler than before. "You're probably wondering who my friends are. This is Celestine, and she's an actual empress! She's from . . . from wherever it is you come from. She says she can fill you in on your family, all the things you don't know. Won't that be fine?" She extended her hands toward Breon, as if she might catch him if he jumped.

Breon wrapped his arms around his knees. As he did so, he felt something lumpy in his pocket. When he pulled it out, he saw that it was the flute Hal had given him. He weighed it in his hands.

Down below, Celestine chose out four of her mage-ish pirates. "I want you to go up and get him. Remember what I said—I don't want the boy harmed in any way. Anything happens to him, you'll regret the day you were born."

Her concern should have been reassuring, even heart-warming, maybe, but it wasn't. She's like the weather on the Indio, Breon thought. Fair to stormy in the blink of an eye.

Now he heard the warriors toiling up the trail toward him. When he peered over the edge, he could see them. Already they were nearly halfway up, but they'd reached a difficult overhang. As he watched, one of them detached a grappling hook from his belt and side-armed it, aiming just above the spot where Breon was hiding. It clanged against the rock, then caught, and held, the rope dangling down, out of sight. Moments later, the rope went taut. They were climbing.

Right. Pirates carry grappling hooks, don't they? Just his luck. Reaching up behind him, he pried at it. But it was wedged in so tightly, he couldn't move it.

But there was another option.

You're not a violent person, he told himself.

You're a lover, not a hater.

Then again, you've always loved the flute.

Breon reached up again, gripped the grappling hook, and listened for music.

A grappling hook is usually not a beloved object, so it didn't come as clearly as he would have liked. Still, he caught a thread of it.

Raising the flute to his lips, Breon began to play a lively tune, a jig of sorts. The warriors climbing toward him froze for a moment. Then the warrior in the lead—the owner of the grappling hook—began to smile. He straightened, stood upright, and began to dance, faster and faster. The warriors behind him backed up, trying to get out of the way, but he slammed into them. They fell, arms pinwheeling, hit the rocks once, twice, then landed on the sand.

Their dancing colleague followed them off the edge. When he landed, he just lay there, his arms and legs twitching to the cadence of the tune.

Three were obviously dead. The fourth was seemingly alive, but broken.

Down below, all of the warriors were moving, shuffling their feet a little. Even Aubrey, still wearing her panic-stricken expression. Only Celestine didn't join in. She just gazed up at Breon like he was a fat, juicy apple, high on the tree, that she couldn't reach.

With the last warrior down, Breon stopped playing. Then, to his horror, the surviving warrior began dragging himself to the foot of the cliff. Despite his shattered limbs, he was still trying to reach him.

Celestine pulled Aubrey closer, and ran a line of flame down Aubrey's arm.

Aubrey screamed and screamed and beat her arm against her side, but the flame didn't go out.

Breon stopped playing and put his hands over his ears, trying to block the sound. But he couldn't. And he couldn't help remembering what it had been like when his own arm had been burned during the interrogation.

"Come down here, boy, or I'll burn your young friend to a cinder, bit by bit," Celestine snarled. "It will take a long time."

"You promised," Aubrey sobbed. "You promised you wouldn't hurt us."

"I promised that I would not hurt *him*," Celestine said. "But I never made any promises about you." She looked up at Breon. "Since you seem to love dancing so much, let's see if your girl is any good at it."

Now she directed flame at Aubrey's feet. Aubrey tried to run, but the flame found her, and she tried to stamp it out, but it just kept burning. So she plunged into the water, but it didn't seem to do any good.

Breon could stand it no longer. Maybe Aubrey had betrayed him, but she didn't deserve this.

"Stop it!" he cried, standing at the edge of the cliff, looking down at the mage. "Stop hurting her!"

"He speaks," Celestine said, with grim satisfaction. "If you want me to stop hurting her, then come down here."

"All right," he said, stuffing the flute back into his pocket. "All right. Just . . . give me a minute."

So Breon descended the way he'd come up, only much faster, slipping and sliding in his hurry so that more than once he almost tumbled head over heels.

Finally, he made it to the beach. Aubrey was writhing on the sand, half in and half out of the water. He hurried over to her, cradling her head, brushing the sand from her cheek.

"I'm sorry, Bree," she said, breathless with pain. "I never meant to be a bad person, but it just happened."

"Never mind," he said, trying to soothe her. He kept thinking about the fire in the dungeon at Chalk Cliffs and wondering if he could have been responsible.

Finally, he looked up at Celestine. "I'm here," he

growled. "That's what you wanted, isn't it? Now heal her."

Celestine shook her head, feigning regret. "I'm sorry, boy. There was a time I could have helped you. I no longer have that gift."

"Can't you at least do something about the pain?" Breon's voice quivered.

She shook her head. "Your girl betrayed you, boy. You don't owe her a thing." When Breon didn't respond, she extended a knife toward him, hilt first. "You can finish her if you like."

Breon stood there, staring at the knife in the mage's hand through a red haze of fury and tears. As if in a dream, he heard a noise, a kind of snap. The air around Celestine shimmered and hardened. Something smacked into it, bounced off, and fell at his feet.

It was an arrow.

That broke Breon out of his reverie. He lunged forward, grabbed the hilt of the knife, and did his best to plunge it into the empress's chest. But the knife slammed into the same barrier, and it flew from Breon's hand.

Then two more of Celestine's warriors had him by the arms, dragging him back from her. Two more *thwack*s, and Breon's captors staggered, staring down at the arrows sticking out of their chests. But they didn't loosen their grip any, even as their blood dripped onto the sand.

Looking past Celestine, Breon could see Aubrey moving, dragging herself out of the water and across the sand toward the empress. He could see that she had something in her fist, a sharp shell, maybe.

But Celestine was focused elsewhere.

"What do we have here?" she said, shading her eyes and staring in the direction the arrows had come from. "A hero?"

"Leave them alone!" somebody shouted from the top of a nearby cliff. "Let them go."

"Or, perhaps, a heroine," Celestine amended.

It was Her Highness.

"Get out of here!" Breon shouted. "Go! Don't be stupid."

"Maybe she can't help herself, boy." Celestine laughed. "You are, after all, a charmer. Is this some kind of love triangle?" She turned to look at Aubrey, who was halfway between the water and her target. "You know," the empress said, "I *hate* love triangles." Gripping her amulet and raising her hand, she immersed Aubrey in flame.

Breon tried to rip free from his captors, but they held him fast, even though they should have been dead on the ground.

Aubrey came to her feet, staggered forward one step, two. She stumbled back as Her Highness's next arrow found its mark, and then Aubrey went down, still burning but now beyond Celestine's reach.

Breon heard three more *thwack*s in quick succession. Another arrow clattered against Celestine's barrier. Two more found their marks among her soldiers.

"Bravo," Celestine said, as if delighted. "I could use more archers like you in my army. How would you like to join my bloodsworn guard?"

"Get back in your boat and leave," Her Highness said, her voice shaking with rage.

"I have every intention of doing that," Celestine said. "But not without the boy. I've gone to a tremendous amount of trouble to find him. But, no worries. You can come with us."

With that, she sent a bolt of flame smashing into the cliff just under the princess's position. Stone shattered and the cliff came down, ending in a pile of rubble at the bottom.

Breon looked from the spot on the cliff where the princess had been to the rockfall at the bottom. He saw nothing moving. It seemed impossible that anyone could have survived that.

"It's so much easier," Celestine said to nobody in particular, "when you don't have to take them alive." She nodded to the pirates pinioning Breon's arms. "Let's get the boy aboard before any more heroes show up."

THE WATER IS WIDE

Halston Matelon half-scrambled, half-fell the last twenty feet from the cliff to the beach. Even as he rolled to his feet, he knew he was too late, but that didn't stop him from charging across the sand to the water's edge and splashing a few yards into the waves.

It was no use. Two hundred yards of gunmetal water separated Hal from the jolly boat, a gulf that grew as the oarsmen strained and pulled. The boat was already halfway to the ship that waited at the mouth of the inlet.

Hal resisted the urge to shake his fist at the fleeing pirates.

Talbot skidded to a stop beside him, spitting out a series of oaths. Shading her eyes, she glared after the boat, which by now was pulling alongside the bigger ship. "Is that them? Do you think they're aboard?"

Hal shook his head. "I don't know. I'm guessing they're either aboard or dead, so maybe we should hope for the former. Is there any chance they'll be intercepted by your navy before they leave the shore waters?"

Hope kindled momentarily in Talbot's eyes, then was as quickly extinguished. "I'd say it was unlikely. We just don't have that many ships, especially this far north of Chalk Cliffs. We have to focus on keeping our eastern ports open and protecting our roads and cities." She released a shaky breath. "This is my fault. It was my idea, to escape by boat. Lyss is scared to death of the water. I should have listened to her."

Hal was only half-listening. He wished he had Lyss's glass so he could get a better look. It looked like they were lifting somebody from the jolly boat up onto the deck. Somebody who was either dead or unconscious. They winched the boat aboard, too, and hastily raised anchor.

They ran the sails up the masts. At first the sails flapped, spilling air, but as the ship turned, they inflated, and she put on speed.

There was nothing remotely magical about Hal, but instinct told him Alyssa Gray Wolf was aboard that ship and quickly moving out of reach.

Hal couldn't watch anymore, so he turned back toward the beach. Bodies littered the sand, all bristling with arrows. From the way they were dressed, Hal guessed they'd come off the ship.

Talbot pulled one of the arrows free and examined it. "Lyss got some shots in, anyway. These arrows are clan-made, and I know it wasn't the busker." She looked up and down the beach. "I count five down."

"Six," Hal said. A charred body lay on the sand at the water's edge, with an arrow centering its chest. Though most of the body had been consumed, it was still smoldering.

Hal squatted next to it, pressing his sleeve over his nose against the stink of burning flesh. From the remains of the clothing, he guessed it was a girl, someone dressed differently from the other bodies on the beach. But not in Highlander spattercloth.

"Unless I'm mistaken, this one was done by magery," he said, sitting back on his heels. "I've seen bodies burned like this on the battlefield."

"That doesn't make sense," Talbot muttered. "Pirates using magery?"

Hal crossed the sand to where several house-sized chunks of rock littered the bottom of the cliff. He could see that it was a new fall—the edges were raw, unvarnished by wind and rain. Head-sized chunks were scattered all the way to the water's edge.

Next to the base of the cliff, he saw two bodies, half-buried in the debris. Again, warriors from the ship, maybe killed in the fall.

"Careful," Talbot called. "It might be unstable."

"It looks like there was an explosion or something. Or more magery." Methodically, he began to root through the rubble, guarding his heart against what he might find. Up against the cliff face, in a spot where two huge boulders stood propped against each other, the sand was spotted with blood. Not a lot of blood, but—

Something glittered from a crevice, nearly at eye level. Hal pulled the object out. It was a pendant, a gold locket, in fact, engraved with a rose. He turned to find Talbot right behind him.

"Do you recognize this?" he asked her.

Talbot licked her cracked lips and nodded. "It belonged—belongs to Lyss."

"Was she wearing it?"

Talbot nodded. "I've never seen her without it, except for when—yes, she was wearing it."

Hal looked up the cliff, then out to where the bodies littered the beach. He swore softly.

"What? What is it?" Talbot snapped.

"I'm thinking Captain Gray was shooting from up here somewhere, and there was an explosion—or a bolt of magic—and she fell."

With that, Talbot began digging through the rubble like a madwoman, until her hands were battered and bleeding. Soon she was leaving her own blood smeared on the rocks. Hal joined in. Side by side, they rolled rocks away.

There wasn't all that much rubble on the beach, and it

soon became clear to Hal that Lyss's body wasn't buried under it. Relief flooded through him.

"Talbot," he said gently.

Talbot looked up from her digging, her face tear-streaked. *"What?"*

"She's not here." He paused, and when she just glared at him, he added, "Do you want to hear my theory?"

Grudgingly, she nodded.

"I think Gray was injured in the fall," he said. "But she was conscious, because she tucked her locket in the niche in the rocks for us to find. She knew that you would know it was hers, and that it meant that she was alive."

From the look on Talbot's face, she liked his theory very much.

"Now let's see what else we can find," he said. They divided up the beach and walked it methodically.

"What I don't get," Talbot said, "is how they tracked us here. It's like they had our scent or something. And why bother with us with the city in their grip? There's plenty to plunder there."

"Could the busker have been in league with the pirates? Maybe he was the one that tipped them off. Maybe they attacked the keep in an effort to rescue him, and this was the pre-arranged meeting place. That would explain why they were so bent on tracking us down."

"No!" Talbot said, and Hal was surprised by her vehemence.

"I know you had him under lock and key, but isn't it

THE WATER IS WIDE

possible that he got word out somehow to—?"

"No." Clearly, Talbot was having none of that.

"Maybe they were after the busker," she said. "But he didn't want to be found." She slid a look at Hal. "Do you want to hear *my* theory?"

"All right."

"I spent a fortnight with the busker. He's a liar, and a charmer, and too fond of the leaf for his own good. I've seen him scared, and I've seen him shoveling scummer."

She paused, and Hal said, "So?"

"So when he saw that ship coming, he was terrified. I'd stake my life on it. When he told us to get out of the boat, he was trying to save the rest of us. And he would have, except Lyss wouldn't jump."

"You could be right, I suppose . . . ," Hal began, but Talbot stopped in her tracks and gripped Hal's arm. "Look at that," she said, pointing down at the sand.

Hal circled around so that he could view the sand from the same angle.

The top line looked like a lover's inscription.

AG + BdT

And, underneath, an arrow pointing toward the sea.

"What the hell does that mean?" Hal said irritably.

Talbot was practically beaming as she traced the letters with her forefinger. "Alyssa Gray plus Breon d'Tarvos. It means they've been taken captive. It means they're still alive. Now all we have to do is figure out how to get them back."

Right, Hal thought, staring out to sea at the spot where the pirate ship had disappeared over the horizon. If Lyss Gray wasn't a soldier he could plan a future with, maybe she was a queen he could serve one day. Once he'd seen to his family's safety.

"It's not good-bye," he said again, this time so softly that it was lost in the sound of the wind and waves.

ACKNOWLEDGMENTS

Writing a book is a lot like having a child. It takes about the same length of time, and for much of that time, you're on your own. Some parts of it are lonely, painful, and disgusting—so that you wonder what made you start down this road in the first place. After all, many people live full and rewarding lives without having written a fantasy novel, let alone a series.

Then there are the other times. Times when you feel that quiver deep in your belly, or when you strike that chord of possibility that tells you that this is the start of something good and true. When answers to the what-if questions come fast and fluidly. These harbingers of joy get you through the other bits.

And then when you deliver that metaphorical child, red and wrinkled, squalling and uncivilized, you find other hands waiting to receive it and love it. Wise women (and some men) stand ready to advise you on how it can reach its full potential.

I continue to benefit from the savvy counsel of my agent, Christopher Schelling, who, having run off to the city decades ago has inexplicably returned to the country, where he grows writers and other creative types (also tomatoes.) Thanks to my foreign rights reps, Chris Lotts and Lara Allen, who have sold my books in so many places that I now want to visit in person.

The publishing team at HarperCollins has worked hard to introduce this new series to the world. Wise woman and senior editor Abby Ranger helps me rein in all the pretty horses and make sure we actually get somewhere without leaving the reader behind. Emily Brenner, Kate Jackson, and Suzanne Murphy have contributed their sagacity and support to this project, while Rose Pleuler offers much-needed assistance.

Managing editorial and copy editing makes sure no detail is overlooked along the way. Thanks to Emily Rader, Bethany Reis, Mark Rifkin, and Josh Weiss.

The design team of Erin Fitzsimmons, Amy Ryan, and Barbara Fitzsimmons from Harper and illustrators Sasha Vinogradova and Alessandro "Talexi" Taini have outdone themselves with covers for the series. Designers, art directors, and illustrators are the gatekeepers who entice readers into my world. It's up to me to make them want to stay in that dangerous place.

The publicity, sales, and marketing staff are critical in getting my work in front of readers. With the Shattered Realms, they have had the dual task of reaching out to fans of the original Seven Realms series as well as finding new readers willing to take a chance on four massive books about a star-crossed queendom. Thanks to the publicity team of Stephanie Hoover and Cindy Hamilton, the marketing team including Julie Yeater, Bess Braswell, and Nellie Kurtzman, and the sales group including Jennifer Wygand, Kathleen Faber, and Andrea Pappenheimer, this spin-off series has received a warm welcome.

As always, thanks to my husband, Rod, intrepid book-hauler and the most responsive webmaster ever, my sons and other early readers, and all of the other writers who offer critique, support, commiseration, sage advice, and the occasional glass of wine. I raise my glass to all of you.

THE SEVEN

THE QUEENDOM
of the FELLS

Shivering Fens

Hallowmere

Rivertown

Eastgate

Dyrnnewater R.

Westgate

Demonai
Camp

Hanale

WATER

Delphi Rd.

Swansea

THE KINGDOM of
TAMRON

Fetters Ford

TAMRON FOREST

Malthus
Shrine

Tamron R. (West branch)

Tamron R.

Tamron
Court

Tamron Rd.

West Rd.

Oden's
Ford

Harbor Rd.

South Rd.

Sand Harbor

South Gate

SOUTHERN ISLANDS

Bruinsport

BRUINSWALLOW

REALMS

FROZEN SE

Invaders Bay

Wizar

Grey Lady

THE VALE

Chalk Cliffs

Fellsmarch

Marisa Pines Camp

Firehole R.

Fortress Rock

Marisa Pines Pass

Way Camp

Hunter's Camp

Queen Court

Alyssa Plateau

The Harlot

Spiritgate

Delphi

KINGDOM of ARDEN

Heartfang Mtns.

Middlesea

North Rd.

Temple Church

Ardenswater

Bittersweet Keep

Ardenscourt

East Rd.

Baston Bay

Ardenswater

Heartfang R.

Bright Stone Keep

Bitter Springs R.

Watergate

Grypr

The Wastes

WE'ENHAVEN

Hidden Bay